# Cinnamon Bun

Ravensdagger

# Contents

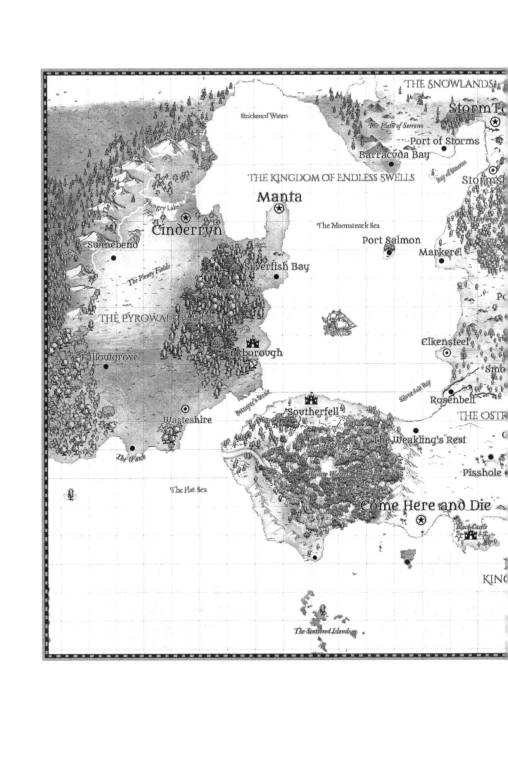

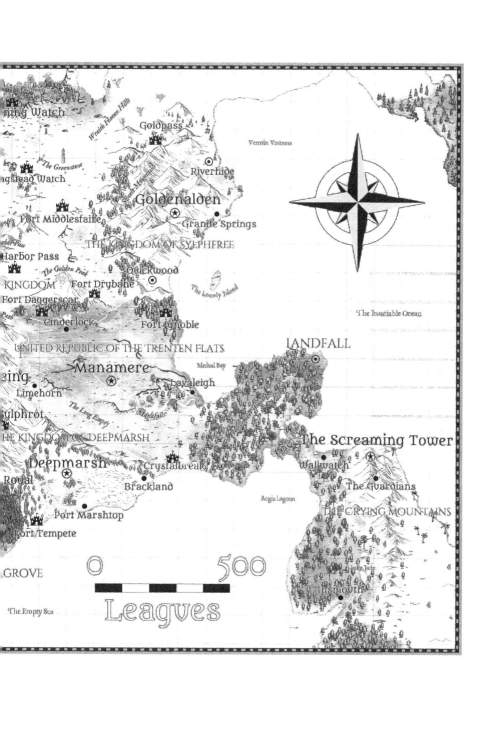

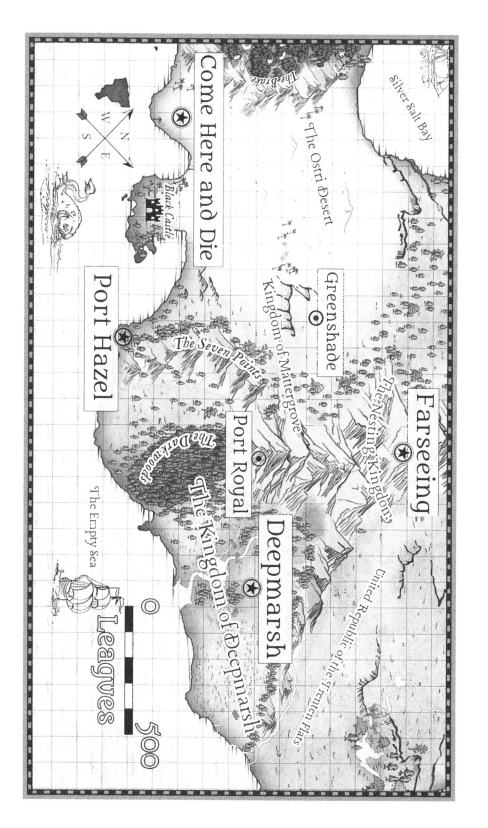

# A Call to Adventure

I was always the sort of girl that looked for the call to adventure, be it in real life or between the pages of a book. So when my time came, I jumped on it.

It all began one fine morning in math class. I was leaning forwards on my desk, elbows down and eyes on the board where our teacher was explaining something about geometric series. It wasn't my favourite teacher and it was certainly not my favourite subject, but I wanted to keep my grades up all the same. I only had a few months to go before high school was over, and then the whole world was going to open up.

A low sound rang out. Sort of like a cowbell being dropped from the top of a skyscraper into a fifty-five-gallon drum.

I jumped in my seat and looked around, but all I found were a few students and friends looking at me curiously. I smiled sheepishly and got some grins in return.

I was about to ask if they had heard the bong noise when it appeared before me. A box, thin and nearly translucent, held in the air by nothing at all and with a simple request on it.

**Bong! A great evil has set its root in the world. You are called upon to save it! Do you accept this quest?**

There were two boxes below that, one labelled 'I accept' the other 'I refuse.' I tilted my head to the side, the box following the motion, then whipped my head to the other side of the desk only for it to glide back to the centre of my vision.

I held back a smile. It couldn't be real.

"Hey," I whispered to the girl next to me. "Do you see that?"

She followed the direction my finger was pointing and stared at the boy sitting one row ahead. "His hair?" she asked.

So, she couldn't see the floaty prompt box. I waved off her questioning look and refocused on the box. The box that offered me a quest. The box that had appeared with a sound no one else could hear. The box that I suppose no one could see. My grin was so wide my cheeks were hurting.

I considered what my parents would say, but they were both struck with wanderlust and were the ones responsible for my desire to see the world.

They would have been tapping the 'I accept' box a million times a second by now.

Grin firmly in place, I reached out and pressed the 'I accept' button.

**`Ding! The world thanks you for your sacrifice!`**

I promptly fell onto my butt.

The world had changed in less time than it took to blink. I wasn't in a sterile classroom anymore with a window overlooking a snowy courtyard or surrounded by about twenty other bored students. No desks, no chairs, no low rumble of distant cars and air exchange systems. Instead, there was birdsong and the croaking of frogs and the gentle murmur of wind through trees.

I hopped to my feet and looked around. I was in a room still. Most of a room. An ex-room. The floor was paved with large flat stones slotted into each other, and the walls were made of a slightly different kind of stone with thick wooden beams running up to the ceiling above.

Tables that had rotted away were left lying around next to crushed chairs and piles of mulch that might have been leaves once. The entire room stank of mould and rot. It reminded me of camping out in the woods when I was a little younger.

Most of one wall was entirely missing.

"Whoa," I said as I moved as close to the edge as I dared.

It was immediately obvious that I was in a tower of some sort, one that rose a level or two above the treeline of the forest beyond. Trees stretched out as far as the eye could see, a sea of swaying green treetops that rose and fell with the dip and rises of the landscape. In the distance was a grey blur that might have been a mountain range that swept into the horizon.

I couldn't see any lakes or rivers but could hear the nearby gurgle of water splashing against stones. Maybe the tower's other side was against the ocean or a river or something. I couldn't tell, and in that moment it didn't matter.

The giddiness rose up in my tummy like an overflowing well, and it burst out as a happy giggle.

"Yes! Yes! Yes!" I shouted to the heavens as I started jumping around the room, arms waving in the air with every cheer. "I made it! I get adventures and dragons and princesses!"

I ran in little circles while giggling and might have boogied down a little, shaking my hips as happy energy coursed through my veins.

"Woo! This is going to be awesome!" My scream sent birds flying into the air all in a flutter.

A bell sounded, light and tinkling, like crystal chimes being struck together.

**Ding! For Completing a Special Action while Devoid of Classes, you have unlocked a new Class!**

My breathing hitched, but if anything the core of excitement in my gut only grew bigger. "A class," I whispered.

**Ding! You are now a Cinnamon Bun!**
*Health + 5*
*Stamina +10*
*Mana +5*
*Resilience +10*
*Flexibility +10*
*Magic +5*

"Really?" I asked the prompt, but its only response was to fade away.

The tropes and stereotypes of a game weren't new to me, of course, but I had never heard of a class called Cinnamon Bun. I had eaten some of those before, in fact, and they certainly didn't taste like something someone could be. But maybe this world was different. I hoped that this world was different.

With dragons and elves and monsters of all sorts! I would be able to grow strong and tough and I'd meet a dragon and ride it into battle and maybe have tea with some dwarves and I was getting ahead of myself... There was usually some menu or status page in the books that I'd read. And so thinking, my mind was flooded with information. Not very much, but some facts and figures and a sort of... memory of a screen. "Whoa."

| Name: Broccoli Bunch | | Race: Human | | | Age: 16 |
|---|---|---|---|---|---|
| Health | 105 | Stamina | 110 | Mana | 105 |
| Resilience | 15 | Flexibility | 15 | Magic | 10 |
| First Class: | Cinnamon Bun | | First Class Level: | | 0 |
| Skill Slots | 0 | | Skill Points | | 0 |
| General Skill Slots | 0 | | General Skill Points | | 0 |

"So cool!" This, of course, prompted more happy dancing. I had a class and an empty skills list and a bunch of numbers that meant more than anything I had worked on in maths class. Also, Magic.

I didn't know what some of them meant, but it didn't matter! I had them and they were mine! A bit of a push and the box with my status and all appeared before my very eyes. I hugged it.

Or, well, I tried to hug it. The box kept juking out of hug reach, even when I started laughing and skipping after it. It was a good box and good boxes deserved all the hugs. Then, with a soap-bubble like pop, the box disappeared.

"Okay, okay, Broc, calm yourself," I said between still escaping giggles. A few deep breaths helped to chill me out. I wanted to sit down, to inspect my super cool new stats and maybe to skip some more because I felt brilliant.

Unfortunately, the tower's floor was a mess. Tables ruined, chairs, all save for one rickety thing in the corner, all busted up. There was a shovel with a flat head leaning against one wall though, and an ancient broom with bristles made from some plant or another.

If I wanted to have a rest, this wasn't the place for it, not unless I cleaned it up a little.

The only exit to the room was behind a stack of fallen stones, each one looking as if they weighed as much as I did.

I pulled up the only seat that looked able to take my weight, then wiped its surface clean.

***Ding! For doing a Special Action in line with your Class, you have unlocked the skill: Cleaning!***

I laughed. A skill! A silly, rather boring skill, but maybe one that would help. It would help even more if I grinded a little, and I did like cleaning.

Nodding to myself, I picked up the broom and shovel and got to work. First making sure that the ground below the opening in the wall was clear of anyone or anything, then I started shovelling up the dead leaves and pushing them out.

A bit of grunting and some sweating had the broken tables busted up even more and stacked up neatly off to one side. The mouldier bits I tossed out. Maybe I would have to build a fire later. Not that I had a lighter or matches, but I could make do.

Then came the sweeping. I swiped at the cobwebs in the corners, swept the floor clean and even dusted off the one usable chair I found.

Every so often I felt a whisper of a 'ding' in the back of my mind, like a distant noise that was just barely audible. A quick bit of focusing revealed that it was my Cleaning skill rising up, and quickly at that.

Probably because of its low level, I decided.

Soon enough the room was as clean as it would be. The mould brushed off the walls with more enthusiasm than skill, the floors swept, the broken furniture sorted and a small table and chair arranged to one side where I could sit down and relax.

I sighed as I flopped onto my seat, the old wood creaking under my weight but not breaking. "Classes!" I decided. That's where I would start.

```
First Class: Cinnamon Bun
Level 0
You are the Cinnamon Bun. Too good for this
world. Too pure. You are the perfect support
and friend to all. Nature itself smiles
upon you.
Cleanse this world of its impurities in
the name of love and justice!
```

I snorted. That wasn't the most helpful description I'd ever seen. Too pure? Well, that... okay, so maybe I was a little naive, sometimes, all my friends said so, and everyone was my friend. But the Class description didn't have to be so smug about it. Also, First Class, which meant that I could maybe unlock a second at some point. Dragon Rider class, here I come!

The Cleaning skill sort of made sense if it was tied to some sort of class ability to cleanse things.

Maybe it was a class that was good against the undead? I certainly hoped so! Seeing a walking skeleton would be creepy. Unless it was a nice gentlemanly skeleton, in which case that was alright.

It wasn't okay to mock or judge others because of their appearance after all.

Humming to myself, I focused on my Cleaning Skill instead.

```
Cleaning
Rank F - 90%
The ability to clean. As this skill rises
in level your ability to Clean will improve!
```

"Well, okay." That was utterly underwhelming. Still, maybe as I got better at it, I would be able to keep myself and the world around me clean too! It was worth it!

I stretched in my new seat then hopped off. It wasn't time for sitting back and relaxing. It was time to do stuff! First, I had a bunch of things to test out!

Trying to figure out if I had an inventory of some sort was fruitless. No amount of shouting 'inventory!' amounted to anything. Then I looked for a handy help menu, but that was absent too. But, after much searching and some head scratching, I found something incredible.

> *You have one (1) Active Quest:*
> **The Hole Down Under**
> *An evil root has plunged into the world.*
> *Find it. Remove it.*

That was it. No waypoints, no hints. Not even a handy-dandy list of rewards. I huffed at the quest box and that was apparently its hint that it wasn't needed anymore. What even was an evil root?

Well, that didn't matter. Maybe it was the sort of quest that would take a long, long time to accomplish. I didn't have that luxury. The sum total of my belongings amounted to a pretty blouse I had bought on sale a week ago, a sturdy pair of shoes I liked, a thick cotton skirt that reached to just below the knees and some warm stockings. And, of course, my underthings.

Not even a jacket.

Fortunately it was warm wherever I was, so I had no need for too much warm clothing. Though a blanket would have been nice. Or a towel.

I had failed hitchhiking one-oh-one already.

Shrugging to myself, I moved to the edge of the hole in the wall and looked down. Two stories from my little nook to the ground, at least judging by the number of windows. The floors looked rather tall. Or maybe that was my newly discovered fear of falling to my death that was talking.

A look over to the blocked doorway confirmed that there was no way I was moving the stones there.

No ropes, no safety equipment, no easy way down.

At least the rocky walls of the tower were rough and had plenty of handholds. It might be possible, easy even, to climb down.

Firming up my resolve, I prepared myself to climb over the edge. My first step into a wild new world!

# Chapter One
# Like You've Seen a Ghost

I swung my foot around, searching for purchase across the stony wall until I felt an outcropping big enough that the toes of my shoe could grab on. Bouncing a few times, I tested my weight and balance on the hold, then gently moved my other foot around while lowering my body.

I had been climbing for a whole ten minutes already, and so far my descent had lowered me by maybe six or so feet. It was hard and slow and a little nerve-wracking. Not having any ropes was the worst part of it.

My original goal had been to climb all the way to the bottom, but there was a window a whole lot closer to the ground and it didn't seem to be blocked by anything, any frame it might have held long gone.

Crossing my fingers - metaphorically, because if I let go of the wall I would go splat - I hoped that there would be a way to move down the tower from within.

It was some long, sweaty work, with the sun straight above and beaming down on my head, but I managed to make it close enough to the side of the window to peek inside.

The room was a mess, with large wooden racks toppled over and part of the floor, wooden this time, burned though. Still, other than a few cobweb-weaving spiders there wasn't much to see.

I stepped on the windowsill and crouched down before placing one foot on the floor. It held my weight with no creaking or bouncing, so I hopped down. I had made it! The door to this room was a splintered mess on the ground, as if someone had burst through in a hurry, and I could kind of guess why.

This was an armoury. There were racks for armour off to one side, with a few scraps of cloth and leather left behind.

Loot!

With an eager giggle I bounced over to the racks and tried picking up some neat looking pauldrons, but the leather was dry and cracked and broke apart almost as soon as I grabbed it. The cloth armour beneath was little better.

This place had been abandoned for a long time, I guessed.

The racks that had tumbled over looked like they were meant to hold weapons on them, spears or swords. I started toeing around the rubble and a couple of pokes with my foot revealed some spearheads lying on the ground, shafts long gone. The racks were made of sturdier wood, or wood that didn't rot, maybe.

And then I found it.

Nearly buried under a pile of wood and coloured nearly the same brown was a sword. Not just any sword, but a huge thing that was longer than my entire arm span.

It took plenty of grunting and lifting and some more sweat to yank it out, but soon enough I held my prize before me. The sword was bent in its middle, and the edge was nicked quite badly, and maybe it was a teensy bit very rusted, but I now had a sword!

I spun around, sword raised above my head in victory and cheered.

"Rwraa," someone, or something, said.

I froze, body going rigid at the sound.

I wasn't alone.

Lowering my new sword, I moved towards the door, carefully avoiding the burnt hole in the ground in case I fell through. I tried to move as silently as I could as I poked my head out into a corridor lined with embrasures on either side. The tower was apparently part of a bigger facility, placed at a corner where two long corridors met. One ended about two dozen meters to my right in a staircase that dropped down, the other passage was blocked by fallen masonry, the light of day shining through the cracks.

"Hello?" I asked.

"Rrer."

The noise was… a growl? Maybe? It sounded more like the kind of noise I'd make if you were to try and poke me awake. It came from the passage with the stairs.

Placing my sword on my shoulder, I moved towards the nearest arrow slit, this one facing the opposite direction from the wall I had scaled down.

There was a town!

Not a big one. I counted fifteen roofs, most just a little lower than the level I was on, and in bad need of some patchwork. Some looked to have been lit on fire a long time ago, timbers showing past missing roof tiles. The building I was in seemed to be a tall wall that circled all the way around the town, another tower placed on the opposite end from where I was.

There was a lot you could tell about people from the kind of house they lived in. All of these had different sorts of shingles, with most of them a sort of dull clay-red. Every house had a chimney and I couldn't see any wires running from home to home.

That confirmed a few things for me. Whoever had lived here was human-sized. The armour helped narrow that down too.

I moved on. There would be plenty of time to explore soon. I was certainly looking forward to it!

The descent to the next floor down was much easier with steps as opposed to rock climbing. I wholeheartedly approved of steps. The bottom floor was a mess. Old soggy papers turned to mulch on the ground, barely leaving an imprint, stains that I hoped weren't blood. Lots of signs that there had been a fire.

There was an exit, at one time, a sort of archway with a large door in it leading into the village, but it had collapsed. And under the pile of rubble from that collapse was the mysterious stranger making all that noise.

I swallowed as I stared at the skeleton stuck under a few choice stones. Glowing eyes fixed onto me and its head and neck wobbled a little, the one arm that wasn't pinned in place wiggling futilely in my direction. "Rraaer," it said.

The room across from the archway where the skeleton was pinned looked like a sort of office space. Big old desks covered in rotting papers and the tattered remains of a flag on one wall. Another wall had had a hole blown through it, revealing a bunch of beds in neat rows with chests next to them.

Nothing that could hurt me.

"Ah, hi?" I asked.

"Rrr," the skeleton replied. He seemed dead set on hurting me.

I held back an inappropriate giggle and moved closer. "Hey there," I said in the same voice I would use to greet a doggy. "You're a nice skeleton, aren't you? Yes you are!"

"Rraararrr!" the skeleton replied. He didn't like that I was coming closer.

"So, magic really is real around here," I said, the giddiness in my tummy returning. "I'm sorry, Mister Skeleton. Didn't mean to disturb your rest."

I should probably have considered burying the poor thing. It was rather pitiful. Then again, I had yet to explore the rest of the tower. Maybe there was a crypt I could put him in? Or a nice graveyard. I considered using my handy dandy new sword, but Mister Skeleton had never done anything to me.

"Is it mister or miss skeleton?" I asked.

"Rrr."

"Hmm," I hummed. "How about Bonesy. Nice and gender—and life—neutral."

"Rraarrara."

"I agree," I said. "It's a fine name." I reached down and patted Bonesy where it couldn't reach its head. "I'll be back."

The office was split into two parts. The front more of a reception area of some sort and the back a more private and secluded office. With the little light coming in from the passage where Bonesy was resting it was hard to tell.

I searched through the desks, prying drawers open with my Greatsword of Prying +1 but only found rotten knick-knacks and some papers that were impossible to read in the low light. I stacked those that looked to be in better shape on the desk nearest the exit.

The big office at the back didn't have much more in it. A few bottles tucked in the desk, still closed and with labels that, when brought to the light, revealed designs of grapes on them. A rusted flask, a dagger that was in even worse shape than my sword.

There was a chest behind the desk, in surprisingly good shape, but I couldn't find a way to open it.

I managed to drag it closer to the front, but the effort wasn't worth it, and my Greatsword of Prying +1 wasn't tough enough to open the chest. All I managed was to make the tip break off when I tried.

Giving up for now, I moved into the barracks.

The mattresses were all filled with rotting hay and the entire room stank of mildew. The smell only grew worse when I found a small bathroom of sorts tucked in the back. Each chest was opened and each of them was a disappointment. They were either empty already or the only things within were old and stinky.

Worn boots, some cloth that resembled swiss cheese, a few belts that were stiffer than my sword. I did find a few coppery coins that had turned green with verdigris spilling out of a pierced sack, and one chest had a haversack that was in decent shape. It was empty, but that changed as soon as I put my newfound coppery wealth in it.

A peek into the bathroom revealed something neat. There was a shower, which confused me until I noticed the stone covered in strange glyphs held by a sort of metal sconce above.

Magic showers! Neat.

I found a sort of pad on the wall that had a corresponding glyph on it but pressing it did nothing.

Pressing and pouting also did nothing. But pressing and pushing with my mind, as if I had to poop really bad, made the glyph above glow and a spray of water came out. It was weak, and lukewarm, and I might have shrieked when it splattered onto my head, but it was water.

I wasn't going to die of dehydration! Yay!

The only other thing of interest was a small cupboard filled with cleaning supplies. A mop that didn't look usable, some clothes that were moth worn but still usable. Another broom and a dustpan and bucket.

Well, I already had some levels in cleaning…

I weighed the value of cleaning out the old barracks against resuming my explorations. In the end, exploration won out handily.

Grinning from ear to ear, I pressed on past Bonesy and down the main corridor inside the wall. A convenient hole in the wall allowed me to squeeze out of the barracks with my haversack and sword in tow.

I had a town to explore! If I was lucky, I would find some food and a place to rest for later. Maybe some clothes and a way to contact people. Oh, and magical tomes, and ancient swords and of course a bunch of new friends!

It was going to be brilliant!

I exited behind a stout little house that was squished between two others. There had been a fence behind it, but it was torn apart at some point long ago. I moved around the house, intending to circle the town and see everything before checking in the houses one by one. A map would have been nice, or a Geography for Dummies book in English.

Instead, as I rounded the corner of the house and moved into an alleyway, I came face-to-back with a floating, white spectre.

It was a person, sorta. A hazy image suspended in the air, their clothes fluttering in a wind that I couldn't feel. I felt colder just watching them. Not a metaphorical cold either.

"H-hello! My name is Broccoli, do you want to be friends?" I asked.

The ghost turned around slowly, its placid, bored face tilting down to look at me. Then its features turned ugly and it screeched.

**You have heard the screech of a fearsome creature! Your soul is shaken.**

I shook. Arms and legs and chest wobbling as the ghost moved in closer, one hand moving back as it got ready to swipe at me.

My sword! I remembered my sword and flung the heavy piece of steel at the ghost, only to see it fly through the monster and bounce on the ground behind it. "Oh, shoot. I'm sorry Mister Ghost I didn't mean to and I'm sorry and oh I don't want to die, I'm leaving now!"

I turned tail and ran.

# Chapter Two

# Who You Gonna Call?

The ghost followed. It didn't make a sound, merely floated at a pace that was just a bit faster than walking, its long cloth-like robes fluttering in an invisible wind behind it as it trailed after me. Still, that look on its face, of indescribable rage and anger never faded, and the soft white glow of its eyes locked onto me and didn't let go.

I ran back through the crack in the wall, then back down the passage. I hoped that it wouldn't follow, but that was dashed when first a hand, then an arm started to push through the wall. The ghost glowed faintly, especially where it was phasing through.

Still, the motion slowed it down.

"Rarr," Bonesy said as I stumbled past him and into the office. Something, I needed something to hurt the ghost. I ran out with a bottle of wine that flew through the ghost's form and smashed against a wall uselessly, the stick—once a chair leg—that I threw next did the same.

I looked around, then picked up Bonesy's head. "Bite him!" I said as I flung the skeletal head at my adversary.

Bonesy 'rawred' as he flew through the air, then, much to my surprise and that of the ghost, the skeletal head chomped down on the ghost's face. "Rarg, ragr, rarre," Bonesy said as he chewed.

I stared, then it clicked. Bonesy was magic. Magic worked on ghosts. It was all rather obvious.

Running into the barracks, I passed the beds and moved into the bathroom. The showerhead glyph was stuck in a metallic basket above, one that wasn't meant to be pried out of the wall, but I had desperation on my side. It came off with a clang and crunch, leaving me with a rusty metal basket and a magical, faintly luminescent stone in it that was still dripping water onto the ground.

The ghost had freed itself from Bonesy's mouthy grasp but not without suffering from my boney friend's cruel ministrations. There were tears in its ghostly form, and whitish vapour was pouring out of it.

I edged closer to the ghost, hoping to slip by it, but the evil-no-good monster blocked my path and spread its arms out as if to give me the deadest hug ever.

"I'm sorry!" I said as I held the showerhead before me. "I just wanted to say hi."

The ghost didn't care, he, it, just advanced on me.

I clocked it in the jaw with my magical showerhead.

The ghost wavered in the air, its face distorted, the anger turned to pain for a moment before returning tenfold. It swiped at me, but I ducked and moved so that a bed was between us. Its next swipe clawed through the mattress with ease.

"I'm really sorry," I said again as I moved up to the ghost and swiped through its entire body with the shower head from head to crotch. There was some resistance… then nothing.

The ghost split apart, both halves smoking as it turned into a fine white dust that spread across the floor.

I sneezed.

**Congratulations! You have murdered 'Sentinel Ghost of Threewells by Darkwood', level 1! Bonus Exp was granted for brutally killing a monster above your level!**

"M-murdered?" I repeated before I tried to grab the box. "That wasn't murder, it was self-defence! Self-defence! Where's my jury of peers?"

"Rar?" Bonesy asked.

"You don't count." I snapped back; then I regretted it. Bonesy had helped a lot. "Sorry. I'm a bit stressed."

I brought my showerhead with me as I moved around, now vigilant for any ghosts. The Sentinel Ghost hadn't seemed all that good at guarding really, but maybe there were more and maybe they patrolled. I would have to sleep with one eye open.

Still, I had learned a few important lessons:

Ghosts weren't magic resistant at all.

They were also scary.

Bonesy's bites were serious business.

This place was probably called Threewells by Darkwood.

A level one ghost was nearly strong enough to end my adventuring career.

I needed to hurry up and level up. Get out there and face the music. Find more ghosts and murd— cleanse their poor souls.

Yup.

That's what I needed to do.

"Hey, Bonesy, you wouldn't mind if I cleaned up around here, right? Right, of course not." Grinding a skill was also a perfectly valid way of spending my time, of course. It was a nice, soothing action and it in no way reminded me that I had almost turned into a ghost myself.

I started with the papers, moving all of them to the chest in the barracks that looked the least worn. They might end up staying dry for longer in there, in case anyone ever wanted to read them. I intended to go over them myself, but I would need to bring them outside for the light and... Later, maybe.

I used the broom and mop as makeshift dusters and ended up sneezing up a storm as the room filled with age-old clouds of dust. By the time I was done and my sneezing fits stopped, I was greeted by a floating box.

**Congratulations! Through repeated actions your Cleaning skill has improved and is now eligible for rank up!**
**Rank E is a free rank!**

A free rank? I thought about my Cleaning skill, and low and behold the menu for it appeared.

*Cleaning*
*Rank F - 100%*
*The ability to clean. As this skill rises in level your ability to Clean will improve!*
*This ability is ready to rank up.*
*Do you wish to increase Cleaning to Rank E?*

"Sure?" I tried.

***Congratulations! Cleaning is now Rank E!***

I blinked at the new box and reopened the skill to see the change.

*Cleaning*
*Rank E - 0%*
*The ability to clean. Your proficiency and instincts for cleanliness have improved!*
*Clean faster, clean better.*

"O-kay," I said. That was nice, I supposed. I hoped that cleaning was one of those skills that was versatile. I had to clean my clothes too at some point, and maybe take a shower later. Still, the progress was nice. I swept all the dust I had kicked up into a neat pile, then used a file folder to scoop it into one of the chests that was now a garbage chest.

Then, out came the showerhead and mop and bucket. The spray was… weak, and my mana ticked down fairly quickly while using it, but it still gave me enough water to start scrubbing the floor.

An hour had passed, maybe more, before I glanced at my skills page again.

*Cleaning*
*Rank E - 06%*

So, about five percent for one room. Which meant… not much. Slower than Rank F, which wasn't too surprising. Shrugging, I looked over the office area. It was far from perfect. There were wet streaks on the ground, and I couldn't do anything about the broken furniture, but it looked like it had been abandoned last year instead of a decade or five ago.

Oh well.

The barracks were next, then the bathroom where I pinched my nose and wished for a nice pair of latex gloves as I cleaned around the wooden latrine hole. At least with the passing of decades anything… biodegradable, had rotted away to nothing.

I wiped the sweat off my brow and looked over the newly cleaned room. There wasn't much I could do about the mattresses, though I had found one that was filled with a slightly less mouldy filling. If I really needed to sleep here, I could use that bed. Maybe.

Shrugging, I turned my efforts to the floor above, though there was little I could do in the armoury except smash the wood into kindling and stack it neatly before mopping up the floor.

*Cleaning*
*Rank E - 14%*

I stared at the skills page for a while, then dismissed it. The sun had passed its zenith and was falling now, the skies not yet turning the yellow-orange of mid-day, but approaching it fast. That was fine. Totally okay.

I wasn't afraid of the dark.

I was afraid of the ghosts living… unliving in it.

"Oh boy," I said. Cleaning was all well and good, but all I was doing was preparing a nice spot for my body to lay. That, and I was hungry. The lukewarm water from the showerhead was handy, but it wouldn't fill my tummy up. "I need a weapon," I said.

I turned towards Bonesy. The skeletal head was resting on one of the desks, mouth working to chew through a piece of rotting wood with wet, mushy noises.

"Any ideas?" I asked the head.

"Rrr."

"Yeah. I can't exactly stick the shower head at the end of a stick and call it a mace. Your head would be a much better weapon."

I blinked.

There was some twine laying around, and cloth that could be used as rope. There was even a broken spear from the armoury, more of a length of wood with a metal cap on the end than anything else, but it was usable.

I got creative!

Nearly an hour and two almost-chewed fingers later, I had a brand-new weapon!

"Wraare!" Bonesy said from his place of pride at the end of my spear. The shaft was stuck through the hole for his spine and into his braincase, and I'd wrapped him in strips of cloth to keep him from rattling around. I didn't want to blind him, though, so I left a gap for his glowing eyes to glare out of.

"I shall dub this weapon… The staff of Bonesy! No, that's silly. The Ghostbuster? The bone stick? The boner club?" I flushed. "Not that last one."

"Rrrr," Bonesy agreed.

Thus armed, I prepared myself to explore once more. My trusty showerhead in my haversack, my Bonesy stick in one hand and all my prayers in mind as I stepped out into the fading daylight.

No ghosts in sight.

I moved slowly around the buildings again, tiptoeing as quietly as I could while taking in the town. The homes were in rough shape but could probably have been renovated and repaired with a bit of love and care. I bet there was a Carpentry skill out there somewhere.

As I rounded the corner, I took in a little plaza with a few smaller homes and a big stone well in the middle. There were more homes than I had initially realized, maybe twenty or twenty-five in all.

It wasn't until I was nearing the main road that I saw the second ghost.

This one looked rather pitiful, floating nearer to the ground, its cloth-like flesh… stuff, all torn up. It seemed to be moving around in a big circle at a slow, shuffling pace. I didn't want to fight it, I really didn't.

"Hey there, Mister Ghosty," I said.

The ghost's floating stopped, and it slowly turned towards me. Its dull eyes searched around then locked onto me. It frowned.

"I don't mean any trouble," I said before raising both hands up in surrender.

The ghost charged.

Well, charge implies rapid movement. The ghost shambled forward like a plastic shopping bag on a windless afternoon. "I'm sorry." I said as I bonked it on the head with Bonesy.

The ghost hit the ground and sort of splattered into dust.

I sneezed again, then looked around to see if anyone or anything had heard. There was only a new box to greet me.

**Congratulations! You have plotted and successfully carried out the homicide of 'Sentinel Ghost of Threewells by Darkwood', level 1! Bonus Exp was granted for killing a monster above your level!**

"No," I squeaked before my hand slapped across my mouth. "It wasn't homicide, I swear," I said.

"Rrre," Bonesy accused.

"No," I squeaked again.

Looking down, I noticed a bit of cloth left on the ground, cloth that shimmered lightly. A poke with my foot didn't do anything except move it about. I carefully picked it up. A loot drop? Inspecting it revealed nothing, but it did shimmer with a certain ethereal quality. I slid it into my haversack and picked my Bonesy stick up again.

There were ghosts around, and no telephone to call the Ghostbusters, which left no one but little old me to take care of things.

I whimpered.

# Chapter Three
# Crime Spree

**Congratulations! You have snuffed out the unlife of 'Sentinel Ghost of Threewells by Darkwood', level 1! Bonus Exp was granted for ending a monster above your level!**

I sniffled and held Bonesy close as I watched the ghost fade away. It was the third ghost I'd killed, the third that had responded to my friendly request with nothing but murder and meanness.

I had moved towards the main street of Threewells, or at least the street that bisected the town from one wall to the next. I tried to keep low and go slow, only poking my head up to peek into windows and try to spot any more ghosts. So far, I had been lucky.

The first few homes were normal enough, with little dining rooms and fireplaces and some quaint furniture. No plates on the tables or signs that people had left in a hurry, so whatever struck the town must have come with some warning.

The fourth house in the row was way larger, with thick double doors and a third floor under its peaked roof. A rusty sign out front hinted that it was a shop of some sort, but the sign was unreadable except for the design that was either a chimney or a well. Probably a well.

I stood up on tippy toes to see into the big window at the front, then dipped down when I caught sight of not one, but two ghosts floating around lazily within. "Oh no," I whispered. "Bonesy, what do I do?"

"Rrrr."

I was climbing back up to take another peek when a ghastly hand tore out of the wall and grabbed my face. Icy coldness seeped into me before I jerked my head back, but the grip was too strong.

Desperate for leverage, I put a foot against the wall and kicked off, tearing myself free of the ghost's grasp, but not without the burning hot sensation of three cuts across my face. I wanted to scream, but that would just make things worse.

I picked Bonesy from where it had rolled and spun to face my attackers.

The second ghost was coming out of the wall slowly, but the first, the one with the bloody hand, was almost out already. Moving through things slowed them down, which meant that this was my chance.

Bonesy swished through the first ghost with a gleeful 'Rreee,' then, after I had caught my balance again, I swiped the bone-topped staff through once more.

The ghost was looking worse for wear, but the attacks had taken time, and now it was joined by its brother. A glance around revealed a third ghost floating towards me from across the street.

I could have stood my ground and fought, but even with one ghost nearly re-dead I didn't like my odds. I aimed for the nearest alleyway and ran.

If my sense of direction wasn't completely off, it led to a spot near the hole in the wall where I had found Bonesy. I stumbled into the backyard of the large building and, after a glance to make sure it was ghostless, spun around.

The three ghosts were lined up now, all of them floating towards me with murder in their eyes.

I licked my lips and tasted the blood from my cheek. My cheek that the ghost's hand had failed to pass through. I was magic.

Or magical enough that they couldn't phase through me. Or they could unphase their hands for the purposes of chopping innocent teenagers up into bite-sized pieces.

I wasn't going to test anything.

The first ghost arrived and was greeted with a smack from Bonesy. The ghost, already injured earlier, broke apart in a fine mist. Its brother ghosts didn't seem to mind all that much, or maybe they were even angrier, but only had one angry facial expression to work with and couldn't display their heightened rage.

I didn't know and didn't care. Bonesy swooshed through the next ghost, first down, then up, then down again. The ghost caught the haft, wood smacking into its hand a couple of feet above its translucent head.

I stared.

The ghost stared.

Bonesy stared at the wall.

With a crunch, the ghost crushed my spear, rendering it down to mere splinters where it had caught it. Then gravity did its thing and dragged Bonesy down through its ghostly body, killing it on the spot.

"Rrar," Bonesy said, rejoicing in its victory.

"W-well done!" I said before the last ghost moved over Bonesy and completely blocked my path to my only weapons. "Ah, can we... negotiate? Please?"

The ghost didn't care.

I could have run, but that would have meant abandoning Bonesy and also I wasn't sure if the backyard had an exit or not, not unless I snuck back into the wall, then up to the second floor, then down the side of the tower again.

It was a bad idea. The ghost could cut me off at any moment.

Instead, I brought my haversack around, the one holding my shower-head, and held it out in front of me. "I'm sorry!" I shouted as I charged at the ghost.

As slow moving as it was, the ghost didn't have time to so much as twitch before I rammed into him.

Cold. So very cold, but also wispy, like standing in front of an air conditioner with nothing on but an oversized t-shirt.

I shot through the ghost, suddenly meeting no resistance. Took two tumbling steps and tripped over Bonesy to land on the ground with a splat. Fortunately, I had my trusty haversack to break my fall. The sack that currently held the very sharp, very pointy showerhead glyph.

"Owie," I whined. Turning around, I looked up in time to see the final ghost fade away into a cloud of whitish dust. "Oh, thank the stars," I said.

**Congratulations! You have caused three (3) enemies ('Sentinel Ghost of Threewells by Darkwood', level 1 x3) to give up the ghost! Bonus Exp was granted for killing three (3) monsters above your level!**
**Bing Bong! Congratulations, your Cinnamon Bun class has reached level 1!**
*Stamina +5*
*Flexibility +5*
**You have gained: One Class Point**

"A what?" I asked. Then a wash of heat running through my entire body distracted me for a moment. It was nice, like being tucked into bed by my mom and getting a warm kiss on the forehead from dad right after.

Still, the sensation faded a moment later and I decided that I had spent enough time staring at the sky as it appeared between two buildings. It was getting darker by the moment. I would need to find shelter soon.

But first...

*Class Points: One*
*Class points are used to upgrade a Class*
*Skill.*

"O-kay?" I wasn't going to waste that on cleaning just yet.

Bonesy was still stuck to a chunk of wood, but the weapon was now more of a mace than a staff or spear. That's what I got for working with sub-par materials.

I walked through the streets with a bit more confidence. I now knew that I could run through ghosts to dispatch them. Sorta. Anyway, they were now on my level, literally. It didn't help that I didn't know how many there were in the town, but that didn't matter.

I moved over to one of the smaller houses I had seen, one of three next to the big. I peek through the window, miraculously still intact, showing nothing of worth, so I pulled the door open.

The squeal of rusty hinges had me tensing, but nothing showed up to eat me. Instead, I found the inside of the house to be a horrible mess. There was a crate to one side, a bunch of things tossed into it, furniture was laying all over the place and the paint over one wall was discoloured as if a painting had been taken.

Looters, maybe? Or people packing up in a hurry?

The home was simple. Four rooms. A small kitchen, a dining area, and a bedroom along one side. There was even a small bathroom tucked away in a corner. It was all messy, horribly, horribly messy.

But I had a skill for that!

I found an old broom and even a feather duster laying around, as well as some soap in a little pan. The items in the house were in far better condition than those outside. Which wasn't saying much, really, the place was mouldy and dirty and draughty.

Still, I started cleaning and exploring. The blankets for the bed were flung out the back door and into a sort of bin I suspected was for composting, judging by the little garden space out back. Then I patted down the thin mattress and found it… usable, if barely. Then came the dusting and the broom and the tossing out of trash, all done with a speed and ease that surprised me a little. Maybe that's what a rank E in Cleaning really meant.

*Cleaning*
*Rank E - 44%*

I blinked at the rise in experience. It was getting close, and I still needed some essentials. Like food.

Screwing up my courage, I snuck out of the house and visited the neighbour's place. It was in a much worse shape, the roof having caved in and obvious water damage ruining the floor. I didn't do much, merely dusted a little, tossed out some things and searched for anything handy, but other than a fire poker that might have served as a non-anti-ghost weapon there wasn't much.

The third house is where I struck gold. Or rather, silver.

This home was a bit bigger than the others, with a cellar below and a second bedroom within and a sort of little workshop in the back. The tools were all gone except for some gardening implements that were more rust than anything else.

The interior was still furnished. Chairs and tables and beds that still had sheets over them. The closets and chests hid some moth-eaten clothes and the little pantry next to the kitchen had some lumps that might have been bread at one time.

At the back were three jars, each filled with liquid gold. "Honey!" I squealed as I brought the glass jars closer. The orangey stuff within looked hard and it was heavy in my hands, but recognizable still. Some prying and sweating later and the jar opened with a pop. A sniff, then a lick proved it to be just that.

I resealed the jar and went back to searching, almost absentmindedly cleaning as I did so.

Everything that looked edible went onto a freshly wiped table. This place was nice. With few windows from which a monster or ghost could see me and enough stuff that I could pass the night.

Choice made, I got to cleaning, and it's thanks to that that I found a loose floorboard. By the time I pried it open with a fire poker it was going dark outside, but not so much that I couldn't marvel at the six pieces of silver I had found.

I was rich! Maybe.

Six silver, a fire poker, three medium-ish sized jars of honey, a jar of vinegar that I suspected was apple cider, three unopened bottles of wine and a block of what I hoped was salt wrapped in waxy paper. Not exactly a feast, but I retrieved a cleanish spoon and took a few scrapes of honey. It was nice and sweet but didn't go so well with the sip of vinegar I tried.

I wasn't going to starve, which was nice. I just had to make sure to survive the night.

I moved blankets over the windows where curtains once hung and made a nice bed for myself with the nicer bundles of clothes I could find in the middle of the living room. Bonesy kept me company, a thin cloth over his face serving to keep it quiet.

"Good night, Bonesy," I said.

"Rrr," the skull replied.

I laid down and thought of my adventure so far. Of discovering a tiny corner of a huge land and of fighting mean ghosts.

The smile wouldn't keep off my face even as I fell asleep while faint glows appeared and faded beyond the windows of my tiny abode.

## Chapter Four
# Dusting Off History

I settled into a routine of sorts. First, I would circle around the house, Bonesy-maul in one hand, fire poker in the other. Then, if I spotted no ghosts, I would try the front door. The people of Threewells must have been very trusting because few of their doors were locked and those that were opened to a swift kick near their handles.

The first three or so homes I snuck into were all fairly similar, but I uncovered little stories and hints of what might have been. A room with a cradle made of delicately twisted wood that had somehow resisted the test of time, a small library with leather bindings that might have once been books in one home. A blacksmith's house, with hammer heads left here and there and a cracked anvil serving as a coffee table.

There weren't any bodies, none that I found, anyway. Just signs that people had left in a hurry. A sickness, maybe? But no, that would have left signs. Maybe the local mine dried up and the community up and left. There were some things that looked expensive that had been left behind though, things too heavy and complicated to carry if you were in a hurry.

I moved back onto the main street, walking a little taller now that I had failed to see any ghosts all morning. I knew there were still some around, but they didn't scare me anymore.

Not much.

Okay, so they still scared me, but I was one tough cookie, I could stand up against a ghost. But probably not two.

I came to the large building where I'd seen two ghosts yesterday and slipped into it. Almost immediately my eyes grew wide and a grin tugged at me. "An inn!" I squealed to Bonesy.

"Rerr," Bonesy agreed.

There were round tables and chairs all around them, a huge hearth against one wall and a long counter at one end with all sorts of bottles on the wall behind it. Rusting lamps hung from the ceiling and the tattered remains of banners were crumpled on the ground. I spun around and took in the room. I could imagine gruff adventurers, pretty elves, stout dwarves and cunning magicians taking a seat and maybe pinching the occasional barmaid's bum.

I giggled in delight, but the sound felt off, wrong in such a dead and vacant place.

I had to explore. And then, maybe I could clean up a little. My Cleaning skill was slowly rising, and I was getting nearer and nearer to the tantalizing prize of Rank D, whatever that would mean.

```
Cleaning
Rank E - 87%
```

Still no other skills, but I knew they would come!

I was itching to get started with the inn, but I decided to explore a tiny bit first. There was a staircase off to one side leading up one floor, with a pretty carved rail and what might have been a carpet once; behind that was the far less decorative staircase into the building's basement.

I went down first, while the sunlight was still angled in such a way that I could see. The basement had a thick door separating it from the rest of the inn, which I found was locked. I frowned at it and kicked the door, even going so far as to lay on my back to deliver a heel-strike next to the brass handle, but that only made the door shudder.

No good.

Still, no ghosts came through, so I was in the clear.

I decided to check the rest of the first floor, then make my way up. The kitchens were big, with a couple of stoves and a big oven off to one side. I found bins that might once have contained flour and wheat and a small pantry where I got to add another jar of honey to my collection. There were also jars of what I thought might be jam, but I wasn't going to take the risk of falling sick with those.

The bathrooms only got a cursory glance and the space behind the counter was empty save for a wooden thing that might have been a cross-bow tucked where the bartender could grab it in a hurry. It really was an inn for adventurers. A sign hung above the racks of bottles, just like the one outside but in better condition. This place was called the 'Well Inn Good' at one time. I barked a laugh at the name and moved on.

The only other rooms were for storage, filled with rotten linens and the moth-eaten remains of blankets and suchlike. One room was a small office with a board on a wall that had little keys on rings sitting pretty on rows of pegs. I tossed them all into my haversack just in case before I moved on.

The steps creaked as I made my way up to the second floor. I had an idea of what to expect. Probably a row of doors on both ends of a corridor, and I was partially correct. There were doors on both sides of the passageway, with ancient paintings hanging off the walls next to lanterns hanging off of hooks.

I made a note to add one to my haversack later. There had been candles here and there and I was sure that a source of light would be handy later.

Each door was opened after some searching for the right key and the small rooms within inspected. Most were small, with a little bed and just enough room to move around in.

Those on the opposite side were a fair bit bigger, with beds big enough for two and little dressers tucked against the walls. I checked all of them but found nothing salvageable.

Then I found the stairs leading to the third floor—and a ghost.

My heart skipped a beat as I took in the lonely form of a ghost hovering in mid-air, its vacant eyes looking out of one of the windows overlooking part of the town I hadn't explored yet. I moved up very carefully, sure not to make a sound and wincing at every creak from the floor.

Half the top floor was a sort of lounge area, with chairs that looked like they had been comfy once and coffee tables with decaying detritus on them. There were only three rooms here, each one way bigger than the rooms below.

They seemed empty, all save one.

The corpse was laying on the bed, legs over the side and torso stretched out. It was old, little more than bones and sinew. I wondered if it's where the ghost came from.

"Hello?" I tried.

The ghost didn't move.

A deaf ghost, or a busy one? I held up Bonesy, ready to strike, then hesitated. This one wasn't trying to hurt me.

I swallowed past my fear and reached out a hand. I touched the ghost's sides, sending chills up my arm. The ghost turned.

We locked eyes.

It had a placid, calm face, not a hint of the anger I say in the others. I felt as if I was being inspected before the ghost dismissed me and returned to staring.

"I'm sorry for bothering you," I whispered, and the ghost nodded. "Um, can you help me?" I asked.

The ghost didn't say or do anything, he just turned and kept staring out the window to something across the street.

I looked around it, careful in case it suddenly moved, and tried to find what it was looking for. It wasn't hard to find. Across the road, and just visible from where we stood between the roofs of two homes, was a dark pit in the ground. The remains of bricks around it hinted at the presence of a well there once. A form floated above. Dark, malevolent and creepy as all heck.

It was a ghost, but one that was dark and broody and probably listened to indie pop.

A ding sounded out in the back of my mind.

Quest Updated!
**The Hole Down Under**
*An evil root has plunged into the world. You have found the hole. Explore it. Find the root. Destroy it.*

"Aww, shucks."

I cleaned the inn from top to bottom, only avoiding the room with the friendly ghost's body because I didn't want to strain our relationship by stepping into his comfort zone. I was nearly done with the second floor when a 'ding' sounded out.

**Congratulations! Through repeated actions your Cleaning skill has improved and is now eligible for rank up!
Rank D is a free rank!**

I whooped and cheered. Finally!

My skill screen came up next, Cleaning front and centre.

*Cleaning*
*Rank E - 100%*
*The ability to clean. Your proficiency and instincts for cleanliness have improved! Clean faster, clean better.*
*This ability is ready to rank up. Do you wish to increase Cleaning to Rank D?*

"Yes please!" I told the menu.

**Congratulations! Cleaning is now Rank D!**
*Cleaning*
*Rank D - 00%*
*The ability to Clean. You are exceptionally good at tidying up and washing off.*

*Effectiveness of cleaning is greatly increased.*

"Neat," I said. I didn't know how that would work out, but it seemed like a valuable skill. Maybe. Maybe I should have spent more time trying to learn how to swing a club or start fires or anything else, but this, exploring and uncovering the story of such an old place? This felt nice.

I moved into the next room, broom and duster and dustpan and trash chest armed and ready.

I left the room ten minutes later and turned around to take it all in. The furniture was spotless, the bed well made, the floor had just a bit of a lustre to it and the air smelled fresher. All that in under ten minutes. It had passed... not in a haze, I knew what I had been doing the entire time, but each step felt so natural and easy.

A giggle escaped. My parents would have flipped if I had been this good at cleaning just a week ago.

*Cleaning*
*Rank D - 03%*

I frowned at that. Only three percent for one room where before it gave quite a bit more than that. Not quite double, but close. At ten minutes per room... a bit of mental math later revealed that I was really bad at math. Also, math was something I could do while working. "Chop-chop, Broccoli, these rooms won't clean themselves!" I said in a gruff voice, as if I was the owner of this inn.

An hour or so later I found myself tidying up the main floor, setting chairs back in place and pushing a hefty pile of dust into a pan that I was going to have to dump in the back. Next, the bathrooms. The stalls were clean enough, but I still splashed some water around and mopped them up, then I used a fresh cloth to clean off the little mirrors above a basin that probably once held water for hand washing.

I stared at my reflection and froze.

I was wearing a smile as I always did, hair pulled back into a not-so-neat ponytail that was tied together with a cloth ribbon. What drew my attention though were the three slashes across my face. One on my right cheek, two on the left. The blood from the forgotten cut had stained my face red and made me look like some sort of ghoulish madwoman. It didn't help that my hair was frazzled and my skin needed a good wash.

That just wouldn't do!

I found a fresh, less disgusting cloth in my sack, wetted it with my trusty showerhead glyph and dabbed at my face, wincing as I reopened the cut a little. I rubbed and rubbed and rubbed until I knew that it was clean, then stared.

And then I stared some more.

It clicked after a moment. I had super-cleaning powers. Of course I could clean my face very well. But I never expected it to clean away skin blemishes and pimples.

This changed everything!

I snorted and tossed the dirty rag aside. Not really. I would never get to show off my pretty skin if I didn't survive the adventure. It was time to get exploring again. There were more houses to see, and a monster ghost to face, and a deep foreboding hole in the ground that apparently hid a great evil, and of course more stuff to clean.

I moved over to the main room, ready to move on when an idea struck me. If I was going to clean the entire town to grind my mad cleaning skills, it would probably be best if I kept notes. A bit of charcoal from the fireplace and a piece of cloth served as a very rudimentary pen and paper.

My map was crude, but it gave me something to aim for. I was going to clean the entire town and get rid of every evil ghost around!

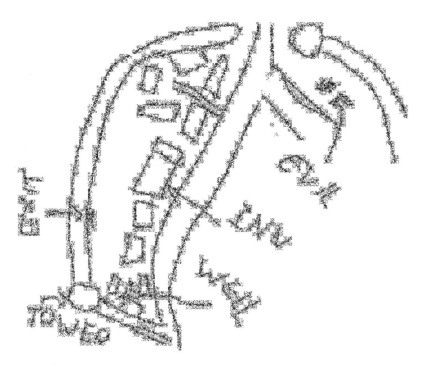

## Chapter Five
# An Insightful Afternoon

```
Cleaning
Rank D - 44%
```

I grinned at the results, wiped my forehead dry of sweat and stretched until my back pop-popped in a most satisfactory way. The sun was starting to dip already. It was crazy how much fun you could have just exploring.

So far, I had covered two of the houses next to the Inn, both of them much bigger than the homes on the Inn's other side. They had enough bedrooms and space for big families, and the quality of the furniture was much better. I even managed to find better brooms and a mop that looked almost brand new and that seemed to stay fresh no matter how much I used it.

A magic mop! Or one that was just really well made.

I had three more homes to work on in this corner of the town—the section that I suspected was reserved for the richer inhabitants—then I would move all the way to the other end in the poorer section where I could see the peaked roof of a church.

Nodding to myself, I stepped out of the last house, Bonesy in my wash bucket and my mop and broom slung over my shoulder.

I should have been paying more attention.

A white hand clawed out towards my face and I squeaked as I bent over backwards to avoid the swipe aimed right at me.

I fell on my bum, then rolled to the side as a claw raked through the ground where I had fallen. My hand shot out and I grabbed Bonesy, swinging the head around to slice through the next swipe aiming for my face.

It worked, making the ghostly hand vanish for a moment before it re-formed. It was a big enough window of time that I was able to roll again, then climb onto my feet. My skirt and blouse were soggy where they had rolled in the grass and my hair had gone wild, but that was secondary to the ghost that turned and tried to claw at me again.

"Not this time, buster," I said as I swiped Bonesy through one arm, then the other, then with a yell that was totally not a squeak, I swished the skeletal head through the ghost from top to bottom.

I panted as the ghost faded away to nothing, leaving only a glowing dust behind that soon sparkled away into darkness. "Oh my goshness," I said as

I tried to calm my beating heart. I looked this way and that, taking in the homes all around me and inspecting everything.

That had been close. Way too close. And so easy to avoid too. All I had to do was stick my head out of the door and look around and I would have been fine. This wasn't home - I had to remind myself - where things weren't out to kill you all day every day.

My grip around Bonesy tightened and I shivered.

**Congratulations! You have made 'Sentinel Ghost of Threewells by Darkwood', level 1, come to a sticky end!**

I stared at the prompt. "Was that a stick pun?" I asked.

Clearly the menu systems in this world were all quite evil. It was something to take my mind off my latest near-death experience… and now I was the one making puns. I groaned and looked up to the sky, taking in the huge blue expanse with the occasional distant birds and the strange balloon in the dista—

I blinked and focused on what looked like a tiny—or very, very distant—oblong balloon. It was brownish grey, with a large red mark on its side and a faint trail of smoke behind it. Not something organic, not with the way it hung motionless in the sky.

"What is that?" I wondered.

*Ding! For repeating a Special Action a sufficient number of times, you have unlocked the general skill: Insight!*

"Holy moly!" I looked around. I hadn't forgotten the whole ghost almost-eating-my-face thing, but this was certainly a nice distraction. "Insight!" I said as I held up Bonesy

*A Skeleton (level ?) head attached to a stick.*

I laughed, then pressed a hand over my mouth to keep the sound low. Looking up, I stared at the tiny distant shape and thought 'insight' as hard as I could.

*An airship.*

"A flip fluffering airship?" I gasped.

There were magical airships around! The world had just gotten a million times cooler. But those were things I'd never get to see if I stayed in this ghost-town…

"Oh no, the puns are catching up."

I shook my head, picked up all of my gear, and moved on to the next house. This one's front door was locked, but the window was completely smashed in. It was pretty easy to climb in then unlock the door from the inside.

There were some bits of furniture left in this house, more so than in others. I made the rounds, checking the kitchen for anything good, then the pantry and the single bedroom and bathroom on the first floor. Nothing. I did find a strange room on the second floor, with large training dummies that were sad and squashed looking where the straw stuffing that had once filled them was rotten away and a rack with some rusty short swords on it. They were probably cheap even before time took its toll. Still, I replaced my fire poker and counted myself lucky.

In the next room over, this one an office with a broken window that had let the elements slip in, I found a small dent atop a desk where the dust was sitting strangely. A bit of poking revealed a hidden compartment, but it only held a silvery key and a bit of ribbon that had rotted away. I tucked it in my sack and kept searching, but to no avail.

Once I was done with the top floor I began grinding.

"Insight."

*A training dummy.*

"Insight!"

*A sword.*

"Insight?"

*A practice pole.*

So, Insight wasn't that useful, at least not at this level. That just meant I now had two skills I could grind! Insight seemed to be increasing by a percentage point with every item I used it on, which was simple enough. But I didn't want to leave my cleaning fall behind.

An hour or so later I carefully, with much snooping around and down and up, moved out of the house and called it done.

*Cleaning*
*Rank D - 68%*

*Insight*
*Rank F - 89%*

Grinning, I moved onto the next home, then the next. Halfway through the first home a big 'ding' resounded in the back of my head and I jumped for joy and spun around with my broom.

**Congratulations! Through repeated actions your Insight skill has improved and is now eligible for rank up!**
**Rank E is a free rank!**

"Woo!" I cheered as I bounced on the spot, only stopping when my broom handle banged on the ceiling and sent a wave of dust clattering down onto my head. I coughed and choked and sputtered and basically lost a lot of the good cheer I'd just garnered.

I accepted the rank up and checked out my crazy new skill.

*Insight*
*Rank E - 00%*
*The Ability to know something. The knowledge*
*you gain is increased.*

"Wow!" I said before focusing on Bonesy who was sitting in a corner to watch me clean.

*A Skeleton (level ?) head poorly attached*
*to a stick.*

"That was… underwhelming." None of the other things I used Insight on revealed much more than what they were with a single word descriptor of their quality or age. I sort of already know that my short sword was rusty. But that was just rank E! Maybe I'd become a real Sherlock Holmes when I hit rank SS+!

My cleaning continued, my skills at housecleaning in a dead city improving to the point where I could clean a whole house in just under an hour or so. I guessed. I would need a watch at some point.

If watches existed.

But airships did, so why not?

I took what little stuff I had found that was useful. A nice silver candle holder with a mirrored hand protector that would keep the light out of the holder's eyes, a pretty painting of a boat on a river with a dragon flying in the background in a nice frame, a few spoons and table knives made of silver, and tossed them all into a rough sack I found that was hole-less. They were the sum total of my riches.

When I found civilization my first stop was going to be an antique's store where I could sell all of the stuff and make enough to fund any future adventures!

I pulled out my map and checked it out. It seemed that I had cleaned and explored the—I was going to call it Western—part of the town completely. The Evil Hole of Great Evil was just to the East of where I was, which was totally off limits because I was pretty sure the only respawn I would get was as a ghost to haunt the next poor adventurer and that wasn't neat.

More grinding!

I had to admit, cleaning had never been so much fun. Or grinding for that matter. There were real, tangible benefits to all of this, and I loved every moment of it except for the moments where I was nearly dying. Those I could do without.

I arrived at the southern end of the town and realized that I would need to update my map a lot. But before that, more sneaking!

Moving between two homes, I kept myself low to the ground, my haversack and cleaning gear and things left next to a house behind to reduce the noise I made as I moved around.

It seemed that at some point the road leading into the town forked and never reconnected, so that the road I had been exploring for the past day and a bit was disconnected from the one I found now. This road ended at a big gate that was left ajar, just enough for someone to walk through if it wasn't for the huge pile of branches stuffed by the entrance.

There was another well, which made three! I was right about the name!

My silent cheering at my discovery froze up when I peeked around a corner and found the old church I had seen a while ago. It was a large building with two bell towers and a small graveyard behind it. One filled with ghosts. A quick snoop revealed five glowing forms wandering in circles.

Five too many.

I still snooped around a little. The buildings nearest the church looked like businesses. A blacksmith's shop, a supply store of some kind, a shop with a stick-like symbol before it. I took note of what I could see, then backed away.

Too much for me to handle at my level.

Maybe it was best that I just… move on. But then that would leave my quest undone, and something niggled at me about it. It didn't have a timer, exactly, but I could tell that the longer I waited the harder things would get.

No. It was best that I stick around and at least try to see what I could do. There was another tower to visit at the far end of town. Close to the evil ghost but not on it. And there were ghosts that I might be able to chat with.

And of course more stuff to explore.

I entered a house as far from the church as could be and did my usual snoop and clean routine. Then, nearly an hour later, as the sun was setting, I used the last rays to update my map, scrubbing out mistakes with some spit and rubbing, and checked on my skill growth.

```
Insight
Rank E - 14%
Cleaning
Rank D - 84%
```

Come morning I would hit Cleaning rank C and probably Insight rank D. Two handy skills to have, but neither combat based. Still, I wasn't without options. I would try to lure some ghosts closer to me and take them out with Bonesy. Insight had come from repetitive actions. Cleaning from a smaller number of actions, but it was a 'class' skill.

Cinnamon Bun was obviously not a combat class, so for a fighting skill I would need a whole lot more repetitions.

I could do it, I knew I could!

"I believe in me!" I said.

"Rrrr," Bonesy agreed. And with that, I packed up and snuck back to the spot I'd slept in the night prior.

## Chapter Six
# Armoured and Ready

I was feeling off as I sat down at a quiet table, Bonesy propped up across from me with a spoon crunching in their mouth.

There was a spoon in my own mouth, metal clinking against my teeth and I wiggled it around and let the lingering taste of honey fade away. It took some thinking, some soul-searching, to figure out exactly what it was that bothered me.

I was lonely.

My entire life had been filled with people. Friends and family and new faces that were just waiting for me to make them smile. We had moved a lot throughout my life, so I was used to parting with friends and making new ones all the time. That had to be it. This town was quiet, no one to talk to, no one to share with.

But that would change! I would accomplish my mission, the very reason I was here, then I would move on and find people. Maybe buy an airship and become sky pirate Broccoli! But without the piracy because taking other people's stuff without permission wasn't nice.

Nodding, I wiped my spoon clean, tossed it into my sack, then got things ready for a whole new day of adventuring. The sun was just starting to peak over the horizon, which meant I had all day.

Hopefully, by the end of the day I would be done exploring the city. Maybe I would even be strong enough to face the Evil Hole in earnest.

We'd see.

For now the plan was simple. Explore every house next to the 'south' wall as best I could, then move over to the shops. Something told me that I would find some much nicer loot there. Then… then I would need to find a way to get rid of all those ghosts near the church.

I would try talking to them first, but if that didn't work, then maybe I could rig up a sort of trap? I was certain there were other magical items around that I could use to injure them. Flicking magic stuff at my adversaries until they poofed wasn't the most glorious tactic, but it might work.

All my gear was prepped, Bonesy 'Rrr'ed' in readiness, and I was determined to make the best of the day.

The first home I scouted was across the street from the inn at an angle. A long, low house with a roof that had once been a vibrant green before decades of missing maintenance took their toll. The door was locked, but a kick solved that problem and opened it right up.

It was dusty and a little tarnished within, but nothing I hadn't seen, or cleaned, before. Surprisingly, there was only a small fireplace tucked in a corner. No kitchen proper. The place felt unlived in. The furniture pushed to the sides; the bedroom too large for the single bed shoved up against the far wall. The bookshelf empty of any interesting looking bindings but filled with broken knick-knacks.

*An ancient jug. Empty.*

I rolled my eyes, dusted the jug and moved on.

The next room was a big office, one with surprisingly few papers, but they were in good shape. There was a huge ledger-like book on the table, one that was entirely untouched by dust or grime and looked as if it had just come off the printing press. I fired an Insight at it.

*Ledger and Accounts of the Well Inn Good, soul bound book.*

Soul bound? That was disturbing. Taking a moment to make sure I was alone, I moved to the big book and poked it. Nothing. Then I fished out a spoon and tried to open the book.

**Warning! This book is Soul Bound!**
*Warning! The Soul Binding on this book has faded. The previous owner has passed away.*
*Do you wish to Bind your Soul to this book?*
**Ledger and Accounts of the Well Inn Good.**

Did I want to play with strange and unknown magics that messed with my soul without any idea of what they did? "Nope," I said.

I dusted around the book, and over and under the desk. There was a rusty key in a drawer. I held it up and stared at it for a moment. If the book was the Inn's ledger, then this key might be for the basement I couldn't get into.

It didn't cost anything to check! Then I remembered that I was an idiot and didn't have to travel all the way over to the inn for that. "Insight."

*Well Inn Good Basement Key.*

"Neat," I said before tossing the key into my sack and moving on. The next house was entirely empty. Not even any furniture left behind. I didn't get much experience in that one. The one right after wasn't a house at all, but a sort of storage place.

The door was barred with a heavy gate that I couldn't break through, and the windows were… well, there weren't any. I pouted at the building, but that didn't do anything, so I marked it on my map and moved on.

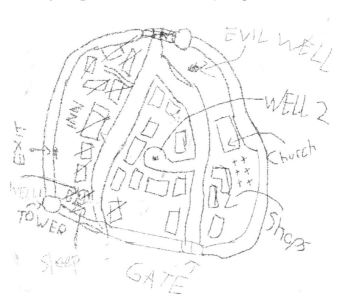

The next two homes were small and simple, but I could see the church through the windows, so I cleared them with as much stealth as possible. It was worth it though as I found some coins under a mattress in what might have been a sock once. One silver, some green disks that were either copper or bronze.

In the second house I found a magical device under one bed.

*Cheap magical wand, old.*

All it did when I pushed magic into it was vibrate. Maybe I could use it to hurt ghosts though, so I tossed it into my sack.

Then it finally happened.

**Congratulations! Through repeated actions your Cleaning skill has improved and is now eligible for rank up!**
**Rank C costs one (1) Class Point**

"What?!" I said once I was done cheering (quietly). I did have a Class Point from when I levelled up, but I was loath to spend it so soon. Wasn't I supposed to sit on skill points forever and never ever use them until I had to fight some big boss?

Oh well, whatever. A lost point at level one wasn't that big a deal, I figured.

**Spend one (1) Class PoWint to raise the Rank of Cleaning to C?**

"Yes please," I said.

*Congratulations! Cleaning is now Rank C!*
*Cleaning*
*Rank C - 00%*
*The ability to Clean. You are exceptionally good at tidying up and washing off. Effectiveness of cleaning is marginally increased. You may now use mana to clean things you touch.*

I stared, then started to giggle, and then, because I didn't want the ghosts across the street to eat me, I slapped a hand over my mouth and ran out of the house.

My next stop was somewhere I was curious about, and where I could practice my new magic. Magic! I had magic! I didn't so much run as skip to the Inn.

The Inn was how I had left it, deserted but surprisingly clean, like a house in bad need of some love ready to be shown off to some prospective buyers. I twirled around, skirt flaring for a moment before I refocused on my task. A bit of searching later, I had the basement key in hand and was fitting it into the lock.

The door opened with a deep groan, revealing a long room with a low ceiling. There were stones with glyphs on them fixed to the beams above, a long table in the middle of the room with a few scraps of what might have been a map, and some crates stacked up to one side. The far wall had big kegs that had probably held the wine and mead and beer that they once served here.

No ghosts, wraiths or even a rodent of unusual size.

I was in the clear to explore.

Deeper in, I found three stands with armour on them, each rack covered in roughly scratched glyphs. The armour looked intact as if they had been completely untouched by the passing of time.

I gasped, already giddy at the idea of using magic, now doubly so if I got to wear cool armour while casting my first spells.

The first two sets looked like something I'd expect a lowly adventurer to wear.

*Simple steel armour, old.*
*Simple steel plate armour, old.*

They were neat but built for someone way bigger than me. And male. The third set was more to my liking.

*Simple armless gambeson, old.*

The thick padded cloth, all of it coloured a sort of beige, would make me look kind of chubby, that that was alright if it meant not being dead. It even had a sort of jacket above it made of a thick leather. A skirt made of long strips of leather with little bronze scales sewn into it hung below.

*Boiled leather jacket, old.*
*Boiled leather skirt, old.*

A glance at the racks and a quick 'Insight' revealed how they had survived so long.

*Magical armour rack.*

I took the armour off the rack and weighted it in my arms for a bit. It was all a little heavier than my usual clothes, but that was fine. "It's such a shame there's no way for me to clean this poor, dirty old armour with a spell," I said with false exasperation.

I focused on my magic - the same stuff I had been using to make water with the showerhead glyph - and pushed it towards the armour. A wash of tiredness swept over me, but that was secondary to what I saw. The dirt and dust flaked off of the armour, the straps took on a faint shine and the cloth looked freshly cleaned.

I laughed aloud as I spun my totally awesome new armour around. I had magic!

First cleaning spells, next, fireballs! A quick check of my stats showed me just how much I had lost which was kind of disconcerting.

*Mana 79/105*

About a quarter of my total mana. Mana which I knew went up by about one a minute. Still, the amount of time it would have taken me to clean the armour as well as the spell had was… probably the same?

I flipped the armour back and forth and looked at how clean it was, then considered how long it would take me to reach the same level of cleanliness by hand. About twenty to thirty minutes? Which was the same time it took to regenerate that mana. So it was a fair trade.

For the sake of practice, I fired off the spell on the skirts and the leather jacket and lost two different amounts of mana, both lower than the gambeson alone. Neat!

"What do you think, Bonesy?" I asked my skeletal friend.

"Rrr," was his bored response.

"Yeah, I guess you saw all sorts of magic in your day, huh?" I told it. "I hope you don't mind, but I need to get dressed, so…" I reached over and turned Bonesy so that it was facing the far wall. As friendly as we were, well, it wasn't so friendly that I'd let it see me getting dressed.

I debated keeping my blouse on or not, but I didn't want the armour to chaff and the soft cotton of my blouse would keep my skin safe. Still, I took it off and winced at how dirty it had become. Oh, if only I had a solution to that.

A few more points of mana down the drain and I had a perfectly spotless blouse. One that I was going to wear over skin that hadn't seen a shower in two-and-a-bit days. Yuck.

Another drain of mana and I gasped. I was… clean. Very clean. I was clean *all over*. "Oh, wow," I said as I shifted around. "That's… refreshing."

Mana 42/105

I shrugged and fired off another cleaning spell at my skirt because I could. Then slid back into my blouse. It felt… itchy. Had I just exfoliated my everything? I had to be careful with this great power.

Still, it wouldn't be right not to share!

"Hey Bonesy, how you like to be the cleanest, leanest skeleton on this side of… wherever we are?"

"Rrr?"

"Uh huh," I said as I placed one finger onto the bony skull and pushed. Magic flowed out of me.

Bonesy shifted, jaw opening, then hanging slack as a ghostly form, just a head and the hint of shoulders, appeared out of the skull.

**Congratulations! You have sent 'Bonesy. Skeletal Bard', level 3, beyond the veil! Bonus Exp was granted for cleansing a monster above your level!**

"Bonesy!" I shouted.

The ghostly afterimage above the skull floated up, taking the shape of a man's face. "Thank you," he whispered before fading away.

My knees crashing into the dusty ground.

"Bonesy! No, no, I'm sorry. I'm sorry."

# Chapter Seven
## Grave

I hit a rock. A spark flew out from the gardening trowel I was using. I grabbed the rock and tossed it aside and returned to digging.

The hole grew. Wet dirt stained my knees and seeped into my dress as I tore into the soggy ground.

My fingers began to hurt. I dug deeper.

The sun burned down onto my back. The hole was a few feet deep now. Not very even, not as deep as some. But enough.

I lowered the package down, wrapped in the cloth of a banner I had found in the guard tower.

I stared for a moment. The words were hard to find until a small smile broke out. "Rarr," I said.

Dirt fell onto the grave, filling it. Then I patted it down.

The gravestone came next. A plaque made from a piece of a door, the stick holding it up once a spear that had saved my life.

*Bonesy*
*An unnamed bard*
*A skeleton*
*A friend*

I wiped my cheeks dry and got up.

The armour I had been so excited about slipped on easily enough. There were knots to tie, and the material pinched in a few places. But as soon as it was all on the material shifted and moved. I felt the faint stir of magic around my body, then nothing.

It fit like a glove.

That was good. I would need it.

There were still only five ghosts. I had a long piece of cord by my side, the end heavy where I had tied my showerhead glyph. I held onto the small 'magic wand' in my other hand. I had a suspicion I wanted to prove.

The grass rustled and shifted as I walked closer to the church, to the graveyard. "Hey!" I called out.

Five heads slowly turned my way, then their faces shifted into disgusting, disfigured expressions as if I had just walked over to them covered in rot and filth.

"Hello," I said. My voice was hoarse, a little raw. I blinked a few times, then coughed to clear my throat. "Hello. My name is Broccoli Bunch," I said even as the first ghosts started to fly towards me, arms and claws outstretched.

"W-would you be my friends?"

The first ghost to reach me grabbed my face, claws digging into the back of my head and cheek.

"I'm sorry," I said.

Cleaning magic shot into the ghost.

The ghost burst apart.

I swung my makeshift flail around in a tight circle, sweeping through the arms of the next ghost to approach again and again, but it was still coming at me.

The magic wand flew through its head and past the body of the ghost behind him. One fell, the other paused as the hole in its torso mended.

I stepped to the side and shoved my hand into the chest of the next ghost. Another pulse of cleaning magic. Two were left. I was down to the last third of my mana.

My spinning flail spun through the already injured ghost as I moved onto the last and most intact of the group. A touch, a burst of mana. It burst apart like a sack of flour with a firecracker inside it.

Then the flail did its job and the final ghost, already torn apart, whooshed onto the ground in a pool of dust. It left behind a thin, ghostly cloth.

My knees hit the ground and I buried my face in my hands. My tears stung when they slid into the open cuts across my cheek.

But I couldn't do it. I couldn't stay and just wallow in my own sadness. I had a quest, a mission to do, and being sad, being down like that, even if, even if I had just killed my only friend. I swallowed, throat thick.

**Congratulations! You have wiped out (5) enemies ('Sentinel Ghost of Threewells by Darkwood', level 1 x5)!**
*Ding! For repeating a Special Action a sufficient number of times, you have unlocked the skill: Makeshift Weapon Proficiency!*

"Neat," I said to no one, because there was no one to hear.

I got up. I wiped my eyes again. I used the last of my mana to clean my face, wiping away the drying blood and allowing a fresh rivulet to slip down my cheek. One more cut and I would have an even number of scars across my cheeks. I snorted, which turned into a giggle, which I stopped before I started crying again.

The shops. The church. Then the evil spirit. Enough time to regain all of my mana and maybe eat some more honey and drink more lukewarm water.

I picked up the ghostly cloth and brought it with me to the edge of the road where my haversack was waiting and tossed it in along with my magic wand. The showerhead I kept. Had to grind those Makeshift Weapon Proficiency levels after all. A gift, of sorts, from Bonesy.

The first stop was a general store, the shelves emptied, some of them tossed to the ground. There were jars here and there, and some lengths of rope that looked decent. I took one and looped it under one arm and over the opposite shoulder. It seemed sturdy enough, and good rope was never a bad thing.

I found a backpack in the back of the store. It was dusty, of course, and a little brittle, but the material seemed nice and tough and hadn't rotten away. I transferred the stuff from my haversack into it, leaving behind some of the less handy things and wrapping others in the cloth I had. I didn't want to make too much noise as I moved, which meant quieting down the rattle of the stuff I carried.

My inventory, if I could call it that without sounding too geeky, consisted of:

- A now-empty haversack
- Two pieces of ghostly cloth
- A key from the house with training dummies
- Four jars of honey
- One jar of vinegar
- Two bottles of wine
- A bottle of water from my showerhead
- One pretty painting boat and dragon
- Some silverware in a cloth
- One silver candleholder with a dozen fresh candles
- A small firestarter
- Some bits and pieces of cloth.
- A length of rope
- My map

Not much of a hoard, but enough, I hoped, to get by. I wondered where and when I had misplaced my rusty short sword. Not that it mattered much.

The next stop was the blacksmith's shop. There was a bell that clunked above the door, just loud enough and close enough to my head that I jumped three feet in the air at the noise. "Oh gosh," I said as my heart pounded away. I shook my head, made sure I was still alone in the shop, then started looking around.

This had to be the workspace of whoever lived in that one home I had found with the broken anvil. It was a busy place, with tools laying all over and strange devices left to rust. From the number of hooks on the wall and the tools around, it was clear that the blacksmith had taken his or her share of them with them. The anvil was gone, but there was a big log where it might have sat. The huge forge at the back had remained, probably easier to move the rest of the building than that one piece.

I didn't clean anything as I moved to a small section that seemed to be made for displaying wares and suchlike to the customers. There was a safe with a key resting in its lock.

"Huh," I said as I easily opened the door and found... ingots of metal and a few knives in leather sheaths. One man's treasure, I guessed. None of the stuff within the safe was rusted, probably owing to the glyphs carved into the sides of the box.

I pulled out one knife and sheath and inspected it visually, then ran a thumb perpendicular to the blade. It sang a little. Sharp.

"Insight."

`A sharp steel woodsman's knife, old.`

I shrugged, tossed one knife into my backpack and looped the other to the belt holding up my leather skirt.

The rest of the shop didn't reveal much of any worth to me.

The third store, the one nearest the gates of the village, had a strange sign above it. A staff with a ball above it and something going around it. Magic, obviously, but what sort was beyond me.

The door opened to a few quick kicks and revealed a sort of clinic, of all things. A pair of beds at the back, both with dirtied sheets on them stained with what might have been blood once. There was a counter with glass jars to one side, and beyond that a small room with mortar and pestles and alembics.

"An alchemist's shop," I realized. "And a medical clinic." It made sense that they would be together. I picked up a bottle and shook it a little. "Insight."

*An expired healing potion, old.*

"Shucks." Not one of them was usable, much to my dismay. I left them behind and explored some more, but most of the good stuff had left with the people living here or had been looted long ago. The second floor of the building had a small bedroom for two and an office space with a strange cabinet on the wall. There were some more tools within, and a single book. All perfectly untouched.

I recognized the glyphs from the safe on the inside of the cabinet. It was locked.

Safe from time the contents might have been, but not from a smack from a rock. The glass burst apart, showering the floor in tinkling pieces that I shied away from. "Sorry," I said to the no doubt long-dead owners as I moved to the cabinet. The book was fresh. Not quite new. In fact, it was worn and well loved.

*Herbs for Healing, Plants for Power*, read the title.

"Huh, neat," I said. "Insight."

*A herbology book.*

I leafed through the pages, taking note of the carefully hand-drawn images of plants on nearly every page and the obviously machine-printed text next to them with descriptions and warnings and uses. There were notes as well, in a cursive hand that was hard to read but still comprehensible if I squinted.

I wrapped it in a bit of old bedsheets I cut off in the bedroom, then placed it in the bottom of my pack.

That was it. There were some homes left to explore, and the church, but that was it for this corner of the town. It was also it for me, at least for that day. The sun hadn't begun to set yet, but I was tired, weary to the bone.

I had one last thing I wanted to look into, then I would be off.

The town was as silent as ever as I crossed it. The only difference now that my head was held high and I welcomed any ghost that would come at me. None did. I reached the hole in the wall where I had first come out into Threewells and shuffled into it. My eyes lingered over where Bonesy had once been, but I moved on.

In the office was the chest I couldn't open. In my hand, the key I had found in the house with the training dummies and spare swords. It was just a hunch, but... The key slotted in, and I spun it around. The lock clicked and the top of the chest popped open with a whump of pressurized air escaping.

I opened the chest to find two binders filled with papers and a leather bandolier, all of its pockets empty.

Well, it was there for the taking. I slipped off my leather jacket, then put on the bandolier so that it would be opposite the coil of rope I had, then I hiked the jacket back on and replaced the rope. There. Now I looked like... well, the gambeson made me look like a marshmallow. A marshmallow with a skirt and a leather jacket.

I smiled faintly at the image I must have presented. Far from the competent explorer I hoped to be. Still, it was good enough for now.

I picked through the binders absently. The pages within were mostly intact, but all of them seemed like dull reports.

I took them anyway. I needed something to keep me company until morning.

## Chapter Eight
# A Look into the Past

I stayed up late to read. The herbology book was still at the bottom of my backpack, forgotten as I read through ancient reports illuminated by the flickering light of a candle.

### Report, Seventh of Harvest
*Apprehended drunk bard at Well Inn Good, began a brawl with local musicians over 'the quality of the music.' Minor property damage evaluated at two sil, three cop. Confined in cell overnight until sober. —Overseer Hardy*

A bard. Was it Bonesy a long time ago?

### Report, Eight of Harvest
*Mana fluctuations detected by local mages including alchemist. No sighting of the adventuring party sent out to the Dunwich dungeon. —Overseer Hardy*

A dungeon? Those were a thing here?

### Report two, Eight of Harvest
*Large mana shifts. Felt them myself. Worried someone might have damaged the dungeon core. Guard rotation C spotted someone in the forests in green. Imperials? This far out? It could explain the shifts in local mana. Doubled the guards just in case. Sent a scout to the Dunwich Dungeon. —Overseer Hardy*

Things were getting interesting, very interesting. A dungeon sounded like a neat place to visit, and there was a lot of talk here about mana as if it was a thing that was just… in the air. I wondered if the mana here was thick or thin and if I would be able to tell the difference.

### Report, Ninth of Harvest
*Dunwich dungeon was destroyed. The shifts in mana are the ley lines snapping apart. Spoke to the mayor. She doesn't want to evacuate but we have no choice, not with Imperials so close and the mana turning like this. No news of the adventuring team sent out. Still have their bard in a cell. Will release him later.*

*More imperial sightings. Hopefully they'll let a group of civilians pass unharmed. —Overseer Hardy*

And that was it. No more reports, just a few blank pages. So there were ley lines for magic. And Bonesy the Bard had been part of an adventuring group. That was kind of neat! Good on him. Not so good was how he had caused trouble at the Inn. He was just as poorly behaved in life as he was in death.

***Ding! For repeating a Special Action a sufficient number of times, you have unlocked the skill: Archaeology!***

I smiled and blew out the candle, then shifted until sleep took me at long last.

I woke up feeling refreshed. Not at my best, and my tummy still rumbled for food that wasn't honey, but the pall of depression was lifted, and I felt my face twisting back into my usual smile. Then I unleashed a blast of cleaning magic at myself and shivered as mana coursed over my body and clothes. It was like taking a shower but better.

Standing up, I stretched, ran through an abridged version of my morning routine—I'd give all of my silver for a toothbrush and paste—then stepped outside after making sure the coast was clear of ghosts.

Today was the day I would take on the wraith. But first, I had a church to explore and a sickly-sweet breakfast to lick.

I strolled across the ghost town, spoon in mouth and attention swivelling around to take in everything. Things had changed in the two short days I had been here. There had been grass when I first came out, but it was brown and feeble and kind of sad. Now bushes were sprouting up everywhere and the grass was thick and lush and vibrant. The entire world seemed more alive, somehow.

Was it because there were fewer ghosts?

I couldn't believe that level one monsters were that strong. But then again, the ghosts couldn't be hurt through normal means. Maybe the animals and such were careful and cautious around them - proving once more than the average animal was smarter than little old me.

The church was a stately building, even with fresh vines climbing up its sides and huge holes poked through its stained-glass windows. It looked like the kind of place that local weddings would be held in, and where a nice old priest would try to help people with their problems and all the old ladies would gather to trade the juiciest gossip.

There was a sense of lost serenity around the building, a sensation that took me a long time to name and would take longer to get used to. It would have felt wrong to scream and shout or fight.

I pushed open the front door and slid into the main hall. It was a single large room with rows of wooden benches all facing a trio of stone altars.

Dust swirled in the air and the light, most of it pouring through the mosaic windows, coloured the entire room in a spectrum of soft blues and greens and reds.

"Hello?" I asked as I moved in. Only silence greeted me. I moved through the room, careful to be as quiet and respectful as I could until I was at the altars. They were all different. Did they practice one faith with many gods here, or were there many religions housed in one church?

The first altar had a small stone chalice built into it, with stone grapes and fruit around its base. The second had a carving of an arm holding an axe engraved atop it and the third had a statue of an archway reaching from one side to the other.

Strange, disparate symbols with meanings I could only guess at. Most buried under a layer of dust. Three quick flashes of magic cleared the altars, leaving them as the only untouched things in the entire room. A strange dichotomy, maybe.

I bowed to the three altars and moved on. There was nothing for me here.

According to my map I still had five houses to explore, but I doubted I would find anything incredible there. No, my goal at that moment was to face the wraith and inspect the hole. I could return to exploring at any time after that.

The monster was hovering over the opened pit, twisting and turning and writhing in the air as if it was wracked with pain. Pain that it almost seemed to enjoy. Now that I was closer, I could hear its delighted howls, the almost ecstatic moans that it made as jolts of… something coursed through it.

Whatever the wraith was feeding on came from the hole. Evil mana, maybe? I could only guess.

My backpack was left on the doorstep of a nearby home. I took a moment to go over my plan, as simple as it was. I was going to go out and attack the wraith, first with the showerhead-flail I had, then by throwing my magic wand through it. Then, if it was sufficiently distracted, I would use my cleaning spell on it.

If things went well that would be enough to clear it out.

The very first step though, of course, was to talk to it.

Maybe it was a nice evil wraith? "Insight."

    An evil wraith (level 2).

Maybe not. But I wouldn't hit someone in the back without at least trying to talk first. Anything else would just be wrong.

I sat back and ate another spoonful of honey as I looked over my many skills.

| Name: Broccoli Bunch | | Race: Human | | | Age: 16 |
|---|---|---|---|---|---|
| Health | 105 | Stamina | 115 | Mana | 105 |
| Resilience | 15 | Flexibility | 20 | Magic | 10 |

| First Class: | Cinnamon Bun | First Class Level: | 1 |
|---|---|---|---|
| Skill Slots | 0 | Skill Points | 0 |

| General Skill Slots | 0 | General Skill Points | 0 |
|---|---|---|---|

| **General Skills** | | **Cinnamon Bun Skills** | |
|---|---|---|---|
| Insight | E - 97% | Cleaning | C - 76% |
| Makeshift Weapon Proficiency | F - 42% | | |
| Archaeology | F - 15% | | |

I was quite the warrior it seemed. "Soon," I whispered in the deepest darkest voice I could manage. It came out squeaky, but it was the thought that counted! "Everyone across all the realms will learn to respect the might of Broccoli the great Cinnamon Bun!"

I might have been able to get Insight up another level, but that didn't feel necessary, or even helpful in a fight. Makeshift weapons would have been a good skill to level, but I wasn't sure how to do that except to fight some more, and there wasn't anything left to fight that I had seen so far.

Well, ghosts didn't generally move very fast. I would try against this one and see how things worked out. Worse case, I was an excellent runner.

I stepped out into the morning sunlight, makeshift flail hanging by my side, mana topped off at max and a determined frown on my face. I walked over to the evil well of evilness until I was only a few dozen paces away. "Hello!" I called out.

The wraith paused in its weird wriggling and turned.

My blood ran cold.

The wraith screamed.

**You have heard the screech of a fearsome creature! Your soul is shaken.**

My breathing hitched and I had a sudden urge to run to the nearest bathroom as the monster tore through the sky towards me. Its hands stretched and shifted, turning into long, scythe-like claws.

I snapped out of it just in time to hop backwards and narrowly avoid the first swing. The wraith screamed again, but this time I was a little more ready for it and managed not to pee my skirts. Instead I flung my showerhead flail at the monster and almost fainted when it bounced off its face.

The wraith flinched back, face leaking the same plumes of dust the ghosts had, though in far smaller quantities.

It spun around and charged at me again.

I rolled out of its path, then tossed the magic wand that merely booped its chest and left only the tiniest of wounds.

Not enough, not nearly enough.

I started spinning the flail around and around until it hummed through the air. The wraith came at me again, its one-track mind not terribly suited to thinking, it seemed. My flail crashed into its hand, a spark of magic burst from the impact, the wraith screeched, though now in pain rather than anger.

"I'm sorry," I said as I lunged closer to it and pressed a hand against its chest. "Clean!"

My mana dropped, then dropped faster as I poured more and more into the attempt to cleanse the monster. A patch formed around my hand, slowly growing and spreading across its body. First a few centimetres, then a few more in an expanding circle.

My mana hit zero.

The world shifted, the corners of my vision going blurry as I stumbled back and fell onto my bum.

The wraith was twisting and screeching, its one remaining clawed arm trying to push back all of its dusty stuff into the massive tear in its chest. It gave up after a moment and started to move towards the hole. Slower now, much slower than its earlier charge.

This was my chance, my opportunity to run back and regroup, to figure out a new strategy and maybe let my mana return to full.

I stumbled to my feet and ran after the wraith, for a certain definition of 'ran.' My stumbling gait didn't stop me from spinning my flail again, and when the ghostly monster started to suck at the evil mana it left itself wide open.

The flail rammed into and through its body, cutting off its lower half to let it float down and turn to so much dust.

It spun around, the back of its claws raking across my face and chest and sending me flying a few feet. "Ouch," I said as I landed on my back. I wanted to stay there for a moment, but huge claws spearing down at me were enough encouragement that I rolled to the side. Just in time, too, as the talons dug into the ground where I had been.

Another smack of the flail, weaker this time and from an awkward angle, was enough to push its hands away. My mana was back to one. One mana.

I slapped my hand on its screeching face and fired off my cleaning spell. It was little more than a short-lived burst, but that was enough to make it race backwards and give me some room. I scrambled back, then got to my feet.

"You are a big, fat meaniehead!" I taunted the monster.

It kind of just stared at me flabbergasted. I was going to need to learn the taunt skill one of these days, if that was even a thing.

Another spin of my flail ended with the shower head smacking the now weakened wraith again, and again, and again.

The fight didn't end in a glorious moment of triumph, but in a constant beatdown, where I delivered blow after blow to an enemy that was less and less capable of fighting back until, finally...

**Congratulations! You have laid 'The Wraith of Threewells by Darkwood', level 2, to rest! Bonus Exp was granted for savaging a monster above your level!**

## Chapter Nine
# Dungeon Dive

**Bing Bong! Congratulations, your Cinnamon Bun class has reached level 2!**
Health + 5
*Resilience +5*
**You have gained: One Class Point**
You have unlocked: One Class Skill Slot

"A skill slot?" I wondered aloud even as a rush of giddiness washed through me. It was like a faint tingling, first in my skin, then my muscles and the insides of my chest, as if someone had placed me in a microwave on high for a few seconds, but without the exploding.

I grinned. I was level two!

Normally, that would have been a time of celebration and dancing and such, but I was right next to a giant evil hole in the ground and it kind of felt unwise to make lots of noise while so close to the scary pit.

Instead, I looked around, took in the bright sunlight streaming down on the sight of the battlefield where I had fought the wraith and soaked in the sun.

The hole didn't drop straight down, not for more than a meter and a half or so. The passage went on into the dark as some sort of tunnel that I couldn't see the end of. I was going to need a ladder or else getting out of there would be complicated.

Fortunately, I had seen one next to the gardening shed of one of the houses I'd explored. Unfortunately it was all the way across town.

There weren't any other options, so I took a leisurely stroll across town, found the ladder where it had been left, tested the rungs a few times to make sure they could hold my weight, then dragged it all the way back.

The moment my foot touched the ground within the hole a prompt appeared before me.

**You are Entering the Wonderland Dungeon**
Dungeon Level 2-4
Your entire party has entered the Dungeon
Seal Dungeon until exit?

"That sounds like an awful idea," I said.

### Dungeon left Unsealed

*Any Person can Enter Dungeon Instance*
*Any Person can Exit Dungeon Instance*
Quest Updated!

### The Hole Down Under

*An evil root has plunged into the world.*
*You have entered the Wonderland Dungeon.*
*Explore it. Find the root. Destroy it.*

I let out a breath I didn't know I was holding and counted myself lucky. It felt as if I had dodged a bullet there. Still, level two to four monsters would probably be really tricky to fight. But maybe I didn't need to fight them?

Dropping my backpack, I searched within until I found the silvery candlestick I had looted and a fresh candle. Then I lost a minute or two with the firestarter until the candle lit up with a spark. I replaced the firestarter and stood back up, the candle holder held before me so that its mirror shield illuminated the path ahead.

The passage was like a borehole, the walls smooth dirt except where the occasional root poked through and the ground tilted down at a slight angle. I tread carefully, always watching where I set my feet in case of traps or pitfalls or anything of the sort. I had read enough about dungeons to know that being careful was the best way to survive them.

The path curved a little, then opened up to a largish room with a wooden door at one end and a monster in the middle. A torch high up on the wall near the door lit everything up with a warm, orange glow.

I froze, taking in the form of a dog-sized rabbit standing on its haunches, milky-white eyes staring at a pocket watch that it, he, held out before him in a big fluffy paw. The rabbit wasn't normal, not just on account of its size and the fact that it was wearing a tattered waistcoat. Its fur was missing in places and its teeth were showing where the flesh around its mouth was rotted off.

I fired off a quick insight as I stood still and wondered what to do.

*A zombie time rabbit (level 2).*

I realized that I might be in something of a pickle. Still, I was Broccoli Bunch and Broccoli Bunch was nothing if not polite. "Ah, hello," I said.

The rabbit's head looked up. Its white eyes locked onto me. The timepiece clicked.

Then the rabbit reappeared in the air right before me, both legs already kicking out into my chest.

I stumbled back, breath whooshing out of me in gasp as I fell onto my backpack and laid down to stare at the dirt ceiling for a moment. "Ouch," I said as soon as I had air in my lungs.

The timepiece clicked. The rabbit appeared above me.

I swept an arm out, hitting the zombie rabbit just hard enough to shove it off to the side and avoid another thumping. Then there was a mad scramble as I slid my arms out of the loops of my backpack and rolled off to the side. I didn't have any weapons except my cleaning magic, and the rabbit could teleport.

It wasn't looking too good. "Mister rabbit, please stop!" I said.

The rabbit turned its white eyes towards me, then pressed on the button next to the timepiece again.

This time I rolled out of the way before it even appeared to kick me again. "Okay, okay, Broc, it's a time travelling zombie bunny rabbit," I said as I shuffled around the room, constantly moving as I kept an eye on the rabbit. "It's an evil time travelling zombie bunny rabbit. K-killing it is okay."

The rabbit's head snapped around to face me, turning way more than its neck should have allowed.

The pocket watch clicked. My hand shot out and wrapped around its furry chest a moment after it appeared before me.

It was heavy, heavy enough that I ended up backing up and bumping into the wall, but I managed to hang on to it long enough to use my one spell.

A wave of cleaning magic tore through the rabbit, its white eyes went glossy and a faint ghostly form shifted out of the body.

"Oh, thank goodness," I said as I let it drop and moved away. That had taken more than a third of my mana, more than a ghost did. But still, it was over. I waited for the 'ding' and the experience points to come in.

The timepiece clicked.

Spinning around, I found the rabbit back in the middle of the room, its head turned towards me with its white eyes set in a glare. "Oh no."

The rabbit bounced across the floor in a straight path for me. I tried to move away, but the room was far too small, so I did the only thing I could think of. I jumped over the rabbit.

**Ding! For doing a Special Action in line with your Class, you have unlocked the skill: Jumping!**

"Not now!" I told the info box.

The rabbit was slow to turn around, which was just what I needed. My hand locked around the timepiece and tore it out of its grip to send it flying against the nearest wall where it burst apart. Then came another wave of cleaning magic.

**Congratulations! You have stuffed a 'Undead White Rabbit Time Mage', level 2!**

I shuffled away from the body of the rabbit as it started to dissolve into motes of whitish light that left nothing behind, even the bits of its timepiece fading away. "I'm sorry," I said before using a bit of mana to clean off my hands. A clink sounded and a key appeared on the ground where the rabbit had been.

*Mana 19/105*

That wasn't very good. I hoped that Dungeon monsters didn't respawn, then I felt bad for calling the rabbit a monster. Sure, it was a time travelling zombie rabbit, but I was the one invading its house. I bet that it used to be a very nice rabbit before it went all zombie and mean.

Maybe that's what the quest was about: Destroy the root of evil in this dungeon and allow it to become a less evil place? It made a sort of sense.

I stared down at my hands, my perfectly clean hands, made that way thanks to some magic and not any effort of my own. Hands that I felt should have been at least a little dirty.

I wasn't some crusader, or the person who got to decide what was right and wrong. I had been asked, by something, to come rid the world of something evil, and that's what I was trying to do, but I didn't want to compromise my morality to do it.

My hands clenched into fists. "So I won't," I decided. I had made friends with all sorts of people already. And maybe I could make even more in this dungeon. Maybe it was an evil place and I couldn't. I didn't know yet, but I would learn, and I would ask the people I met to be friends first before I ever raised a fist against them.

I nodded. "Right!" My choice was… not made, because that had been my path already, but reaffirmed.

*Jumping*
*Rank F - 00%*
*The ability to jump. As this skill rises*
*in level your ability to jump will improve!*

A glance at my new skill didn't reveal all that much. It wasn't... well, it wasn't Fireball. Jumping could be useful... maybe? For getting to high places?

"My skills are really lame," I whined.

Still, it was a skill, and at rank F it wasn't that handy. I skipped over to the door, then looked at the experience change. It had gone up a full percent. Maybe I could grind it here before moving on, then. I had another skill that was nearly at the next level too.

The door to the next area had a large lock on it. It didn't take a genius to see that it was the key that had dropped from the rabbit. Next to the door was a little table with a potion bottle and a cake on it. The cake had 'EAT ME' written on it in big letters, the bottle had a small tag with 'DRINK THIS' scribbled on it. I fired off two quick Insights.

"Is that... is that an Alice in Wonderland reference?" I asked aloud. "Insight."

*A poisoned cake.*
*A poisoned shrinking potion.*

I eyed the cake and the potion, then carefully took the potion and brought it back to my backpack to tuck it away. There was a chance it would come in handy later. Then I checked my notifications.

**Congratulations! Through repeated actions your Insight skill has improved and is now eligible for rank up!**
**Rank D is a free rank!**

That was an easy choice to make.

*Insight*
*Rank D - 00%*
*The Ability to know something. The knowledge*
*you gain is further increased.*

I stretched, jumped on the spot a few times, then looked to the door as I slid my backpack back on. I didn't know how ready I was to face off the rest of the dungeon, but I wouldn't learn that until I tried. I got my makeshift flail ready just in case I ran into more zombies or ghosts, then unlocked the door to step out into the rest of the dungeon.

My breath caught.

The passageway continued for a few feet, then opened up onto a railless balcony overlooking a large hole. It was maybe ten or twenty meters wide, with an opened top that revealed the bright green sky above There were other platforms at different levels, with huge, bulbous mushrooms growing in a spiralling ring all around the sides of the shaft. It seemed as if the level I was on was the highest one around.

It was pretty, with glowing moss along the walls, little trees sticking out here and there with huge caterpillars on them and pretty pink clouds floating above. Pretty, surreal, and nothing like the world I had left when I entered the dungeon.

"Whoa," I said as I moved to the edge of the ledge and looked down. Every quarter turn of the shaft had a hole drilled into the wall, some with elaborate arches, others quite plain. All the way down to the bottom where a field of grass was waiting and a large vine-covered archway. It would have looked idyllic if the pervasive sense of wrong wasn't so strong whenever I looked at the tunnel behind that arch.

That had to be my objective then.

And the only way to reach it was to jump from mushroom to mushroom. Maybe Jumping wasn't a waste of skill after all.

## Chapter Ten
# Mushroom Hop

I stood at the very edge of the balcony and looked down at the big mushroom just a few feet down. A few feet down and a few feet away. And between me and the big fluffy looking mushroom was a two storey drop to a rocky field.

"Okay, it's okay, it's obviously a path," I said to myself as I looked at all the big bouncy-looking mushrooms all lined up in a curve that led to the next platform down. This was a… risk.

And risks could be bad.

I shook my head, then unwound one of my ropes. It was more than long enough to make it from where I was to the next platform. I created a loop, set a knot into it, and hung the rope off of a rocky outcropping. A few really hard tugs without so much as a creak and I figured it could hold my weight.

Then I tied the rope around my waist. If I fell it would hurt. Hitting the ground all the way down would hurt more.

I jumped on the spot a few times to unlimber myself, made sure that my backpack was nice and snug, then I jumped.

I didn't expect the mushroom to deflate on landing, then burst back to its full size.

My knees shot up into my chest and I barely had time to kick at the next mushroom down.

I landed on the third bum-first with a scream that echoed across the dungeon. I managed to flip once, my backpack flopping around, my legs kicking out to find purchase. My hand scraped the wall and I belly flopped onto the fourth mushroom down.

It shot me back into the air where I had plenty of time to see the platform coming before I landed on it face first.

"Ouch," I said as I laid on the ground, cheek pressed down, butt in the air and knees and wrists lancing with pain. That had been, I decided, a horrible idea. A no-good, very bad, super dumb idea.

*Health 107/110*

I climbed to my hands and knees, straightened my skirt back down from where it had flipped, then crawled away from the edge when one foot slipped over it. "Nope," I said. "Not until Jumping is way higher."

I took a moment to relax and calm my racing heart, then stood up and undid the rope around my waist. I tied it to a rock and took in my surroundings.

There wasn't much to see. This ledge was about half a floor lower than the entrance ledge with a rocky archway filled with vines that partially hid a wooden door. The ground was one large slab of stone with a small sconce at the end with an unlit brazier on it. There was a sign hanging from the door, I cleared the vines before it.

*Out for tea*
*—Maddy the Hatter*

Did someone live here? Just in case, I knocked carefully on the door and waited a moment. When no answer came after my third knock, I opened the door and looked within. "Hello?"

The inside was a corridor. The ground was packed earth, the walls were rough stone that might have been chiselled to be a little more uniform, but not enough to prevent creeping vines from climbing all the way up to the ceiling.

A few glyph-covered stones hung in little iron cages, the rocks glowing blue and green and red and lighting up the corridor quite nicely.

I checked for traps, wished I had a ten-foot pole, then moved in. Nothing shot out of the walls, there were no time travelling critters and I couldn't hear anything except for a faint and distant clicking.

Careful not to make too much noise, I retrieved my showerhead flail and held it close by my side as I moved on.

The corridor opened up to a field of sorts, a small hill surrounded on three sides by hedges that climbed up and up and up. The green sky had three bright suns in it, all of them carefully moving around and making the entire area bright and cheery while throwing my shadow around in weird ways.

A large door stood open on the far hedge, some twenty meters away. And between me and that door, right atop the hill, was a large skeleton sitting with his legs sprawled out. He had an upside-down top hat on his head and was bringing a teacup up against his mouth with a faint clinking noise.

Two animals sat next to him on a blanket laid out atop the hill. One was a calico cat, with patches of fur missing, the other a long green snake that was missing an eye and quite a few scales.

"Hello!" I said as I waved to the group. "Ah, it's a nice afternoon for tea, isn't it?"

The skeleton stared at me without any eyes to see. His long legs gathered up to his chest and his toes dug into the blanket before he stood up straight and tall.

"Insight," I whispered as I took in the three before me.

```
Maddy   the   Hatter,   Skeleton   Milliner
(level 4).
Zombie snake (level 2).
Zombie cat (level 2).
```

I smiled at Maddy. "Do you like tea?" I asked. It seemed like a good place to start a conversation. He could invite me to tea, and I had some honey to share, and we could chit and chat and become the best of friends.

Maddy threw his cup to the ground where it shattered. The door behind me shut with a dull boom and the clunk of a lock engaging sounded out.

Reaching up, the skeleton removed his hat and reached an arm into it. Out came a big floppy wizard's hat, all purple and covered with uneven yellow stars. He placed the hat atop the snake. Then he pulled out a second hat, a nurse's cap with a big red cross on the front which he slapped onto the cat's head.

"Um?" I asked.

```
Zombie Hedge Wizard snake (level 2).
Zombie Nursing cat (level 2).
```

"Oh," I said. "That's really neat!"

Maddy spun on a heel, quite literally, and stomped off the hill, slamming the door in the hedge behind him with a loud clatter and bang.

"Did I say something wrong?" I asked the almost-cute zombie animals.

The snake opened its mouth wide and a fireball shot out of it.

I 'eeped' and hopped over the rather slow-moving projectile and heard it boom against the wall behind me. Then it opened its mouth again and a second fireball started to form.

"Oh, shoot."

At least this time I knew what to do.

I tossed my backpack off and started running and jumped over another fireball. They weren't very big, and they only moved as fast as a dodgeball thrown by, well, me. Easy enough to avoid. But they were fireballs.

I started spinning my flail around. I didn't have all that much mana, not enough for two zombies as tough as the time rabbit at least. There was a pattern to the fireballs. They would launch, then slow down once they were a few feet from the snake. Then it would close its mouth, stare at me, and ready the next one.

A pattern!

I waited for the next fireball which I somewhat nimbly sidestepped, the warmth of it washing past me as if I had walked by an open oven but with less cookies and more fiery death. The moment the snake closed his mouth I rushed up the hill and brought my flail down.

It smacked the snake right on the head like a very hard, very rude boop.

"Hah!" I shouted before reaching down to pull out my knife. I didn't want to do it, but it seemed as if I had no choice. At least I could reason that you couldn't kill something that was already dead.

A blur of white barrelled into me, claws swinging this way and that with a cattish howl that sent me tumbling bum over teakettle down the hill. When I regained my feet, it was to find the zombie snake completely healed… well, mostly healed, it was still very dead, but now bandages were wrapped around it and it had a few plasters on its snout.

I took a moment to regroup while the snake shook its head and glared at me with its one eye. I had overlooked the calico, which was apparently a very bad idea. There was a clear theme here. The hats gave the zombies classes or something similar. No wonder Maddy was level four!

The snake was a wizard, which meant fireballs for days. The calico cat was a nurse, which meant healing and first aid for the snake.

That made everything a whole lot harder.

I had to focus on the healer.

With a huff, I picked up my flail and charged for the cat, only to pause as I had to jump over a fresh fireball. And that, right there, explained their gimmick. If I ran after the cat the snake would pelt me with fireballs. Focus the snake and the cat would hit me instead.

Tricksy zombie animals were not my forte.

I charged after the nurse cat who turned tail and darted away, moving faster and slower as if to bait me into getting hit by one of the fireballs raining down on me. Then, the moment the latest fireball shot past, I turned and hopped up the hill in three bounds and brought my flail down on the snake again.

As expected, there was a screeching yowl and a ball of angry kitty shot towards me.

So I hugged it.

"Cleaning hug!" I shouted, because attack names are important. A bit of mana left me and washed over the kitty.

## Congratulations! You have eliminated Zombie Nursing cat, level 2!

I wanted to whoop in delight as a ghostly cat purred out of the nurse, but then a fireball struck me in the chest, and I went rolling down the hill again.

This time the snake was playing for keeps. Fireballs, much smaller than before were raining down towards me, each one moving way faster than the big cumbersome ones from before.

I ran, breath catching in my throat as I panted and patted down my chest. The gambeson and leather coat were singed and smoking a little, but they weren't too damaged.

I ran over to a large stone off to one side, jumped over it, and landed in a crouch that ended with my back pressed against the cool rock and my chest heaving.

That had been… well it had been terrifying.

The snap and crackle of fireballs hitting the stone stopped a moment later. "Are you done, mister snake?" I asked. "I really don't want to have to fight."

I dropped my flail for a moment, tugged my knife out of its sheath and transferred it to my left hand before grabbing my flail again. Maybe I could throw the knife at the snake and distract it?

I checked my menus for anything handy and was surprised to find a message waiting for me.

## Congratulations! Through repeated actions your Jumping skill has improved and is now eligible for rank up!
## Rank E is a free rank!

"That was fast." Maybe dodging fireballs gave more experience than just skipping around?

### *Congratulations! Jumping is now Rank E!*
*Jumping*
*Rank E - 00%*
*The ability to jump. You can now jump further and higher than before.*

I was about to dig into that when a hiss sounded from right above me. I looked up to find the snake with its floppy wizard hat staring down at me, mouth opened and fireball growing.

My knife-wielding hand shot up and the sharp steel dug into the monster's pallet.

I cringed back as the snake flopped around, then began to turn to dust. The hat glowed and disappeared with a soap-bubble pop.

I leaned my head back against the stone, eyes closed as adrenaline coursed through me.

"Note to self: snakes are sneaky."

## Chapter Eleven
# Wearing Many Hats

I didn't get any loot from the snake and cat, but I did pack up the blanket that had been on the hill. It was nice and thick and smelled like freshly cut grass, and no one knew when they might need a towel.

I checked my status while rolling up the blanket.

```
Health 101/110
Stamina 115/115
Mana 22/105
```

My health and mana both went up by about one a minute. That didn't mean that I could survive being dropped to one health. When I'd been cut before I was aware of my health dropping by a point or two before going back up. That probably meant that the number was an indicator of health, not some ephemeral... *thing* tied to me.

Still, I was healing faster in this world than back home, and I didn't have any skills associated with it, so that was probably normal.

The door to the exit hadn't unlocked, which only left one way to go.

Before running off though, I took a moment to find a decently flat rock and a sheet of paper from my backpack and some coal with a sharp tip.

Soon enough I had a somewhat rough map of the dungeon so far. Now I couldn't get lost! Or if I did get lost, I could ask someone how to get to the exit and use the map for reference. I just hoped that zombie animals couldn't read, the last thing the world needed was an invasion of zombie critters.

I rolled up my map and stuffed it in my sack. Out came a jar of honey and I had lunch while enjoying the surreal triple suns above for a few minutes.

```
Health 107/110
Stamina 115/115
Mana 28/105
```

"It'll have to do," I said as I got up. This time I faced the door equipped for battle. Flail in one hand, free hand on the knife I moved to my bandoleer, and eyes narrowed like Clint Eastwood just before he called someone a bad word.

I pushed open the door in the hedges and peeked in. There was another corridor, this one surrounded by hedges on both sides and with a cobblestone path down the centre.

No signs of the mean skeleton with the hats, or of any zombie critters.

I stepped in and looked around. There didn't seem to be any traps, but the hedges could hide anything, and the cobbles looked too much like pressure plates for my liking. I stuck to walking on the grass for now.

The path veered off to the right after a little bit then took a sharp turn. I stopped and stared. The hedges shrunk. They went from towering walls of green to being no higher than my hip in the space of three steps.

That was interesting, but what was far more arresting was what I could see in the distance. Water. An entire ocean of water as far as the eye could see.

I was on an island, with not too distant shores where the sea was smacking against stones and there was a small cottage-like home a few hundred meters away. Or maybe it was closer? It looked... off.

The hedges around me formed a short wall around a garden with flowers and ponds and large, decorative rocks. But everything was tiny. The biggest flower was no bigger than my pinkie, the trees along the edges were only a bit taller than I was and the pond could be walked over.

In the centre of it all was Maddy, sitting at a white, wrought-iron table that barely reached his shins. The skeleton held a minuscule teacup by its mouth as it sat on a chair that looked like it had been made for dolls, not people.

There were three other guests at the table. A large hedgehog, a big ol' tortoise and a Shetland pony. Each zombie had a small teacup before them.

"Hello," I said. "Or, ah, maybe I should say 'rarr?' That's in skeleton, right?"

I might have said something offensive because Maddy stood up and flipped the tiny table right over the tortoise's head, the tiny teapot cracking and breaking across the glass with a tinkle that filled the sudden, awkward silence. He reached up into his hat and pulled out three more bits of headwear.

"Oh no," I said as he placed one on each zombie animal's head.

The hedgehog got a chef's hat, the pony a bright yellow construction helmet and the tortoise had its head wrapped in ninja bandages with a forehead protector at the front, one that had a sideways chess piece on it.

"I didn't come here to fight!" I said.

Maddy the skeleton didn't seem to care. He got up and stomped off towards the home, arriving at it sooner than he should have. He reached way up, grabbed the handle and opened the door. A moment later it slammed shut.

The zombie animals all turned around until I could see the milky white of their eyes.

    Zombie Chef hedgehog (level 2).
    Zombie Construction pony (level 2).
    Zombie Ninja tortoise (level 2).

"Oh no," I said as they started to move. The pony clip-clopped away from me before it disappeared behind a row of hedges. The hedgehog began to move towards me with a slow, waddling gait and the tortoise…

Something grabbed me by the back of the ankle, then squeezed.

I screamed and kicked out my foot, sending the tortoise flying across the garden. It had snuck up on me. Then again, it was a ninja. I was going to have to keep an eye out for sneak attacks.

My backpack fell with a clunk and I began to backpedal away from the advancing hedgehog. It was only about the size of a smaller dog, but that still brought it up to my shin, and with everything else in the garden looking so tiny it looked formidable indeed.

Kicking it seemed like a bad idea. It was missing plenty of its quills, but I was sure it wouldn't feel good to try and punt it away.

I started spinning my flail around and around until I felt it brushing against the hedge wall behind me. "Mister hedgehog, I'm warning you," I said. "I'm going to smack you if you don't stop moving close to me."

The hedgehog kept shuffling forwards.

My flail swung around and thunked unto the hedgehog with a yucky crunching sound.

Then it caught on fire. I pulled my flail back and looked away from the mess it had made of mister hedgehog. Zombies were not very tough, not even zombie hedgehogs

**Congratulations! You have cooked Zombie Chef hedgehog, level 2!**

That was nice and good, but now I had to deal with a flail that was on fire. Swinging it around only seemed to make it worse, the cord that made up the chain of it burning more and more. Soon it was going to burn up completely and I'd be left weaponless. The pond! I just had to—That's when a spinning green disk flew out of a hedge and cracked against the back of my knees.

I fell onto my back with an 'oomph' and saw the tortoise crawling away at a tortoise-y pace to go hide under a hedge.

"Not, nice," I coughed as I got back to my feet. That had hurt, but it hadn't injured me, at least.

A glance to the side showed that my flail wasn't much of a flail anymore. The showerhead was warped a bit, the stone within cracked and the rope was still burning, what was left of it, at least. I had taken out one of the three zombies, but at an incredible cost.

There was a distant clunk-clunk sound that had me getting up a whole lot faster. Just in time too, as a rock the size of my head landed where I had been laying.

I started looking around, trying to trace the source of the sound. It was probably why I caught the tortoise slowly sneaking up behind me with a gardening trowel in its mouth. A very sharp-looking trowel.

"Oh no you don't!" I said as I ran over to the ninja tortoise and jumped.

Both feet crashed into the tortoise's back, squishing it flat before I bounced off. A quick spin around and I got ready to do the same thing again when, with a poof, three more tortoises appeared.

"Clones," I growled. I was getting very very miffed about all this running around and trying to kill me stuff. It had stopped being funny. I took a running leap and stomped first one clone, then the next, then the next, bouncing from one shell to the next like an Italian plumber.

Three of the clones poofed away, then the final tortoise began to fade into motes.

## Congratulations! You have assassinated Zombie Ninja tortoise, level 2!

Two down.

It wasn't a nice feeling, knowing that killing these poor zombies was becoming so routine. Well, not routine, but common. The ghosts were different, less tangible and more obviously evil. These critters were kind of cute if I ignored the smell of rotting meat around them and the more zombie-ish parts of their anatomy. Cute animals missing an ear were still cute. Cute animals with hanging entrails… not so much.

Something went 'clunk-clunk' again and I dove to the side. A moment later a rock flew past where I had been standing, impacted the ground with a dull thud, then bounced into the pond with a splash.

I looked in the direction the rock had come from and saw a wooden pole swinging back down behind a hedge.

"I saw you!" I said as I ran over. I had my knife out, but really, really hoped that I could talk to the pony because stabbing a cute little zombie pony would be like stabbing my childhood and that just wasn't cool.

I rounded a hedge and skid to a stop.

The pony, yellow hat and all, was standing next to a trebuchet, and before it, pointing right at me, was a ballista.

I never backpedalled so fast in my life.

The ballista fired with a 'twang' as a blur shot past me and into the distance. "Look, mister pony, I don't want to hurt you, but you're not giving me any choice here," I said.

The sounds of what I suspect was a ballista being reloaded filtered over to me. No good.

I wasn't about to run back around the hedge, which left up and over the only option. With a running start, I charged towards the hedge and leapt into the air. My skill must have helped, either making my legs supernaturally strong or telling gravity to mind its own business for a moment, because I moved as if I had just bounced off a springboard.

A wide-eyed pony looked up a moment before I crashed into it feet first. By the time I had recovered from my jump the pony was only a memory.

## Congratulations! You have demolished Zombie Construction pony, level 2!

Part of me wanted to cheer, to jump and skip and be super happy that I had won another fight. I tamped down on that little voice, stood back up and bowed towards where the zombie pony had been. "I'm sorry," I said.

Being happy over the death of something, even something already mostly dead, wasn't cool.

I looked around the garden once I was done paying my respects and found that my efforts had been rewarded. Where the zombie ninja tortoise had faded away was a hat. It looked like an old British soldier's helmet, with a dome in the middle, a large flat brim and a turtle-pattern all across its surface. A pair of leather straps under it showed how it was meant to hang on to the wearer's head, and the inside was padded with more leather.

"Thank you," I said to the zombie tortoise, even if it couldn't hear me.

*Shelled kettle hat, new.*

My new hat was quite comfortable once it was strapped down nice and tight. I'm sure I made for a dashing figure. I wiggled my head a little to make sure everything was neat and fit right, then hopped on the spot a few times to make sure it wouldn't just fly off my head. It seemed nice.

Which meant it was time for me to continue on my adventure.

A bit of exploration around the garden revealed that the entrance had locked behind me already. There wasn't anything else on the island except for the massively oversized house in its middle.

*Health 110/110*
*Stamina 115/115*
*Mana 39/105*

Not nearly as good as I wanted, but it would have to do.

I picked up my backpack, holding it by the straps, then reached up and turned the door handle.

## Chapter Twelve
# Tea Time

The door opened with a long, low creak to reveal a room that immediately made me feel tiny. It was a living room that could have belonged to any one of the homes I had recently explored in Threewells. There was a rotting carpet on the ground, chairs with missing legs placed around a stone fireplace, a few tables and shelves that were covered in dust and no lack of rotting refuse just piled into the corners.

Where things got strange was when I stepped in and actually took in the size of everything. I could have fit three Broccolis side by side on any one of the chairs, the ceiling was five meters above and even the smallest table stopped next to my shoulders.

I felt like a mouse that had wandered into a bear's den.

Slowly, carefully, I lowered my backpack next to the door then moved in. I had my knife by my side, even though I didn't really know how—or even wanted to—use it, and my other hand tingled with cleaning magic just waiting to be released. I was crossing the entrance to a bedroom, the door left ajar, when the entrance door slammed shut.

I 'eeked' and jumped five feet up and nearly lost my heart from the fright. I crouched and hoped that nothing was going to pop up to eat me. It took some time for my heart to decide that it wanted to stay in my chest.

The bedroom was clear, though the bed itself was big enough for an entire family to sleep on and I could easily crawl under it on my hands and knees if I wanted. There wasn't anything there for me, so I moved on.

I found Maddy the mad skeleton sitting in the dining room. Only his head and shoulders stood out above the tall table, and his feet dangled a foot off the ground where he was perched on the edge of an enormous chair. Three more zombie animals were at the table. A red furred fox, a sickly goat and a big fork-tongued lizard.

Maddy was trying, in vain, to lift a kettle the size of his torso up when he saw me enter.

"Hello, Maddy," I said.

There were no doors here, no place for Maddy to escape to. Something told me that this was the end of the line for one of us.

The skeleton stood up onto his chair, then climbed atop the table with more alacrity than I thought a skeleton ought to have. He yanked his hat off, and from its depths pulled out three more hats.

"Oh no," I said as I started to run.

A large wig landed on the zombie fox's head just as I reached the creature and yanked at its tail. It flopped to the ground with a clatter, a gavel spinning out of its mouth a moment before I goomba-stomped it flat.

**Congratulations! You have rendered the final judgement on Zombie Judge fox, level 2!**

The other two zombie animals landed with a clatter of hooves and a... bounce?

I turned and fired off two quick Insights before taking them in with my own eyes.

*A zombie Viking goat (level 2).*
*A zombie Clown lizard (level 2).*

The goat had a big red helmet on, two large horns that were definitely not goat-like sticking out of the sides and a round shield was strapped to its back.

The lizard...

I stared at the clown makeup slathered with more enthusiasm than skill across the lizard's green scales and the big honking nose on the end of its snout. A red wig sat atop its head, wobbling to and fro as the lizard balanced on its hindlegs atop a big, multi-coloured ball.

"That doesn't even make sense," I said.

They charged. There was no gimmick here, no tricksy trick. The goat lowered its head and charged right at me and the lizard followed suit.

I spun on my heel and dashed back towards the living room, narrowly avoiding a thrown knife that sunk into the doorway with a dull thunk as I passed it. The lizard was juggling knives and that wasn't fair!

The goat's hooves skittered across the ground as it turned the corner, losing enough traction that the lizard overtook it on its huge ball.

I darted into the bedroom, then ducked behind the door. A moment later the lizard zoomed into the room. "Got you!" I said as I moved out, pulling the door shut behind me and feeling a wave of satisfaction wash over me as it clicked shut.

The satisfaction left when a hard head rammed into my tummy and sent me flying.

I landed with a roll, coughing for all I was worth as the goat, only visible from the corner of my eye, backed away and stomped a hoof like a bull after a matador.

*Health 93/110*

That had taken a chunk out of me. I wasn't sure if I would be able to stand again, and I had lost my knife somewhere after being punted. Hooves clattering on wood announced the goat's next charge.

I rolled, just barely avoiding the attack that had the zombie slowing down and turning to face me again. "You made one mistake, mister Goat," I said as I got onto shaky legs. "You left your gate open."

Spinning around, I ran back towards the dining room.

The goat followed.

When it sounded close, I ducked to the side and saw it shoot past me and deeper into the living room. That was my chance! I darted into the dining room, ran to one of the chairs and with both hands on the edge of it, jumped.

I landed in a crouch on the edge of the chair and had only just gotten my balance back when the goat rammed one of the legs. The crunch of rotten wood giving way sounded out and the entire platform shook and started to tumble to the side.

I ran, gaining some momentum before I jumped and, with an arm over the edge to help me up, managed to roll onto the table then onto my feet.

Maddy was standing across from me, something akin to surprise on his skeletal face. "Now what?" I asked him.

The goat bleated angrily below and I heard it move to another chair. It might be able to climb up, which didn't leave me much time. It was my turn to charge at an adversary. Maddy reached into his hat and pulled out all sorts of hats that he flung at me. Shakos and cowboy hats and police caps. All dodged or batted away until, finally, I was in front of the mad hatter and slapped him hard across the chest.

"Clean!" I screamed.

Magic, all the magic I had left, poured into the skeleton.

I took a couple of steps back, wary and uncertain.

Maddy placed his top hat back on, then tipped it to me a moment before he and his hats began to fade into motes of light.

**Congratulations! You have wiped three opponents ('Zombie Viking goat', level 2, 'Zombie Clown lizard', level 2, 'Maddy the Hatter, Skeleton Milliner', level 4)! Bonus Exp was granted for cleaning a monster above your level!**

"Heh, got all of them!" I cheered as Maddy faded away completely. A tea-cup and kettle landed where he had fallen.

**Bing Bong! Congratulations, your Cinnamon Bun class has reached level 3!**
*Stamina +10*
*Flexibility +5*
**You have gained: One Class Point**

"Woo!" I cheered as wonderful little tingles ran up my spine and made me feel light as a feather. I was still tired, the constant fighting and adrenaline taking their toll, but I was also energized by my victory. It was a strange feeling, but one I welcomed.

**Dungeon Alert:**
*First Floor Boss Defeated. 24 hours until respawn.*
*Second Floor Unlocked.*

"Even better!"

**Congratulations! Through repeated actions your Jumping skill has improved and is now eligible for rank up!**
**Rank D is a free rank!**
*Jumping*
*Rank D - 00%*
*The Ability to jump. Your reflexes and timing for jumps has increased. You can now jump higher and further.*

And the giddiness just grew as more gifts were rained down onto me. I calmed down a moment of two later, my tiredness catching up to me. Seeing that Maddy was just a construct helped a lot.

I suppose it meant that I could leave and return and fight all of the same monsters again and again. If I recalled books with dungeons though, there would be new tricks and traps next time, and being overconfident could lead to me walking right into a pile of trouble. Also, Maddie's hats felt… randomly assigned. Maybe I would get a really poor match-up next time.

It was probably best that I learn when to quit and when to move on.

Next was checking out my loot.

*An enchanted teacup, new.*
*An enchanted teapot, new.*

Not as handy as my awesome new hat, but they might be valuable. The cup and kettle were both a beige colour, with tiny animals etched into the side. They looked… well, they were tiny zombie animals, but maybe someone that didn't know would think they were just poorly drawn.

I held my prizes close to my chest and started trekking over towards the door when everything wiggled and waved and the world spun. Then, between one blink and the next, I was at the entrance of the level, back to the door that still had Maddy's sign on it and front facing the drop in the middle of the dungeon.

"Oh," I said. A look down showed my backpack, unceremoniously dumped by my side, and my teacup and pot were both still pressed against my chest. Even my knife was returned to me, left on the ground by my foot. "That was kind. Thank you, dungeon!" I said.

No response came.

I decided that a break was in order and settled down next to the wall with my back to it. Out came the honey jar and a spoon and soon I was lick-licking my way through a tasty and well-earned treat.

| Name: Broccoli Bunch | | Race: Human | | | Age: 16 |
|---|---|---|---|---|---|
| Health | 110 | Stamina | 125 | Mana | 105 |
| Resilience | 20 | Flexibility | 25 | Magic | 10 |

| First Class: | Cinnamon Bun | First Class Level: | 3 |
|---|---|---|---|
| Skill Slots | 0 | Skill Points | 0 |

| General Skill Slots | 0 | General Skill Points | 0 |
|---|---|---|---|

| General Skills | | Cinnamon Bun Skills | |
|---|---|---|---|
| Insight | D - 48% | Cleaning | C - 76% |
| Makeshift Weapon Proficiency | F - 72% | Jumping | D - 00% |
| Archaeology | F - 35% | | |

"Hrm, my Cleaning skill is getting close to Rank B. That might be handy. And Jumping is actually pretty nifty. I look forward to getting it up to C to find out what it does! What do you think, mister Menu?" I asked.

The box didn't say anything, but I like to think that it appreciated the attention.

Then my eyes alighted on my race and I stared. "Well, that's new," I said. Or was it? Had I just not been paying attention last time? Did it matter at all? I was going to have to ask someone the next time I found myself in a more civilised place.

I finished up my honey a few minutes later and pulled out a bottle of lukewarm water to sip at, then just kind of sat back and relaxed. I was getting the hang of the adventurer's life. At least, I hoped I was.

The future had so much in store here! I was going to become super strong and respected and I was going to make a ton of friends and one day I'd ride a dragon. I smiled as I leaned my head back against the wall and just let my imagination run wild…

A distant whisper of wind startled me awake and I looked around bleary eyed. There wasn't anyone around, just the huge empty dungeon.

I climbed back to my feet, legs kind of ache-y from the way I had been sitting back until I stretched and tried to get my blood flowing again.

*Health 110/110*
*Stamina 125/125*
*Mana 105/105*

"At least my nap wasn't all bed, huh?" I asked my status menu while hiding a grin behind a hand.

It must have been shy because it popped away soon after. The poor thing. This time my trip down the mushroom path was as easy as pie. I could feel the difference the rank up had made with my jumping skill. It was so much easier to guess when the exact right moment to land would come up and when and how to bend my knees and shift my weight just so.

I landed with a huge smile on my face and skipped over to the second door of the dungeon. It was time to move onto the next part of the adventure!

# Chapter Thirteen
# Off With Her Head

I stepped into the next room of the dungeon, my eyes roaming across clean stone floors and walls decorated with banners of red and black, each with a different symbol piece on its surface. A heart, a diamond, a club and a spade. The room led to a smaller door that had a sign hanging next to it.

*Doth not disturbe*
*—By the royal decree of the Queene of Hearts*

"Well, that's ominous," I said. I wasn't going to knock if they didn't want to be disturbed, but I doubted just standing around was going to do me any good. I carefully opened the door—the sign didn't say I couldn't go in, only that I couldn't cause a disturbance—and peeked around.

It was a courtroom, with balconies along the sides looking down at a box where the guilty could stand. Off to one side of the main floor was a large guillotine and next to that the judge's platform. The door opened onto the balcony level, where they circled around the entire courtroom. There were people!

Well, not people-people. The room was filled with four dozen square people, each one very thin but quite large and dressed in either black or red. I saw spears and swords hanging from hips or standing by their sides. They looked like playing cards with arms and legs and heads sticking out.

In the judge's area below was an ostentatious throne on which a large woman sat, her head covered in an elaborate red wig with a pair of crowns on it with plenty of little hearts. Before her, in the box reserved for the guilty was a younger looking person with the same bodily dimensions. He was unarmed, hands manacled together by large chains

It didn't take a genius to figure out what was happening here, the jack was being judged by the queen for having committed some crime.

A few of the people turned my way when the door clicked shut behind me. I froze, then waved while smiling sheepishly. They turned back to watch the show.

People that didn't instantly want to kill me!

I moved over as quietly as I could and found a spot where I could look over the rails while keeping a few feet's distance between me and the others.

"Sir Jack of Spades," the queen said in a high-pitched voice like a mom calling a kid that was on the second floor. "You are accused of the crime of grand theft cake. How do you plead?"

The Jack of Spades stood up tall and proud. "I plead… not guilty."

"Then you're a liar then?" the queen asked in the same high tones. She picked up a fan and began waving it towards her face. A face smeared in what looked a lot like cake.

"I am not, your Majesty. I am a loyal Jack."

"Then how, pray tell, did my cake go missing. It was by my side, and then it was not. Were you not guarding my person?" she asked.

"I was, your majesty, and no one approached you or the royal confectionary."

"Then where, is, my, cake?" the queen asked as she snapped her fan shut and pointed it quite dramatically at the Jack.

"Your majesty," the Jack said. "I suspect you ate it."

A gasp sounded out across the entire courtroom.

What? I could see the cake stains all over her face from where I stood. This entire thing was obviously a sham! But then, should I really interfere?

"Off! Off with his head!" the queen shouted.

"Wait!" I called out.

My voice quieted all the murmurs and I suddenly found myself the centre of a whole lot of attention. I swallowed and inspected the nearest person just in case.

*A Cardstock Man, Three of Hearts (level 2).*

Not too strong, but there were so many. I couldn't stand against them. The smart thing to do would be to apologize and stay quiet.

The smart thing.

But not the right thing.

"I think that the Jack of Spades is innocent!" I called.

"Innocent? Innocent!" the queen shouted. "Come down here, fool child, and stand before me so that I might see your fool face!"

I huffed, screwed up my courage, and leapt off the ledge. I sailed through the air for a couple of long seconds before landing and rolling to bleed off momentum. I got to my feet and stood before the queen.

She looked a lot taller from the ground floor with her imposing throne around her. Not that she was tall, all the cardstock people were pretty short, the tallest one was barely as tall as I was.

The queen seemed to notice as much. "Ace! Bring out the measuring staff. This interloper seems… tall for this courtroom."

"Is that a problem?" I asked.

"The law dictates that none who are taller than the staff of judgement may stand within this room and be suffered to live," the queen said. "Foolish girl child, you ought to know your place."

I was nervous for a moment as a Cardstock person walked over to me, but when he placed the staff next to me it was clear that I was a few centimetres shorter.

The queen's eyes narrowed, but she nodded and waved the Ace away. "Very well, plead the case of the Jack. Plead it well and perhaps he, and you, shall leave this place unharmed."

"I…" I paused to swallow. I couldn't just point to her face and say the cake was still there. "Your most majestic of majesties. It is difficult to prove a negative, so I will suggest an alternative sentencing. If the queen has her cake, does the Jack truly deserve to lose his head?"

The queen considered that for a moment. "Yes, yes he does, for having taken the cake in the first place."

"Ah, okay then," I said.

"So you're willing to stand aside and allow this fool to be judged properly?" the queen said, her voice reaching whole new levels of haughty.

"What if I bring the queen a replacement cake?" I asked.

The queen's eyes lit up. "A replacement, you say."

"Yes, your majesty. A cake unlike any to be found in your hallowed halls."

The queen set aside her fan and picked up a gavel which she banged onto the arm of her throne a few times. "Very well! The court shall recess for one hour! Upon the end of which either a new cake shall be eaten, or you will both be judged as cake thieves of the highest order and will lose your heads!"

I swallowed and shot an insight at the queen.

*The Cardstock Queen of Hearts (level 3).*

Tough. Not as dangerous as Maddy, according to whatever gave things levels, but dangerous all the same. And she had guards and a whole kingdom at her beck and call.

"I'll be back!" I said.

This time I took the stairs and shot out of the room, only just picking up my backpack on the way out.

My plan was simple, but it relied on a few things that I wasn't certain about. Notably, that I could return to the courtroom without having to re-fight the first-floor boss Maddy all over again. The mushrooms were a bit tricky, but with my newfound jumping skills I made it up with little trouble. Then it was through the entrance where I found no time-travel bunnies, but I did find a plate with a cake on it. A cake with the words Eat-Me written on them.

I sniffed the cake and poked a corner with a pinkie. It was nice and moist still. A cleaning spell took care of my dirty finger for one whole point of mana.

*A poisoned cake of enlargening.*

It… wasn't a deadly poison then. Still… yes, there was a solution there. One that the dungeon has obviously planned with this cake at its centre. It was like a big puzzle! I wondered if there was a similar solution to Maddy's part of the dungeon that I had just missed.

The return trip was a lot harder. Balancing a cake while bouncing around was no easy feat. Still, I made it to the courtroom door and opened it with an elbow, breathing a sigh of relief when it opened without fuss or muss.

"What took you so long?" the queen screeched from her royal throne; her fingers were tapping a beat upon the royal arm-rest and she seemed utterly impatient even if it had probably taken me less than ten minutes to go up and come back.

"I bring you your royal cake, your majesty," I said with a careful bow.

"Ace," the queen said.

The Ace card, still holding the staff, returned to my side and carefully took the cake. I shifted on the spot, waiting as the Ace brought the cake closer to the queen, then deposited it upon a table brought forth by two numbers.

"I'm sorry if this doesn't work out," I told the Jack of Spades.

The Jack looked at me, then smiled. "You are a brave one, to stand for what is right rather than what is easy. I thank you."

That had warm fuzzies rumbling in my tummy and when I turned to the queen it was with a smile upon my lips.

"I will now taste this… cake and decide on its value. If it is of poor quality, then we shall see about shortening your heads!" The queen dipped a silver fork into the cake, then took a careful bite. She chewed as if thinking, then took another bite. "Ace, bring me the royal milk!"

The card person bowed a little then moved off, returning a moment later with a silver platter with a glass cup. The queen pinched it between two fingers and tossed the entire contents down her mouth.

I held back a grin. The queen was growing bigger by the moment. "Here's your chance," I told the Jack. "Your majesty!" I said. "You've eaten too much cake."

"What?!" she said, her attention suddenly all on me. She took another forkful of cake but had a hard time on account of the fork becoming smaller in her hands. "What is the meaning of this?"

"Your greed has made you fat!" I accused, putting a bit of theatricality into it because it was fun. The gasps from the court-viewers had me holding back a giggle. "Look, soon you'll be too big for this courtroom."

The Ace stepped up and brought the staff next to the queen. She was, indeed, too big for the room, even sitting down she was half a head taller. "What nonsense is this?" she demanded to know.

But it was too late. The murmurs in the crowd had turned into suspicion and someone started to raise the large blade of the guillotine with loud squeaks of a pulley. "She is right!" the Jack of Spades said as two other Jacks came to undo his manacles. "The queen has broken the law. Off with her head!"

"I cannot break the law, I am the law!" The queen shouted.

It was drowned out in a chorus of 'off with her head!' and a flood of number cards grabbed the queen and started dragging her ever larger body towards the gallows.

I couldn't watch. I knew that they were all constructs, but the idea of seeing someone's head just... no, it was too much. The queen's protests died with the sound of steel slicing through bone and I had to swallow to keep my gorge from rising.

Then a ding sounded out and I opened my eyes.

**Dungeon Alert:**
*Second Floor Boss Defeated.*
*24 hours until respawn.*
*Dungeon Boss Room Unlocked!*

I was out in the main shaft of the Dungeon again, the green sky above and the door to the courtroom closed behind me. That... had only taken an hour or so, I judged.

**Congratulations! Through repeated actions your Insight skill has improved and is now eligible for rank up!**
**Rank C costs one (1) General Point**

"Ohh, shiny!" I said a moment before a spade landed on my head.

# Chapter Fourteen

# A Very High Cinnamon Bun

"Ow," I said.

Then I touched the bump on my head. "Oww!"

I was crouching down on the second-floor platform, both hands pressing down on a nice lump with my eyes closed. It took a while before the pain ebbed away and I dared to open my eyes and look down at just what had bonked my head.

There was a spade on the ground, just sort of lying there, with a cross-shaped handle and a shaft made of a whitish wood. The metal bit at the end looked nice and new and there was a big 'J' embossed on the plate.

"Really?" I asked.

The Dungeon was being very rude with its rewards. Still, a new… weapon of sorts was better than nothing. I wondered if it counted as makeshift? It was a good thing that my reward hadn't been a mace.

I picked up the spade and swung it around a little to test its weight and balance. I could tell from my experimental swings that I knew nothing about swinging any sort of weapon around. "Insight."

*A Spade of Jacks, new.*

"Huh. Okay, so a sort of gift for finishing the last room by helping Jack. I wonder if clearing the room in other ways gives other rewards? Do you know, mister Menu?"

The Insight information box popped away. Poor mister Menu was so shy. I shook my head and pulled up the screen for Insight.

*Insight*
*Rank D - 100%*
*The Ability to know something. The knowledge you gain is further increased.*
*You have no General Skill Points! You cannot increase Insight to Rank C!*

"What's a general skill point?" I wondered aloud. It wasn't a Class Skill Point. I had two of those just sitting around and trying to think about clicking them to Insight just made my head feel fuzzy. So that wasn't it. Oh well, a question to ask someone once I was out of here and found civilisation.

"Well, onwards," I said as I hiked my backpack back on.

The path down was filled with mushy mushrooms to skip from. I was a little less careful this time since I was so close to the ground floor already. I was pretty sure that with Jumping at rank D I could survive the fall mostly unhurt, and each mushroom down made that a little more likely.

Then a caterpillar stuck its head out from behind one of the mushrooms and blew a thick plume of pinkish smoke at me.

I waved a hand before my face, but the thick smoggy smoke was already down my throat. That was one rude caterpillar.

It pulled out a large hookah and took another big puff, cheeks ground big as it got ready to spray me again.

Then I landed on its head.

## Congratulations! You have smoked Hookapillar, level 2!

I landed at the base of the Dungeon's pillar coughing like mad. My first step missed the ground and when I stumbled and tried to reach the wall it was to find it a whole foot further than I had thought. It didn't help that everything felt like it was spinning just a little bit, like one of those tea-cup rides at amusement parks but really slowly.

"I-insight," I said, aiming the skill onto myself.

*A very high Cinnamon Bun (level 3).*

I... I had taken drugs? Was this the peer pressure my family had warned me about. My mom would be... mildly disappointed that I had smoked something without taking the proper precautions. There was only so much disappointment a mostly-ex hippie could give when it came to the subject of drugs. I'd seen my parents' pictures of their time at Woodstock.

Oh no, I was thinking in tangents!

Was it the drugs?

Was I a delinquent now? I didn't look good in black and wearing spikes would make me less huggable!

"Menu!" I said and grabbed at it when it appeared. "Quick, I need a drug resistance power, quick!"

The menu popped away with what I imagined, or hoped I imagined, was a huff of annoyance.

It was okay, I could figure it out.

I started pacing the bottom of the dungeon, eating a circle around the small hill in the middle while taking big, huge gulps of air to clear my system. A few glances here and there and the occasional snoop behind some of the sharp rocks surrounding the clearing didn't reveal much at all. I decided that I might as well waste time productively and sat down with my back to the wall and took out my map making gear, which was mostly the same bit of coal and my dungeon map.

Adding the additional rooms and some details ate up nearly half an hour.

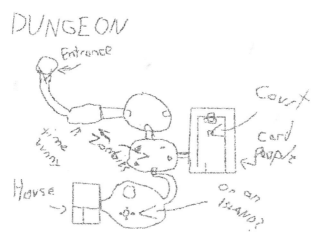

"Yep," I said as I looked over my work. "That's certainly almost a map." I stuffed it away and considered napping, but I had a strange sort of energy and was starting to be really hungry. "Insight."

*A very buzzed Cinnamon Bun (level 3).*

That would have to do.

I got up, tossed my backpack back on and moved over to the archway set in the far wall. Carefully carved stones formed a delicate arch which was filled to the very brim with climbing vines and all sorts of plants. They were so thick in the passage that I couldn't see more than a foot into the tunnel.

Was I meant to hack my way through? That didn't feel right. Every other challenge in the dungeon had a non-violent answer to it. Maybe I was meant to use the shrinking potion?

I poked at the wall of vines with my spade and watched, fascinated, as they all receded away like curtains being pulled aside on a stage. It revealed a long, dark path. "Spooky," I said.

Lights began to appear in the tunnel, first in the distance, then closer and closer, each new point of light a little brighter until I could make out the flickering of torches tied to the walls. Soon, a pair of torches just a few meters into the tunnel lit up with a crackling woosh.

"Neat."

I stepped into the passageway and walked along it, making sure to always have one foot on solid ground and keeping an eye out for traps. I even took one of the torches out of its sconce and held it aloft like a real adventurer would, or at least those in my books.

The long tunnel led into a room that reminded me a little of the dungeon's main area, only there were no big colourful mushrooms here and the ceiling above was covered in sharp stones jutting downwards.

In the centre of the room, monoliths loomed up in a circle that reminded me of Stonehenge without the caps. The room smelled faintly like ammonia, but the constant breeze made the smell come and go even as it rustled the dry grass growing between the stones on the ground.

"Hello?" I asked aloud.

The place looked dangerous. A clear and obvious shift from the otherwise bright and almost cheery atmosphere of the rest of the dungeon.

"My, oh my, a late-night snack."

I spun around, searching for the source of the voice but finding nothing.

"I'm not over there," came a whisper from behind me.

I turned again and found only an orangey wisp fading away so fast that I wasn't sure I had actually seen anything. "Um, hi, my name is Broccoli," I said.

"Are you as scrumptious as your name implies?" the voice said. Every word came from a new direction and I gave up trying to trace it.

"I'm not for eating, I'm for making friends with," I told the person. "We could be friends too if you stop with the weird voice thing. Unless you can't? I'm sorry. If you can't help yourself then we can still be friends, I promise I won't judge."

I slowly lowered my backpack next to one of the pillars and stood with nothing but my spade in one hand, the tip poking into the grass between my feet.

"Oh, you are a... treat."

Something bit my bum. Hard teeth sinking through the material of my skirt and into my skin before I shrieked and jumped five feet into the air.

"So tasty, and those reactions. Lovely!"

This time I saw the thing, a quick insight going off even as I pressed a hand to my butt and tried not to cry.

It was a cat, or the head of a cat. It had one malevolent green eye, the other white and milky. Its huge mouth was twisted in a cruel smirk before it slipped into the shadows.

*The zombie of Cheshire, Boss (level 5).*

Level five? But this was a level two to four dungeon? Had the prompt lied or was the Cheshire cat the end boss?

"Y-you know, touching a girl like that without permission is exceptionally rude."

"Oh? Have I been rude?" the cat purred. The rumble was so deep I felt it in my chest.

Something brushed past between my legs, soft and furry, like a cat begging for attention. I swung my spade around but hit only empty air before teeth sank into my thigh.

I screamed, my hand shooting out and firing a cleaning spell into the first thing I touched.

"Tingly," Cheshire said from the shadows, all the shadows. "But that only adds to the flavour, doesn't it?"

"S-stop hiding!" I screamed while my hand shakily took stock of my wounds. Blood was flowing freely down my inner thigh and into my socks. Not too much, but more than I ever wanted to see.

"Hrmm, if the snack asks so politely," Cheshire said.

He appeared in the middle of the stone circle, a huge orange furred cat covered in black stripes with a large cattish grin that looked like it could chew me whole.

I jumped to the side a moment before the cat charged at me mouth wide open to take a nibble out of me. The jaw snapped shut, and with that snap the cat disappeared like sand in the wind.

I couldn't do it. The cat was too big, the level difference way too large. I looked to the exit and saw that the passage was still unblocked. It was just down a couple of hundred meters of narrow tunnel that I was certain the cat could shoot through with ease.

"Darn it," I said.

A whisper of a rough tongue moving over lips was the only warning I had, but it was enough for me to duck out of the way of another attempt from the huge cat to chow on me.

I kicked upwards, putting all of my jumping skill into the act of kicking the Cheshire only for the cat to spin out of the path of my kick as if I had announced it days ago.

"Such a slow little kitten," the Cheshire said mockingly. "Do continue to struggle though. I enjoy the game."

"I won't let you eat me!" I swore at the cat. Rolling to my feet, I ran over to my backpack and started rooting within, the task made harder by the spade in my hand.

"More toys?" the cat asked.

I pulled out the wrong thing, my magic wand instead of what I was looking for, but I still flung it at the orange cat when it stuck its head out of the nearest corner.

"Naughty, naughty!" he said before slinking back.

Then I found it.

I tossed it into my left hand and held on tight as I started looking for the cat. "Come at me, you unfunny Garfield wannabe!" I shouted. I... was still not very good at taunting. I blamed the wet throbbing of my thigh.

The Cheshire giggled maniacally. "Come at you? Very well."

The cat came around one of the pillars and rushed right at me. My spade swished through the air, but all it did was bonk the cat on the head. Then I punched out with my left hand, right at the cat's open mouth.

I hit its rough tongue with a wet squelch and probably didn't so much as leave a bruise. Teeth, long and dagger-like, snapped around my shoulder and armpit.

I screamed, my entire body trashing as the cat's tongue ran over my arm and it made disgustingly pleased sounds. My spade came down again and again on its big ugly head, but it didn't seem to do anything. I wanted to unleash my magic, but had to keep it back, for just a little while.

The potion bottle in my hand burst. I felt the juice of it mix with the cat's saliva. My spade hit the ground with a clatter, and I reached up to grab the cat by a fistful of its fur.

"You are not friend material!" I shouted as the cat's eyes went wide and it began to shrink. The monster tried to go intangible, but my arm, still in its mouth, fired a tiny burst of cleaning magic at its zombie flesh and it returned to normal.

It shrunk and shrunk. I had to squeeze my arm out of its throat, but its slick saliva helped with that.

It was no bigger than a kitten now, a ball of orange-black fluff that I held by the scruff.

"I will eat you!" it squeaked.

I glared. "Eat this."

A burst, a full half of my remaining mana, shot into the kitty and it burst apart into a shower of orange motes.

**Ding! Ding! Ding! Congratulations, you have defeated Dungeon Boss: Zombie Cheshire, level 5! For defeating an enemy above your level, bonus exp is gained! For defeating a Dungeon boss, bonus exp is gained!**

"Not now," I told the menu. The pile of notifications faded away a moment later, still there, but out of sight.

I crashed to my knees and cried as I cradled my arm to my side. My thigh was no better. It hurt, hurt more than anything I had ever felt before. But for all that it hurt it was an impotent pain, one I couldn't do anything about.

I pushed a bit of my mana into my body, and all that accomplished was wiping the wounds clean and reopening them to the sting of fresh air.

So I decided that the best thing to do was to have a sit and cry for a bit.

# Chapter Fifteen

# The Last One Smiling

*Health 59/110*
*Stamina 115/115*
*Mana 37/105*

I was worried. For a few long minutes, my health had slowly but sure-ly ticked down every few seconds, going from a not very healthy seventy something to the low sixties. Now it had stopped and held at fifty-nine for a few minutes, or as close as I could reckon.

"Okay, okay," I said as I shifted to the side and opened my backpack. I found the blanket I had nabbed from the first floor and set it down before using it as a spot to sit on. "I'm ready, Mister Menu."

**Bing Bong! Congratulations, your Cinnamon Bun class has reached level 4!**
Health + 5
Resilience +5
**You have gained: One Class Point**
You have unlocked: One Class Skill Slot

That was nice. I glanced at my status as soon as the giddiness washing through me passed.

*Health 64/115*
*Stamina 115/115*
*Mana 38/105*

That was really nice, even if I didn't feel all that much better. Still, I would take it. Another level, another skill point and another class skill. That last could be very useful if I got something that wasn't Cleaning or Jumping.

"Next one, mister Menu," I said.

**Congratulations! Through repeated actions your Makeshift Weapon Proficiency skill has improved and is now eligible for rank up!**
**Rank E is a free rank!**
*Makeshift Weapon Proficiency*
*Rank E - 00%*
*The ability to use non-weapons as weapons.*

*Your ability to find and use makeshift weapons has improved.*

"That'll be handy," I said as I patted my spade. It hadn't served all that well in the last fight, but I was sure that would change eventually. Plus a spade just seemed useful to have. "What's after that, mister Menu?"

I found a jar of honey and a spoon while I waited for the next pop up.

**Dungeon Cleared!**
*All adversaries with The Wonderland Dungeon Defeated.*
*All Bosses Defeated.*
*Broccoli Bunch, Cinnamon bun, level 4 is awarded the Wonderlander class.*
*All class slots filled.*
**Replace current class with Wonderlander?**
*Replacing your current class will reset your level 0.*

"Heck no!" I said as fast as I could. No way was I going to get reset to level zero just like that.

**Class: Wonderlander set in abeyance until Class Slot becomes available.**

I hummed as I considered that. It seemed as if my earlier hunch about multiple classes was right. That raised the question though, how did you get a second class? Maybe it would happen when I hit level one hundred. That seemed almost reasonable. At my current rate I would be… long dead because I ran into something scary that gobbled me up.

Oh well, I thought, maybe I'd figure it out later.

*Health 65/115*
*Stamina 115/115*
*Mana 39/105*

My health was rising, that was excellent news. I wasn't going to die!

My mood somewhat improved, I got to my feet, wincing at the pull of mending flesh over my thigh. Packing everything back up into my backpack and crossing half the room to retrieve my magic wand was a huge pain in the butt. Literally. But I got everything sorted and took another look at the room.

There were now two glowing portals between two sets of the stone monoliths. I should probably have noticed those earlier.

One had a blurry image or what I recognized as Threewells, just outside of the dungeon. The other was a hazy image of a small room with a stone pillar at its middle. Atop the pillar, and covered in glowing roots, was an egg of sorts.

```
Quest Updated!
You have found the Evil Root. Destroy it
to Cleanse the Land!
```

"Oh," I said as I took in the pulsing form. My hand reached out and brushed against the portal, slipping through it without so much as a whisper, though I felt something tingling under my skin, as if I was using my cleaning spell without actually using it. Funky.

I closed my eyes and stepped through, then opened them again.

I was now in a much smaller room, tight, even, with dirt walls and large, cruel-looking roots crawling across the ground and up the plinth.

"Whoa," I said as I moved closer to the egg-thing in the middle. It was too round to be an actual egg, and too glowy and see-through as well. I felt... funny, just standing next to it.

```
Health 97/115
Stamina 135/115
Mana 275/105
```

"Oh, yikes," I said as I took in my stats. That was probably not supposed to happen. No complaining about the faster healing though, and I did feel oodles better. I fired an 'insight' at the orb, then the freaky roots.

```
The Dungeon Core for the Wonderland
Dungeon.
An Evil Root.
```

"Well, that's simple enough, isn't it," I said.

I poked the evil root and fired a blast of cleaning magic into it, then, when that did nothing, a stronger blast that lowered my mana down to the low two-hundreds.

When that didn't work, I gave it a smack with the edge of my spade.

It didn't even leave a mark.

```
Quest Update!
You have found the Evil Root. You are too
```

```
weak to Destroy the Evil Root. Break the
Core and let the Root Starve.
```

"That sounds wildly dangerous," I said to the quest menu.

The menu merely shifted to the side as if to say, 'there's the core, get smacking.'

Something about the smooth motions of the quest menu, the way it seemed to be more reactive, told me that it wasn't mister Menu. I was going to call it miss Menu not to confuse the two.

"Well, here goes," I said as I poked the core and fired a cleaning spell into it. If that didn't work, then it was back to using the spade.

The magic washed across the core, starting from where my finger touched it, then racing all the way to the other side as a glowing ring before returning. Then, with a glass-like crunch, the core cracked. At first just a small little hairline, then it expanded and raced across the surface, like the videos I'd seen of Antarctic ice breaking apart.

**Dungeon Warning**
**Dungeon Stability Failing.**
*Evacuate.*

"Oh, shoot," I said as I turned tail and ran. I dove through the first portal, then almost tripped when the ground of the boss room heaved underfoot. The sharp rocks above, stalactites? Mites? Loosened and began to crash to the ground around me like thrown spears and the monoliths trembled.

I hung onto the straps of my backpack and jumped through the portal to the exit.

It snapped away just as I was about to pass through.

"Ohhh, shoot, that's very not good," I said as I spun around and started running for the tunnel.

Part of the floor jutted up and I jumped over it, clearing a good ten feet before landing in a sprint. If jumping was faster than running, then that's what I would do. My sack bounced atop my back with every hop, but I didn't have time to ditch it.

I exploded out into the main dungeon shaft to find that the sky above was hazy and warped, like a television with a bunch of magnets stuck to it. The walls were trembling here too, loose stones clattering to the ground with crunches that would have been loud if they weren't competing with the entire world going full apocalypse.I bounced from mushroom to mushroom, moving as fast as I could with no concern for safety because safety was for when the world wasn't literally falling apart. The tunnel into the time bunny room was broken, part of the floor and ceiling cracked so bad I had to take off my backpack and fling in through before I leaped down the remaining hole feet-first.

Something caught at my neck and my hat fell off just as the ceiling rumbled and the opening started to close.

I reached in and yanked my hat back a moment before the whole thing shuddered to a close.

"Close," I gasped before jumping to my feet, grabbing my backpack, and running.

I took the ladder two rungs at a time and set foot in Threewells once more just as the shaft behind me collapsed, the world shifted sideways and a wave of what I could only assume was pure magic burst through the air like a bomb going off.

My knees gave out and I collapsed in a heap, gasping for air like a fish out of water.

"Hah," I said. Then another laugh escaped. "Haha… hahaha!" Soon I was rolling on the ground, not because I was tired, but because the adrenaline coursing through me made me feel lightheaded and funny and everything was hilarious.

**Quest Complete!**
*The world thanks you for your sacrifice!*

That only made me laugh harder, even if it wasn't funny.

**Wonderland Dungeon Core Destroyed!**
**You have gained: Two General Points**

I was laughing so hard by then that I was seriously worried, at the very back of my mind, that I might pee myself. My legs were kicking the ground and I was clutching at my sides and rolling.

**Congratulations! Through repeated actions your Jumping skill has improved and is now eligible for rank up!**
**Rank C costs one (1) Class Point**

But like all good things the fit of maniacal laughter came to an end.

I sat up, then dusted my skirt before checking it for damage. There were a few holes punched into the leather of my armoured skirt, and the cotton of my normal skirt fared little better. My stockings were… pretty much ruined. Fortunately it wasn't cold out wherever I was. Not compared to back home.

Stretching as I stood up, I took in the town. There were more plants and such than I remembered, and the air felt vibrant somehow, thick with magic. It was nice. The sky was a burnt orange above, fading slowly into darkness.

I looked down and took in the large crater where the dungeon had been. There wasn't much left there. Then my eyes picked up something laying at my feet. "Insight?"

*An enchanted Cheshire Cat's Collar, new.*

Loot from the final boss, perhaps. I picked it up and examined it. The collar was offensively orange, with thin black lines across it and a little pendant at the front that looked like a smiling kitty mouth.

"Okay then," I said as I shoved it in my backpack. A thing for later. Right now I had to… do…

I looked around, then down to my hands.

"Now what?"

*A New Quest!*
**Pruning the Evil**
*Evil Roots Remain! Dungeons across Dirt are Infected! Destroy them!*

"Okay, so that's a 'what'," I said. I took a few steps, then paused. I wasn't sure where to go, what to do. The last hour had been… a lot. Too much even. All I wanted now was my bed, and, and maybe my mom and my dad. We could have a family hug and mom would burn the supper and dad would complain about the environment and then the price of gas and—

"Focus Broccoli," I said. "Focus. You did it. You took out a whole dungeon. You're awesome. Now you just need to… to make friends."

Right. That was a goal, one even better than some silly no-reward quest. I would find some really cool people and we'd form an awesome party and have the greatest adventures together!

In the meantime, I could check out a few last things in the town. Check up on that nice ghost in the inn, look into that one building with the big locked door, then, then maybe I'd spend the night in Threewells one last time before hitting the road.

Resolve all firmed up, I allowed a smile to cross my face and strolled across the town, checking in at all the houses I had missed along the way.

Not much remained of them, the houses nearest the side I had decided to call the North were all in much worse repair, with caved in roofs and walls with holes torn into them. There wasn't even a ghost snooping around to scare poor level one adventurers.

The Inn was as I remembered it. I stepped in and looked around, then made my way all the way up to the top floor. "Mister Ghost?" I called out.

But there was nothing. My wispy friend was gone.

On the bed where a corpse had lain was now a small ring that looked to be made of bronze.

*Bronze ring of cleared soul.*

I picked it up with a cloth and stuffed it away. I kind of wanted to try it out, it was certainly laid out the way someone would leave a gift, but I didn't dare put on any sort of soul-related rings. I had read Lord of the Rings, I knew better. Broccoli would not be a pretty Gollum.

The sun was nearly completely down. Rather than venture out to my tiny hidey hole I found one of the less disgusting beds, fired off a few dozen mana's worth of cleaning magic into it, then flopped down.

I was asleep almost as soon as my head hit the mattress.

## Chapter Sixteen
# Ready Check

My backpack was nearly completely packed with everything I thought I should bring. It didn't amount to all that much. Some provisions, a few tools, and some extras, but not as much survival gear as I would have wanted to have before setting out for a long trek through an unfamiliar forest.

Before anything though, I had some points to assign. Insight and Jumping were both at rank D and had enough experience points—or whatever was used to fill their meters—to rank up. I had a suspicion that skills were not supposed to grow as quickly as mine did. A side effect of using non-combat skills in a fight? Makeshift Weapons Proficiency certainly wasn't growing quickly.

Oh well. I leaned against the headboard of the bed I had picked for myself, a silver spoonful of honey in my mouth. The sweetness helped calm the grumbles in my tummy. Those weren't helping me think much.

I had two general skill points, earned from the Dungeon, and three class skill points. The class skill points were uncommon but came fairly steadily. The general skills points, if they all required blowing up a dungeon, were not nearly as easy to get.

That meant using one on Insight was a big risk. But it might lead to a big reward too. My other options right then were a weapon's skill and Archaeology or any future skill I might or might not obtain.

It was worth it, I thought. Insight was handy already. Having it be better seemed like a good idea.

Getting Jumping to Rank C, on the other hand, was a choice so brain-dead easy that I didn't even really need to think about it.

```
Jumping
Rank C - 00%
The Ability to jump. Your reflexes and
timing for jumps has increased. You can
now jump higher and further. You may now
expend Stamina to increase the power of
your jumps.
```

"Oh, shiny," I said. So Rank C unlocked a secondary ability yet again. Was this a pattern? Two was too few to know. But three results…

*Insight*

*Rank C - 00%*

*The Ability to know something. The knowledge*
*you gain is further increased. You may now*
*expend Mana to discover hidden knowledge.*

"Oh, now that is beautiful!" I said before rolling off the bed. I rooted around in my backpack while licking at the spoon still in my mouth like a very hard lollipop. Soon, I had a row of objects on the crumpled mattress awaiting inspection.

There was the collar from the Dungeon boss, my hat, the soul ring I had found in the next room over, the magic wand I'd been flinging around, and the tea set from Maddy.

"Insight!" I said as I pointed at the collar and pushed some mana... somewhere. It somehow felt right to pull it towards my head, which was a little strange, but the information I got spoke for itself.

*An enchanted Cheshire Cat's Collar of Rare*
*quality, new. Allows the user to summon a*
*spirit cat once a day.*

"A what?" I asked aloud before shaking my head. No, that was for later. A glance at my mana status showed that it was down a good ten points. A fair bit, but not too much. I had noticed my magical cleaning costing less and less over time, so maybe that would decrease with experience.

Next was my hat.

*Shelled kettle hat of Uncommon quality,*
*new.*

"Well, I like it regardless of its quality. It's fashionable." I picked up the hat and plopped it onto my head. Only four points of mana this time. A correlation between magical items and plain ones?

*Bronze ring of Cleared Soul of Uncommon*
*quality, old. Protects the wearer's soul*
*from minor to mild soul manipulations.*

I put the ring on in a hurry. "Thank you, mister Ghost," I said as I felt the ring shift to fit just right on my left middle finger. It was plain, just a rough bronze ring, but a bit of a rub and some cleaning magic and it shone quite prettily.

*Vibrating Magic Wand of Cure Hysteria of Common quality, old.*

I tilted my head to the side as I examined the foot-long magic stick. It was made of old, smooth wood with a gnarl at one end and some runes or glyphs carved into it. Maybe the owner suffered from hysteria? Was it a common sickness around here? Well, I wasn't going to throw the wand away. I'd try to sell it if I found anyone interested. In the backpack it went.

*Enchanted Teacup, Uncommon quality, new. Keeps tea warm as long as a small amount of mana is fed into the cup.*
*Enchanted Tea Kettle, Uncommon quality, new. Will boil water rapidly if mana is fed through the handle.*

Tea! I liked tea, and the set looked fairly robust for what they were. I would still wrap both in cloth when I packed them away. This meant that I could boil water anywhere! Very handy. Maybe I could check my herbology book later for some local plants that made good tea.

Smug satisfaction radiating through me, I packed all my stuff away and hiked my backpack onto my shoulders.

I had two more stops for the day, then I would be off for real. The storage room that I couldn't figure out how to enter, and the second tower to the 'North' of the city. I was hoping for a nice view of the surroundings

I stuck my head out of the inn before exiting because I was a clever girl and remembered my lessons—especially when I nearly lost my head to learn them—then I hiked over to the storage building.

It was as I remembered it. The door was tough, not even shifting when I kicked it. I considered ramming the wall in with a long log or something, but that was just silly. Then I noticed that a few of the roof's tiles had gone missing.

No time like the present to test a new skill!

Stamina was a resource my class seemed to like. I got a bunch every other level up. I didn't know if that meant something or not, but it seemed important. I would need to find out if a magic class gave heaps of mana and stuff every level to compare.

Licking my lips, I set my backpack down, then tensed the muscles of my thighs and squatted to jump as high as I could. I paused before launching myself into the air as I felt a sort of… question from my own body, a sense of it asking me 'how much' that was at once utterly bizarre and somehow completely natural. It was like sitting on my hand for a few minutes then trying to pick my nose.

Or something.

I noticed my stamina dropping to nearly half a bare moment before I took off.

Then I screamed as my leap took me over the lip of the roof and almost sent me flying over the other side of the building. I was lucky, and a foot caught on the very tip of the roof. Then I was unlucky because that arrested my momentum too quickly and I ended up slamming into the roof. I slid down along with a few loose tiles until I crashed unceremoniously on the ground on the opposite side of the building. I barely got my feet under me before going splat.

"That," I said to the open sky. "Was a bad idea."

I groaned as I got to my feet and huffed when I saw that I had just shaved half a dozen points off of my health. No injuries, but maybe I'd get a nice bruise for my silliness.

"Nevermind this place. It's a stupid storeroom anyway," I muttered as I glared at the building.

My next attempt, because I was apparently unable to give up on something once I started, had me using a whole lot less stamina, just enough to land on the very edge of the roof. After that it was all carefully shifting across the top until I gave up and tore some tiles out to peek within.

Even with the sun at my back there wasn't much light to see with. Still, I could make out big boxes, shelves covered in dusty knick-knacks and some barrels. Nothing really inspiring.

"Dang it, Broccoli," I said. "Do you really need to sneak into the room just to see what's in it? You have places to be!"

Despite my own protests against myself, I was soon tearing a hole through the roof and jumping down. It was a good thing I was so skinny or else it would've been tricky to squeeze in.

The storage room was a dusty mess that had my Cleaning skill itching to get to work, but I wanted to save the mana and didn't want dust all over while I snooped. And I found… nothing. Empty crates, barrels that sounded hollow, rotten remains of sacks that had been chewed through by generations of mice.

The door, at least, could be unlocked from the inside. It was the only thing that prevented my pout from being absolutely devastating as I stomped out of the silly storage shack and picked up my backpack with a huff.

Spade in hand, I stomped away, not even closing the door behind me to save the next poor idiot like me the trouble of climbing in. It wasn't fair. The heroine was supposed to find some hidden treasure while looting the last remaining place, it was just good storytelling.

But then, this world didn't work on storytelling rules. Or maybe it did, and I wasn't the heroine.

Well, if that was the case, I'd find the hero and be their best friend.

I reached the last destination I wanted to explore in good time and slowed down to be sure I wasn't going to be surprised by a wandering ghost. The final tower seemed smaller than its twin, a little thinner on the sides.

Not that that was a bad thing. Ancient towers were to be enjoyed regardless of size.

The large wooden door at its base creaked open with some prying, revealing a small corridor that led into the walls and a stairwell at the end. A few barrels were sitting around, but some snooping revealed that they only held rotten sticks that might have been torches.

The second floor had a row of jail cells, iron bars completely rusted through. There were glyphs on the walls and floor, but I didn't want to go poking at the symbols inside a cell in case they were meant to hold a prisoner. Accidentally locking myself up in a tower and waiting for some prince to save me was not my style.

I climbed up another floor to a small room with a few chairs and a table. Maybe a lounge area for the guards on duty? A breakroom? A ladder in the corner led to a trapdoor in the ceiling. I was a little wary of the rungs of the ladder, but they held my weight with only a lot of creaking.

The trapdoor required some banging and moving before it finally opened with a squelch, decades of rotting leaves pouring down onto my head and face until I had it completely opened. Cleaning, of course, was the greatest skill and fixed the faceful of rotten leaves with a tiny burst of magic.

I clambered out and stood up. The wind was stronger above everything and without the protection of the town's walls. Still, it meant I had a beautiful view of the surroundings.

There were forests all around, but I could see the winding line of a river to the south. The forest continued to the south for a long, long way, a sea of undulating green as far as I could see. The north was a whole lot more interesting. The horizon to my right was dark with a large spot where all the trees seemed almost black. It looked very far away though. To the left was a distant series of plateaus over a lake, or maybe a swamp. I made a note to avoid that because it was mosquito season.

Directly in the direction I had dubbed north was a mountain that rose to a flat top as if some giant had smashed it with a hammer. There was a city there. Big enough that I could see it from what must have been half a hundred kilometres away. There were even tiny shapes floating in the sky around it. Airships.

I grinned.

I had a destination now!

## Chapter Seventeen
# The Road Untravelled

What was left of the road wasn't all that great. I suspected that the road had once been compacted dirt with cobbles above it, but nature and time and a complete lack of maintenance had taken their toll. Now that path was torn apart by younger trees, roots, fallen branches and more bushes than you could shake a stick at.

There had been a few homes close to the road and some paths leading off into the forest, but they were worn far worse than anything within Threewells and I didn't think it was worth snooping around them.

Navigating through the woods would have been, if not impossible, then at least very hard.

So I cheated.

"Hup!" I said as I spent a trickle of stamina and burst from one branch to another. I wasn't using the branches near the top, but instead the much thicker ones by the base of the trees. Fortunately, most of the trees along the road had grown horizontally to catch the sunlight pouring over the path instead of growing upwards and competing with the other trees. It made for much easier travelling.

Plus, I got to feel like a ninja.

My mood was riding pretty high. The air was fresh, the sun was shining, I got to bounce from tree to tree and I felt like I was making good time for someone that wasn't too used to travelling through a forest.

I paused on my next leap and looked down. Something red had caught my eye off to the side of the road.

There was a bush. Well, there were lots of bushes, but this one had big plump red berries growing out between its branches. Big berries that probably didn't taste like honey.

I let myself drop from the branch I was on and landed with a crunch that didn't carry over the birdsong and the rustle of wind across treetops. I hiked up my backpack to make sure it was on snug and moved over to the bush. A few of the lower berries seemed to be missing, so something was eating them, and a few friendly bees were buzzing around.

"Hello, mister Bee," I told one that buzzed closer to my face. "No worries, I won't disturb your bee-sness."

I giggled as I used insight on a berry.

A red berry.

"Wow, thanks," I said before I tried again with some mana.

A red berry, common, fresh.

"Wasted skill that one," I muttered. I set down my backpack, then rooted around until I found the cloth-wrapped book. I hadn't really read anything out of the herbology book yet, but this seemed like the time for it.

I hopped up—because using my Jumping skill as much as I could was not only smart, it was fun—and found a spot to sit on a low hanging branch before cracking open the book. The hand-drawn pictures weren't coloured, but they were very pretty, and the notes next to them hinted at what colours the flowers and berries and roots within were supposed to be.

Flipping through the pages to find berry bushes took a few minutes, but the prize was worth it.

### Red Chokerberry

*These berries, which grow on Red Chokerberry bushes, have a few interesting qualities. Mashed and mixed with sugar it is a perfectly palatable snack and can be used to feed pets and woodland animals. Turned into a paste and left to dry, the berries will darken and if consumed can affect the eater's respiratory canals. In low doses can assist those with specific breathing problems while exacerbating others.*

I read the rest of the page, then read through the warnings and preparations that could turn the plant into a poison or a cure for some specific ailments. It was at once interesting and kind of scary. Still, the book said they were safe.

Hopping down, I ambled over to the bush and plucked a couple of the juicier looking berries, then popped them into my mouth.

They were bitter, but also tangy, like ripe oranges.

And they weren't honey!

***Ding! For doing a Special Action in line with your Class, you have unlocked the skill: Gardening!***

"Whut?" I said, bits of red berry juicy spitting out of my mouth. I swallowed. "But all I did was eat berries!" I said. "Delicious, delicious berries."

I brought up the menu for my new skill while I ate more berries.

*Gardening*
*Rank F - 05%*
*The ability to find, identify, and cultivate plant life.*

It wasn't Fireball or Magic Missile or anything that I really wanted, but it could come in handy. Especially if it meant more food!

I packed the book away but placed it near the top of my backpack for easy access. Then I found a cloth and wrapped a few berries for later. It was time to hit the road again.

Time passed in a comfortable haze. Other than the occasional jump that I almost missed, there wasn't much to make the trip exciting. I kept jumping over the road, made sure to keep the distant mountain in sight, and generally fell into a sort of meditative pace where trees passed and time sank away.

I saw chipmunks and squirrels and the occasional daring rabbit. There were big paw prints that probably belonged to bears in the mud, and I heard a howl from afar once, but it didn't worry me too much.

The road curved as it climbed up a hill and I found myself without trees to jump from. I landed and stretched a little. My legs weren't cramping, but they were a little stiff from the constant jumping.

The sun was starting to set above, but it was still a few hours until sundown and I still had plenty of time to find a spot to camp.

I started hiking, the steep incline of the road harder on my legs than the constant jumping had been. I was going to have great calves by the time my adventure was over.

Reaching into one of the pockets on the side of my backpack, I pulled out the Cheshire Choker and fiddled with it as I walked.

> An enchanted Cheshire Cat's Collar of Rare quality, new. Allows the user to summon a spirit cat once a day.

I had mana to spare. I pushed some into the collar and… and nothing happened.

Maybe I was supposed to wear it? I wasn't the kind of girl that wore collars though. I tried wearing it as a bracelet, but that didn't work.

"Stupid Cheshire Cat," I grumbled as I undid the latch on the collar and placed it around my neck. It fit nice and snug, with the smiling kitty mouth dangling over my sternum. I probably looked quite silly.

A bit of focus and some spare mana pushed into the collar and I felt my reserves draining, more and more until they had dropped nearly seventy points in one go.

I slowed down as a sparkly cloud formed before me at chest height. It twisted, spun, then was sucked in as if a blackhole had opened up in the world. I felt myself being pulled in, and the ring on my finger grew cold, but nothing changed in the world around me.

A popping sounded out from the spot before me, like someone pulling a cork, and a cat appeared. No, not a cat. A kitten. It was a ball of semi-transparent fluff and cuteness that dangled in the air and looked around with the kind of lack of interest that was common among kitties.

It took one look at me, then walked through the air in my direction.

"I-Insight," I said before reaching for it.

*A spirit cat companion, bound to Broccoli Bunch.*

"Holy granola muffins, I have a kitty summon," I squealed as I picked the kitty out of the air. It was soft, there and yet not. Like the ghosts I had touched but warm instead of cold. I spun around once, then saw the unamused look the kitty was giving me and hugged it close instead.

This was the best day ever.

"Oh, you're a cute little thing, aren't you? Yes, you are," I told the kitty as I rubbed my nose against theirs. I bit of a peek under its tail that earned me a very indignant look and I had solved one small mystery. "Do you have a name, miss kitty?"

The kitty made a meowing motion, but no noise.

I hummed as I started walking again. "You're not very noisy, huh?" I asked it. "Okay, then I'll give you a name! For free!"

The kitty started at me, so I cradled it against my chest and started rubbing against her tummy.

"How about… hrm, can't go with the classics here, they don't have Saturday Morning cartoons. Unless they do. Ah, I know. I'll call you Orange. Because it's your colour and it's a fruit while my name is a veggie, and no one can make mean rhymes with your name."

The newly dubbed Orange seemed completely ambivalent to her name.

I got to the top of the hill I was walking on and took in the sights before me. The road wasn't taking a straight path towards the mountain but was veering off towards what I chose to call the West. Towards the swampy areas. I wanted to take a straight path towards the city, but that would have meant trekking through untraced paths.

The road might reconnect with another at some point, which might mean people. No one spent as much time building a cobbled road as the one I was on only for it to lead nowhere.

Still petting Orange, I tried to take in the whole world out ahead of me, but there wasn't too much to see. Then I spotted smoke way off in the distance to the West, way too far for me to reach it in a day, but still present. People!

Or a random brush fire, but I was hoping for people.

"Come on, Orange!" I said as I continued my trek.

An hour or two later the woods turned darker and darker and I was beginning to look for a place to rest. Staying out in the open was an option, but not one I was fond of. I soon found a small clearing with a stream running downhill through it. A stone bridge crossed the rocky rivulet, being in the same rough condition as the road running across it. The place sounded nice, the constant flowing murmur of water a sort of quiet lullaby that made it seem nice and peaceful. A good place for a rest.

I placed Orange on the ground and watched as she trampled around and sniffed at the grass and stuff around her. I could almost pretend she was a real cat until a bug spooked her and she floated a meter into the air and stayed there.

Shaking my head, I let my new friend have her fun and explored a little while I collected branches and whipped at the grass next to the road to make a decently sized clearing. Then I stacked the branches and found some rocks from the edge of the stream. It was like camping again, only without a tent and without parental supervision and with a much greater chance of running into zombie bears at night.

Hopefully they were afraid of fire.

The sun was setting for real as I sat down on my blanket next to the fire and pulled my herbology book out and started reading through it while eating supper. Supper being more berries and some honey.

Orange took a nap hovering a centimetre or two over my chest curled up in a little ball. It felt as if I could unsummon her at will but keeping her around didn't seem to cost anything so I enjoyed the company without complaint.

I searched for flowers and plants that the book said made for good tea and left leaves in the pages that had good candidates. Then, while a small fire crackled merrily next to me, I let the warmth of the flames and the exhaustion of a long day overwhelm me at last.

# Chapter Eighteen

# Pick a Pixie

I woke up a little sore but otherwise well-rested. Some bouncing around and a few stretches unlimbered all of my limbs, then a burst of cleaning magic woke me up better than a shower could ever manage.

Not that I wouldn't take a shower if I was given the opportunity.

Orange plodded after me as I unmade camp, stuffed my book away, fetched a wine bottle to fill it with water, and generally got ready for the day while the morning was still fresh.

I was wary of drinking stream water, but a burst of cleaning magic directed at the bottle cleared out all the wiggly little things floating within. Hopefully that counted as filtering of a sort.

My morning business taken care of—thank goodness for Cleaning Rank C! No toilet paper, no problem! —I set Orange atop my hat, slid on my backpack, and made sure that the fire I had started was well and truly dead before continuing my trek.

I wasn't just going to walk today though. Oh no. I had a plan and a small list!

I had spent some time thinking the night before as I stared up at the stars and rested my eyes from all my reading. The herbology book suggested that there were plenty of plants that grew in the wild that had good, helpful properties which I could use in a pinch.

Nothing super great, but some plants could be used as ingredients in healing potions and others could be brewed into teas that did all sorts of things. Some seemed mundane (Rasperberry tea helped with cramps) while others were outright fantastic (Sweet Artemisia's roots could be dried and then boiled into a tea that let you see in the dark!).

I had my eyes peeled on the ground, only occasionally hopping to the air to avoid parts of the road that were made unpassable by small trees and bushes. Every so often I'd detour just a little bit to look at some flowers and give them a sniff and a pat if they were doing a good job at being pretty.

"Orange, look!" I said maybe an hour into the day when I spotted a small patch of white flowers with big yellow centres. They were sitting in a small spot where the sun slipped through the old trees all around.

I skipped over and squatted next to the flowers. The air smelled like bitter citrus, a smell that seemed to be attracting all of the local bees. A bit of leafing through my book and I was able to match the flower to a drawing, and even the description of its smell was spot on.

### Feverfew

*This wild plant is one of the most commonly used cures for headaches and fever-like symptoms in many hamlets. The leaves, once dried for a few days, can be used to make a simple tea or broth that will reduce fever symptoms.*

"Cool," I said before I started snipping some of the nicer leaves off of the long green stems and piled them atop my spade which was serving as a sort of plate. I tied it all together as a small bushel with a bit of stem, then fired off a cleaning spell to get rid of any yucky stuff. Animals pee in the woods after all.

The package of leaves went into one pocket of my bandoleer.

"Thank you!" I said to the flower before giving it a grateful bow and standing back up. Orange rejoined me a moment later and returned to her spot atop my hat.

The morning was very productive, I found some common plants that I would have recognized back home, like chamomile and milk thistle, and two more strange plants before noon.

### Marsh Rose

*The buds of this uncommon plant are a precious resource for travellers. Boiled, they produce a fragrant and flowery tea that can cure scurvy-like symptoms and can reportedly prevent the user from catching any infectious illnesses. When eaten raw the buds act as a powerful aphrodisiac.*

### Bloody Dandelion

*A dangerous plant to handle for the novice or unwary. Bloody Dandelions can draw their petals in rapidly and snip the tip of a clumsy herbalist's finger right off. The flower can be used for blood replenishing potions, iron-will potions, and tinctures for curing skin-related ailments.*

The page about the kind of creepy dandelions had a small recipe scribbled into it for a kind of potion that only required some heating and mixing and that would work as a very slow acting health potion as long as it was drunk while still warm. I wasn't sure how I felt about that, but it was better to have the scary blood flower healing potion when you needed it than not.

I was happy with my haul for the morning, so when the sun was at its peak above, Orange and I found a nice clearing next to the foods and stopped for a sit.

"So, what's it like being a spirit kitty?" I asked Orange as I filled my enchanted kettle with the last of my water and then tossed in some chamomile blossoms into it. I focused a bit and watched with a growing smile as the water bubbled and boiled within seconds. It cost me half a dozen points of mana, but it was worth it.

I let the tea steep for a moment, poured myself a cup, then, because I could, I added a pinch of honey.

"Ahh," I said as I took a long sip. A few berries made my lunch a thousand times better.

Orange stared at me, but she didn't want any tea or even a nibble of a berry, she just wanted to plop herself down on my lap for a snooze, and I was okay with that.

I was just thinking of packing up when I heard a flutter of wings, then another. It was as if a flock of panicked chickens were rushing my way. I didn't even have time to jump to my feet before they were there.

Not chickens, I realized right away. Fairies!

They were small, vaguely humanoid little creatures that looked to be naked except for the occasional twine bandoleer or leafy belt. Some of them had sticks with pinecones at the tip like spears or small chipped teeth and fangs with stems around their base serving as swords and knives.

They glowed every colour of the rainbow, lighting up the clearing in a dancing parade of brilliant lights that spun and whirled and made me dizzy just from watching. I had a hard time keeping count of them, but there couldn't be more than two dozen. "Hello!" I said.

The little fairies fluttered away from me, then returned in force when I waved a little.

One of them, brighter than the others, floated right up to me and stood with his hands on his little hips and his chest puffed out. "Chirp," he said.

"Ah, I don't speak that," I explained. "Insight," I said next while pushing a bit of mana into it.

    A blue forest pixie (level 6).

It was two levels above me! But it looked so small and delicate. "Chirp chiirr," he said, then waved at the forests around him.

"Do you need help with anything in the forest? Oh, are you welcoming me?" I asked.

The pixie shook its tiny head, pointed at me, then pointed away.

My heart sank. "You want me to leave?" I asked.

The pixie nodded. "Chrr chirp!" he said, quite obviously pleased with himself.

I pouted but nodded to him all the same. Then I saw that a few of the other pixies were eyeing the jar of honey sticking out of my bag with pure, pixie-ish greed in their little eyes. I reached down and took the jar, then popped the lid off. "I'll just take one last bite for the road," I said as I stuck my spoon into the jar.

Every pixie eye in the clearing followed my spoon as it scraped a bit of honey off the top, then moved up towards my mouth. I paused, then turned the spoon around towards the pixie leader. "Do pixies like honey?" I asked.

It nodded violently.

"Ah. Okay. Do pixies trade? If I give you the rest of this jar, would you let me stay in your forest a little bit?"

The pixies all wavered at that, then, with a 'chip chip' from their leader, they fell into a big huddle, their glows almost melding into each other as they all chirped and chittered. I picked up Orange, who was still dozing so hard she was more liquid than cat, and placed her in the biggest pocket of my bandoleer, right over my chest.

The pixie leader came back, then chipped and chittered at a million miles an hour while gesturing at me, the jar, then the road and finally himself.

It took some trying, but I finally understood what he was saying. "You'll escort me?" I asked.

The pixie nodded and I couldn't help but grin. They weren't human, and they seemed a little primitive, but I had made friends anyway. And all it cost was a bit of honey. I replaced the lid on the jar, and stuffed it into my back-pack, ignoring the incensed and indignant looks from all the pixies, looks that disappeared when I pulled out an unopened jar and twisted the cap off. "Here you go!" I said.

The pixie gestured at the jar and it floated out of my grasp and into the air. Then he dove into it head-first, somehow making the hard honey turn liquid and melty a moment before splashing in.

The others gathered around, and I saw them taking big fistsful of honey and stuffing them into their tiny faces.

It was a sight to see, so many teeny tiny gluttons gorging themselves on honey as if it was the best thing ever. They made cute little nomming nois-es as they chowed down and some of them floated down to the ground, their wings too sticky to fly.

I made myself another cup of tea while they had their little party. Soon, more pixies joined, smaller, shier ones that darted in, took some honey, then zipped away into the canopy above. I sipped my tea while I enjoyed the lightshow. It wasn't as if I was in any hurry, and seeing my new friends having fun was a blast.

But then it was over, and the lead pixie floated back up to me. He was slathered in honey and had one arm stuck in his mouth to the elbow like a big lollipop. He pointed and I nodded. "Lead the way," I said as I stood up and picked up my bag.

He eyed the sack, then licked his lips.

"My new friends are greedy, aren't they?" I said.

The pixie huffed and crossed his arms.

"I'll give you the half full jar once we reach the edge of your territory, is that fair?"

"Chirupt!" He said before spinning around me a few times. The pixie shot ahead, then twisted around as if waiting for me to hurry up.

"Bye everyone!" I called to all the pixies. A good quarter of them were on the ground, hands rubbing across tummies that were fat with food babies. Some of them waved lazily at me so I waved right back before I stepped out of the little clearing and back onto the road. "Lead the way, Mister Blue," I said.

The pixie tapped a dirty finger to his chin, then chirped an affirmative. I think it meant that he liked the name. Though really, he was more of a golden-brown and blue now.

New friend guiding me, I set off on the road again, my mood as floaty and happy as the pixie next to me.

# Chapter Nineteen

# Blue Skies

Mister Blue the glowing blue pixie was a good travelling companion. Sure, I couldn't understand what he was saying unless he pantomimed it for me with many 'chips' and the occasional 'bleek,' but we made do.

We kept to the road, travelling at a much slower pace than I was used to even though Mister Blue was much faster than I was and would likely outpace me even at my best. Truth was, I was enjoying the company a little too much to want to hurry towards our inevitable departure.

"And then what happened?" I asked.

Mister Blue had been telling me of some great, ferocious monster that had invaded his forest and that he had single-handedly defeated. He gestured grandly, both arms before him scissoring up and down to mimic the jaws of the great beast. "Chirrrr!" he roared savagely, as if someone had stepped on a squeaky toy.

Mister Blue flew around and faced where he had been, hands on his hips and body straight as if imitating a real-life Superman. The floating certainly helped the look. The lack of clothes did not. He waved his hand in a banishing gesture, and a crack of lightning shot from his fingers to the ground with a firecracker pop.

Orange jumped within the pocket of my bandoleer, the noise enough to awaken her and drag unamused eyes over to Mister Blue, who was now pretending to be the great beast scampering away.

I watched, a hand pressed over my mouth as Orange floated up behind Mister Blue and started stalking him through the air. Mister Blue was orating his victory with many a chirp when he turned around and froze in mid-flight.

Orange wiggled her little kitty bum, then pounced.

What followed was a chase scene out of a cartoon, with Orange darting this way and that through the air, her little paw-paws running as fast as they could while Mister Blue flew circles around me.

The tables turned when Mister Blue spun around and started flying after Orange while static shocks ran across his body with little Geiger-counter-like tics.

Giggling, I put an end to the game by snatching Orange out of the air by the scruff of her neck and sliding her back into her spot in my bandoleer.

She glared at Mister Blue, who preened in the air—quite proud of himself—but at least the fight was over.

"So, Mister Blue," I said some little time later. "I've been looking for rare and valuable plants. Mostly for making tea, but I wouldn't mind finding flowers that I could sell later, or that might be helpful. Since this is your territory, do you happen to know of anything like that?"

The pixie tapped at his chin and floated alongside me while making a strange humming noise. Then he nodded and zipped ahead. I lost sight of him almost as soon as he dipped into the forest and chose not to try and follow.

Instead I slowed my walk down a little but kept moving.

My patience was rewarded when Mister Blue came chittering back while pointing at something I couldn't see.

Grinning, I followed after him as he flew at a much more sedate pace through the woods and over thick brambles. The woods grew darker as he led me away from the road, then up a fairly steep hill that would have been impossible to travel without Jumping from big rock to big rock.

I tried to keep an eye on more or less the direction the road was in, in case I got lost. But that soon faded away when Mister Blue chirped in victory and circled around a bush. It was growing on a patch of healthy-looking dirt under a rocky overhang. Its vines were a deep, wine red and its leaves were a faded crimson. Each flower had seven large petals around a waxy stem in the middle. And atop of that was a faint, flickering blue flame.

"Whoa," I said as I watched the three dozen or so burning flowers lighting up the rocky alcove. "So pretty," I said.

The air smelled like the sulphur of a recently struck match, but also like… oatmeal. It was a distinct scent that took me a while to place, though it certainly wasn't bad.

I lowered my pack and pulled out my book. Pages flew by as I searched for the plant that I was certain I had seen illustrated already. Mister Blue hovered over my shoulder and 'bleeked' appreciatively at all the pretty pictures.

"Ah hah," I said as I landed on the right page.

### Seven-Petal Candle Flower

*An exceptionally rare find across most lands. The seven-petal candle flower is actually a flowering bush, one most commonly found in areas that have had a recent influx of mana. They only grow in secluded, darkened areas and can be exceptionally difficult to reach when found. However, finding them is made easy by the faint blue glow given off by the flame atop their flowers.*

I was getting excited, especially as I read on.

*This plant has numerous uses, though many of them are niche at best. The leaves make for a tea prized by some tribes for its ability to temporarily make one immune to fire. The stem of the flower can be used in a multitude of fire-resistance potions of various strengths, as well as tinctures to heal burn wounds. The stems can be chewed to heighten one's awareness of fire-attuned mana. The flame, if frozen through magical means, can be used to create a catalyst called the Flaming Tongue which allows the user to commune with fire elementals and may be the most valuable part of the plant.*

"Whoa."

*When gathering, start from the flower and work down. The flame is easily snuffed out by feeding it non fire-attuned mana. Care must be taken with the main stem of the flower which is highly flammable, though difficult to light. Store the clipped parts of the plant in a dark, humid location.*

There was no way I could freeze the flames off the tips. Which was too bad, but the rest sounded simple enough. A careful jolt of cleaning magic made the flames on one flower sputter away, releasing a refreshing burnt-breakfast scent in the air. Then, with my knife held by the back of the blade, I snipped off the flower and placed everything on a clean patch of rock.

Orange batted one of the stems around playfully, and I let her as I focused on my work. Soon I had harvested a quarter of the plant and decided that I had taken my share.

**Congratulations! Through repeated actions your Gardening skill has improved and is now eligible for rank up! Rank E is a free rank!**

"I'll take that," I said with a delighted giggle.

*Gardening*
*Rank E - 00%*
*The ability to find and cultivate plant life. Your instincts for dealing with plants have sharpened.*

I thanked the plant, then Mister Blue for helping me find it, and packed everything up as quickly as I could without losing anything. A bit of cleaning my hands later and replacing Orange onto my shoulder, and I was ready to move again.

Mister Blue was kind enough to lead me all the way back to the road, but soon he stopped and spun around me a few times, 'bleeking' and 'chirping' sadly.

"Oh," I said as I realized what he was trying to say. "Is this the end of the road for us?" I asked.

Mister Blue stopped before me and nodded.

I... didn't want to go back to being alone. But I knew it wouldn't be forever. And I had Orange now, even though we had yet to really bond. "Okay," I said as I lowered my backpack. I fished around for one of the filled jars of honey at the bottom, then placed it on the road next to me. That left me with one and a half jars, more than enough to last me a long while. "I wish I could hug you goodbye," I said.

"Bleek!" Mister Blue said before he blinked to stand right before me and wrapped his arms across my chest. He couldn't even reach from one side to the other, but the gesture was heartwarming all the same. I patted him on his head with two fingers and held back a sniffle.

"Chii, chirup!" He said as he backed away. He gave one last glare to Orange, then waved at me before darting away. His prize bobbed in the air behind him as he disappeared into the woods.

I wiped my eyes, licked my lips, and kept on walking.

Nothing kept Broccoli Bunch down, not even losing a fun new friend that she had just made! I would find more friends along the way; I just knew it.

At least the parting had only been bittersweet. I could visit Mister Blue again in the future, maybe with even more honey. I laughed and imagined how heroic he would look coming to all of his friends with a second full jar of honey behind him. Unless he snuck it away to enjoy it all for himself, the little ruffian!

The woods started to change as I moved through them. The air wasn't quite as vibrant and the trees weren't as brilliantly green and full of life, even the birdsong wasn't quite as chirpy and happy.

I hopped up to the branches of a nearby tree to be higher and took in the world around me as far as I could see. That wasn't very much, as it turned out. I was in something of a dip in the landscape with hills all around. The distant rumble of a river or stream sounding just a few hundred meters away.

Looking up, I caught sight of a plume of smoke, then realized that it was a few of them meeting together to form one column, but it was still far away. Too far to reach before the sun set.

I hopped over to the next tree, then the next, aiming for the top of the hill where my line of sight wouldn't be nearly as obstructed. Maybe there was a town like Threewells out there, but inhabited?

I paused between one jump and the next when I heard something below. At first I thought it was some creature moving through the woods, but creatures didn't swear so much.

"Why am I always ze one sent out to clear ze path?" someone said after saying some words that were very impolite.

"Ze question ought to be why I got picked to babysit you," another, deeper, voice said.

People! Close enough for their voices to carry even. I jumped in their direction a few times, aware that I was moving back towards the road and the river at the bottom of the hill.

"Zere's a nettle bush over zere," the gruffer voice said. It was clearer now that I was closer. It definitely sounded like a man.

"Zut. Could have told me earlier, I've got some of zose ball zings stuck to my pants." The other voice was also distinctly male, though it sounded a few years younger.

I was getting so excited I almost missed my next jump.

"Good luck removing zem. Zey're a right pain to get out. Also, zey're called 'burrs', not 'ball zings'."

Grinning from ear to ear, I dropped down first one branch, then another, until I could see my new potential friends. They had long knives that were flashing out as they cut through the branches and brambles across the road. One of them was focused on chopping while the other tossed the branches to the side.

At first I thought they were human, but a look at their smooth, greenish skin, thick legs and squat features revealed otherwise. Their clothes had strange cuts to fit their strange proportions, but looked fine otherwise, the sort of thick robust clothing you would want to wear for trekking through the woods. One—the older, I guessed by the better quality of his equipment—had articulated leather and metal armour over his legs and shoulders and a breastplate gleamed under his jacket.

A bored Grenoil Swamp Ranger (level ?).
A nervous Grenoil Fencer (level 9).

I had just met a pair of frog people!

With one last hop, I landed on the road before the two wide-eyed adventurers and grinned.

# Chapter Twenty
# A Ribbiting Meeting

I took a deep breath, raring to start talking to my new potential friends. I had so many things to say. Entire days of pent up talking ready to be unleashed. Instead, all that escaped my lips was a breathy giggle. I flushed, coughed into my closed fist, and tried again.

"Hello! My name is Broccoli Bunch and I want to be your friend. Welcome to this forest, do you come here often? What's it like being a frog person? Wait, no, was that racist? Speciesist? I'm sorry I've never met someone who wasn't human before and I don't know how to act around you so if I'm accidentally rude please tell me and I'll try to fix it!"

I slapped a hand over my mouth and tried to think of ways to not embarrass myself any further when the frog-person—the grenoil?—with the more articulate armour spoke out. "Hail, human," he said while raising an empty palm my way.

"Do all humans speak zat much?" the other grenoil said.

The ranger shook his head. "Shush, Donat." Focusing back on me, he nodded his head and made a gesture with both arms that I couldn't decipher. "We weren't expecting to see a friendly face, human. What brings you to zese dark woods?"

"I'm lost," I said, a little sheepishly. "I kind of just ended up here and I've been following this road to try and find people for a couple of days now. Then I found you, so I guess that plan worked out!"

"Indeed," the ranger agreed.

"So is it just the two of you? Not that there's anything wrong with there being just two of you. I'm all alone and that's… well it's alright, I guess. But what I mean to ask is, are there even more people around here? A town or a city or a big gathering place of people? I have some things I'd like to sell, and I want to learn more about this place. And I want to eat something that isn't honey. Oh, and I want to make even more friends."

The ranger raised one webbed hand and I stopped. I might have been talking a lot. "You can come back to our camp with us," he said. "Zere are others there zat might want to take a look at you."

"We're going to bring it back with us?" the fencer asked.

"What are our other options? Let it leave and perhaps jeopardize ze expedition?" Ranger said before shaking his big wide head. His hood didn't move much with the motions, which was a little strange.

"Donat, get behind it. I'll take ze lead," the Ranger said.

"Oh, I'm being escorted!" I said. "So, do these woods belong to your people? Was I trespassing? I'm sorry if that's the case."

So, the younger-looking grenoil was called Donat. I waved at him then started walking down the path which they had done a good job of clearing of brush. It was still uneven, with roots poking through the cobbles and making the large flat stones sit all crookedly across the path.

"Zese woods belong to no kingdom," the ranger said. "None that still stands. Now please be quiet, we don't need to attract trouble."

"But I only found you two because you were talking so loud," I said.

"Exactly."

I adjusted my gambeson and coat and tried to make myself presentable, then fired off a few small cleaning spells to make sure I was nice and neat. Donat and the other ranger didn't seem to notice, or if they did they didn't mind.

Maybe I could help them clean up later too, their boots were all muddy and there was a certain smell to them that kind of hinted that they needed a bath. Not that I would say that to anyone, it was very rude.

We started walking and I was about to introduce myself when Donat started talking. "So, uh, ze human, it's a man human, right?"

"No, you idiot, it's a female," the ranger said. "Did you hatch yesterday? Look at ze lumps on its chest."

"I zought zose were muscles," Donat said.

I looked down at my chest, then back around to stare at Donat.

"Ah, chests are taboo with humans, right?"

The ranger sighed. "Just with ze female humans. Zey compete with each other to see who has ze biggest because it helps zem attract mates. Zey don't croon at each other. Well, some do, but it's not ze same."

"Weird." Donat was tilting his head from one side to the other, his entire upper body following the motion since he didn't really have much of a neck. "Why are zey taboo?" he asked me.

"It's because… they just are." I crossed my arms and tried to find something to say to defend myself, and my chest, while the ranger ahead of me called out.

"Oi zere! We're back."

I looked ahead of the Ranger and felt my grin growing huge. There were more frog people! Some were sitting around a little clearing along the edge of the road while one of them was setting up a tent. Most were around a small campfire on which a cauldron was hanging off a rack. The wind shifted, and with it came the mouth-watering smell of some sort of stew.

One of the frog people was skinning a small critter off to one side. It looked icky, but the thought of eating some fresh meat pushed that aside for now.

Donat raced ahead, arm gesturing back in my direction. "Emeric, Ari-anne, we found a human!" he said.

The entire group gathered before me, with only the ranger staying behind me instead of joining the others. I smiled and took them all in.

The ranger and Donat I knew already, both in leather armour over perfectly usable clothes. Among the frog people I was now meeting were two that I suspected might be girl frogs. Frogettes? They were slimmer, with smoother skin and faces that weren't quite as wide, though they seemed taller than the boy frogs. One had armour similar to the ranger, but with articulated metal gauntlets and a shirt made of fine scales.

The other was wearing thick cloth robes made of a deep blue material that were open at the front, revealing plain clothes underneath. She had a staff but was just holding it by her side with familiar ease.

A wizard? A wizard!

The other two were boy frogs. One in more leather and steel gear, with two swords held by his hips, and the other had strange armour made of overlapping plates over his shoulders and hips, with a helmet that had a sort of U-shaped crest at the front. A samurai frog! All of them except for Donat had bandoleers, kind of like mine but with medals and pins on them.

I bowed to the group. "Hello!" I said catching a few of them off guard. "My name is Broccoli Bunch, let's be friends!"

"Oh, swamp-gas, she speaks our tongue," the younger looking frog-girl said.

The samurai turned a glare onto him. "You did not question it before bringing it here?" he asked, voice gruff and no-nonsense. Donat, who I was realizing seemed rather young-looking compared to all the rest, backed up a step.

"I'm a she, actually," I said. "And Donat did talk about my chest a lot."

One of the frogs, the one with the two swords, made a croaking noise that was similar to a snort.

The samurai shook his head. "Donat, your being here is a privilege. It's not too late to fetch someone else to carry through a dungeon." I noticed that he pronounced every word very carefully, enunciated every syllable just so.

"I'm ze one at fault here," the ranger said. "I chose to bring ze human to ze camp."

The samurai glared over at the ranger, then huffed. "Very well. Tie it up. Search through its things."

"Eh?" I asked. "I'm sorry mister samurai but tying people up is not a good way of making friends. I'd even argue that it's counterproductive."

"Cease your yammering," the samurai said.

I took a small step back. There was something pressing against me, a sort of weight that was trying to drag me down and... and I wasn't going to let this mean samurai frog talk down to me like that. It's not how things worked. "No."

The samurai was about to turn away when I spoke. He whipped around to stare at me as if I had said something incomprehensible. Then one of the others, the one with the two swords, started chuckling.

I crossed my arms. "Mister samurai, if you're not going to be nice then that's your prerogative. You won't make many friends that way, but I won't tell you how to live your life. But telling me to be quiet and threatening to tie me up won't intimidate me. I don't abide by bullies."

Now three of the others were holding back chuckles and the one with the two swords was openly laughing. "Do you know who I am?" The samurai said.

"No? How would I, you haven't introduced yourselves. I'm Broccoli, by the way. In case you didn't hear." I waved at the others and some of them waved back. There were some mixed reactions. Donat seemed nervous of the samurai still, the ranger didn't seem to care either way. The one with two swords waved back and grinned, as did the non-wizard girl frog. The wizard and the others were looking longingly back at the fire and at the stew set next to it.

"I am—" the samurai began.

"Hey, can I have some stew? I have some things I could trade."

"Oh, what sort of zings?" the one with two swords said.

"Ah, honey? I've got, oh I've got two bottles of wine that I found." I said, remembering the two bottles I was still carrying with me. "And I have a bunch of herbs. If one of you is an alchemist, you might be interested in those. I could make some tea?"

"Wine would be nice," the ranger said.

"We will not get drunk on the job!" the samurai roared.

"Two bottles shared between seven won't be enough to get anyone drunk, except maybe ze tadpole," the ranger said.

"Hey!" Donat protested.

The group broke up, most moving to the logs around the little fire pit while the non-wizard girl stirred the stew and then poked the brazier with a stick. Donat was pointed to the unmade tents with instructions not to poke his own eyes out. I guess being the youngest in the group wasn't fun, but maybe he had to learn how to put up the tent.

These frog people weren't humans, but they seemed cultured and nice enough. Their clothes had a professional look to them and were tailored to fit their non-human proportions, so they had to come from a place with tailor-frogs, which meant a larger community out there.

"This is highly unprofessional!" the samurai said.

"Oh, stuff it, Leo," the twin-sword frog said. He gestured to a log not too far off to the side. "Sit, friend, and be welcome at our fire. As long as you cause no harm, none shall befall you."

I mentally 'ohhed' at how cool that greeting sounded even as I took off my backpack and set it on the ground next to me. "Thank you for sharing your fire. It's been forever since I've seen anyone. Meeting people who are friendly is really nice."

"I can imagine," he said. "You said you were Broccoli Bunch, yes?" At my nod, he smiled then patted a webbed hand against his chest. "I am Emeric. Ze fine wizard here is Arianne. You met Pierre, our ranger and scout. Ze young lady across from you is Valeria. Our friend at ze tents who likes your chest is Donat, and ze grumpy one is Leo."

"My name is Leonard Chand'nuit," the samurai said. He shifted the hilt of his big sword around and crouched down on a log next to Emeric. "I will be keeping an eye on you, human. Know that I will not allow you to interfere with this party's business."

"Okay," I said. My mind was reeling trying to keep all the names straight. "It's a pleasure to meet you all. I might have a hard time with all of your names. I hope you don't mind."

"Hey, it's no problem," the frog girl across from me, Valerie said.

I fired off a few inspects on each of them in a hurry.

*A relaxed Sword-Dancer (level ??).*

That was Emeric, of course. His class sounded really neat.

*An amused Marsh Wizard (level ??).*

Arianne, whose full lips were curled up in a slight smile.

*A hungry Fencer (level ??).*

That was Valerie, who was eyeing the stew the way a wolf might eye a steak.

And then I used Insight on Leonard.

*A frigid Samurai of the Moonless Night (level ???).*

Three question marks. Did that mean he was even stronger than all the others? That sort of made sense. He certainly felt that he deserved more respect. Maybe being a higher level earned people more honour and such by default? It was... sort of fair. More so than respecting someone because they were rich or born with the right family name.

"Ah, you're all very strong," I said as I rooted around my bag and pulled out one of the wine bottles I had. I didn't know anything about wine, but I hoped that it was good. It had been aging for quite some time.

I handed the bottle to Arianne, my hand brushing against hers for just a moment. It was moist and kind of slippery, which was a weird but not uncomfortable feeling.

"Would you mind if we Observed you?" Emeric asked. "Just as a precaution."

I froze. "Is that like using Insight?" I asked.

The wizard next to me laughed, it was a strange, gurgle-y sound. "Insight is a variation of Observe and Inspect, yes," she said. "It's a bit of a faux-pas to use zat sort of skill on someone without permission."

"Oh no," I said before pressing my hands over my face. "I'm so sorry!"

Emeric laughed it off, but Leonard next to him narrowed his eyes with suspicion. "It's nothing," Emeric said.

Arianne looked at me, and then her eyes widened. "She's a Cinnamon Bun, level four," she said.

That earned me a bunch of looks. "Is that bad?" I asked.

"How are you still alive?" Valerie asked.

I had the impression that I was going to have to do some explaining.

## Chapter Twenty-One
# Tiny Fish Huge Pond

"Um," I said as I tried to deal with the question. How was I still alive? Was this place really that dangerous? Sure, the ghosts were scary, and there were bears and things, maybe, but nothing I had seen topped the evil ghosts or the monsters in the dungeon. "Well, mostly I just fought ghosts, some zombies and that was it, really. I've been eating berries and honey for the most part. Is that what you meant?"

Arianne shook her head. "Ghosts aren't too common, but zey are easily dispatched by most. It's ze sombrals, ze pixies, and ze dryads zat are ze issues here."

I stared at her, then at the others around the fire. Donat had rejoined the circle, plopping himself down right on the ground without even a log to sit on. Emeric was still wearing a smile, but next to him, Leonard the mean samurai was glaring suspiciously. Valerie was the only one ignoring me as she focused on the stew. The ranger was… gone? I couldn't see him, and I never noticed him leaving. Neat!

"Well," I said. "I never saw any dryads, and I don't know what sombrals are. I did meet a whole lot of pixies though. They were nice."

"Nice?" Arianne asked. "I have seen zem melt the flesh off of creatures an order of magnitude bigger zan zey are wiz zeir magic. Each pixie has a different and mostly unique set of spells zat zey will use to tear you apart."

"Uh." I shrugged. "I offered them some honey to let me stay in their territory. Then I gave their leader a second jar to escort me around for a day."

"You—" Emeric started to croak with laughter. "Oh, zat's priceless. Hear zat, Leo. No need to scare off ze pixies with your big sword. Just give zem honey!"

"She could be lying," the samurai said.

I nodded, which set him to blinking at me. "I could be. But that wouldn't be very nice of me. I have some honey left over if you want to try it for yourself. It would be a real shame if you hurt the pixies just because of a little misunderstanding."

Arianne looked like she wanted to pat me, but she didn't which was good. People were always doing that, and it was very rude.

"Can you tell me about the sombrals and the dryads?" I asked.

"Are you going to offer zem some honey as well?" Emeric asked.

"I might. But I don't know what dryads or sombrals eat. Maybe they don't like honey or can get some themselves."

"Sombrals," Arianne began in a tone that sounded an awful lot like some of my teachers. "Are one of the monsters native to the Darkwoods. Dryads, on ze other hand, are common across ze whole world. Zey tend to be wherever zere are large forests. Donat, tell Broccoli about sombrals."

The young grenoil jumped, looked around, then rubbed at his face where his nose would be as a human. "Ah, right, sombrals. Second tier monsters. Scary, big, zey like ze taste of fresh grenoil meat. Do you know what a wolf is?" I nodded and he continued. "Right. sombrals are like wolves if wolves were made of shadows and didn't need to sleep. Zey aren't as big as some kinds of wolves, but zat only means zat zey are sneakier."

"And how do you fight zem?" Arianne asked Donat. She was leading him on, making him recite information that he was probably already supposed to know.

"Fireworks. Zey don't like it. Light magic is best. But we don't have zat. Hitting zem on the head works too. Zey are not like ghosts who are immune to physical harm. But zey do resist it better."

"Can't you just run away?" I asked. I didn't want to go around booping any poor wolves on the head for doing what was in their nature.

"No," Donat said with a shake of his head. "Sombrals are blind. Zey can't see. But zeir sense of smell is incredible and zey will hunt you for days if zey must. You can run to find a better place to fight. Or into a town with lots of people if it's close, but zey can't be outrun in zis forest. Zey hunt in packs and will try to encircle you if zey can."

"Scary," I said. "I guess I'm lucky I never ran into them."

"Zat's the strange part," Emeric said. "Zey would track you down by your scent. How did you avoid zat?"

I thought about it for a few moments, but the answer was pretty obvious. "I am very clean," I said. "I have the cleaning skill, so I shouldn't have much of a smell at all."

Emeric blinked his big froggy eyes at me, then tilted back and laughed, his feet thumping on the ground as he croaked and gurgled with mirth.

"Tch," Leonard said. "I would call what you did clever if it was not so obvious that you merely managed to avoid death through sheer dumb luck."

"Now now, Leonard," Arianne said. "It's good information to have. We might be able to use it ourselves."

"Stew's ready!" Valerie declared. "Hey, tadpole, get ze bowls and such."

Donat grumbled, but he ran off to the tents in a hurry at the sight of Valerie's glare and soon returned with a stack of tin bowls and a handful of wooden spoons. He passed them around, then got shoved aside by Valerie when he reached for the ladle. The frog girl started filling everyone's bowls, and I got to go first for some reason. Maybe some sort of guest custom.

I sat back down, tummy gurgling as I took in deep breaths of the vapours coming off of the stew. It smelled so good my eyes nearly rolled back into my head. Still, I noticed that the others were waiting before digging in.

Pierre the sneaky ranger walked out of the woods as if he had just been standing in plain sight all along and took a bowl of his own. He was the last to sit down.

"May our wills be the will of the world," they all intoned at more or less the same time. Then they started digging in.

"You don't worship the world tree?" Valerie asked between two bites.

I shook my head and hoped that wouldn't cause any troubles. I forgot all about that as I put the spoon in my mouth and the savoury taste of meaty juices and some sort of potato-like root filled my mouth with an explosion of flavour. "This is so good!" I said when I swallowed. I might have burnt my tongue and throat, but it was worth it.

Valerie made a gesture my way, a sort of thumbs up, but her thumb was webbed so it came out weird. Still, I understood what she meant and didn't blame her if she didn't want to stop eating for even a moment.

I slurped down a few more bites then started scooping up some of the meat and vegetables out of the juice. Some were crunchy, which was strange, but not too bad.

"Needs more roach," Donat said.

"Hard to find out here," Arianne said.

I wondered what they meant. Then I looked into my bowl and saw that thumb-sized and very dead bug in my stew. Another floated up to the surface next to it. "Ah," I said. I debated losing my supper all over the campfire, but then held back. It had been really good until then. I picked up another bug on my spoon, then placed it in my mouth and chewed.

It crunched and crunched and I just couldn't do it knowing what it was.

"I, I'm full," I lied as I pushed the bowl to Valerie. If there were tears in my eyes at losing such a delicious meal she didn't comment.

The girl smiled wide and took my bowl without protest to chug it all down. Emeric's eyes were turned up as if to say he knew exactly what had happened and thought it was hilarious.

"So, um, dryads?" I asked.

"If you run into a dryad, you'll know," Leonard said. "They are immensely dangerous, usually past their second tier, though you might find younger ones around. They can kill an entire squadron of ill-prepared troops. But, for the most part, they will not hurt or hunt you if you make an effort to avoid them and are careful about not cutting down trees in their presence."

"So they're peaceful?" I asked.

Arianne shook her head and swallowed. "No. Zey are merely not aggressive. Do not confuse ze two."

"The pixies weren't aggressive at first and they became friends," I said. "Maybe you're just approaching them the wrong way?" I wondered.

"Oh, please do try to make friends with a dryad," Leonard said. "As long as I am there to watch, of course."

I harrumphed and reached into my bandoleer to pull out Orange. The kitty had been sleeping all afternoon, but the motion of taking her out woke her up. She looked around at all the people around us and shook to fluff out her fur.

"What's zat?" Donat asked.

"This is Orange," I said. "She's a spirit cat."

"Did you find it in ze wild?" Arianne asked as she stared at Orange with an intense look. Her eyes opened wider after a moment. "Ah, a summon."

"What a useless summon," Leonard said.

Orange glared at him.

"Watch out Leo, it might scratch you," Emeric said. "Where did you find a spirit cat? Attracted it with some honey?"

"No, I got her from an item," I said.

"Cute," he replied. "Not zat useful, but a handy companion. And perhaps it will grow into a large and fearsome tabby cat in a decade or two."

"Well I like her," I said as I pulled Orange in for a quick snuggle. She, being a proper kitty, objected to the display of love and squirmed out of my grasp to run away. She didn't go far and was soon distracted by some swaying leaves. "So," I asked as I refocused. "What are you guys doing out here? Is there a village or something nearby?"

"I was zinking of asking you ze same. What is a level four Cinnamon Bun, whatever zat may be, doing out in zese woods?" Arianne asked. She set her bowl aside then hugged her staff close, fingers running across the well-worn wood.

"I'm a bit lost," I admitted.

Emeric chuckled. "A little, yes. You can stay wiz us tonight. Tomorrow we will point you to Rockstack. It's a small outpost run by a few guilds. If you're as clever as you look, you'll be able to find work. Maybe one day you can join the Exploration Guild."

"Is that who you are?" I asked. "Members of an exploration guild?" That sounded so cool! Like an adventurer's guild, but with less killing rats in someone's basement and more exploring tombs and looking for cool places.

"Zat we are," Emeric said. "Myself, Arianne, Pierre, and most recently Valerie are all members of ze same exploration team. Leo here is a senior member who joined our team for zis expedition because we'll be exploring a more dangerous place, and Donat tagged along because we need someone close to reaching zeir class evolution if we find a dungeon."

"So cool," I said. I now had about a million questions to ask! "What are you guys looking for?"

"She isn't part of our group," Leonard said. "Don't spill confidential information."

"She might have come across what we're looking for. At least she might save us some fruitless searching," Emeric argued back.

The samurai considered this for a moment, then nodded. "Very well."

Emeric smiled triumphantly. "We are looking for a lost town zat was once occupied by humans. Zere is nearly no human presence left here, and it was a frontier town when it fell, so we don't know where it is. But someone discovered something interesting in zat town and we want to see it."

Frowning, I considered what he'd said. A human town around here. The only one I had seen so far was… "Are you talking about Threewells?" I asked.

In a blink there was a hand clasped over each of my shoulders.

# Chapter Twenty-Two

# A Long Talk Off a Short Pier

"Tell us everything you know about Threewells," Leonard demanded.

Up until that moment I had seen the dour samurai as a sort of… pompous and somewhat rude man that was in a bad mood. Just a normal person who had rolled off the wrong side of the bed that morning. He wasn't a threat because he could talk, he could be reasoned with.

Now he was in my face, hands gripped over my shoulders and holding on so tight that I couldn't move. Something told me that bonking him on the head wouldn't do anything to him. That, and there was a force pushing down on me.

I could hardly hear Emeric's protests over the roaring in my ears.

Then I remembered that I was Broccoli Bunch, and Broccoli Bunch said nope to bullying. "I won't tell you anything if you're going to act like a bully," I told him. "If you want, I could trade you some information, but with how rude you're being I think I'll just keep it to myself." I crossed my arms. "So there."

Leonard let go of my shoulders but didn't back away. He opened his mouth to say something, paused, then stroked his chin. "A trade would be acceptable," he said. "What do you know of the Exploration Guild?"

"Um. Nothing?" I said. "Nothing beyond what I can guess, at least."

"Oh boy," Valerie said before she moved back to the cauldron and started scraping stew off the bottom.

Leonard pulled the log he had been using as a seat closer with hardly any effort. "The Exploration Guild is an old and storied society. It transcends the boundaries of race and species and serves many. Kingdoms rely on it to find new lands and resources; merchants rely on us to find precious materials and to scout new roads. Most important of all, we are often the first to delve into new dungeons to discover the will of the world."

"That's impressive," I said. The feverish light in his eyes kind of disturbed me a little, but it did genuinely sound interesting.

Leonard nodded. "It truly is. As impressive as we are, we still lose members. New Dungeons can be creative and dangerous, exploring faraway lands means being far from help, or encountering threats never seen before. Information is what we seek, and information is what keeps us alive. Like you learning about dryads and sombrals and knowing to avoid them."

It kind of clicked, not that there was much work needed for that. "That's why you want to know about Threewells," I said.

"Yes, he replied simply. "You asked for trade. I do not know how valuable your information is. But some of it might be the difference between the life and death of this party of overconfident fools."

"Um, are they your responsibility?" I asked.

He nodded. "They are. But I am but one grenoil, I cannot be everywhere at once."

"Well, okay then." I wasn't sure what to think of Leonard anymore. That was both annoying and kind of confusing. But he wanted to know what I knew, and I wasn't averse to sharing. "Let me just fetch something." I opened my backpack and retrieved my map of Threewells. The map of the dungeon I left behind, maybe I could use it to bargain for something else. Maybe some food. "Here."

Leonard took my crude map and his eyes widened a little. "This is Threewells?" he asked.

"Yup, I explored most of the town while I was there," I said, a bit of pride sneaking into my voice.

Emeric laughed. "Full of surprises zis one. We should keep her!"

"Oh no," Arianne said. "I'm not going to abide to ze party having a pet human."

The two bickered back and forth, but my focus was mostly on Leonard who was looking over the entirety of my map with more care than I thought it deserved.

"This is shoddy work," he said, and my tiny kernel of pride deflated and died. "It's not accurate to the maps of Threewells I have seen. The houses are all there, but their locations are slightly off. And the art is… questionable at best. These words, what language are they in?"

"Um. English?" I said. "You can't read?"

"Of course I can read!" Leonard said over the laughter of Valerie and Emeric. Even Donat seemed to want to laugh. "I don't speak this 'Henglish' of yours."

"But we're speaking it now," I said.

Arianne looked at me curiously. "Do you have a translation skill?" she asked.

I shook my head.

"Any magical jewellery zat may be soul-bound?" she asked next, this time looking at my hand with the bronze ring.

"Well, yes." But unless my Insight skill was dead wrong there was no way that my ring was translating for me. Did that mean that I just… knew how to speak frog? I didn't have much time to wonder about it.

"You shouldn't just put on strange jewellery," Leonard said. "At this rate it is a miracle you're not dead already. Donat, fetch me a paper and an ink-well!" The younger grenoil jumped to it. "Very well, for the map, if you help me recreate it in a less… childish hand, then I will give you one gold."

Emeric whistled. "Suddenly being generous," he said.

"A lesser gold," Leonard added even as Donat returned with a small satchel. The samurai pulled out a wooden board with an inkwell built into it and then a long feather and some yellowish paper. "Do you accept?" he asked.

"Um, okay, sure." Gold was good. Maybe. Probably. Did I want my new friends to know that I had no idea how the money here worked?

"Good." Leonard reached to his belt and pulled at the drawstrings of a pouch. He flicked a coin at me that I caught out of the air. It was small, about the size of a dime but thicker, and it was heavy. I stuffed it into my backpack in a hurry. "Now, translate this."

I did as he asked, translating all the little notes I had made for myself while he copied the map with quick, sure strokes of his plume. His notes were tiny little inscriptions in the margins and sides of the buildings and places I had marked.

"I can tell you about the buildings I explored too," I said.

"Go on."

"In exchange for the right to spend the night here," I added.

The samurai looked up at me and narrowed his eyes. "Very well."

"Am I the only one zat expects her to slowly fleece him of everything he's worth?" Emeric asked. He smiled at me then got up to his feet. "I'll leave you to it. Donat, fetch some blankets and finish setting up ze second tent. Broccoli can sleep wiz ze girls. We'll set up a watch and put up torch-es before ze sun sets."

That last comment had me looking up to a sky that was putting on its night-time colours. "Ah, darn, the day's almost over."

"Indeed. Now, tell me of these places," Leonard demanded again.

So I did, each home earning a small notation next to it as he moved across the town. "And that's the main tower. The one I came in from," I said. "Nothing on the third floor. You can only get to it by scaling the outside wall. Ah, but there are offices on the first floor, I found a lot of papers and stuffed them in a chest in the barracks."

"… good," Leonard said. "Documents from a fallen city might interest some buyers at the guild."

"How much would you give for, say, the ledger of the guard captain? All the reports leading up to the fall of the town?"

Leonard looked at me. He sighed. "I have misjudged you. For that, I would give a young fool… a letter of recommendation to the guild. As well as four lesser gold."

"Ask for more," Arianne said.

"Mind your own business," Leonard grumped at her. To me he said. "What made you explore the town so much? At your level it's an incredible risk."

"I needed stuff. Food and supplies. And I like exploring, it's fun." I grinned at the flummoxed look on the samurai's face. It was as if he'd swallowed a fly. Only probably not, he would like swallowing flies, I suspected.

He shook his head. "Perhaps the letter of recommendation would be too much. The amount of time spent beating the stupid out of you would cost our instructors far too much."

"No, no, I'll take the letter," I said. The guild sounded neat. "And the gold too. Oh, and some food. But nothing with bugs in it."

"Hey, nothing wrong with some crunch in your lunch," Valerie said.

Arianne shook her head. "Humans don't usually like eating insects.

The look of confused betrayal I received from Valerie had me holding back giggles. "Just enough food for the road, at least until I reach that outpost you mentioned. Unless you'd let me come with you?"

"No," Leonard said. "There is no chance of that happening." He said it with enough conviction that I decided not to test him. "We can offer you some food, yes. But only after I see the books."

I pulled out the two binders filled with reports. It was going to be nice to not have that weight on my back. Or maybe just to replace it with proper food. I handed them over to Leonard who brushed a thumb across the cover, then leafed through the reports. Most, I knew, were exceptionally boring, but he seemed not to care.

"Six lesser gold. I won't have my honour besmirched by short-changing even a fool." He carefully set the binders aside. "Tell me more about the town."

"Ah, which parts?" I asked.

"The so-called evil hole you mentioned," he said. I sat up straighter and wondered what kind of goodies I could get for my dungeon map. "It sounds like the entrance to a young dungeon."

"We felt a mana surge," Arianne mentioned.

Leonard nodded at that. "We did. Someone might have destroyed the dungeon after you left. Not an easy feat."

"Is that bad?" I asked.

I shrank back as all three still around the fire looked at me.

"Destroying a dungeon is," Arianne began. "A crime of ze highest order. One who breaks a core must in turn be broken, for it means going against ze world's will."

"The world's will?" I asked.

"It's a miracle you know how to read and write," Leonard said. "With the pitiful education you've no doubt received. Typical of a human."

"What Leonard is trying to say," Arianne said with some bite. "Is zat ze world needs mana to sustain itself. Not all of it. You can live in a mana-free area your entire life. But you will be made uncomfortable by it. Injuries will take longer to heal, and you will no doubt die younger with fewer offspring. Dungeons, when zey appears, bring lots of clean mana to an area, and wiz zat comes the lure of ze dungeon boss."

"You mean… the class thing?"

"Not completely clueless, then," Leonard muttered.

"Yes, killing a boss grants you a class. Zat's why our group has zree fencers in it. Zere's a boss zat grants ze fencing class near ze capital. A lower levelled one, at zat. It is farmed regularly."

"Oh," I said. "Wait, three?"

"Emeric was a fencer until his class evolved. Valerie also reached ze level for a class evolution, but she remained a fencer."

"So cool," I said under my breath. "Do you know what Cinnamon Bun evolves into?"

"No, I've never heard of ze class," Arianne said. "Was it a natural one? That is, one you grew into?"

"I guess so."

"Zen it being strange isn't surprising in ze least. Uncommon, but not surprising."

"What can you tell us about the dungeon?" Leonard asked.

I shook my head and smiled. "Nothing, nothing at all."

## Chapter Twenty-Three
# Friendmaking

Emeric insisted that I didn't need to help prepare for the night, though I did help a little anyway. The look on Donat's face when I cleaned the cauldron with a tap of my fingers was worth the half dozen points of mana I spent.

The tents weren't the sort of tents I was used to. In fact, there were little more than canvas sheets with a few holes here and there that had flaps covering them. Ropes strung out between the nearest trees held them up, and little ties on the canvas allowed parts of it to be folded in to form walls around three sides.

It would keep the rain off, if it rained, and the wind too, but that was about it. Still, no weird retractable sticks to deal with, so it wasn't all bad. I was given a spot in the middle of Valerie and Arianne and a few extra blankets that were less than fresh until a couple of cleaning spells fixed them up.

"Zat's a handy little spell," Arianne said as she watched me lay out a blanket to sleep on and another to cover myself. I had my own too, so I would be nice and snug all night. It was like a sleepover but outside and with strangers!

"It's great!" I said. "I never got to see much magic, so I was super excited when I got my own spell."

Arianne's smile was at once demure and extremely amused. "Well zen, do you want to see some more?"

"Yes!" I said before scrambling to my feet and following after her. Magic was awesome because it was magic. Even after using my cleaning spell a hundred times I couldn't get over how cool it was. "Can you teach me about magic?"

"I can, a little. But zen we must sleep. Tomorrow will be a long day. What do you know so far?"

"Um. I can push magic into stuff, and then I lose some mana. Then things happen."

Arianne tittered. "I have my work cut out for me, zen." She walked us over to the edge of the clearing. "Zere are two types of spells… no. zere are many, many types of spells, but only two matter for you. You can worry about ze ozers later."

"So what are the two, then?" I asked. I was bouncing on the balls of my feet as the marsh wizard raised her staff and narrowed her eyes in focus.

"Ze light of my soul illuminates," she said while making a cupping gesture in the air under the end of her staff. A spark appeared, then formed into a baseball-sized ball of whitish light that began to fall. "Ze will of the world captures." The light started to dim. "Ze weight of my will determines ze path."

And just like that the ball stopped falling and hovered in place, releasing a whitish light that was weaker than a torch, but that was pure and clear. "Cool," I whispered.

"Zat is for the sombrals. Zey dislike ze light," Arianne explained. "Zat was one type of magic. A spell zat I cast using my own mana by controlling it, zen I tied it to zis place so zat it hovers."

"So if I chanted like that, would it do the same thing?" I asked. I was trying to memorize the chant just in case. I wanted light balls. I could hang them all over the place and people would comment on them and tell others of how cool Broccoli Bunch's balls were.

"No, ze chant is to help. Do you know what a… mnemonic is?"

"Like a song to remember something?"

"Yes, zat's exactly right. Many practitioners use zem. Some have very misleading chants to trick opponents. Zey are just to help you remember and to help you move ze mana ze right way at ze right time. I can cast zis spell wizout because I have been practicing it a lot, but to demonstrate it is easier wiz ze chant."

"Okay, so you take your mana and then you make a light ball?"

Arianne shook her head, then paused. "Yes. But zat is too simple. Zere is a specific shape ze mana must take. Zere is some leeway, but not too much. Ozerwise ze spell fails. Zat is where ze ozer kind of spell comes in. Skills."

Arianne tapped her staff to the ground and a clod of mud rose up, then twisted around itself until it took the shape of a small muddy frog person that barely came up to my shin. It wobbled around on unsteady legs, then collapsed into a heap of mud.

"Zat is a Golem spell. To cast it would take me a minute. Maybe two, if I want to avoid mistakes. But by using a skill like Earth Magic Manipulation it becomes trivial." She smiled at me. "Do you understand?"

Right, I knew that using magic skills came with an instinct for it. My cleaning magic was the same way. I didn't really have to think too hard on it and the spell just kind of formed immediately and worked on the first try.

Did that mean that someone without the cleaning skill could use my spell? Probably, but as Arianne said, it would be difficult. I could see why. The amount of mana used in each cleaning spell was slightly different, which probably meant that the spell was a tiny bit different too.

So, using skills to cast spells was like having a calculator do the math for you. Or maybe a computer solving your physics problems. Casting it yourself was like doing it by hand. But that meant that you could still do it by hand.

"Wait, does that mean I can learn Fireball?"

Arianne sighed. "Zey always want ze fireballs. No, Arianne, don't cover ze enemy in mud, light zem on fire. Always ze same."

"Oh, I'm sorry," I said. I might have touched on a sensitive topic. "I think mudballs are cool too. All magic is cool, and you're a wizard, which means you're cool by default."

Arianne shook her head from side to side, a strange swaying motion with the way her neck was made. "Go rest. You're going to have a long walk tomorrow," she said before placing a hand on my head and ruffling my hair like a big meanie.

I woke up with a jaw-shattering yawn, then stretched my arms and legs out every which way. It took a moment for me to realize where I was, but the strange croaking snores of the girls next to me helped a bunch. A glance out of the tent revealed that the sun was rising, and that morning was here and the faint clinks of metal against metal and the crackle of a fire suggested that someone was up.

I slid out of my blankets and searched for my armour and stuff. I had slept in it before but now, with a whole party of strong adventurers around, I felt safe enough to just sleep in my normal things.

All dressed up and ready, I slid out of the tent and stood up tall to take in a deep lungful of morning air.

"Up already?"

I finished my stretch with a few sways of my hip to get my lower back settled, then bounced on the spot a few times. "Yup!" I said.

Emeric and Leonard were both sitting around the fire while a small metal pan was sitting with a slice of bread on it and a pot sat next to it with what looked like beans boiling merrily away.

"Is that breakfast?" I asked.

"Favourite meal of ze day?" Emeric asked as he stirred the beans.

"I've been eating nothing but honey and berries for a while, any meal is my favourite if it's got neither. Not that I dislike either, it's just too much is too much."

Leonard made a croaky snort. "Unprepared child," he said.

I sat next to them and waited, tummy growing fiercer by the minute, as breakfast was prepared. It was nice. Emeric filled three bowls up, mine almost to the brim, then he placed some toast atop the bowl, and we got down to eating in quiet, only the morning birdsong to accompany my oms and noms.

"We'll be leaving soon enough," Emeric said. "I got grumpy here to draw you a basic map and zere are supplies in zat sack over there." He gestured to a bag off to the side. "Some canned goods, a few little things. Our last loaf of proper bread. Ah, and some hardtack. It tastes awful but it will keep you fed."

"I... can't come with you?" I asked. I kept my eyes on my now-empty bowl.

I saw Emeric shake his head from the corner of my eye. "No. We're not just going to Threewells. The Dungeon there, if it's still active, would be outrageously dangerous for someone at your level. And we have to move quickly."

"I can move quickly," I said.

He smiled. "Nope. You get yourself back to Rockstack. There are some nice folk over there, some will be willing to keep an eye on you, maybe even get you a job. Ask for Juliette, she runs the inn. She ought to have some work for you."

"If you are dead set on being a fool, then head over to Port Royal," Leonard said. He handed over a folded piece of parchment with a red wax seal on the front. "My name has some weight there. The people at the headquarters of the Exploration Guild might see something in you if you don't act like such a foo— don't break the seal!"

I froze, fingers caught fiddling with the seal before I let go of it and gave him a sheepish smile. "It's still attached," I said.

"Idiot," Leonard said. "I'm going to wake the others."

Emeric watched him go, then turned to me with a huge smile. "I think he really likes you."

"I do not!" Leonard roared, which probably helped in waking all the others more than anything else he did.

"He's nice under all that gruffness," I said. "I kind of wish I could come with you; I hate making friends and then losing them right away."

"You'll make good friends one day. No worries," Emeric said. He rooted around in a bag and found another tin of beans which he opened with a casual flick of a knife across its top. "Maybe you'll start your own party?"

"That would be wonderful," I said. It would be! Just me and some close friends, heading out on mysterious adventures to discover hidden things. We'd meet dragons and ride them into battle, and it would be awesome.

"Wait," I said. "You have beans that come in tins?"

"Yes?" Emeric said. "They're good for travelling, which we do a lot of. You can buy them in most guild supply stores. They're not meant for civilians, but they'll sell you some if you don't mind the mark-up."

The others woke up one after the other, some with more alacrity than the rest. Arianne was not a morning person and kind of just flopped next to Emeric until he pushed a bowl into her hands. Valerie zeroed in on breakfast and scarfed it down, then bounced around while undoing the tents and gathering all of their things in a hyperactive hurry.

And then it was time to go. Donat and Pierre, who had been sneaky all night, waited by the roadside. Leonard was deep in a map and Valerie was rubbing a tired Arianne's back. Emeric reached a froggy hand out to me. "Goodbye, Broccoli," he said.

"Bye Emeric," I replied right back.

We shook and I waved goodbye to the others as the party formed up and started walking and hopping away.

I swallowed thickly, put on a smile, and got my stuff. I still had a ways to go. But maybe I would see them again. It would be neat to be part of the same group as them, maybe. Time would tell.

*Ding! For repeating a Special Action a sufficient number of times, you have unlocked the general skill: Friendmaking*

I laughed as I set off into the unknown.

# Chapter Twenty-Four

# Rockstack

I moved with a skip to my step. "So, Mister Menu, feel free to tell me about yourself," I said to the box floating before me. "I'm sorry that I haven't spoken to you in a while. I was sort of busy. Then again, I know that you're kind of shy when you're on the job."

The menu popped away, letting me see the long, treacherous road ahead. A thought made it come back.

"Now, now, no running away!" I chided. "I need to grind my new skill. You're the one who gave it to me. Or at least, I think you are. It doesn't feel like something Miss Menu would do."

The box just displayed the same thing it had for the past twenty minutes or so.

```
Friendmaking
Rank F - 13%
The ability to make friends. As you practice
this skill your ability to make friends
will improve.
```

"Come on, I need to get this skill super high so that I can make all the friends!" I told the menu box. "Maybe we can try hugging again?"

The box popped away.

"No fun!" I called after it.

Shaking my head, I refocused on the road and kept on walking. I had an eye open for any interesting plants, but so far all I had found was a nice spread of chamomile to top up my tea reserves. There were other plants along the road, but none that had properties that interested me.

I wasn't about to start carrying around poisons if I could avoid it. That just wasn't a very nice thing to do.

I hopped up to a low hanging branch, then started jumping from tree to tree without using any stamina. It was good practice in case I had to make a run for it.

"Mister Menu, can I see my profile please?"

| Name: Broccoli Bunch | | Race: Human | | | Age: 16 |
|---|---|---|---|---|---|
| Health | 115 | Stamina | 125 | Mana | 105 |
| Resilience | 25 | Flexibility | 25 | Magic | 10 |

| First Class: | Cinnamon Bun | First Class Level: | 4 |
|---|---|---|---|
| Skill Slots | 0 | Skill Points | 2 |

| General Skill Slots | 0 | General Skill Points | 1 |
|---|---|---|---|

| General Skills | | Cinnamon Bun Skills | |
|---|---|---|---|
| Insight | C - 17% | Cleaning | C - 93% |
| Makeshift Weapon Proficiency | E - 04% | Jumping | C - 57% |
| Archaeology | F - 39% | Gardening | E - 13% |
| Friendmaking | F - 13% | | |

Cleaning was reaching the edge of Rank B. I wasn't exactly grinding it ceaselessly, but I was trying to make sure that my mana was never completely topped off just so that I didn't waste any time.

Jumping was plodding along as well. It might overtake Cleaning at some point in the near future. My general skills, on the other hand, were falling behind. Insight was the only one slowly ticking up, but the rest? I would need to find a way to get them up a few ranks.

It seemed as though the main barrier for skill growth wasn't experience points at all. Sure, it could take days to get a skill up to max experience, but that didn't matter if you were going to rely on that skill your entire life. It was the hard limit imposed by skill points that slowed everything down.

A month of dedicated practice would be more than enough for me to get every skill up to the highest level they could go, I suspected. Then I would be stuck waiting forever to level up and get just one more skill point to spend. It felt like an almost artificial restriction on what I could accomplish.

Annoying, but understandable. If skills allowed the user to become super strong with only minimal effort and some grinding, then they would be completely broken.

The road forked.

I paused at the intersection and took in the two diverging paths. One to my left, deeper into the forests, one straight ahead towards the marshes. Neither towards the mountain city that I assumed was Port Royal.

I shuffled around to take off my backpack, then grabbed the map Leonard had drawn for me. It showed the camp, the road, and indicated the fork with an arrow pointing ahead and towards Rockstack which was, according to the map, not too terribly far. I had crossed half the distance already.

The left path continued and ended with a big skull and crossbones symbol. I wondered what was over there. It was pretty clear that Leonard thought it would be too dangerous for me, but he also seemed to think that tying my own shoes was beyond me.

"I'll go check later," I decided as I replaced the map into my sack.

Mid-day came and went. I probably should have stopped for lunch, especially now that I actually had supplies, but instead I stopped for a quick break behind a bush, then after cleaning up, pulled some still-soft-ish bread from the supplies sack I had and nibbled away at it while walking.

If I was within only half a day's distance from Rockstack, then it was worth it to rush back over. There might be an inn, and people too. As much as I was enjoying my time on the road, having a roof over my head, a warm meal in my tummy, and a hot shower before bed sounded heavenly.

I was finishing up the last of my bread when I caught sight of smoke between the trees ahead. I paused along the road, then climbed up a tree to see a little better. Not one smokestack, but about five, all of them joining together hundreds of meters above.

It had to be Rockstack!

My steps were a whole lot faster after I hit the ground. I wanted to make it to the town, and I wanted to get there now!

Then the road I had been travelling on for a few days now ended. No more cobbles, no more path, not even some flattened dirt to show where it could have been. I took out Leonard's map and eyed it for a moment. It said to continue, but I had been expecting to follow the road for a while.

I ran ahead a ways, skipping over brush and bushes until, between one step and the next, I caught sight of a new road ahead.

The stones were well-placed and untouched by roots. The sides had deep ditches with thin rivulets of water at the bottom. The road was even wide enough that two cars might have been able to drive on it side-by-side without issue.

"Whoa," I said as I took it in with a growing smile. Well-maintained roads meant civilisation!

I checked Leonard's map one last time, turned to the left, and started jogging.

That didn't last very long. I might have been working out a whole lot more, but that didn't mean I was in shape. The weight of the backpack didn't help, or so I told myself. My jog turned into a fast walk, then an easy, more stable pace as the terrain grew a little hilly.

And then, at long last, I crested a hill and saw Rockstack.

The first and most obvious thing, the only thing I could see, actually, was the wall. It was a solid barrier of living tree trunks, each one as thick around as my arm-span and nearly completely branchless. What few branches were there all stuck out like the spiny thorns of a cactus.

Huge, bulbous bowls sat atop the walls, each one made of some dark bark and big enough to fit half a dozen Broccolis. They reminded me a little of coconuts, only they were perfectly distanced all around the wall.

I squinted and took in the form of two guards by the arch of the doors. Each one was only about as third as tall as the wall. There was even a small moat going around it, and the forest near the town had been cut back to create a big clearing full of tree stumps.

I reshouldered my backpack, made sure Orange was sitting pretty in my bandoleer and walked over to the gate.

The guards were both grenoil like those in the Exploration Guild party, only they didn't seem quite as intimidating. They had cheap spears and thick gambesons with a bit of scale mail that seemed ill-fitting.

"Hello!" I called out to them as I got closer.

*A bored Grenoil Fencer (level ?).*
*A bored Grenoil Hunter (level ?).*

"Hail, traveller," the hunter said. He seemed to snap himself awake as I came closer. "What business do you have in Rockstack? Ah, I mean, Royal Outpost Seven?"

I stopped when I was still a dozen steps away from them just in case they got nervous. "This isn't Rockstack?" I asked.

The fencer sighed. "It is. At least, zat's what everyone calls it. Official name is Royal Outpost Seven. Not zat you look like an inspector."

"Well okay then," I said. "I'm here to find a place to rest, and maybe a way to get to Port Royal?"

The hunter nodded. "Zat's fair. Might take a while before ze next caravan passes zrough. As for ze place to rest, go ask Juliette at ze Inn. You can't miss it."

"It's on the main road?" I asked.

They both laughed, croaky chuckles that calmed down after a moment. "Miss, zere are only seven buildings here. If you can't afford an inn room zen it's off to the tents with you."

"Oh," I said. "If there are so few buildings, then what are the walls for?" I asked.

"Keep zings zat want to eat you out at night. Had a high-ranking Wood Mage show up when ze outpost was still fresh. Built ze walls in a few minutes is what I heard."

The fencer shook his head. "It took hours," he said. "Zis idiot is just trying to impress you."

"Whoa, that's still awesome!" I said. "I have a Gardening Skill; do you think I could do that?"

The hunter looked at his buddy and it was clear he was trying not to laugh. "Yeah, sure. Go on in kid."

I did as he said, running through the arch and into Rockstack. My eyes went huge as I tried to take it all in at once. There were people here, and a ring of buildings that all looked strange and unique, but what caught my eye right away was the huge structure right in the middle of the sort of square that made up the centre of the outpost.

It was a stack of rocks. Sort of like the little stacks someone bored might make by balancing one rock atop another, only this stack was ten meters tall and had rocks that would more appropriately be called boulders. There were three stacks, each one arching up at the top and meeting in the middle at a shiny black stone covered in little golden flecks.

Fool's gold, if I had to guess, but pretty all the same.

I tore my eyes away from the strange sorta-sculpture and took in the rest. The guards were right; there were only seven proper buildings in the outpost. There was a huge inn to one side, then three little shops with second floors that probably had apartments. Then a big blacksmith's shop. There was a huge home that looked like it belonged to someone important, and lastly two large buildings that were both square and boring-looking, as if someone had built a fantasy office building out in the middle of nowhere.

There were a few people around, all grenoil and all minding their own business, so I decided to do the same.

"Where do I start...?" I wondered aloud.

The obvious answer was, of course, the Inn. That's where all the best adventures began, after all. The Inn was a long building with a huge front. Three stories tall and completely out of place in the middle of nowhere like this. It was a bit strange to see such a large building so far from a proper village, but maybe there were enough travellers to make it viable.

There was a sign on the front with a frog jumping into a mug and the words Hop on Inn after it.

Grinning, I held on to my backpack by the straps and ran over to the building, every part of me ready for my first chance to see the inside of a working inn.

The doors were, disappointingly, normal, but the moment I stepped through the threshold I was inundated with the sound of glasses clinking, people talking in low murmurs, the strumming of a lute and the mixed smells of sweaty people and fresh food.

I had found a small paradise.

# Chapter Twenty-Five

# The Hop On Inn

I knew that staring was rude, but I couldn't help myself. There were just so many people, and no two were the same. I didn't mean that the people within were all dressed in strange ways, though there was certainly some of that, I meant that at a glance I counted five different species of people all sitting at different tables and doing… whatever it was adventurers did in an inn.

There was a table with three small people that had translucent wings, all sitting on stools which were taller to accommodate their height. They wore tight-fitting uniforms in dark blues that looked like dress uniforms for officers back home, with medals and tassels on their shoulders and cute little caps.

A bigger table off to one side had a mixed group. Grenoils and a human and a large person with a hunched back and legs that bent the wrong way. They had long, long arms tucked against their side, and their entire body was covered in beige wraps of cloth that did nothing to hide their strange proportions. They even had goggles on.

Someone squawked. "Look at the newbie," and I realised they were talking about me.

It had come from a table with four bird people at it. Their arms were actual wings that ended in taloned hands and their uncovered legs were covered in fine feathers.

"Sorry," I said with a sheepish smile before I skipped over to the counter.

Behind the bar was a large grenoil who stood like a queen surveilling her people, hands carefully cleaning out a mug with a corner of her apron until she caught sight of me and looked me up and down. "You look lost, girlie," she said.

"Ah, I was, I think, until now." I gestured to one of the stools near her. "Can I sit here?"

She croaked. "Go ahead."

I smiled at her and plopped myself down. "Um, I'm looking for a miss Juliette. Do you know her?"

"It's Misses, and I know her better zan anyone. Who's asking?" She filled up a mug with something from a tap and sent it sliding across the counter just as a barmaid passed to pick it up.

"Eh, I am? I met a team from the Exploration Guild in the woods. Emeric said that I should ask you about a place to stay, and maybe work." I smiled hopefully.

She eyed me up and down. "I'm not a charity, no matter what zat idiot Emeric thinks."

I shook my head. "No, no, that's okay. If you don't have work, then I'll find something. Um, do you sell food?"

"Of course we sell food!" she roared. "Nine cop for ze best meal you've ever eaten."

"Are there bugs in it?" I asked as I started reaching into my bag. I had three little pouches made from some cloth I'd knotted together. One for each sort of coin I'd found. I pulled out the copper pouch and emptied it on the counter, then counted them out. "Ah, I only have eight," I said.

Juliette eyed my meagre copper coin supply, then snapped a hand out and stuffed them somewhere so fast that I couldn't see where they went. "You're too zin," she said before moving back. There was an opening at the back in the wall, a window into a busy kitchen where a couple of gren-oil and one of those cloth-wrapped people were cooking up a storm. Juliette screamed a few numbers at them before returning to me. "You said you were looking for work?" she asked.

"Um, yeah! I'm just level four though, so I can't do too much."

Juliette shook her big head. "What is someone like you doing out here? Trying to get yourself killed?"

"No, I got lost. Sorry?"

"Tch. Fine. What can you do?"

I beamed at her. "I can clean, and I can cook and bake a little, and I've got the Gardening skill."

"You have ze cooking or baking skills?" she asked.

"No," I said with a shake.

"Zen you're useless in my kitchen. Go ask Dylan if he needs the help." At my confused look she elaborated. "He's ze alchemist. If you can't find him in zis pisshole zen you're hopeless."

"That sounds great!" I said. "Um, do you have rooms here? With showers?"

"We do. Two lesser sil a night." She glared at me. "We have smaller rooms too. No showers, but zere is a communal shower for our guests. One sil a night."

"Okay, great. How much copper is a sil worth?" I was going to need to get the hang of their money system sooner or later.

Juliette pressed a hand over her face. "Emeric, damn you," she muttered. "Nancy! You're in charge for a moment," she called out. A barmaid on the floor made that thumbs-up gesture Valerie had made before.

The large frog woman walked back to the window just as a platter appeared then she returned and placed it before me.

My eyes widened at the bounty. There was a big potato with a slice cut into it to release some steam and a square of butter melting away atop it. Some stew in a stone bowl that didn't have any bugs in it that I could tell. Some slices of sausage with a sauce over them that was still smoking and half of a round loaf of bread that looked crisp and fresh. There were even some veggies to the side.

Juliette, who I decided then and there was the best frog person ever, placed a big mug of milk next to my plate.

I picked up the fork next to the plate and started taking big bites of everything. "Oh, oh this is so good," I said.

"Don't talk wiz your mouth full," Juliette grumbled, but there was a spark of joy in her eyes. Maybe. Reading grenoil moods wasn't my forte.

"But it's so good," I said after swallowing. I tried a bite of everything, and it was all delicious. Even the milk was fresh and yummy.

"Tch," Juliette said. She reached under the counter for something, then came up with a handful of coins. She laid them out in a row. The first was a copper coin, then a small nickel-sized silver coin, then a quarter-sized coin that was also silver. Finally she placed a gold coin like the one Leonard had given me at the end. "Cop, lesser silver, pure sil, lesser gold. Zere are ozer coins. Gold galleons and ze like. I'm not fool enough to keep zem here. And ozer places have zeir own currencies. Your coins are worzless too far West or past ze mountains to ze east."

"Okay," I said as I chowed down. It was hard to focus with all the yummy flavours running across my tongue, but I made the effort anyway.

"Ten cop to a lesser sil, ten of those to a pure sil, ten of those to a lesser gold," she explained.

"So… a thousand copper to one lesser gold?" I asked.

She nodded. "Zat's right."

"So, for one lesser gold I could buy… a hundred and forty of these meals. Minus the tip."

Juliette laughed and swept the coins off the table. "You'd be a good customer if you did."

I smiled. I was truly tempted. "How much does most work pay, by the hour, I mean?"

"By ze hour? I pay my barmaids two sil a day. Ze cooks four," she said.

"Oh, okay," I said. "How much does a loaf of bread cost?"

"A loaf of…" she shook her head again. "Here, four cop. In a proper city and most towns, one or two."

"Things are expensive here?" I asked before using a chunk of bread to dab at the stew.

Juliette nodded. "Ay, zey are. We're far from any town zat can supply us. Most zings we need are brought in from Port Royal and some of ze towns along ze way. No farms means no local crops."

That made sense. I supposed that the outpost had other sources of income, or at least something to attract people to it temporarily. It didn't seem like a permanent place yet. Maybe one day it would become a proper town, with farms and livestock and normal villagers. I looked around the bar and all I saw were people that looked ready for adventure.

"So, I need a place to sleep," I said.

"One sil a night," Juliette said.

"Ah, okay," I agreed. "Do you need anyone to help you clean and stuff like that?" I asked her.

She snorted. "I always do. You could stay in ze tents if you want. Zey cost two cop a night. But if you wake up naked and wizout anyzing to your name, zat's your problem."

"Right, your inn seems much nicer," I said. "I have some things to sell. I should go do that soon to afford a room."

Juliette grabbed a rag and started rubbing at her counter absentmindedly. "Ze first room down zat corridor," she said with a nod to the side. "Go clean it. I'll give you a cop if it's to my liking."

A copper, which was a tenth of the value of a small room. "How many rooms does your inn have?" I asked.

"Forty," she said with a growing smile. "But I wouldn't pay you more for caring for ze bigger rooms."

"Right," I said. I looked down and was disappointed to find that all of my food was gone. I shoved the sadness aside by reminding myself that I could afford hundreds of these meals now thanks to Leonard. "Um, I'm supposed to go to Port Royal, are there ways to get there?"

"Yes. You walk. You ride wiz a caravan. You hire a mage to teleport you," Juliette said.

"Teleport?" I asked with wonder.

"Zat's usually a few lesser gold for ze distance between here and Port Royal. Triple it here because no mage will want to take you."

I winced. "Okay. How about the caravan option?"

"Ze last caravan arrived yesterday morning. Ze next one arrives in a week. Ze guards for it have all been hired already from ze local adventurers, so you'd need to buy passage to go wiz zem. A few sil. More for food."

A week then. A week to gather things and make some money to be able to live in a proper city. A week to explore and meet people and make friends. I grinned at Juliette. "Brilliant!"

I hopped off the stool and moved over to the side towards the room she had pointed out. "I'll get to cleaning then," I said as I held my bag to the side. "Can I put this somewhere?"

She took the bag and stuffed it behind the bar. "Cleaning zings are in the cupboard under ze stairs."

"Got it!" I said.

I found the room and slid in with a broom and some rags. It was a small space, with a simple undecorated bed to one side, a chair and desk at the far end and a tiny window overlooking the back of the inn.

I could see the tents she had mentioned. They weren't actual tents, but small squat buildings with cloth walls and roofs. Some had the sides rolled up to reveal hammocks all in a row within. There was what I suspected was a latrine at the far end, a human man coming out and hopping around as he buckled his belt. Not very fancy. A room would be much nicer, even if it was simple.

My plan so far was pretty simple, but I could go over it again and again as I swept the floor and did the bed and rubbed the top of the desk free of dust. Get a room, then spend the night. In the morning try to sell all of my loot. Then maybe I could work in the inn. That did sound kind of cool.

But I also wanted to see the world around the outpost and maybe find more cool stuff! The adventurers here had to be around for something. Maybe I could help?

I wiped my brow and looked over my work. It was good enough.

I set aside all of the cleaning stuff and went to fetch Juliette. "Problem?" she asked. "Don't tell me you don't know how to do ze bed. I swear children zese days are…" she stopped when she stood by the door. "Did… did you polish ze floor?"

The floor looked clean, nice and well cared for and just a little sparkly. "I just cleaned it," I said.

"And ze bed?"

The bed looked fresh and welcoming. It even smelled nice, like fresh hay. Probably because that's what was in the mattress. "I made it right, right?" I asked. "Um, I can try harder, if you want."

Juliette eyed me. "You have the Cleaning skill zen. Good. One cop a room," she said.

I grinned. "Okay!"

# Chapter Twenty-Six
# Selling for a Bargain

I woke up with birdsong in my ear and a smile on my face.

The room I had been given had a small window, barely bigger than my head, but enough that—when I had left it open for the draft of fresh night air—it let in plenty of noise. People talking, laughing and starting their day. Birds darting around with wild whistles and the bark of a happy dog.

I stretched in my bed, then let all of my limbs go floppy and loose so that I could enjoy the sensation of being in a bed.

Beds, I decided, were the best.

I wanted to just… stay there forever, but I was a busy bun with busy bun things to do! With a sigh, I tossed off my blankets, then hopped to my feet and stretched a little more. I found all of my clothes—conveniently left draped all over the room's one chair—and got dressed up and ready to go.

I debated wearing my armour, but in the end chose not to. It would feel good to go without for a day and if I wanted to buy clothes or equipment later it would be a hassle to take it all off. I still carried my bandoleer and my backpack though.

"Orange!" I called out. No kitty appeared. A look under the bed revealed nothing, nor did a peak in the dresser provided with the room. I shrugged and pushed a bit of mana into my necklace. I wasn't sure how it worked, exactly, but I figured it might just get me my kitty companion back.

A moment later a ball formed in the air before me and a disgruntled Orange poofed into existence. She looked around, then glared at me.

"Oops," I said. "Sorry, Orange, but I'm heading out and I think you should come!"

Orange huffed, but she still took pride of place on my shoulder and refused to budge even as I ran my fingers through my hair to unknot it, then tied it in a neat ponytail. Preparations for the morning done, I fired off a nice burst of cleaning magic at myself and grinned.

"Let's go take on the world, Orange!" I said.

The Inn's main floor was a chaotic hive of activity. More people than could possibly be rooming at the inn were swarming the tables, shouting over each other, laughing at unheard jokes and basically drowning the floor in raucous noise.

Nancy, the nice barmaid, stopped by me, a tray on her head and two in each arm. "If you're not in a hurry love, zen you'd best wait in your rooms for breakfast."

"Ah, okay!" I tried to say, but she was already moving through the crowd, avoiding elbows and snapping her long tongue into the face of any boy with questing fingers. It was impressive to see her go, but I had a bunch of other things to do and breakfast could wait. Maybe lunchtime would mean a calmer inn.

Stepping out into the full sunlight of the morning was, for just a moment, completely blinding, but I enjoyed the light before taking my bearings of the world around me.

There were a bunch of carriages hitched to big ol' horses. The wagons were empty except for the benches by their sides. That was plain enough and other than a passing thought to petting the horses I didn't pay them any mind. The gigantic frogs, on the other hand, those had me pausing.

These weren't dressed like the grenoil. In fact, they were naked except for a bunch of harnesses strapped all over them with big sacks that looked full of stuff. A grenoil, looking tiny next to the giant frogs, was checking the harnesses when I approached. "Eh, hello sir," I said.

He turned and brought a hand up to adjust the straw hat he was wearing. "Yes ma'am?"

"What's that?" I asked, pointing to the giant frog. It didn't look sapient at first glance.

"Never seen a toad before, huh?" he asked.

"That's a toad," I said. "It's huge! The toads where I'm from are no bigger than Orange." I pointed to my shoulder cat as an explanation.

The man laughed. "Ay, zey're big bastards. Nice though. Zey might try to gobble you up, but a swift kick or two and zey'll let ya out. We use 'em to carry stuff. Good for hauling. 'Specially 'cross ze terrain 'round here. Lot's a mud. Horses get stuck, so we use toads when we can."

"Wow," I said. "That's cool. Where do you go with them?"

"Ze dungeon, of course," he said. He tipped his hat at me. "Need to get back to it before ze delvers finish eatin'."

I waved him goodbye and went the long way around the toads. There looked to be a half dozen of them, with more being brought over from the other side of the outpost. They probably had a corral of some sort for them and the horses.

I took in all the shops that the outpost had to offer. There was a grand total of three of them, which wasn't that impressive. Still, it seemed like Rockstack was made to cater to adventurers and the like, so I expected the shops to maybe have better gear and such.

The blacksmith's shop was the one to the far left, so I chose to start there. A snoop through the windows revealed stacks of swords and spears and all sorts of weapons left alongside racks of armour.

I opened the door and was assailed with the shriek of metal-on-stone, drowning out the jingle of the little bell above the door.

"If you brought it last night, it's not ready yet!" someone screamed over the din from the back of the shop.

"Um, no!" I called back. "I'm just here to look around."

The whirring noise continued, but I could hear someone moving. I prepared a nice smile to welcome them. The smith was a big bird person, her white feathers turned black with grime and her entire front covered by a thick apron. "If you're not here to buy," she squawked, "Then be elsewhere." She emphasised every word with a swing from an unfinished sword.

"Oh, okay," I said before backing up and out of sword-reach. I turned around, careful not to knock anything over with my backpack, and ran out of there. Maybe I could try again when she wasn't so busy. It wouldn't do to dismiss a potential friend just because they were a little gruff.

I'd try again tomorrow!

My next destination was the general store next to the blacksmith's shop. This one had a much bigger floorspace filled with shelves laden with stuff. Most of the things on display were strange twists on the ordinary. Cans of food with tabs on them next to paper-wrapped strips of jerky. Jars of salt and boxes of soap.

There were non-food things too. Stacks of baskets, sacks, and flasks all in neat rows. There were scales for sale (2 sil) and a barrel filled with long wooden poles (3 cop ea.) next to a stack of torches. There were little bands with stones sewn into the front labelled as genuine runelights going for a silver each next to Fur-B-Gone magic razors.

I smiled at the older looking grenoil behind the counter as I continued to browse. The ads on the walls caught my eyes with their colourful displays. 'Croaker's Delight' was apparently a brand of cigars and 'Deep Delve Wax' a sort of wax to put on leather that was guaranteed to make it waterproof.

Then at the back I found rolls of dark pelt (Sombral Skin, 1sil/yd) and bits of bark in a box labelled Dryad bark that was going for a few copper an ounce.

I had to hold back a laugh at the strange, yet magical feel of the place. So many ordinary things right next to extraordinary ones. Then I saw the glass display near the counter with books inside and I rushed over. "Ohh," I said as I took them in.

"Interested, missy?" the old grenoil asked. "I've got Ze basics and nothing but, I'm afraid. Flare's Compendium of Basic Magics, Ze Deep Dungeon Delvers' Dictionary and a few others besides. I've got skill scrolls too. Fireball and Mana Manipulation. Some martial art guides."

I snapped to attention. "Fireball?" I asked.

The grenoil croaked a laugh. "Indeed!" He reached into a cubby-hole filled rack behind him and pulled out a scroll which he placed on the table. The end caps were simple wood, but they had little fire carvings marked on them. "Zese are three sil each," he said.

I winced at that. I could afford them but there were other things I would need and— "I'll take it."

The shopkeep grinned and placed the scroll to the side. "Anyzing else?"

"Um, the book on basic magics, how much is that?"

"Zree lesser gold," he said with a straight face.

That was over three hundred meals over at the inn. That was three hundred nights in my tiny room with the nice bed. Were books really that expensive? "I'll think about it," I said. "Um, I do have some things to sell," I said as I put my backpack down.

"Show me, show me. I trade a lot in monster drops here," he said.

The first thing I placed were the parts of the plants I had collected. "Um, these are from plants that I ran across on the way here. Blood Dandelion, Red Chokerberry…" I paused as the shopkeep waved his hand in a 'no' sort of gesture.

"Sorry miss, I could buy zese off of you. I can see what zey're worth after all, but Dylan next door would give you a fairer price for your flowers. I would merely resell zem to him with a mark-up."

"Oh," I said. "That's very honest of you. Thank you!"

He shook his big froggy head. "No no, it behoves one to be honest in his dealings. And zis outpost is almost entirely populated wiz dungeon divers and explorers. A bad reputation amongst zem would hurt more zan just my bottom line."

"Well, thank you anyway," I said. "What about ghost cloth?" I reached into my back and pulled out two squares of ghostly cloth.

"Zis I'm more familiar with. An uncommon material from a common foe. Zey would be farmed but farming ghosts is tricky business. Zese are in nice condition," he said as he examined the cloth then ran a hand over it. "Good enough. Not ze market for it here, but I can send it to my guild affiliates for a tidy profit. I'll give you two sil each."

Better than nothing. "Okay," I said.

The shopkeep stared at me then rolled his eyes. "You're supposed to offer five, zen we meet at zree," he said.

"Oh."

He set the cloth aside and I wasn't sure if I had just been tricked or not. "Alright. I also have this painting that I found." I placed the small painting of a dragon and a boat on the counter. I had been dragging it around for a while, frame and all, but it was small and light. I took off the sheet covering it and let the shopkeep look at it. "Do you have a skill to know what things are?" I asked. "I have Insight."

*A moderately high-quality painting of a dragon over a fishing boat, old.*

"I have Appraise, which is similar. Not as... insightful, pardon ze pun, but better at judging ze value of zings. Zis painting is worth forty sil, for example."

"Really?" I asked.

"Yes, I'll give you ten."

My shoulders slumped. "Oh, okay."

The shopkeeper sighed. "Fine, twenty."

I grinned big and proud at him. I had made so much!

"Okay, twenty-five, but not a sil more." He set it aside with a huff.

"Thank you!" I said. The next item up was a small pile of silverware.

The shopkeeper looked at them all quickly, then shrugged one shoulder. "Two cop each. Some are worth more, others less. Zese I can sell to zose coming in here, or bundle with my meal and survival packages and call some of zem higher quality."

"Okay," I said. "This is my last item," I said as I placed my magic wand on the table.

The shopkeep made a strange face.

"It's a wand of cure hysteria. It still works. I used it." To kill ghosts, but he didn't need to know that.

"No. Find a shop zat... specializes in zat kind of zing. Not here."

"Oh, okay," I said.

A quick tally later and I was leaving with twenty-six more silver and forty copper and, best of all, a scroll of Fireball!

I was going to set so many things on fire!

## Chapter Twenty-Seven
# Planting the Seeds of a Quest

I wanted to start learning how to cast fireball, but I had other things to do, like check in on the next—and last—shop in Rockstack.

The alchemist shop had the same sign hanging off the front as the alchemist shop in Threewells, a staff with a ball spinning around it. This one had two balls and I couldn't remember if it was the same for the last I'd seen. Maybe it meant something?

There was light within, so I pushed open the door and came to a stop in a small waiting area. To my left was what looked like a clinic with one of those faerie looking people buzzing around on four wings, they looked like a boy-faerie, but I couldn't quite be sure. To the right was another door and next to it a window set into the wall with a counter jutting out, like a drive-through window at a fast-food place only probably not at all like that.

The faerie person buzzed over, then landed daintily by the entrance of the clinic. "Can I assist you, human?" he asked. The voice was definitely a boy's.

"Eh? Ah, yeah. I'm looking for a Dylan. I have alchemical stuff to sell. Plants and things."

The faerie nodded quickly. "Of course. Just one moment then," he said before taking to the air and casually drifting to the window and knocking on its frame. "Dylan, you unprofessional oaf, you have a customer," the faerie said. He turned back to me. "He should be with you momentarily. Is there anything else I can assist you with?"

"Ah, maybe? I've never met someone like you, but you seem nice. What's your, um, species?"

One of the faerie's little eyebrows perked up. "I'm a Sylph. Try reading a book if you find yourself lacking in knowledge, it might help." He looked at me for a while. "Maybe more than one book."

I watched the Sylph flutter back to his side of the clinic and held back a huff. That had sounded positively rude, but maybe Sylphs were just naturally brusque, and the advice itself wasn't that bad. Maybe there was a Planeswalking for Dummies book out there?

I ambled closer to the window and peeked into the next room over. It was a mess. There were tables and counters all over, all of them covered in pouches and jars full of glowy stuff and boxes that had been labelled with things, then had those labels scratched out and replaced by others in sloppier and sloppier handwriting.

There were tools too. Alembics and what looked like Bunsen burners, kettles with long necks and glass bottles with loopy tubes sticking out of them like something from a mad scientist's wet dream. There were racks to the side filled with finger-sized bottles that had paper labels with things like 'health' and 'water resistance' glued to them.

I couldn't decide if I should have been excited at the prospect of magic potions or kind if disgusted at how messy the place making them was.

"I'm coming, I'm coming," a man's voice said a moment before someone, presumably Dylan, came around a corner and placed a bunch of empty vials on a table already covered in stuff. I winced as one of them went off the edge and exploded in a crackle of glass. "Oh no!"

"Do you need help cleaning that?" I asked.

"No no, it's all well," Dylan said as he abandoned the table and came closer. He had a bit of a limp as he walked, I noticed, then I saw the glasses perched across his froggy face and I had to hold back a giggle at how big they made his eyes look. "I'm Dylan. How can I help?"

"Ah, hello Dylan. My name is Broccoli Bunch, and I would love to be your friend."

"Zat's nice?" Dylan said. "I don't sell zat kind of potion zough."

There were friendship potions? "What? No, no, I mean… Oh, shucks, nevermind. I have some plants that I picked up that I thought you might be interested in."

"Plants can be good," Dylan said as he wiped the window's counter clean with a sleeve. "Show me what you've got!"

I nodded and pulled out a small cloth with some drying Red Chokerberries.

Dylan took then, sniffed at the pile, then popped one into his mouth. "Mmm, still good. But not what I'm looking for, I'm afraid."

"Ah, okay," I said. I pushed the cloth aside, then because I could I plopped one of the berries into my mouth.

Next came a few blood dandelion buds. Dylan made a content sound and poked them with the tip of a finger. "Much better. One moment." He left, then returned with a scale which he set to one side and a pen and paper. A few moments later he nodded. "Seven cop for all of it."

I was a little disappointed, but then again it had only taken me moments to gather. I could get a lot more easily enough. If a barmaid made two silver a day, then I could easily make just as much with dandelions alone.

"You're not interested in chamomile or milk thistle?" I asked and he shook his head. "Okay then. I have some march rose buds."

"Oh, zose would be worz somezing in Port Royal. Zey make fine nutrition potions, scurvy cures and… marital assistance potions. I can't give you much here zough. Ze locals are all dungeon divers and ze like, zey are in good healz until zey're not. Two cop each?"

"Darn," I said. Still, I didn't have any use for the buds. They were to prevent scurvy and acted as an aphrodisiac, and I had inn food now and I wasn't married so I didn't need them, and they would go bad eventually.

Six copper coins were added to a small pile, bringing my total up to thirteen copper. Enough for a good meal.

"And this is the last plant I have that might interest you," I said as I placed the stems and leaves of the seven-petal candle flower I had found onto the counter.

Dylan cooed, a strange sound from a froggy throat. "Seven-Petal. Where did you find it?"

"On the road here. I asked a pixie and it helped me," I said.

"A… pixie? Well, I suppose zey would know. A rare find! And valuable. Freud-Slip doesn't have many fire-based traps, but it does use zem on occasion."

"Freud-Slip?" I repeated.

"Ze Dungeon in the swamps to ze south. Ze one ze delvers are all here for? Is zat not what you came for?" he asked.

I shook my head. "Nope. Just got a little lost. I'll probably be leaving with the next caravan to Port Royal, but until then I'll be around the outpost."

Dylan tapped his chin for a moment, then looked down at all the stems and leaves I had brought him. "Twenty sil for ze lot," he said. "And I have a request. You're a human. Humans like quests, yes?"

"I am and I'll listen if you have something for me to do," I said as I gleefully watched my wealth grow. I was now up to a whopping twenty silver and thirteen copper. "I'd love a proper quest."

"Are you wiz any guild?" he asked.

"Not yet, but I want to join the exploration guild maybe."

"Zen zis will be right up your alley, as ze humans say. Zere was a dungeon called Dunwich not too far from here some time ago. When we came here, we rediscovered where it used to be, but it was destroyed long ago. Ze negative mana around ze area has made it unwelcoming to most and zere are a few apparitions in the area. It's not too dangerous, but it isn't safe. A plant grows zere called ze Two-Lipped Tulip."

"Wait a moment," I said before searching through my back, out came my herbology book which I placed on the counter to search through.

"Zat is a very nice book. Forty sil."

"Nope," I said with a grin. Dylan didn't even look disappointed that I had refused. It took some leafing (hah!) but I found the right page. There was an illustration of two flowers. The first a tulip that had strangely curved flowers that did look like lips. The second a similar plant, but the flower was gaping open to reveal a pair of fangs dribbling with liquids that I bet weren't good for anyone's health.

### Two-Lipped Tulip

*A plant that actively seeks out areas with rot-aspect mana, or places with negative mana. They grow quickly and should be considered a weed, though unless they are near populated areas it may be best to leave them alone as they are known to purify an area's mana though at an incredibly slow pace. The flower can whip around and 'bite' animals and unwary herbalists, injecting them with a weak to mild venom that will drain the person's health over time.*

*The flower contains a pair of sacks that hold their venom. The liquid is a great contact poison but can also be used in strengthening potions and as a base for drain-based potions such as 'drain disease.'*

"These look kind of dangerous to mess with," I said.

"A little. I will give you one sil per poison gland. Zere are two per flower. I need no more zan fifty for now."

"That's a good amount of silver," I said. "What do you need them for?"

The alchemist shrugged. "Some for experimentation, but most will go towards drain-madness potions. We need many for ze local dungeons. It's still young but it is dangerous."

"I'll think about it," I said.

We soon shook over the plants I had already sold to him and I walked out accompanied by the happy jingle of a couple of pouches full of silver.

The inn, when I walked in, was completely empty except for the two barmaids and Juliette sitting by the bar. "Where is everyone?" I asked as I moved closer.

Juliette snorted. "Gone. Ze lot of zem. Zey are here for ze dungeon and wiz no travel to and from it at night ze only time for zem to work is now."

"How does that work, dungeon diving for a living, I mean?" I asked as I took a seat next to Juliette and sighed as I got the weight off my feet.

"Zey go in, zey find zings, zey come out and pay ze taxes on zem, zen zey sell it all to the guilds for some tidy profits. Zen zey come here and make my inn a mess. You can clean ze rooms zat are unlocked. Same price as last time."

"I might do that. Dylan gave me a quest though, and I wanna try my hand at it. Maybe after I've met some of the adventurers, they seem nice. Oh, and I bought a fireball scroll!"

"Cast zat indoors and you can sleep outdoors, wiz an empty stomach," Juliette said.

I pouted at her, but it bounced off her tough maternal hide to no effect. "Fine, fine. Maybe later. Can I have lunch or is it too late?"

"It is never too late for lunch in my inn," Juliette said. "As long as you have ze coin for it."

I nodded and watched with an eager smile as she got up and waddled over to the kitchens. I hadn't even placed an order, but I trusted anything she brought would be super delicious.

Nancy the barmaid shifted over one seat to be next to me. "Be careful around ze divers. Some of zem are not ze sort of people you would want around a young woman. Zey might not look it, but zey kill for a living. And when some of zem don't come back. It's not always ze dungeon's fault."

"I'll keep that in mind," I said truthfully. Then Juliette was returning with lunch and my focus turned to chowing down.

# Chapter Twenty-Eight

# JourneyBun

I stared at Mister Menu, reading and re-reading what was written on his bluish surface. The broom in my hand was a little slack and if Juliette made the rounds to see how things were going with the cleaning, she would probably have been disappointed to see me slacking off.

**Congratulations! Through repeated actions your Cleaning skill has improved and is now eligible for rank up!**
**Rank B costs two (2) Class Points**

"Two class points?" I whined. That was so many! In fact, that was every point I had left, and I had no idea when my next level-up would come around.

Jumping was going to rank-up soon too, would it cost two points to get it to rank B? That was awful! I would be stalled forever.

I pouted at Mister Menu while I finished up my cleaning work. Only a bit over a dozen rooms had been left unlocked, which meant I was making a lot less money per day cleaning than I had expected. Enough for a meal at the inn or to rent a room for the night, but not both. I had enough coins set aside to last a long while, but I was going to start spending more than I was making.

Returning to the main floor, I found Juliette tidying up around the bar. "I'm done," I said. "fourteen rooms in all."

"Do you want ze coins now?" she asked.

"Can you use them to cover for another night? The same room and all?"

Juliette nodded absently. "Fourteen for ze room and a meal. Just one."

"Really? Thank you, Juliette! You're the best," I said, my mood lifting considerably. "Hey, do you know about rank B skills?"

"Rank B? Ah," Juliette said. "You cleaning has gotten better?"

I nodded vigorously. "Yup! Just a few minutes ago."

The big frog matron returned to her work, passing a cloth between bottles to dust them off. It was work that I could probably have done, but then Juliette would be left with nothing to do. "How do your skill ranks display zemselves?"

"Eh?"

"Do zey appear as colours? Numbers? Shapes?" she asked.

"Um, they show up as ranks? Rank F at the start, then they go backwards through the alphabet."

Juliette made a noncommittal sound. "Very well. Every person sees zem differently. Well, mostly differently. I see ze letters and numbers of ze first language I learned. But my ranks feel like… bottles being filled."

That kind of made sense. If someone didn't know how to read, they still needed to be able to interact with their system. "So each person's system is unique?"

"As unique as you are a unique human," Juliette said. "Zat is to say, most humans have legs, two arms and a head, but zey are not grenoil. Most people from a place will have similar, what did you call it, systems."

"Neat," I said. "So do others need class points to raise their ranks, or whatever?"

"Zey do. Ze name for each rank when you don't know ze people you're dealing wiz is novice, intermediary, apprentice, disciple, journeyman, expert, master. Zere are some above zat, but you won't see zem anytime soon."

I sang the alphabet song in my head a few times to get all the letters and names right. "So, to get to disciple you need a skill point?"

"Yes, zat's right."

"And journeyman needs two?" I asked.

Juliette nodded. "Zen expert needs three, and master five."

"Five?!" I asked. "That's five levels worth of points."

"Above master needs even more," she said. "Which is why you won't see skills zat high."

I slumped onto the bar's surface, letting the overwhelming despair get to me. "It's going to take forever before I'm super powerful," I muttered. "So much work."

Juliette croaked and tossed a dirty rag onto my head. "My bar is a happy place. Go be mopey elsewhere."

I huffed at her but cleaned her rag all the same then left it on the counter next to me as I got up. "You're right. I need to think a little and maybe go on an adventure again! Ah… wait, do you know what Cleaning does at journeyman level?"

"No. Now go. Supper won't be served for anozer four hours. Not until ze adventurers return."

I waved Juliette goodbye as I ran off to my room and started looking for my things. I hadn't made my choice about Cleaning's rank B yet. The numbers were still working themselves out in my head, but that didn't mean that I couldn't do other things. Dylan's little quest sounded like an easy enough task.

I'd get to explore a little beyond the outpost, and I'd maybe make enough silver to… buy myself something nice. Like that book on basic magics. Oh! And I could practice fireball while out of the outpost. The lands around here were pretty marshy, so it was unlikely I'd light the whole world on fire.

Probably.

I was grinning as I set Orange on my bed then started slipping on my armour and gear. In no time at all I was ready and set for adventure! Then I realized that I didn't need all my stuff if I was returning, so I left some things behind. I brought my shovel, my herbology book, the firestarter and a candle and some food and water for the trip. My silver and gold I tucked under the mattress. If I needed more than the ninety-odd coppers I had on me I could always return.

"Let's go, Orange!" I said to my kitty companion.

The archway into the outpost was guarded by the same two bored-looking grenoil as the last time. "Hello boys," I said as I approached them. "I was wondering if maybe you could help me with some directions?"

"I've nothing better to do," one of them said as he leaned into his spear. "It's a long walk to ze dungeon from here zough."

"No no, I need to find the, ah, Dunwich dungeon place. I'm going flower picking."

"Flower— whatever. It's to ze west and north of here. Can't really miss it. Ze whole place stinks of rot. Follow ze smell." He pointed off in a direction that I suspected was northwest. Which… after looking around, made me realize that the big city—Port Royal—that I had been using as my north was actually to the northeast.

"Oh, I have a map," I said before pulling Leonard's map from my bandoleer. "Could you tell me where it is on that?"

He looked at it, then at me. "You see ze big skull and crossbones?" he asked. When I nodded, he continued, "It's zere."

"Do you know anything about the place?" I asked. It wouldn't hurt to know what I was getting into. Leonard certainly seemed to think that knowledge was important for an explorer and I was willing to bow to his experiences on the matter even if he had been a big grump.

The guard who had been the least talkative so far nodded. "Group of divers went a week or two back. Came back right startled zey did. Said zere wasn't anyzing worz looting zere zough."

"Zere used to be a dungeon zere before some filzy dog broke its core. World curse zem. Ze area has bad air, but most monsters know better zan to stick around."

"Spooky," I said. "And awesome! I wanted to know why Leonard didn't want me to go there. I guess I'll find out! Thank you, mister guard." I smiled at the pair then spun on one heel and marched off.

My pack was lighter on my back and I had a full tummy, which was enough of a change that I could move a whole lot faster than before. That, and instead of the meandering kind of lost way I had scurried across the forest a few days ago, I now knew more or less where I was going, which was very helpful.

As soon as I was out of the clearing around Rockstack I took to the trees and climbed the tallest one I could until I was standing on a branch that let me see over the swaying forest all around.

Northwest, as it turned out, was towards a range of big mountainous hills. Not big pillars of stone like the mountains to the Northeast, but still impressively big hills with windswept tops and a distinct lack of plant life.

I could see a cliffside up ahead that was going to be tricky to climb up. "Seems that's where we're going," I told Orange as I walked off the branch and plummeted to the ground with a whoop.

I landed in a skill-enhanced crouch like a superhero and instantly felt a thousand times cooler. "Hey, Mister Menu, is there a 'cool' skill I can unlock? Pretty please?" I asked.

The menu didn't deign to answer.

Shrugging, I started walking, mind contemplating different things like superhero landings and how hard they would be to do with pants on. It would be super embarrassing to land in front of some bad guys only to have the inseam of my pants tear open. I vowed to avoid doing that.

Reaching into my pack, I pulled out the fireball scroll and unrolled it a little. The advantage of a proper scroll was that with both hands I could reveal only as much of the text as needed, though reading and jumping proved to be too complicated after I nearly ran into a bush.

Grumbling, I set aside the scroll for later. There were just so many things I wanted to do, but so little time to do them in. Maybe I could learn some time magic to give myself more hours in the day in which to do stuff.

My jumps grew a bit riskier as the number of trees around me started to dwindle, soon I was forced to land and start walking across rough stony ground, feet brushing over brown grass that barely reached my ankles.

I took a deep gulp of breath, expecting to get a lungful of fresh mountain-y air but... not. The air was off. Not something I could pin right away, not until I remembered what Dylan said about negative mana being strong in the area. Did that mean that negative mana was an actual thing, or was it just an absence of mana? Like a shadow being an absence of light?

The more I learned about my strange new home the more I realized I didn't know much at all.

I used a bit of mana on my shoes, cleaning them of dirt and dust and mud in an instant, then I kept an eye on my status while I started climbing uphill. I didn't have a timepiece on me, but it felt as if it took far, far longer than usual for my mana to tick up one point.

Scary indeed. I could imagine that people used to a more or less fixed return on the amount of mana they had would be spooked by the change. Or maybe it was something else about the area that had them scared?

I arrived at a spot where the uphill climb shifted from a slight slope that was good for the calves to a rising cliff that rose half a dozen meters above me, all jagged stones and rough rock walls that seemed impassable at first glance.

But the cliff probably wasn't expecting the intrepid Broccoli Bunch to tackle it!

I crouched down while scanning for a nice spot on the wall, then I found a place where I could land—just a small ledge about a third of the way up. There was another outcropping a little higher than that too, one I could use for a final hop to the top.

The first jump had me just barely overshooting the ledge, and I found myself hugging the wall to avoid going splat. After calming myself down I jumped up another meter and a bit to the second outcropping, then shot upwards to the top.

It was only when I was at the top of the cliff that I noticed the path leading up it to the side.

Oops?

Shrugging, I started following the road, probably one dug in place to allow for carts to get to and from the dungeon. I was getting just a little excited at the idea of exploring a whole new place, even if there wasn't much to see there.

## Chapter Twenty-Nine
# Mad Hare

The Dunwich site was kind of strange. I didn't just mean that the air felt off, which it certainly did, but there was a sense that everything was just a little too… light. I bounced on the spot a few times and tried to pinpoint the feeling, but it wasn't easy.

Once, when I was a much smaller Broccoli, my parents and I had gone camping near a mountain. We went hiking one day and spent the whole afternoon climbing towards the peak. It was a big slopey mountain, so the climb wasn't too rough, and there were well-trodden paths leading all the way up. As we got closer to the top the air felt harder to breath, lighter. The air around Dunwich felt the same, but without the altitude to explain it.

That, and there was a stench to the air, as if someone had farted nearby and I was only catching stinky whiffs of it when the wind shifted.

I scrunched up my nose and started looking around. The Two-Lipped Tulips might be hard to find. I hoped they weren't. It had taken a few hours to arrive, and I suspected that it would take a couple more to get back to Rockstack. I didn't want to be stuck in the woods at night.

The path ahead turned one final time and the ground evened out onto a plateau. To my left I had a spectacular view of the Darkwoods, a sea of trees stretching out to the distance, with marshes to the East and mountains stretching out to the North. I even caught a glimpse of what might have been a huge lake way off in the distance to the South.

Those things were all far away though. I focused on what was to my right.

There were a few buildings still standing even against the test of time. The nearest pair were wooden shacks with tiled roofs, just like the buildings in Threewells. The final building, this one further on the plateau, was a huge construct of corrugated tin, with a rusty metal roof and huge streaks of muck on its sides.

The tin building looked like an abandoned warehouse from back home, strangely out of place in a world where I expected everything to be made of wood and brick. It just made me want to explore it even more!

Orange jumped off my shoulder and started walking in the air before me as I made my way towards the first little shack. There were big windows on the front of it, windows that had been broken inwards some time ago. The door was a few meters away, left to rot on the stony ground.

"Yikes," I said as I moved into the darkened interior and took it all in. There were chairs and a table and a couple of bunk beds at the back. A small cast iron fireplace sat to one side and there was a tiny little closet against one wall. Not even a bathroom.

The place had seen better days. No chests, no floorboards to hide any- thing under, and a tug at the creaky door of the fireplace just revealed an- cient coal sitting on a pile of brownish ash.

"A bunk house then," I muttered. "Probably for the adventurers com- ing to the dungeon."

Orange ran back to me and I picked her up to set her on my shoulder. I poked my head out of the front door to make sure there wasn't anything mean around, then left the bunk house and headed for the next.

This one was in worse condition than even the bunkhouse had been. It was a small home, with two floors and a tower built into the side that rose up even higher. A guard station, maybe? Or a more permanent residence?

Either way, I found the door smashed in and moved into the darkened interior. The place had a pair of offices at the front and, as I moved to- wards the back, I found a small clinic with a tall bed and some rusty tools left on the floor. There had been tables and desks and chairs and other things here, but most had been broken or kicked aside. Footprints on the dusty floor suggested that it hadn't happened all that long ago.

The adventurers from Rockstack? That was a distinct possibility.

The second floor had a few small bedrooms and access to the tower proper. It was on the top floor that I got my first glimpse of what had to be the Dunwich dungeon itself, or the place it had been.

The Dungeon's entrance was shaped a little like a mining shaft, a deep dark hole in the walls of a rocky outcropping. Wooden beams formed a rough archway around the entrance, all of them scorched black as if some- thing had exploded out of the hole.

The ground around the dungeon was blackened by fire and the few bits of vegetation around it were all skeletal and dead.

"I am not going in there," I said to Orange. I had seen horror movies be- fore, I knew what happened to cute girls going down dark shafts.

I was on my way down the tower when I heard a strange sound, a sort of yowling roar as if someone stepped on the tail of a giant cat.

**You have heard the screech of a creature of madness! Your mind is shaken.**

I stumbled down the next few steps and had to hang onto the creaky rails to prevent myself from falling even further. The world swayed.

I giggled because it had been such a funny noise.

I was smiling so hard it hurt when I made my way to the first floor and stepped out without so much as looking around. I didn't need to look around because looking too much was just silly.

Orange moved ahead of me and blocked my path, so I stepped around her.

She floated before me and blocked my path again. "Get out of my way, you stupid cat," I said.

I blinked.

Orange gave me a kitty glare.

Shaking my head, I tried to refocus and found my mind all fuzzy and strange. My next step had me stumbling sideways until I bumped into the house and just clung to the wall for balance. "What?" I wondered.

The noise, the screech. It had to have done something. I re-read the warning mister Menu had given me with mounting horror.

"Oh, that's bad," I said. I knew it was bad, and yet I wanted to either start laughing or curl up in a ball and scream and I couldn't decide which to do.

Orange pushed herself against my neck and I felt her entire body rumbling with a gentle purr. Had she been trying to stop me? But stop me from what? The madness had only lasted a little bit, but it had been pulling me towards something, making everything but the idea of walking over to it seem like a distraction at best.

Very spooky.

I took a deep breath to resettle myself, then fired a small bust of cleaning magic aimed at myself just to freshen up.

It was like wiping away the fog on a window. As my cleaning magic moved through me, I felt it pushing into my head and the cobwebs cleared up. It wasn't as if my thoughts returned to me so much as the strangeness receded.

Had I just cleaned away insanity?

A glance at my status had me wincing.

```
Health 111/115
Stamina 84/125
Mana 76/105
```

I had lost health to that scream, not to mention the heavy cost to my mana reserves to wipe the insanity away. And yet I still didn't have the slightest clue what the thing screeching at me had been.

The options I had were pretty simple. I could return to Rockstack right away. The few silvers I'd get from finding the Tulips might not be worth all the trouble. Or I could look for the thing making the noise and at least see what it was.

The third option, and the one I chose, was to push off the wall and head over to the next building.

I did so slowly, cautious of the world around me and wary of anything that made any noise. I was going to snoop around that final building and at least try to get an idea of what had happened here.

The Dunwich site was kind of creepy, but in the full light of day there wasn't anything to worry about.

Something scuffed against a rock and I turned around towards the dungeon entrance to see a monster waddling out from behind a rock. It was about the size of a big dog, with, at a glance, seven feet and three arms that ended in long-fingered hands. Its mouth reached from just below the hole where a nose should have been to its upper chest, a gaping pit in its front that dribbled with saliva.

Pale skin chafed against a rock as it wiggled against it, the stone digging into flesh that peeled off in lumps. It opened its mouth wider and a pair of long tentacles slid out of it to rub at its side.

"Nope," I muttered.

*A hungry Dunwich Abomination (level 8).*

"Nopity, nope, nope, nope."

The abomination must have heard me because it turned its strangely dog-like head my way and locked eyes with me. Much to my growing horror, the monster's skin began to shift and warp and between one moment and the next it turned the same colour as the stones behind it and became nearly impossible to see from afar. That was, until it started wobbling towards me.

"Oh shoot!" I said as I turned and started running away.

The abomination screamed. It sounded human.

**You have heard the screech of a creature of madness! Your mind is shaken.**

I stumbled forwards, then came to a slow stop. Why had I been running? It was probably a nice monster. And it was hungry. I could feed it!

Cleaning magic burst through me and my mind cleared in fits and starts. The abomination was closer.

I ran, putting every effort into outpacing and outdistancing the monster on my tail. There were some rocks ahead which I thought to weave through, until they started to wiggle and move my way.

"Oh no. No, no," I said between pants.

A leap brought me over the line of abominations and let me shoot past them, but I could tell that they were still right on my heels.

The cliffs were ahead, a dip in the ground that would lead me to the forests below. I didn't have time for the normal path, not when it meant looping back and forth a few times.

This bun was not going to get caught by any number of tentacle monsters.

I shot off the side of the cliff with a squeak, my stamina reserves dipping down as I tried to make get as far from the cliff's edge as I could.

I crashed into a tree.

Something screeched behind me before a sickening splat sounded out across the region.

**Congratulations! You have caused Dunwich Abomination, level 7, to drop dead! Bonus Exp was granted for splattering a monster above your level!**

Luckily for me, I had aimed at a large pine, so other than a body-full of sharp needles, I was mostly okay as the tree bent back with the impact then swayed to return to its original position.

Turning, I looked at the top of the hill to see six abominations all standing in a row and glaring at me. "Hah, Made it!" I called back.

They sprouted large, deformed wings.

"Oh, that's not cool," I said as I started to scramble down the tree. Forget the flowers and forget Dunwich. It was a silly place for silly people, and I didn't want to be anywhere near it. It would suck to tell Dylan that I had failed, but better to fail a small quest than get tentacle monstered.

The abominations landed in the woods just as I hit the ground and the chase continued.

Trees blurred past as I ran deeper and deeper into the forest, my path hampered every few meters by fallen trees and thick brush. The abominations weren't as fast, but they just barrelled through the bushes in their way, not even breaking their flailing stride.

And that's when I ran face first into a very angry tree.

# Chapter Thirty
# A Very Handsome Tree

I stared at the tree.

The tree glared right back.

*An irritated Dryad Tree Tender (level ??).*

I knew that I should have maybe been a bit more worried about the abominations following behind me, because... well, the because was rather obvious, they were angry madness-inducing tentacle monsters which wanted to eat me, that was a lot of reasons to avoid them.

Still, I had just literally run into a tree person and I could at the very least apologize.

The tree man was tall, with bark-brown skin that was rough and textured over his shoulders and sides and pecs, but over the more flexible muscles it looked smooth like the skin of a tree just beneath its bark, it even had a soft green look to it. His hair was long and whippy, like the branches of a willow and his legs were thick and literally trunk-like.

He also had a really nice six pack and the kind of squarish shovel-like jaw that I was really digging. "Hey," I said before running my fingers through my hair to straighten it up a little. "Sorry for running into you, Mister Dryad, sir," I said.

The tree-man's eyes narrowed.

"Tell you what," I said as I kept my eyes on his and not on his chest. "How about we go out for lunch. I'll pay. To apologize. I'm sure they have vegan meals at the inn."

Judging by the increasingly irritated look on the dryad's face it was clear that I wasn't very good at the whole flirting thing. Unfortunately, my only wingmen were a group of monsters that decided to interrupt my moment by bursting through the bushes behind me, tentacles whipping out ahead of them.

I jumped away, making it to the lower branches of a tree a little ways away before turning around and holding my shovel close to my chest. I couldn't just leave Mister Dryad to be swarmed by the abominations, not when he was going to be outnumbered six to one.

The dryad's hand shot out, catching the whipping tentacles of the abomination in the lead before he yanked the monster closer. His other arm shot forwards, fist burying itself into the monster up to the wrist.

The abomination struggled, its many hands grasping at the dryad, at first to find purchase, then with increasing desperation until thorny vines burst out from under its skin and started wrapping around its body.

I had to look away. The sight of the abomination, already on the gross side, being mulched by thorns the size of daggers, was just too much.

**Congratulations! Your ally has made Dunwich Abomination, level 8, push up daisies! Bonus Exp was granted for eliminating a monster above your level! Due to not being the primary combatant your reward is reduced!**

Mister Dryad grabbed the next abomination and started doing terrible things to it, but there were four others, and they did not take kindly to their friends being pulped. Tentacles whipped out towards Mister Dryad and one of the monsters clamped down around his leg with its big nasty teeth.

I couldn't just watch.

Screwing up my courage, I reminded myself that the abominations were big mean monsters and that it was okay to fight them. Sure, I had been the one to invade their home, but they were over-reacting with their long chase and their madness-inducing screams.

I jumped off the branch I was on and landed on the head of the rear-most abomination, sending it planting face-first into the ground before I bounced off and landed next to it. My spade came down on its head with a clang so hard it made my hands rattle.

It didn't seem to do much to hurt the monster, but it did distract it.

Then a tentacle grabbed me by the ankle and started dragging me towards one of the other abominations.

"Oh no, no no no," I said as I spun around and bonked the abomination behind me on the noggin. It didn't do much.

I chopped at the tentacle with the edge of my spade, then hit it again and again until it sliced off with a wet squelch and I was free to shoot up and into the trees above.

Mister Dryad had used the distraction to take out another one of the monsters. The two I had distracted waddled after me as I circled around Mister Dryad while he finished off their friend. The moment he was done, he turned to the abominations that weren't looking his way and crashed into them like a falling tree.

It didn't take very long from there.

**Congratulations! Your team has eliminated five opponents (Dunwich Abomination, level 7 x3; Dunwich Abomination, level 8; Dunwich Abomination, level 9)! Bonus Exp was granted for killing a monster above your level! Due to not being the primary combatant your reward is reduced!**
**Bing Bong! Congratulations, your Cinnamon Bun class has reached level 5!**
*Mana +10*
*Magic +10*
**You have gained: One Class Point**

I landed on the ground next to Mister Dryad and panted with a mix of exhilaration and adrenaline-fueled desperation that was only just fading. Then the smell of all the abominations hit me and I gagged.

It had been easy to ignore the stench when I was busy running for my life, but now that I had a moment to relax, I had no choice but to endure the stink. It was like inhaling raw sewage. My stomach surged, and it was all I could do not to lose my breakfast.

Mister Dryad didn't seem to enjoy it any more than I did, not if the way he stomped off was any indication.

I followed after him, both of us moving upwind from the corpses of the abominations that were even now rotting at an accelerated pace. I could celebrate the level up when I wasn't choking on stinky air.

Mister Dryad walked a little ways away, then turned around to face me with his big arms crossed over his chest.

I smiled sheepishly at him and rubbed a hand behind my neck. "So, ah, I'm sorry about all of that. I didn't mean to bring those things into your home. They kind of followed me. If there's anything I can do to make it up to you, please tell me! I want to be friends!"

The tree person glared.

"I really am sorry," I said. "I was looking for some flowers when they kind of ambushed me, and the forest seemed like the safest place to run off to. But I learned my lesson! I'll be a lot more careful next time I go snooping around." It looked down towards my feet, then I caught sight of something from the corner of my eye and gasped. "You're injured!" I said.

Mister Dryads thick legs were covered in small scratches, the sort that would probably heal over in a little while. Those had to be from the tentacles. The wounds that caught my eye were the large, jagged bite marks around his knee and calves. They looked deep and there was something leaking out of them.

I stumbled forwards and Mister Dryad stepped back.

Looking up, I met his eye, then gestured to his leg. "Let me see, please? I can clean out the wound, at least, and I have some cloth to bandage it up."

The tree looked at me for a long time, then slowly nodded.

Smiling, I got down on one knee before him while slipping off my backpack. I regretted not buying any healing potions while I was at the alchemist's shop. Maybe some salve of sorts. It would have been the smart thing to do, but doing the smart thing wasn't always something I was good at.

I carefully pressed a hand next to the bite and winced a little as I took it in from up close. The bark-like skin was split open, each jagged hole liberally smeared with some sort of putrid purplish… stuff. I didn't want to touch it. There was also something coming out of the wound, brownish and sticky looking. Sap? That would make sense.

I idly wondered if Mister Dryad could make me some maple syrup, then banished the thought.

A glance at my status showed that I had plenty of mana, so I fired off a powerful burst of cleaning magic aiming for the wounds and the gunk within them.

The purplish stuff fizzled away as my magic rushed to it. Mister Dryad shifted but didn't object otherwise. He did protest when I pulled out some long strips of cloth from my backpack and started tying them around his leg. "Hey, you can't just leave this uncovered. It'll get all infected and then it'll take forever to heal. I don't know what kind of infections work on a tree person, but I bet they're not fun."

He paused and let me bind his wound with my makeshift bandage. I made sure to leave a cute little bow on the end, that way he could impress all the cute dryad girls. It would show off his manly 'look at me injuries' side, and also his cute feminine side. I wondered if he'd let me play with his willowy hair. I bet I could make it look really cool if I braided it.

"So, what does a handsome treeboy like you do for fun around here?" I asked.

Mister Dryad looked at me for a long, long time, then he opened his mouth. "… Fun?"

I blinked. "Eh? You can talk?" I asked.

He nodded with the kind of speed you'd expect from a tree—which was to say, fairly slowly.

"Oh, wow. Okay, cool! I didn't know dryads could talk. This is really neat."

He pointed to me. "…Talk."

"Yes! I can talk too, of course."

"… Too… much," he finished.

I almost collapsed. "No! I don't talk too much! I talk just enough, I swear. I'm sorry, it's just when I meet someone new I want to know everything about them so sometimes I ask too many questions and I guess I do come on a little strongly, don't I?"

He nodded slowly again. He turned around a little, looking deeper into the woods and I had the impression that he was getting bored with the conversation.

"S-so, I'm looking for a flower," I said. "Actually, wait, I never got your name!"

He sighed, a noise like wind ruffling through leaves.

"Was that your name?" I asked. "Oh right, I'm being silly again. My name is Broccoli Bunch. Like the veggie!"

"…No." He shifted a little. "Oak."

"Your name's Oak? That's a great name for a treeboy! I'm Broccoli, but I already told you that. So, ah, I'm wondering if you could help me. Not that you need to, you've helped me a ton already today."

Oak closed his eyes and I had the impression that he might have been praying to whatever a tree prayed to. "…Help?" he asked.

"Yes! I'm looking for a flower."

Oak tilted his head to the side, then he waved his arm across the ground and all sorts of little wildflowers sprouted out of the soil and bloomed to life, their colourful petals turning a patch of the dreary forest into a brilliant rainbow patch full of life.

"Whoa," I said as I knelt down to poke at the flowers. I recognized them vaguely as common cornflowers and poppies. "Pretty!"

"…Flowers."

"Yes, they are," I agreed with a beaming smile. I set my backpack down, careful not to squish any of Oak's flowers, and pulled out my herbology book.

Oak frowned at it. "…Dead brother."

I froze. The book had, admittedly, probably been made from a tree of one sort or another. "I'm sorry," I said. "I found this a while ago. I can't say whether it was made with respect to your brother or not."

Oak considered that, then shrugged.

I opened to the dog-eared page with the Two-Lipped Tulips and showed it to Oak. "This is what I'm looking for," I said.

He looked for a long time. "…Weed. Cull."

"Cull? You want to get rid of this kind of flower?" I asked.

He nodded.

"Well then, maybe we can help each other!"

## Chapter Thirty-One
# In Which Broccoli Gives the Locals Weaponry

Oak led me back towards the Dunwich site, something that would have made me nervous if I hadn't seen him tear an abomination apart with his bare hands.

"So, where are those flowers?" I asked as I skipped along behind my new buddy. I decided that even though we were a boy and a girl walking through a forest together it didn't count as a date. Sure, he had given me flowers, but I didn't think there was any romantic intent behind the gesture.

Too bad. Oak was kind of cute for a tree.

Oak, being a tree… man of few words, pointed to the cliffs ahead, then to the rocky areas around their base. "Weeds," he said.

"Neat. So, what do you consider a weed? I would have thought that all plants would be good plants for you."

Oak gave me a strange look, one I recognized as the 'you're being very dumb' look people gave me sometimes. "Weeds… bad."

"Well, that does explain some things, I guess."

We ambled past the first cliff and to a rocky bit of terrain next to it where the ground was covered in sharp rocks and craggy bits of dirt that seemed super dry from afar. The trees there were few and far between, all of them leafless and emaciated. Oak pointed to one of them, then to its base. "Weed."

I moved closer and saw what he meant. There was a Two-Lipped Tulip growing around and into a dying tree, its long, thorny roots coiled around the tree's bark while a few of its fanged flowers were biting into it.

The instructions in my book only said that I should be careful not to get bitten myself. I thought it would be fairly simple, but by the look of it the plant was more like a snake than merely a very angry bush.

I reached out with my spade and poked at the stems before taking a long step back.

Flowers snapped at the air where my spade had been.

"Yikes. That is one nasty flower," I said.

"Weed," Oak repeated.

"You got that right. I wouldn't want any of those in my garden. I kind of need the flowers though. Tricky."

"No... touch," he warned. After a moment he decided to add to his warning. "Bite."

I looked up to the tree then, with a careless shrug, hopped up and onto one of the lower branches. It creaked under my weight but didn't crack. With the edge of my spade serving as an axe, I chopped off a long branch and tossed it next to Oak before joining him.

"Cut... brother?" Oak asked. He didn't look pleased at how I had treated his... brother, but he didn't look ready for violence either.

"Sorry, but with this I can help your brother." It swished the branch in the air a few times, making sure that it was still fairly sturdy. Then I whipped it into the bush, skimming just over the top and slicing through a dozen stems. Some of the flowers bit into the wood, but that only helped to tear them out.

I grinned as I swiped again and cut through more of the bush. It didn't go as well the second time, but that was alright.

"See, you just need the right tool."

"Tool," Oak repeated as he stared at the long branch. He looked at the tulips again. "Cannot... touch."

"Right, so you make something to touch it from afar for you." I brought the branch closer, then pried some of the flowers off the haft with my knife. They came off with a few deft flicks. I pulled out my old haversack from my backpack and tossed the flowers into it. The tough old material would probably handle a few bitey flowers.

Oak looked at my stick for a long time. "Tool," he said again.

"Yeah. A spear would be better though."

"Spear?"

I nodded. Dryads probably didn't have much use for spears and the like, but it could come in handy. "It's a long stick, nice and tough, and at the end you have a spearhead. That's, ah, like a leaf, but very sharp and hard. That way you can cut things from far away." I wiggled my spade around. It wasn't exactly spear-like, but it was close enough.

Oak tilted his head to the side and swayed a little as he thought, then he bent down and touched the ground. Out came a long pole, as tall as he was, and at its end a long wavy leaf made of wood.

"Can I see?" I asked as I gestured to the spear.

Oak let me take his spear and examine it. It was kind of neat, though the leaf bit was a little bit too flexible still, and not nearly sharp enough. It looked flimsy, too flexible and whippy.

"Here, make the sharp bits like this," I said as I showed him my knife. "And if you can, a little bit less flexible. I think some flexibility is good, but not too much. But I'm not a spear person."

Oak studied the metal blade, then poked his finger with it a few times. "Tool," he repeated.

"That's right!"

His next spear was much nicer, with a slightly thinner haft and with a sharp wooden point that had little veiny imprints on it. It was deceptively sharp and a fair bit heavier, though not so much that it was hard to swing around.

"Nice," I said as I weighed it and sliced at the air inexpertly. A few swipes at the bush sent bits of it flying as it cut through. "Insight."

*A living spear of uncommon quality, new.*

"Good work, Oak!" I said.

Oak nodded and made a second spear for himself, this one much longer and heavier. We got to work chopping up the plant from afar, then Oak approached it and stomped on the flower-less bush a few times. He really didn't like weeds.

The dryad touched the dying tree with a palm, then moved forwards and wrapped his arms around it in a deep hug.

The branches shifted and the tree's colour lightened from the rotting brown it had been. Tiny buds sprouted all along its branches and opened up to reveal pinkie-sized leaves.

Oak backed away and picked up his spear. "Healed," he said.

"Wow, that was great!" I walked up to the tree, making sure that I didn't step into any biting flowers, then gave it a hug too. A burst of cleaning magic shot into it and I saw bits of flower poof out of its base and disintegrate in the air. Had they been stuck in the tree's base?

"No... healing?" Oak asked.

"Me? Not really, no. All I can do is clean. And holy heck did that ever cost a lot of mana. I'll have to be more careful with the next one!" I grinned at my new buddy and then got to work picking up flowers from the ground. Oak had trampled a few and we had both chopped some up with our new spears, but it was okay, there were plenty more tulip bushes around.

As we moved over to the next tree, I tried explaining other tools to Oak. He didn't seem to care much for most of them, but when I explained what bows were, he paid a lot of attention. "They're like a curved branch with a string between the two ends that's kept tense. So when you pull back on the string and then let go it snaps back into place. If you put a smaller stick, an arrow, against the string it'll fly really far. Oh, but you need fletching. Um, that's like a feather on the end, but I'm sure a leaf would work in a pinch."

Oak nodded slowly. "Tools," he said.

"Yes," I agreed. "Tools are really handy. You can hunt things with a bow, though I guess you don't need that if you can just grab things with like, roots and suchlike."

I wasn't sure how many flowers I collected, but it had to be close to fifty because my haversack was filled to the brim. I shut the bag closed and made a knot with its drawstring before flinging it over my back.

A glance at the sky revealed that it had begun to put on its night colours. It was far past the time for me to head out. I hefted my new spear and gave Oak a big smile. "I need to go, Oak, but maybe we'll see each other again someday."

Oak looked at me with none of the tension and annoyance he had when I first bumped into him. "Grow," he said.

**Congratulations! Through repeated actions your Friendmaking skill has improved and is now eligible for rank up! Rank E is a free rank!**

I laughed aloud and gave Oak a big, clumsy hug. "I will!" I said as I took off.

The trek back was just a little melancholic, but it was fun all the same. The path grew darker by the minute, until I could hardly see a step ahead of me. I considered finding a place to hide in the trees for the night, or taking out a candle and just walking, but then something stirred over my chest and a yawning Orange poked her head out from my bandoleer.

"Wow, you're very good at sleeping," I said.

She gave me a flat look before gazing around.

"Yeah, we're not exactly lost, but making it back will be tricky. I can't see very well."

Orange made a huffing gesture, though it was soundless, then bounded off my chest and walked ahead of me. She glowed. It was faint, but still more than enough to light the path ahead.

"Awesome," I said.

The kitty turned and gave me a look as if to say 'I know.'

We arrived at Rockstack to find the gates closed and barred, but the walls weren't so tall that I couldn't just jump up to one of their uneven sides, then up to the very top.

The outpost was lit up by a hundred candles flickering in the night. Laughter and light flowed out of the Hop on Inn and a sea of firefly-like lights moved around the tents that took up the back of the outpost. The shops were darker, but some still had light pouring out of their top floors.

I landed in a crouch inside the walls and shifted my packs around as I walked towards the inn. The talking and music and sounds of cutlery grew louder as I approached, as did the scent of delicious food wafting through the air.

Grinning, I plucked Orange out of the air and set her on my shoulder, then pushed my way into the inn. I wasn't home, exactly, but it was a nice place to be. I had had a tiny adventure for the day and was more than ready for a heavy meal and a long sleep.

I found a seat by the bar and slumped down. "Food please," I asked as I fished out some coppers from my bag.

"You're alive?" Juliette asked. "I was almost starting to get worried. Where were you?"

"Near the Dunwich site," I said. A few heads turned my way, some eyeing my strange spear, others my well-worn but clean gear. I wished I could read minds, if only to know what they thought of me, but I dismissed that thought soon enough.

Juliette shook her head as she placed a mug of something warm before me. "I'll get you somezing to eat, you fool girl."

"Hey, I'm not that foolish! I levelled up after all."

"Humph. Zen we'll get you a meal to celebrate wiz."

I leaned onto the counter, eyes closed as I soaked into the ambiance of the inn and the warmth of the hearth that warmed my back even from across the room. "That would be nice, really nice," I said.

# Chapter Thirty-Two
# Hop on Out

I arrived at the main room of the Hop on Inn, tummy protesting its lack of breakfast and the rest of me still miffed that I wasn't in bed. I was so tired that my feet dragged and I had a hard time keeping my eyes open, but I had stuff to do, so I couldn't just laze around all morning.

The room was nearly empty of delvers, only a few of them sitting at the back and minding their own business while the barmaid swept the floor or replaced chairs. Juliette was in her spot behind the bar, idly flipping through a big book and making notes with quick twitches of a quill. Her own version of the ledger I had found in Threewells, maybe?

"Heya," I said as I slumped into a seat before her. I was only wearing my normal clothes because putting on my armour was too much to ask for before breakfast time. "Food, please," I said before I let a handful of coppers clatter onto the counter.

Juliette snort-croaked.

My head landed on the bar and I might have snoozed because the next thing I knew there was a plateful of eggs and strips of meat and bread waiting for me. That energized me a bit. Juliette obviously hired the very best cooks because the food she served always tasted exceptional.

"So, what are you doing today?" Juliette asked.

"I don't know," I said after I swallowed. "Dylan gave me a quest yesterday, but it's done. I guess I can go hand that in. But after that, I have no idea. Dunwich was way too scary, I'm not going back there until I'm at least level one hundred."

Juliette hummed. "I'll see you in some decades zen," she said. "If you're not going to do anyzing productive, zen you should consider heading out to Port Royal early."

"You mentioned that the next caravan isn't leaving for nearly a week," I said.

The barkeep started to clean her counter, a habitual gesture, I noticed. "Zere's a group leaving today for Port Royal. Just a small one. More danger, but you wouldn't have to wait as much, and I zink zat maybe more danger doesn't scare you."

"Really? Do you know when they're heading out exactly? From where?"

Juliette nodded. "Come back in a few hours, I'll introduce you to zeir leader. Zat is, if you decide to go."

"I'll think on it," I said as I returned to my meal. I was done all too soon and had to argue with myself not to order another helping out of sheer gluttonous greed. Back to my room I found Orange sleeping on my still warm pillow. I slid on all of my gear, put on my backpack and plopped my hat on. Orange went into my bandoleer again with minimal protest.

The weather had taken a turn for the grey, the skies hanging low overhead and the air strong with the scent of oncoming rain. The cheery people I had seen yesterday were all gone, and the few folk still hanging around the outpost moved around in a hurry.

I had a few things to get rid of. The plants for Dylan the alchemist came first though. Stepping into the clinic with a spear and a spade was a little strange, but it didn't seem to bother anyone since there was no one to bother. The sylph I had seen last time was nowhere to be found.

A few knocks on the window to Dylan's section of the shop summoned the clumsy grenoil alchemist. "Yes yes?" he asked.

"Hey Dylan," I said before plopping the haversack full of flowers onto the counter. "I got your quest done," I said.

"Truly?" He eyed my sack, then opened the top to peak within. "Incredible. And such a large haul. I'll need to count these. A moment please."

I didn't get to protest as he moved to the far end of his lab space, shoved things aside on one of his counters and dumped out all of the flowers. He didn't even flinch when one of them chomped on his gloved hands.

I heard him mutter as he counted the pile, then nod before coming back. "Seventy-eight in all. Some are damaged. I'd give you less for zem, but you brought more zan I expected in one go. You're quite good. Did you want ze excess back?"

"Ah, no? I wouldn't know what to do with them. But maybe we could trade them? I ran into these creepy monsters called Abominations out there and I realized after that I didn't have so much as a healing potion."

"Zat's foolhardy," Dylan said. "A good potion can be ze difference between life and death." His mouth turned down in a scowl and he limped off, coming back a moment later with five bottles. Two were plain old glass bottles with cork tops, but the other three were strange. They looked like three separate bottles that had had their tops fused together into one opening. "Two health potions. Common quality. Forties. Zree trifectas. Twenties."

"Um. Are the numbers the price?" I asked.

Dylan stared. "You're not familiar wiz potions?" When I shook my head, he went on to explain. "Ze number given to a potion is how much impact it will have, usually as a flat percentage. A good potion maker will round it down."

"So those forties give forty percent of my health back?"

He nodded. "Depending on ze severity of ze injury. Zese won't regrow limbs, but zey will assist in ze healing process. Scrapes, minor burns, bruising and such."

"And the weird three bottle potions?" I pointed at the three he had set to the side.

"Trifectas are generally weaker and more expensive, zey are also prized more by ze sort of people who have run-ins wiz Abominations while picking flowers. Zey will increase all of your main stats wizout interfering wiz each ozer. Some potions can do zat. You don't want to take a healing potion, zen learn zat when mixed wiz your water breathing potion it turns into a poison in your stomach."

"Yikes," I said. "Does that happen a lot?"

"No," Dylan said. "But it has happened before. Zat's why trifectas are popular. Also, zey help wiz many zings at once. Most delvers zat are low on heath are low on ozer zings too."

"That makes sense. So the potions for the extra flowers?" I asked.

"And for my peace of mind," Dylan said. He rooted around under the counter and then plopped down a single gold coin. "And zis is yours, for ze flowers you delivered."

"Thanks Dylan," I said as I picked the coin up and clasped it close. That was a thousand copper right there. A hundred nights at an inn. Totally worth almost getting tentacle monstered. "I'll see you around!" I said once I was done stashing away the potions. One of the trifecta potions went into my bandoleer for easy access and the rest were dropped into my backpack with some cloth wraps around them to keep them nice and safe.

It had started to drizzle a little while I was inside, just a faint misting of rain that stopped and restarted twice in the time it took me to walk over to the general goods store. I considered selling my spear at the blacksmith's shop, but the lady working there didn't seem all that friendly to begin with.

"Hello," I called out over the jingle of bells over the door.

The old grenoil by the counter looked up and gave her a big smile. "Ah, hello zere, young miss," he said. "Looking for anyzing in particular, or just looking?"

"A bit of both," I admitted. "I need stuff for a long trek. I'll be heading over to Port Royal later."

"Ah, zen you will need some zings, yes. Are you walking or taking a carriage?"

"Um, walking, I think."

He nodded at that. "Zen food, a tent if you don't have one, a pot to cook in. Do you have a warm blanket?"

"I do, but another wouldn't hurt. Do you have all of that equipment stored in a way that I can carry?"

He smiled wider and moved off to the back with a 'one moment' called over his shoulder. He returned with a backpack with a rolled-up tarp above it and a pot hanging off one side. "Zis is what zey call a traveller's pack in any proper city. Everyzing you need for a week on ze road. Ze food isn't tasty, but it's nourishing enough, and it's light."

We both undid the pack together and what followed was a quick flurry of adding and removing things. I didn't need some of the things he had added like water purifying tablets, but wanted others, like a proper flask and one of those nifty magic lights meant to be strapped to one's forehead.

I made a small tally of all my gear, just to keep track of it because for some reason the world didn't have handy inventories for everyone to use which was just totally unfair.

- One and a half jars of honey
- One silver candle holder with a dozen fresh candles
- A small firestarter
- Two blankets
- Some bits and pieces of cloth
- A length of rope
- Herbology book
- 79 Copper coins
- 50 lesser silver coins
- 8 lesser gold coins
- A sack full of hardtack and beans
- Two healing potions (40)
- Three Trifecta potions (20)
- A magic headlamp
- One waterproof tent
- A poncho
- A tiny compass.

That—as well as the things I was wearing, my spear and my spade—was the sum-total of the things I had. Not that much, but way more than I had started with. I thanked the shopkeeper, handed over a few silvers and told him to keep my beaten old backpack. The new one was a little bit snugger anyway, which would make it easier to jump with.

My final stop was the inn. "Hey Juliette," I said to the older grenoil lady who had moved out from behind her bar to chat with someone I didn't recognize.

"Broccoli," Juliette said. "You're almost late. Zis is Milread, she's ze leader of ze party heading over to Port Royal."

I looked Milread up and down, she looked like a bird-person, like the blacksmith. Tall, almost a full head taller than me, with a sharp nose and inhuman eyes set in an otherwise ordinary, if pretty, face. Her uncovered arms had long brown and black feathers sticking out of them with sharp talons at the end and her bare feet were rough and ended in huge claws. "Hey there, lil' human. Never seen a harpy before?"

"Ah, not really from up close," I admitted.

"If you come with, you'll be seeing plenty of me, at least. Juliette says you're good people, and she's never done wrong by me yet."

"Oh, I just helped her a little with the cleaning, not much else, really," I said before looking at Juliette. The woman huffed.

"Broccoli's a good kid," she said. "Actually, before you go. Broccoli, can you do me a favour?"

"Sure thing," I said.

Juliette reached down the front of her apron and pulled out a letter with a waxy seal on the front. "Zere is an inn near ze east gate of Port Royal. Can't miss it. Ze owner is called Julien. He is my oaf of a husband. Give him zis, yes? I made a note to give you a room for ze night."

"Thank you!" I said as I took the letter and immediately stashed it away in my backpack. Then I wrapped my arms around the wide-eyed grenoil. "Thank you for everything, Juliette, I had a lot of fun! I hope we see each other again!"

"You ready to go?" Milread asked. "The others are waiting."

"Yes, I'm coming. I bought everything I need for a few days of walking. Are there a lot of us?"

"Calm down, little chick, you'll have plenty of time to make friends," Milread said, and I instantly knew I was going to like her.

# Chapter Thirty-Three

# The First Step in a Short Journey

"Hi! My name is Broccoli Bunch!" I declared with one arm raised to head height and waving. "This is Orange," I said as I raised my other hand to show off my cute kitty companion. Orange glared at my new potential friends.

There were three of them, two if I didn't count Milread. Both were grenoil, one a boy and the other a girl.

"Hello", the man said with a nod of his big froggy head. He had a neat speckled pattern across his skin that I had never seen on a grenoil before and a pair of strange goggles hanging around his neck. Other than that, he looked like a business grenoil that had taken a tumble into some mud.

The girl grenoil looked a lot younger and a whole lot sadder. Her focus was almost entirely on the ground underfoot, one hand absently rubbing at the pommel of her rapier-like sword.

"You two ready to head out?" Milread asked. When she got nods from both of them, she turned towards a one-horse wagon sitting in the middle of the road. "Well then, we just need to settle, and we can be off. Broccoli, you missed it, but I'm charging a sil for the trip. It's mostly to keep Missy fed."

"Is Missy the horse?" I guessed as I took in the horse hitched to the wagon, she—I guessed her gender because a boy horse called Missy would be a little strange—looked like a perfectly ordinary horse.

"That's right. Missy will save us some walking," Milread said. "I hope one of you feels like holding the reins, I hate wearing gloves." She wiggled her hands to show the long talons she had.

The two grenoil found some coins to hand over to Milread, and I did the same. One sil wasn't much for a multi-day trip. In fact, that was a great place to start a conversation. "So, Milread, why are you heading to Port Royal?" I asked.

"I'm a courier. I go from Port Royal to this outpost to Fort Tempete and then Deepmarsh and back. Round trip takes about two weeks. It's a living." The harpy flapped her arms and kicked off the ground to land on the forward part of the wagon where a bench was built into it.

The other two hopped onto the back so I decided to join her at the front.

"All aboard?" Milread asked. "If you forgot something back here, it's not my problem." She grabbed the reins from a hook next to which a lantern was hanging and handed them over to me. "You've done this before?" she asked.

"Nope, but I like horses," I said as I took the reins. "Yah!" I screamed as I whipped the long leather cords.

When the wagon finally stopped, I ended up being sat in the back with the grenoil man.

The floor of the wagon wasn't very comfortable, especially since it was a small wagon with only two wheels and I was sitting right on top of the axle so that—even across the flattened ground in the outpost—my bum was bouncing all over the place and was going to get sore in no time.

I ended up pulling out all the blankets I had and placing them on the floor to act as padding. The grenoil across from me harrumphed then did the same, pulling out a thick quilt from his pack and sitting on it with a humph.

We moved past the gates of the outpost and I waved to the two guards who looked just as bored today as they did the day before. One of them even waved back.

And then we were on the road.

"So, why were you in Rockstack?" I asked the grenoil man.

The grenoil looked at me. "You're a chatty one, aren't you?" he asked.

"Yup! I sure am."

"Great. I was here for ze dungeon. I got what I came for, so now I'm heading home." He leaned against the wooden sides of the wagon, then shifted to try and get comfortable.

"You live in Port Royal?" I asked. "Ohh, I didn't get your name. I'm sorry. I'm Broccoli Bunch."

"Severin Bleriot," he said. "And no, I don't."

The grenoil girl leaned back a bit. "I'm Noemi," she said.

"This is great," I said. "I'm making so many friends today." The wagon went over a rut on the road and I laughed as I had to grab the edge to stop from tumbling around.

"World's tits, what kind of potion is she on?" Noemi muttered. I don't think I was supposed to hear that, so I didn't comment. I wasn't on any sort of potion, not unless friendship was a drug, in which case I was an addict.

"So, mister Severin, if you're not from Port Royal, where are you from?" I asked. We were moving at a fairly slow pace, no faster than I could walk really, but without any of the effort that came from walking. If it wasn't for all the friend-making potential on the trip, I might have found it a little boring.

The older grenoil closed his eyes. "I'm from Deepmarsh," he said.

"That's twice now I've heard about Deepmarsh, is that a town nearby?"

Severin opened his eyes and stared at me. "It's ze capital of ze kingdom. Ze Kingdom of Deepmarsh… Ze Kingdom we're in right now."

My smile became a little fixed. "I kind of got lost," I said. "And I didn't exactly have a map, you know?"

Milread looked over her shoulder. "Why didn't you just open your map?"

"My map?" I asked.

The harpy sighed. "I know not everyone uses it, but did you really not know? Focus on the idea of a map, your magic should take care of the rest."

I did as she asked, because even if it was a joke, and it didn't feel like one, there was nothing to lose. It took a bit of focus, but I felt as if I had an option just waiting there that I had never toyed with, like an itch that I didn't notice until it was suddenly the only thing I could focus on.

"You have got to be kidding me," I said as I stared. I could see all of Threewells and the curving path I took to get from where I had appeared all the way to Rockstack. "I had a map the entire time? Does it auto-update? That is, if I leave, and the area changes, will my map reflect that if I don't know about it?"

"No, it doesn't work zat way," Severin said. I had the impression he was enjoying my disbelief. "What level are you at? I don't recall seeing you wiz ze other delvers."

"I'm level five," I said, my attention still on the map. It was obvious that the scale was off, but it was pretty accurate as far as I could tell. Everything I had seen was there, with big gaps for the places I hadn't really explored except from afar. "Gosh I could have used this this past week."

"A poorly educated human, you must be from Mattergrove," Severin said. "I assume zat you're heading to Port Royal to find passage back home?"

I looked away from the map for a moment to refocus on Severin. "Eh? No, no, I'm heading there to join the exploration guild and make a ton of friends!"

"Ah, an explorer. I suppose zat would make us rivals," Severin said.

"Rivals?" I asked.

He nodded. "Ze exploration and delvers guilds have been at each ozer's zroats for generations. It's mostly harmless, zough I'm sure some eyes were browned in a bar fight or two over ze years."

"I guess that's okay," I said. "As long as it means we can still be friends."

Severin pressed his hands over his face. "Lady Hawk, would it be possible for your horse to move any faster?" he asked.

"Don't be grumpy, you old frog," Milread said. "The kid isn't that bad. She's just trying to make nice."

"Tch, fine. My apologies, miss Bunch. I did not mean to be short wiz you."

"It's okay," I said. "I come on a little strong sometimes. But I get so excited when I meet new people. I just want to be their friend right away, but most people need a bit of work before they're ready for that."

"I... see?" Severin said. "Well, you have two days to get used to us and us to you."

"Joy," Noemi muttered. It earned her a wing in the ribs from Milread.

I tried to be nice and stayed quiet for a little bit. Instead of talking I scratched Orange, who had crawled down to my lap at some point, behind the ears as I took in the fresh air and lack of sunshine. The skies were still a dreary grey and the roads were covered in little puddles, but at least the rain hadn't returned. The forests were... forests. I had been seeing forests all day.

"So, what class are you, Severin?" I asked by accident. The question had just kind of slipped out.

The grenoil croaked. "I'm a Mudmancer."

"Like a mud wizard?" I asked. "That's neat. So is it its own... branch of magic or is it a combo or like, earth and water? Wait, where's your staff?"

"I do not need to carry around a large stick to validate my masculinity," Severin said. He flicked his hand and a wand appeared between his fingers, a long piece of dark wood with silvery carvings all along its sides and a metal band near the handle.

"I carry a spear," I said before poking my spear with my foot. "I wonder what that says about my masculinity?" Milread snorted and even Noemi chuckled.

I had made my friends laugh! Bun one, lack of friends, zero!

"So, does having a wand help you cast spells?" I asked.

"You don't know anyzing about magic, do you?" he asked.

"Nobody taught me," I said. "If you want you could teach me, I'm an avid listener!"

His wand flicked away back into his sleeve. "Teachers are paid," he said.

"I have some coins," I said before pulling out my little pouch of coppers.

Severin eyed the pouch, then me for a moment. "I suppose it's ze choice between talking myself or hearing you prattle all ze way over to Port Royal, isn't it?"

"I am an excellent prattler." I reached into my pack and found my scroll of fireball and held it up. "Would this help any?" I asked.

He took it from me and unfolded it with an expert flick. It wasn't his first magic scroll, I guessed. "Yes actually, zis would. You've been trying to learn zis spell?"

"I wish I could start to try. I don't know the first thing about casting spells so I'm mostly just getting confused by all the diagrams."

The wagon bumped and hitched along the road for nearly a full minute before Severin made up his mind. "Very well. Two sil for two days of teaching. To be paid ze moment you cast your first fireball. It's a weak spell, a beginner one, it should be easy enough."

I scooted over so that I was on Severin's side and could see the scroll at the same time as him. He looked a little uncomfortable at that but didn't protest. "Okay! I'm ready to learn. I really want my next general skill to be fireball or something awesome like that."

"Zat would take some time, depending on your class."

"My class matters?" I asked.

He nodded. "You will tend towards skills zat suit your class most of ze time. You're a…" He narrowed his eyes at me. "Cinnamon Bun? Never heard of zat one, but it doesn't sound like a magic-focused class."

I thought that snooping at a person's class was rude, but Severin didn't seem to care. "I don't think it is. It's more like a… bard class, but without the music, I think."

"A social class zen," he said. "Learning a magic skill will be complicated zen, but not impossible. At ze very least you can make ze effort to cast zis spell, skill or no." He rolled the scroll up until only the first dozen lines were visible. "Zis one is outside of my specialty, but I zink teaching it will be simple. But if you know nothing about magic zen we will not skip ahead."

"I'm ready to learn! I said.

## Chapter Thirty-Four
# The Embers of Magic

Milread and Noemi were both listening as Severin, who insisted that I sit across from him, spoke to me. They must have thought it was just as interesting as I did.

"Magic is ze application of mana towards a specific task. Mana, in its natural state, will reflect ze environment it is in and zat environment will in turn reflect ze mana zat suffuses it. Ze great Ostri Desert has six sand-aspect dungeons wizin it zat keep ze climate inhospitably warm and dry. Ze Darkwoods we are in is home to a dungeon zat releases marsh-aspect mana."

"So dungeons give off mana that matches the environment?" I asked. "There are fire dungeons near volcanos and such?"

Severin made a wibbly-wobbly gesture. "Yes and no. Zis is a chicken and egg problem. You are familiar wiz ze analogy?" at my nod he continued. "Ze world produces all mana. Dungeons conduct zis mana to ze surface, like wells. Somewhere along zat path, the mana begins to resemble the environment.

Some dungeons don't match zeir location's ambient mana at first glance. Which is usually because mana always has two aspects. Zere is ze physical and ze metaphysical, but one of zese doesn't matter when casting somezing as infantile as fireball. It is enough zat you are aware zat mana has aspects zat are needed to cast a spell. Ze more complex parts you can learn at anozer time."

I shifted on the spot, eager to get to the more hands-on part of the lesson, but also curious to learn more. In the end it came down to Severin's preference, if he wanted to get to the practical parts I was okay with that. "I'm ready," I said.

"Calm down," he said. "We will get zrough ze basic zeory first. Mana aspects are important, it indicates how mana will behave. Ze same spell construct zat you use for fireball can be used for a windball or pureball spell wiz only slight tweaks to ze structure. If you want to cast an actual fireball, zen you need to take your natural mana and shift its aspect to zat of fire. Or you could do ze same to ze mana in ze air around us."

"I could conjure fireballs from nothing? Without touching my own mana… pool thing?" That sounded like it had a lot of very useful applications. Machine-gunning fireballs at my foes was a big 'yes' on the list of things I wanted to be able to do. As long as those foes were very mean and evil and okay to hurt and had already rejected all offers of friendship, of course. Maybe if I found them in the act of eating a baby or something.

"Yes. When you're a level forty archmagus you can do whatever you like with the mana in ze air around you," Severin said.

Noemi snorted a laugh. It didn't hold her mood up for long, but she did laugh.

"So, to re-explain as I am sure I will have to do many times. Mana has what we call aspects, mirrors of certain parts of nature. Fire-aspect mana is wild and ferocious. Water is tepid and calm and flows rather zan breaking. Earth is firm and tough. Zere are hundreds of aspects. Some people like to tie zem to a wheel of colours to see which aspect is near which ozer."

"Like… fire is red, water is blue?" I asked.

"Yes, exactly. Zose people are idiots. Mana doesn't care about colours or any such zing. Some aspects are bizarre. If you meet someone wiz insect aspect mana, run."

"O-kay?" I said. "So what kind of mana do I have? And how do I burn things with it?"

Milread turned around on the bench to face me. "You're not burning anything on my wagon, right?"

I shook my head violently from side to side until she looked back towards the road.

No fireballs on the wooden wagon. Noted.

"Give me your hand," Severin said.

"What?" I asked.

"Your hand." He gestured with his. "Put it in mine."

I placed my hand in his. He had calloused fingers that were at once wet and rough as they wrapped around my much smaller hands. "Like this?" I said and it was absolutely not a squeak. I was a bun of the world. I had held hands with boys (my dad counted!) before. This was nothing.

"Push mana towards your hands. You know how to do zis, yes?" he asked.

"Like when casting a skill? Yeah, I can do that." I pushed some mana towards my hands until my fingers tingled.

"More," he said, his mouth set in a big froggy scowl.

I pushed some more until my whole hand was tingly, as if I had sat on them for a few minutes and they had gone to sleep, but with less loss of sensation and a lot more magic. It felt as if my hand wanted to do something and do it right now.

"You use cleaning magic a lot?" he asked. At my nod, he went on. "It shows. You have cleaning aspect mana."

"Is that… good? Special? Rare and really awesome?" I asked as he let go of my hands and I took them back. I let the mana I had accumulated go as a burst of cleaning magic into the floor of the wagon that left it nice and shiny.

He made a dismissive noise. "It's not uncommon. Usually for ze serving staff. Cleaning aspect is close to holy, light and water aspects. Casting your fireballs will be tricky."

"Aww," I said. "So, how do I do it anyway?" I wasn't going to quit at the first setback!

"Fire aspect mana is needed first and foremost. Fire mana tends to consume a lot and grow rapidly. It moves quickly and burns hot. Take your mana and make it do zose zings. Zere are no indicators for whezer or not you have it right. Get it close and it should work for ze spell. As I said, fireball is a beginner spell, it is very forgiving if your mana control is lacking."

I focused on a hand, then looked up. "I have no idea how to do any of that."

Severin rubbed at the spot where his nose would be were he a human. "Look," he said. He brought his hand between us, then let me watch as a shimmering haze formed around it. It became more solid, then started to look a bit like gelatine that was wet and see-through. "Mud aspect. My mana's natural state. And now, fire." The shimmering mana stuff twisted and warped and was soon shivering a whole lot, then it started to wiggle as if in a heat haze, the edges flickering like tongues of fire.

"Awesome," I said as I stared at the nearly transparent flames. "So, I do that with my mana and then I get fireballs?" I asked.

"You do zis wiz your mana," he said before wiggling his hand as if to dry it, the mana fading away in moments. "And zen I teach you ze way to twist your mana into ze spell."

"Cool!" I said.

What followed was an hour of the wagon bumping along and moving at a decent clip through the forests while I stared at my hand and scowled fiercely at it. At some point I even upgraded the scowl to a full-blown pout but that didn't help much.

The skies, already dark and grey, opened up and let loose a torrent of rain that came down on us like a tipped-over bucket. Milread said some very unkind words to the sky as she pulled out a poncho from her pack and covered her arms so that her feathery arms wouldn't get wet. The grenoil with us didn't seem to care much about the rain.

I didn't mind it much myself, it was a warmer rain, a bit like taking a luke-warm shower, and the passage under some trees broke apart the raindrops in a neat way. I still took out my own poncho and settled it on my shoulders with the hood up and my hat atop it. In the end the rain was only a mild inconvenience, and one that came in handy when my hands started glowing. "Oh, look, look!" I said as I waved my hand at Severin.

The grenoil snorted. "Ze first step and it only took you an hour. I should have asked to be paid whezer you learned ze spell or not."

I laughed and stared at my glowing hand. My mana wasn't as muddy as Severin's. Instead it kind of flowed out like water and had an incandescence to it. "Praise the sun," I muttered under my breath.

"Guys, we have trouble," Milread said.

I snapped to attention, the glow in my hand poofing away along with a couple of points of mana as I looked around the woods and tried to spot the trouble. Fortunately, the trouble was easy to find. Unfortunately, it was all around us.

Pretty glowing lights bobbed out of the gloomy woods, most concentrated before the wagon but some flitting along the forests to our sides or daring to cross the ditches alongside the road to zip behind us.

"Pixies," Milread growled. She stood up on her bench and reached for her sword. I saw Noemi do the same and Severin's wand appeared in his hand. "Severin, you can do barrier magic?"

"I can."

"Good. Get the cart some cover from their lightning attacks. In this rain they'll be a nightmare to deal with. Noemi, rearguard. I'll focus on the bigger groups." Milread pulled off the hood of her poncho and made a growling noise deep in her throat as her long black-brown hair began to be plastered across her face.

"You're going to kill them?" I asked as I tracked the glowing motes.

"They're pests," Milread said. "They won't leave us alone and there's no outrunning them, not in this weather. One pothole and we'll be in a ditch when they come to pick us off. It's best to make a stand. They'll break before we do, don't worry."

"We could negotiate? Try talking to them?" I asked.

Milread snorted.

I opened my pack and rummaged around in a hurry. I found what I was looking for and stood up, hands tight around the last full jar of honey I had. I could do something here. I could stop my new friends from killing the pixies. I knew I could do it.

I looked at the determined cast to Milread's face and the resigned look on Noemi's. Both of them moved off the seat of the wagon, Milread patting Missy's sides as the horse shifted at the sight of so many moving lights.

That's when I jumped forwards and landed a dozen feet ahead of the wagon, my feet splattering into a muddy puddle halfway between my new friends and the biggest group of pixies.

"No! You idiot, get back here!" Milread cried. "I swear Juliette's going to charge me double if you die."

I flung my arm behind me, gesturing her back but keeping my eyes focused on the milling pixies. "No!" I said. "Stay back. Just, please? Trust me? I know what I'm doing." I licked my lips and whispered. "I hope."

The pixie swarm broke up into a grid wall, each pixie keeping about half a meter's space between themselves and the next pixie until they formed a Christmas-light barrier in the air before us. Simple, but effective.

I put on my most cheerful smile as I greeted them. "Hello pixies. My name is Broccoli Bunch, and I want to be your friend." I looked around, searching for their leader until I found the biggest in the lot. She, because there was a definite feminine cast to her features, was glowing a bright green and wore an intricate dress made of knotted leaves and vines over her tiny figure.

The leader pixie zoomed forwards towards me with a big scowl on her face. Her tiny arm slashed the air and a line of fire whipped out to slash into the ground a step ahead of where I was.

I stopped and stared wide-eyed at the glowing green ball. "H-hey now, that was uncalled for," I said as I raised a hand before me to ward off the spray of mud. I made sure to keep my voice soft and gentle, as if I was dealing with a dangerous animal, which I suppose I might have been. "We don't want trouble. We don't want to hurt any of you."

"Get back here, Broccoli!" Milread yelled. "You can't negotiate with pests." A glance over my shoulder revealed that she was bouncing on her feet, ready to charge over to me. She had a pair of swords out, steel flashing in the rain.

The pixie's eyes narrowed, and I could see the warmth radiating off of her. Milread was really making this complicated. "I'm sorry about my friend. She's… ah, not from around here? Anyway…" I brought my prize forwards and displayed it to all the pixies. "You guys like honey, right?" I shook the jar a little.

I was suddenly the focus of a whole lot of attention, but the mean green pixie shook her head.

"You… don't?" I asked. Just to be sure, I slowly popped the lid opened and stuck a finger into the warm gooey stuff, then pulled it out. A long sticky line dribbled to the ground before I put my finger in my mouth. "Mmm, you really sure?" I said, mouth all sticky.

"Broccoli, what are you doing?" Milread hissed.

"I'm making friends," I said with as much cheer in my voice as I could manage. It hid the slight tremble well.

This was dangerous. Probably not as dangerous as fighting the pixies off, but this put me right in the middle of the pack where I would be the first to go. I didn't hold any delusions about surviving against thirty angry pixies flinging spells at me all at once.

"So… how would you guys like to share this entire jar of honey?" I asked. "In exchange, you let us go without trouble. It's too wet for fighting anyway."

I saw a few nods, but the lead pixie huffed and gestured at me with a burning hand. It was a violent back-and-forth motion, as if stabbing someone, then she pointed at me and then the jar.

"You want to just take it?" I asked.

She nodded. A cruel little smiled played out across her lips.

"But then I might drop it. And then no one would get the honey." I let go of the jar for a moment, then caught it again.

There were lots of dismayed squeaks and chirps at that.

"How about I give you this jar right now?" I said. "And then you can all decide on whether or not we can go?"

The pixies started bickering and chirping at each other, most congregating in a big huddle as they abandoned their formation. The leader was apparently very much against the idea, but a lot of the other pixies really wanted my jar of honey.

"By the way," I said, cutting off some of the chatter. "We're really sorry to have disturbed you. We didn't mean to trespass into your territory, but we need to get out of the rain and the place we're going to is down this road. If we knew it was your home, I think we would have found some other path."

The pixies chirped and some danced around the others until finally a decision was made and the green pixie leader, wearing a pout that was impressive only because of how resigned it made her look, approached and signed at me a few times, then towards the jar and finally down the road.

I grinned, my shoulders relaxing. "Here you go!" I said as I carefully placed the jar on the ground between us and took three long steps back. "It was a pleasure doing business with you!"

A flight of pixies zoomed in and snatched it off the ground before rushing off into the forest. There were squeaks and chirps as the formation broke up to follow them.

The green pixie remained for a long time, looking at me with narrowed eyes while a few of her companions milled around behind her. "Bleek," she said to me before darting off after her friends.

"You," Milread said from right behind me, her words almost drowned out by the splash of rainfall. "Are an idiot. A brave idiot, but an idiot all the same."

I grinned at her. "I won't deny it," I said.

# Chapter Thirty-Five
# A Spark in the Night

Setting up a tent in the rain was not the most fun thing to do. Getting all the poles in place, moving the tarp around, not getting tangled in the lines, it was all the frustrating end of a frustrating day. My blankets—which I had left on the floor of the wagon—were both sodden and wet. My cleaning spell took care of some of it, but it wasn't a drying spell; they were still wet.

I stepped out of my tent, rain pinging off my hat with a constant rap-tap-tap beat and took in our tiny camp. Milread had driven the wagon all the way up to a small cliff area that was higher off the ground than the rest of the forest. It meant that we got to sleep next to a wall of stones that did a decent job of keeping off the rain.

There was a bit of a divot sliced into the rock, probably by some previous travellers. It served as a good spot to set up a little fire pit with all our tents in a circle around. The wagon was pushed into the trees to one side and Missy was left to graze opposite it.

Basically, the camp was tight, cramped even, but it made sense to set it up that way. Our fire wouldn't be visible from afar and if we had to fight something, we would have a wall by our backs.

I wished that such considerations didn't matter. That we could all just enjoy a nice fire and a warm meal before snuggling into a warm bed.

The others were all huddled around the anaemic fire in the pit. It wasn't much, just a few tiny licks of flame from some twigs and a small block of rune-covered wood that Milread had tossed in. It was growing though, and even with the tiny bit of warmth pouring out of it, the fire was welcome.

"I…" I started to say before three pairs of eyes looked towards me.

The others had not been happy with me after the thing with the pixies, Milread most of all. It had worked out, in the end, and no one had died. That didn't matter to her. It had been silly and foolish and I could have been hurt with one wrong word. She wasn't wrong, not entirely, but I didn't think I had been all that wrong in the way I acted either.

I tried again. "I can make tea. Chamomile, if you want?"

"Fire's not hot enough yet," Noemi said.

I pulled out my tea kettle, tucked under my arm since I had left my tent. "Enchanted tea set," I said. "Can't do much more than boil water, but, well…" I sat down on a log that had been there long before we arrived.

"Sure," Severin said. He had a set of camping utensils next to him, one a tin mug that he handed over to me.

I added the herbs I had and let it fill with rainwater as we waited.

"Rainwater's not good for drinking around here," Milread said as she tossed in a log and sent up a small plume of embers that quickly died.

"Cleaning spell," I explained.

"Ah."

I sat around and waited for enough water to fill the kettle. At the rate it was raining it wouldn't take long. "I'm sorry," I said.

Milread looked up from the fire. "You've said that already," she said.

"I mean it this time."

Noemi scoffed and got up. "I'll get the food," she said.

Milread eyed me for a good long while, until I felt like squirming under her hawkish gaze. "Next time you listen. Or you at least tell me of your fool plan before trying anything. I'm responsible for the lot of you. Severin and Noemi know what they're about, they're past their first rank, but you're no better than a kid. Plus, Juliette would turn my head into a mantlepiece if you died under my watch."

"I'm… sorry," I repeated. "I didn't mean to scare you. I just, I just really don't like fighting."

"Then find a nice city with big walls and stay in it," Milread said. "Out here you fight or you die."

It was quiet for a good long while after that. No, not quiet. There was the croak of hundreds of frogs, the occasional cry of a distant coyote, and that incessant pitter patter of rain on leaves. I brought my feet up onto the log so that I could hug my knees close to my chest for a bit of warmth.

Noemi returned with a sack that she dropped next to the growing fire. She placed a pot next to her, the lib scrapping and pinging with every motion. "I'm cooking," she said.

"Got the skill?" Milread asked.

"At apprentice. Got better?" Noemi asked.

"Don't even have it," Milread said.

Severin just shook his head.

The grenoil woman started opening cans and adding spices to the pot. It stirred it all together then added it to the top of the fire. "Going to take a bit," she said. "Could use a hotter fire too."

"Right," Milread asked. She poked the fire one last time and then tossed the stick she was using onto the flames. "We need more wood if we'll keep this going all night. And we need to set up a watch. Severin, can you do mage lights?"

"For the sombrals? Of course," the mage said. He huffed as he got to his feet. I noticed that he had tossed his boots at some point, but he didn't seem to mind having his feet in the mud. He moved over to Milread and they both ambled off into the woods around our camp until I could just barely hear them from the crackle of branches and the shift of cloth.

"So, um, Noemi, right?" I asked.

"Do you really have to?" Noemi asked right back.

"Have to what?"

"Do this whole thing where you try to chat me up. If you were a grenoil boy I'd think you were a flirt."

I shook my head, bits of rain slipping off my hat. "No. I just want to make friends."

Noemi sighed. "Yeah, that's nice. Make friends with someone else."

I wasn't sure what to say to that. I fumbled through a few openers, but none seemed to fit, and a direct response would just be so rude. I wondered if my Friendmaking skill could be of any use, but it felt more like a passive sort of thing. "So, why are you heading to Port Royal?" I asked.

Noemi paused in the stirring of our supper. Her knuckles tightened around the spoon, but she never looked away from her work. "I have family who died. I'm going to their funeral. Are you happy now that you know?"

"I'm sorry," I said.

"Good. You can apologize by keeping quiet."

I swallowed and looked away. The kettle was halfway full, leaves floating in lukewarm water. I fired an absent cleaning spell, then sighed when it made the flower buds I had left in the water poof away. It wasn't my night.

The tea was boiling and my mana was slowly dropping when the others returned. They settled down and I poured a cup for Severin then myself. The others begged off, but I left the kettle close, just in case.

"This isn't bad," Severin said as he took a sip.

"Thanks," I said.

Milread shook some water off of her hood. "We're setting up rotations. Broccoli, you're up first. I have some watch candles. You wake me when the wax hits the ring and the flame changes colour a little. Severin, you're taking the late middle, Noemi, the last. We can change things around tomorrow." She pulled a small fat candle from a pocket and, with the tip of a talon, made three marks around it before setting it to the side.

"You trust her not to sleep?" Noemi asked.

I stiffened.

"Yeah. I'll wake up for my watch either way," Milread said.

"Hrm," was Noemi's response. "Food's ready."

We were each given a decent bowlful of some sort of stew. No actual meat, just different cuts of veggies in a sort of gravy with some spices. It was a little light on solids but tasted good all the same. I was one of the first to finish eating. "I'll clean up," I said. "I've got cleaning at, um, disciple rank."

"Thanks," Milread said. "I'm going to get some shut-eye. Good night." She left her bowl on the log she had been perched on and walked off to her tent. Noemi soon did the same.

"Do you think I can practice magic?" I asked Severin as I gathered all the utensils and pots.

The older grenoil gave me his empty bowl, then refilled his mug with the last of the tea. "I don't see why not. Don't cast anyzing and you should be fine. Your light is no brighter zan the fire."

"Neat," I said.

Soon I was wishing him a good night and settling in as best I could next to the fire. I took a moment to fetch my spear, just in case. The candle Milread had left was lit with a twig and burned merrily despite the occasional raindrop that landed on it. Magic, maybe, or some clever alchemy?

I focused on a hand. My right, because that was my dominant hand for day to day stuff. Magic moved into my limb until it tingled, then I pushed a little more. It was like shoving some of that dough stuff kids played with through a strainer. It didn't flow out of the body easily and pushing too much made my chest feel a little empty in a way that spending all of my mana didn't.

My mana didn't dip down though, not unless I lost control of the mana and it slipped out of my grasp. So, the number in my status was the amount of mana I could control, not the amount I had in my body? No, that didn't feel exactly right.

Eventually I grew a little bored with just making my hand glow. Even shutting it off and bringing it back as quickly as I could grew tiresome, and it felt as if I was straining something inside of my hand when I did so. Like a new muscle, maybe.

I formed the mana into a ball, then, when that didn't work at all, I satisfied myself by cupping a blob of mana in my hand. Severin had said that my magic was cleaning aspect. That sounded... strange. I had grown up on stories with the usual magical elements. Fire, water, earth, air and so on. Cleaning was definitely not one of those.

Maybe magic didn't care about what I thought was usual and I would just have to deal with it.

I tried to make my mana turn into fire mana. Severin had made it look easy, but it was far from it.

At first I tried to make my mana look like fire, but that only made it bob around like jelly. Thinking hot thoughts didn't work and getting angry was hard because I wasn't an angry person. The hottest my emotions ever ran was mildly miffed. Maybe I'd manage to unlock mildly miffed aspect mana, but a mildly-miffedball didn't sound as awesome as a fireball.

I looked at the fire before me, then jumped when I saw that it was dying.

Getting to my hands and knees, I blew at the embers until they were nice and hot again, then added more sticks and branches to the fire until it was crackling merrily away.

Maybe that was it. I had to treat my mana as a tiny fire?

I spend an hour or so—occasionally looking around to the woods—trying to nurture a small fire in the palm of my hand.

By the time Milread woke up I had almost seen a flicker.

"You're still awake?" Milread asked. She looked around, then scowled. "It's still raining."

"It is, and I am," I said. "Is it time for me to sleep now?"

"Yeah, get some shut-eye. You'll need it."

I slid into my tent and, after wasting some mana cleaning myself off, fell asleep under my moist blankets. It was a long night.

## Chapter Thirty-Six
# I Just Want to Set the World on Fire

The rain didn't let up until halfway into the morning. By then we were trudging along in our wagon, bumping over potholes, and generally just travelling on a long road that seemed to twist and turn all over the place.

The ditches along the sides were full, a heavy current of muddy rain-water gurgling past us except where the road dipped and we had to pass through huge, but fortunately shallow, puddles.

There were fewer trees as we travelled. The forests turned thin and the ground all around us became a marshy vista filled with the low drone of mosquitoes and flies and other bugs. Fortunately, Milread had a magic in-sect-repellent rune device that she activated to shoo off the bugs. It would have been a nightmare otherwise.

I focused on my hand again, first came the pushing of mana out of the… I was going to call them mana pores because that's what they felt like, then the concentrating of my mana into a flat shape on the surface of my palm, then I thought fiery thoughts and let my mana sort of just… burn.

"You're getting better," Severin said as he eyed the fuzzy mana in my hand. "Zat's not perfect fire aspect mana, but it might be close enough."

"Really?" I asked. The lapse in concentration made my mana construct, if it could be called that, fizzle out and take a few points of mana with it. "I've been practicing very hard."

"Yes. It's almost enough to make up for your deficiency."

"Hey!" I said. "I'm not that bad, am I?" I asked.

Severin made a wiggly motion with his hand. "You're no prodigy. Per-haps had you started wiz holy or light spells you would be better. And you're not exactly in a school environment. Zat might mitigate some of your slowness to learn."

I resisted the urge to pout. "I'm trying my best," I said. And I really was. There wasn't anything else to do while bumping along in the back of the wagon. I could have practiced my other skills but most of those weren't easy to do. Talking had… not been fruitful. Noemi still refused to open up and Milread had remained coolly professional.

I was beginning to think that people in this world were just not as friend-ly as people back home. Maybe they didn't trust as easily, maybe there was some prejudice at play that I wasn't aware of.

Did the 'why' matter?

If it was hard to make friends then I just had to work harder at it, that was all.

Severin pulled out a small notebook from his pack, opened it to a fresh page, then fished out a strange quill with a bulb near its middle filled with ink. He scratched out a quick design then turned it around to show me. "Zis is ze side profile of a fireball spell. Side profiles are deceptively simple and useless for complex spells, but for somezing as simple as fireball it will do."

The drawing looked like a ball with a long tail behind it, like a comet, maybe. "That does look fireball-ish," I said.

"Most spells won't look like zeir final product at ze creation stage. But fireball is, as I said, simple. It's made of two parts. One, if you squint. Ze main payload and ze propellant. Have you ever seen a firework?"

"Yes, a few times," I said. Some in person and I had seen plenty on TV and online.

"Do you know how zey work?" he asked next.

"Um." I tried to imagine what a firework's internals looked like. "There's a fuse, then some powder that burns through a... nozzle? And then after it takes off it eventually explodes? I guess there might be a fuse inside too?"

Severin made a huffing noise. "Zat's mostly correct, yes. Fireball is similar. Only ze entire zing in a mana construct. Let me show you."

"Hey hey, what did I say about no fire on my wagon?" Milread said.

Severin scoffed. "I am no fool. She only needs to see, zere is no need to use fire-mana for it." He reached out with his hand and held it palm up between us. Mana rushed out it and formed into a perfect ball, then a coil came out of that and formed a long, spiralling cone. "Zis is what a fireball looks like. Once formed, you will ze mana at the base to react and it goes off."

The wizard moved his hand over the edge of the wagon and fired off his spell. The mana, now looking like a ball of muddy... stuff, shot off into the marshes and splattered against a tree with a dull thump.

"Cool!" I said. I wondered if that could be done with cleaning magic? Something to try next time I ran into some ghosties!

"A ball of mana-constructed mud like zat won't do much to harm an enemy. But many creatures are weak to fire. I suggest trying to form ze spell with your natural mana first. A ball of cleaning mana won't do anyzing bad to anyone."

"Awesome!" I said as I jumped to my feet, then windmilled my arms around to stay upright. "I'm going to practice as I walk, I can't stand being on my bum any longer."

The others didn't seem to mind as I hopped off the side of the wagon and landed on the ground with barely a bend in my knees, the kind of acrobatics that would have hurt just a week ago. I hopped along next to the wagon, jumping from clear spot to clear spot along the road with only the occasional splash of mud to accompany my jumps. My jumping skill was nearly at Rank B.

*Jumping*
*Rank C - 77%*

Jumping wasn't as practical in my day-to-day as Cleaning was, but it did give me the ability to run away from big scary monsters that Cleaning just didn't. My other class skill, Gardening, wasn't directly useful in combat at all. Though it was close to its own rank up too.

If I had a couple of days to just practice all of my skills, I was sure I could get them all to top rank. Actually, maybe I could get the others to help a little? Makeshift Weapons Proficiency might go up with some sparring and I could definitely use some help there. Insight… wasn't going to rank up anytime soon, so I could just let that rank up organically.

Between hops I toyed with my magic, forming my mana into a ball, then trying to give it a tail of sorts, but all I really succeeded in doing was making the blob distend into a longer, less shapely blob.

Magic was tricky and hard. Which, I suppose, was only fair. It was magic, after all.

We started moving uphill, which meant less water in the ditches and the puddles in the road were easier to avoid. Not that I did. Puddles were for jumping in, after all.

I stopped advancing when I reached the top of the hill. I felt my mouth opening wide in a big 'o' of surprise before a huge grin took over.

Our destination was right ahead of us. Still a little ways away, of course, but close enough that if I squinted, I could make out the shapes of the bigger towers and the huge, multi-levelled walls encircling the city.

Port Royal was huge, with towers all along one side and a large dock on the other where ships were hanging in the air, their big balloons bobbing just enough that I could see them moving from where I was.

The path to the sky port was cut into the mountainside, a series of switchbacks that lead off from a small town at the very base of the mountain the port was built into.

"We can see the Port!" I called back to the others.

Milread gave me a knowing smile and even Noemi looked up from staring at the road to take in the city behind me.

"Still half a day's travel," Milread said. That dampened my mood a little and I turned to inspect the road we would have to take to get there.

I couldn't see all of it, of course. Even if the forest was a bit thinner, there were still thousands of trees around. The road seemed to zig and zag around a lot, avoiding the larger untamed areas that looked a little too swampy for my taste.

The only settlement I could see was the town at the base of the mountain, but I did spot a road leading off to the east and into the distant woods that way. I was practically shaking in my shoes when I jumped back onto the wagon. "I can't wait to see what the city is like. And airships! Airships are the best."

Milread snorted. "Sure. Won't argue with that. The best ones are made in Farseeing, of course."

"Farseeing?" I asked.

"Ze harpy capital," Severin answered. "Along the unimaginatively named Harpy Mountains. Port Royal is at the base of that mountain range, though it is Deepmarsh territory, not Nesting."

"Oh, neat," I said. A world map was going to be one of my first purchases because I was getting lost just talking to them. "What's Port Royal like?"

"Bit messy," Milread said. "Lots of folks from plenty of places. Most of the expensive goods from Deepmarsh make it to the port eventually, then they're shipped elsewhere. And the opposite is also true, you have stuff from all over the world passing through Port Royal. Lots of strange folk with strange customs. Keep your hands to yourself and stick to the cleaner parts of the city and you'll be fine."

"I can't wait! Can you tell me anything about the Exploration Guild? I was thinking of joining them, but that's mostly on a whim."

Milread hummed. "Mostly good folk. You could do well for yourself and they might give you some training on how not to get yourself killed. Risky work, but the pay can be great. The guild works across a couple of nations, so if you like traveling they might do good by you. I work for the Courier's Union, we use the Exploration Guild to chart out new paths sometimes."

"Zere are some problems wiz any guild. Not just the fees and hierarchies. Ze Exploration Guild is relatively small for all zat it is spread out. The Guards Guild is bigger and safer, the Delvers more cut-throat but you'll make more coins. The Monster Slayers will grant you access to plenty of training, but you will probably die young as most of zeir members do."

"I would like to avoid dying if at all possible," I said. "Maybe I'll give the Exploration Guild a try, then see how I feel after that. I do like the idea of seeing the world and just being sort of… free. Exploration Guild people work in parties, right? Like a group of friends?"

"That they do, and I wish you the best," Milread said. She pointed ahead of us and towards a bit of a bend in the road. "We're stopping there for a minute. Missy needs a breather and I need lunch. Noemi, you good to cook again?"

"If you have ingredients I can use," she said.

"I've got some cans, some hardtack, a couple of other things," I interjected. "I could forage a bit, if you want. I've got a skill for it, though it's kind of low ranked."

"Huh," Milread said. "Alright. Maybe we'll take a longer break then, get a good meal in, and go for longer later. I want to arrive at the Port before nightfall. If we move too fast, we might end up camping within running distance of the town."

"Wouldn't it make sense to push on, zen?" Severin asked.

Milread snorted. "That's what everyone says. Then you end up pushing through the forest at night and go off the road or get ambushed. Trust me, one extra night under the stars won't hurt anyone, but I'll be making that choice later. For now, I'll set up some traps and maybe catch us some meat. Broccoli, get to foraging. Noemi, tend the fire and get cooking. Severin, can you keep watch and care for Missy for a bit?"

We rolled into a small camping spot next to the road, and just like that our group broke up.

# Chapter Thirty-Seven

# Let me Level With You

I hummed as I picked berries as quickly as I could, plucking them off the branches and placing them on a cloth I had spread out on the mossy ground. When I had collected a whole bunch, I knotted up the cloth into a sort of baggy and tied a neat bow at the top.

### Cloudberries

*These berries grow on tough bushes that are quite common across most marshy areas and bogs. They are a delicacy in certain northern territories. Hard to cultivate in an artificial environment. They require a few specific temperature ranges and a precise acidity level in the ground to grow. The bushes will often create foggy clouds around them that might disguise their presence.*

*The berries are edible by most humanoids and are quite tasty if fresh. They don't keep for long. The berry's juice has a very weak lightening effect that makes the eater weigh less. This can be heightened with a few alchemical processes. It's also one of the main ingredients in cloud tinctures and smokescreen vials.*

The only thing better than yummy berries were magic yummy berries.

I hopped on the spot a few times but didn't feel any lighter. Maybe it took some time for the magic to settle in? Whatever. I was happy for the snack already.

Bending down, I picked up my baggy of berries, then gave the bush a pat. "Thank you," I said.

**Congratulations! Through repeated actions your Gardening skill has improved and is now eligible for rank up!**
**Rank D is a free rank!**

"Oh, sweet!" I said.

**Bing Bong! Congratulations, your Cinnamon Bun class has reached level 6!**
*Health +5*
*Resilience +5*
**You have gained: One Class Point**
You have unlocked: One Class Skill Slot

… Eh?

I ran back to camp to find everyone sitting around the campfire, all of them looking to be in a good mood. Milread was skinning a rabbit while Noemi stirred a pot full of something that smelled scrumptious.

"Guys!" I said as I ran over, then paused to pant and catch my breath. "Guys, I levelled up!"

The three of them paused, then Severin nodded. "Congratulations."

"No," I said. "I mean, I just levelled up, like that. I didn't kill anything."

"That's great?" Milread said. She sounded a bit confused. Which was good because I was very confused.

"I just got a rank up in my gardening skill, for picking some berries. Um, I found some cloudberries, by the way. And then I got a level up. How?"

Severin and Milread looked at each other while Noemi kept stirring the pot. "That's how levels work," Milread said.

"But every level I got so far was from combat with stuff," I said.

She perked one eyebrow at that. "That's unusual for a non-combat class. Most of the time you'll level up from doing things in line with your class. I'm a Sword Sweeper. I get levels from fighting and practicing with a sword. But if I were a Baker, I'd get levels from baking."

Severin shook his head. "You could get levels from baking wiz your current class as well. It would just take an order of magnitude more work zen usual. You said you received a rank up, Broccoli?" he asked.

"With Gardening, yeah," I said.

"Well, zere you go. Zat pushed you past ze experience you needed to level. Didn't anyone teach you zis before?"

"No," I said. "I thought that I would need to fight for every level." I found a spot to sit down next to the fire and placed the berries close to Noemi. Then I handed her a little bundle of fresh parsley that I had gathered earlier. My book didn't have much on it other than its use as a cooking spice, which was enough for me.

Noemi hummed as she sniffed the herbs then tossed a sprig or two into the stew. The berry bag she opened and then re-tied. I supposed that berries didn't fit in with the current lunch.

I shook my head and refocused. The surprise at levelling had robbed me of the chance to bask in the glow of levelling up. The pleasant tingles were still coursing through me, but they were faint now.

So, I could level up from things outside of combat. Did that mean that I could just sit back, find some cleaning work, and maybe tend to a small garden and just live a happy, quiet life? I did want that. A nice little house with a pretty garden full of flowers. Two kids and a loving husband and a big dog and a couple of cats.

That had been my dream once. But now, in this world, my sights had changed a little. The thought didn't appeal as much as it had just a few weeks ago.

Now I wanted… I didn't know. Not yet.

Well, I did want an airship.

A big one.

With a garden on it. And a house. And a little park area for my dog and my cat and my two kids. My husband and I could both rock tricorns.

Friends first, new dreams second.

Lunch passed in no time at all. Noemi gave us all a big portion of meaty stew and some hardtack that became a lot more palatable once dipped in the hot greasy juices, and then Milread passed around a skin with what I thought was juice at first but discovered, with much sputtering, was actually strong wine.

And then we were off again, the wagon loaded back up and bumping off while everyone took turns nibbling at a quickly dwindling supply of cloudberries.

"These are worth a fortune back home," Milread said as she stuffed a handful of berries into her mouth. "There's this whole thing about being as thin and light as you can be. I love my sister harpies, but by the world can some of them ever be vain."

"Are non-harpies allowed in harpy lands?" I asked. It was a bit off-topic, but I was really curious. If the best airships were harpy-made (according to Milread the harpy, there might be some bias there, just like how I believed that the best maple syrup was from home), then it made sense to learn all about them as soon as I could.

"Of course," Milread said. "Unless you're a Sylph. Not that there are any laws against being a twinkly little faerie, it's just, well, they don't get the warmest welcome."

I looked at Severin, the question obvious in my eyes. He sighed. "Ze Sylphs and ze Harpies have been at each ozer's throats for two generations now. Zey compete over land and territory and dungeons. It's quite a spectacle."

"What about Deepmarsh, do they have enemies?" I asked.

"The Trenten people," Severin said with a growing scowl. "Zey pushed into our territory some time ago before zey were repelled. Ze tensions between us and zem have been strong ever since."

"Oh no," I said. I didn't want to get caught up in some big war. "I hope that things get mended."

Severin snorted. "Don't concern yourself over it. Your time would be better spent practicing your magic."

"That's not a bad idea," I said. "I have an open skill slot now. I could get something magic related to fill it!"

I got back to forming magical blobs of cleaning magic in my hand then watching them deform and break apart when my control slipped. It was a bit of a pain in the butt, but I figured I was going to get the hang of it one day.

Time moved on, seconds counted by the steady clip-clop of Missy's hooves across the road. We crossed a couple of forks in the path and then we rode past first a hut, then a couple of little cottages, and finally little farmsteads along the sides of the roads.

There were big areas cleared of trees and with planks running over the ground where rice was growing and some spots that looked drier with barley stalks waving in the wind. We even crossed a few fenced off areas with big cows and bulls. Then an entire field filled with cockroaches the size of greyhounds (the dogs) and beetles the size of greyhounds (the buses).

There were big muddy pillars with a few grenoil in overalls and straw hats walking around them with shovels. They were patting the sides of the pillars while another group were tapping a spigot into the side of one of the muddy towers.

A termite farm.

"Oh, eww," I said before snapping my attention back to working on my magic. If I didn't think about where the food I was going to eat came from then it couldn't hurt me.

When I next looked up, it was to see that the sky was starting to turn orange. There were plenty of lights on the horizon though, both from Port Royal above and from a tiny village that was coming up ahead.

"Bottom's Rest," Milread said, probably for my benefit since I was the only one that had never been to Port Royal before. "That's where we're stopping for the night. If you guys want to split, this is the place. I'm only heading up the mountain in the morning. Missy needs a rest before trying that climb."

"Zen I think it's where we'll part ways," Severin said. "It was an enjoyable ride."

"Hmm," Noemi said.

I swallowed and nodded. "Yeah, I guess it was. A tiny adventure. Um, Severin, I never did cast fireball, but you taught me a bunch, do you... well."

"Keep your silver," Severin said. "You'll need it more zan I will, I have no doubt."

"Thank you!" I said. "If we ever meet again, I'll be sure to show you how good I've become at magic, alright?"

He croaked in what I thought was delight. "We shall see."

Missy pulled the wagon up to the large wooden gates of the little village and got in line behind a few farmers and a single fancier carriage. Each vehicle was inspected in turn, but it was a quick affair, more of a formality than anything.

Milread pulled out some documents that showed that she was a courier and the guards, after looking at it for a while, let us pass without trouble.

Bottoms Rest was a small village, maybe twice the size of Threewells but with a lot more shops and a bigger inn. That's where Milread led the wagon with Noemi's help and stopped before the stone building. "This is it," the harpy said.

I hesitated a little before jumping off the wagon and looking around. The town was fairly quiet, though there was a murmur of conversation from within the inn. It made sense, what with the sun just about to set.

I spun around when Milread tapped me on the shoulder. "You be safe, alright, kid?" she asked.

Smiling, I stepped up to the taller harpy woman and gave her a quick hug. "Thanks for the ride," I said.

She squawked in protest and shoved me off with a ruffle of feathers. "None of that, brat. I'm not the hugging sort. Go try with Severin. We'll see us when our paths next cross, world willing."

I smiled to keep the melancholy away and found Severin climbing out the back of the wagon. He was in the perfect position to hug as he came down. "Bye Severin," I said. "You were a great teacher."

To my surprise he returned the hug with a good pat on the back. "Of course I was. Anyone would be a good teacher to someone so poorly educated as you." He laughed. "If you're heading up, zen you'll want to follow me a little more. I'm taking ze carts up."

"Oh," I said. I didn't know that there were carts leading to the top, but it made sense.

Then it was time to say bye to Noemi.

"Hey," I said. "Um. I'm sorry if I came on a little strong. I just wanted to be friends. But I'm glad we got to meet anyway."

"Sometimes people don't want friends," she said.

"Isn't that when you need a friend the most?" I asked. I gave her a quick hug, then backed away. "I hope we meet again someday," I said.

Then it was time to be off. I had an entire city to explore!

# Chapter Thirty-Eight
# Port Royal

I had two choices on how to reach Port Royal. Three, really. I could walk all the way up the switchback path, I could pay three copper to ride in a carriage pulled by a team of oxen with other passengers and some cargo, or I could pay a silver, the equivalent of half a day's work for a normal person, to ride in a cable car that travelled up some towers and all the way up to the city proper.

I pressed my face against the glass off the cable car to take in as much of Port Royal as I could while I approached. The city was built on three large plateaus, each one ending at a sheer cliff face with a small wall all around it.

The city itself was a sea of red roofs sprinkled with the occasional bronze or blue or green. Off to the East were a series of five big towers that stuck out of the mountain side and cast long shadows across the port. And, barely visible on the west side, was the actual port. It overlooked a large chasm, bridges spanning the gap with ropes dangling down to the airships docked below.

That was going to be the third place I would visit. First Juliette's husband's inn, then the Exploration Guild's headquarters, then the airship docks so that I could gawk at all the pretty flying ships.

The cable car stopped with a clunk and the young grenoil manning the controls opened the door and doffed his big floppy hat. "We've arrived, ladies and gents," he said.

I was one of the first off, backpack bouncing behind me as I landed on the cable car's platform. We had stopped above a little staging area next to the main gates. There looked to be places where lines of people would wait during the day to be let into the city, but—late as it was getting—those were all empty and only a few guards stood around attentively waiting for the next person to climb the hill.

"Thanks for the ride!" I called over my shoulder as I skipped over to the huge gates.

"Hello ma'am," the nearest guard said. "First time in Port Royal?"

"It is!" I said.

He nodded his helmeted head. "Welcome to Port Royal. I'm going to Inspect you and your items, after which, if you're not carrying anything suspect, you'll be allowed to enter. Do you understand?"

"I do," I said.

His eyes glowed in the depths of his helmet and they twitched to my backpack, then up and down my body. I felt like I had just been x-rayed or something and had to resist the urge to cross my arms over my chest.

"You're good to go. Welcome to Port Royal."

Smiling, I passed first the guards, then the gates, before coming to a stop. The area right after the entrance was an open plaza. A little fountain standing in the middle of a square lined with shops and homes, not one of them less than two stories tall. Lanterns hung on poles alongside the streets, giving everything a cheery golden glow.

People of all sorts walked around or chatted. Some were packing up stalls with blue cloth roofs while others sat next to the fountain and enjoyed the evening air. Most, I noticed right away, were grenoil, but there were a few harpies and some sylphs and even a couple of humans.

I grinned as I started walking deeper into the city. That's when the scent hit me. Or rather, the stench. There had to be an open sewer somewhere because the place smelled like poop.

It still wasn't as bad as a rotting Dunwich abomination, though.

Someone laughed from behind me and I turned to see a guard that was a good foot shorter than me standing next to one by the gates. "Always fun to see country folk take in the Port Royal air," he said.

"Does it always smell so… like this?" I asked.

He nodded. "It's the steam vents, mostly. Smells worse in the Scumways, not that you look the sort to go venturing down there. I'm told it's the sulphur in the ground or some such."

"Right," I said. "Um, I need to get to the inn by the east gate. Do you know where that is?"

"East gate? That's to the East." He pointed to his right and down one of the roads. "That way, then you take a right onto Tripping Lane and up to Central. That cuts through the city West to East. Can't miss the gate from there."

"That way, Tripping Lane, Central. Got it!" I said. "Why's it called Tripping Lane?"

The guard shrugged. "Heard the earth mage who made the road was off his rocker on Mattergrove wine. The entire road was bumpy and every step on the side paths was different to the next. Some noble tripped and broke his nose. They've fixed it after that, no worries."

"Okay, neat! Thank you guard person!" I waved over my shoulder as I started towards the inn. The roads were very tight, much more so than anything back home. It was obvious that they hadn't planned around cars and the like. But I could see lines criss-crossing above and even the occasional cable car whizzing by so maybe they didn't need to worry about that.

The cable cars weren't the only unexpected thing. There were pipes all over. Some gurgling with water, others smoking as hot steam rattled through them. The few people out and about who had stopped to chat had to scream over the constant clanking of pipes and the occasional shrill whistle.

The houses, and I only guessed that because plenty of them had clothes out to hang and candlelight flickering within, were all pressed together with hardly any room between them, it made navigating the steep road like walking through a narrow chasm.

I did enjoy the architecture though. The homes all had stone walls on their first floors and everything above that was covered in wooden planks. The roofs had shiny red tiles that gleamed in the orange light of the evening and more than one home was freshly painted in blues and yellows and turquoise.

I almost missed Tripping Lane because of how my head was on a swivel to take in as much as I could. The road was, disappointingly, pretty normal, though there were a few pubs with some rowdy customers at both ends.

Central was much wider than any of the other roads I'd been on, with a patch of greenery down the middle and enough space that the people walking about had plenty of room around them. I shifted to the middle of the road, looked both ways, then started heading eastward and towards a large gate some hundred meters away. All the buildings along the street were either shops with big windows showing off their goods or very pretty homes with little fences and tiny gardens out front.

A low rumble from above had me craning my neck up and then gasping as an airship flew past so close that I could make out the individual planks of its hull. Brackish, blue-grey smoke poured out of a pair of engines in two nacelles at its sides as the ship veered around in the air and aimed towards the docks.

"This place is awesome," I muttered.

The East Gate was manned, just like the front gate, and I could see that the homes and businesses on its other side were far nicer than those I had passed so far, with actual lots around them and lamps that weren't quite so far apart.

"Hello ma'am," one of the guards at the gate said. "Do you have business on the East side?"

"I think so," I said. "I'm looking for an inn. The owner is called Julien. I have a letter for him."

"Courier's guild?" he asked.

I shook my head. "Exploration, but not yet, I'm just delivering the letter for a friend."

He looked me up and down, then fixated on Orange who had poked her head out of my bandoleer to look around.

"Right, go on in," he said. "Third building to your right, you can't miss it."

"Thank you!" I said as I shot past him and skipped along the road until I came to the front of a building that couldn't be anything but an inn. It had a huge front, with three stories topped by a steep bronze-coloured roof with a couple of chimneys poking out the top. A glance through the chequered windows revealed a bunch of people sitting at round tables and finishing up their evening meals.

A sign hung over the door. Rock Inn and Roll Inn.

I walked in with a snort at the name only to be assaulted by a barrage of fresh scents. I had forgotten how bad Port Royal smelled over the course of my short walk. The Inn, in complete contrast to it, smelled heavenly. There had to be some magic keeping the nasty smells away.

"May I help you?" a young grenoil girl asked as she watched me just breathe in through my nose to commit the smells to memory.

I shook myself to refocus and fired a small burst of cleaning magic at my clothes. I wanted them to smell like the inn, not the sewers outside. "Yes, yes you can!" I said. "I'm looking for Julien."

"Julien? He's at ze counter," she said as she half-turned to point.

There were two grenoil behind the bar, one was far too young, and too female, to be Juliette's husband. The other was a big fat frog, the biggest I had ever seen, with a blindingly white apron around his tummy that was straining under his girth and a smile so huge it could have swallowed me whole.

He was talking to a customer that looked to be on his way out, picking a hat off of a rack built into the end of the bar to hand it over to the client who left with a wave over his shoulder.

I stepped aside to let the man pass, then walked over to the bar. "Hello, sir," I said as I moved over to the bar. "May I sit?"

He blinked big froggy eyes at me and gestured. "Sit away! Zere's always a free seat at my bar!"

I plopped myself down, removed my hat, and with a deft flick, completely missed the hat rack on the corner and sent my hat flying down a hall that, I suspect, led to the washrooms.

"Oh no!"

***Ding! For doing a Special Action in line with your Class, you have unlocked the skill: Cute!***

I froze.

No. No! Cute wasn't a skill, and I wasn't cute. I was attractive and pretty but not cute.

"Are you okay lass?" Julien asked.

"I-I ah, ah, I… shucks," I said. I could freak out about it later. Instead, I pulled out Julien's letter and handed it over to him. "This is for you."

He looked at the letter, then his eyes widened and his smile grew tenfold as he saw the seal atop it. "From my dearest Juliette!"

"Yeah, she, she wanted me to deliver that to you," I said. I absently pulled a silver coin from one of the pouches of my bandoleer and set it on the counter. "If you have a moment, I'd like a meal too. I need to… to drown my sorrows in delicious food."

"Ah, keep you coin girl. Juliette would have my head if I treated someone who did a favour for her wrong," he said before popping the seal and unfolding the letter. He moved back and cackled as he read, a sound that had a few of his staff shivering in what I suspected was horror. "She called me an oaf!" he said with glee.

My eyes met those of the barmaid, and she shook her head. "I'll get you some supper," she said.

I nodded and then let my head thunk onto the counter. Cute. Cute. I wanted Fireball. Or… or literally anything else.

**Ding! Two of your current skills are eligible for Merging: Cute, Friendmaking.**

"Merging?" I asked Mister Menu, a kernel of hope flickering to life in my chest.

**Merging skills will reset merged skill to the lowest rank. All skill and general points will be refunded. You may pick which**

**slot the new skill will occupy as long as
there is an available slot and the new
skill matches class requirements.**

That sounded… brilliant! I liked Friendmaking, it had potential, but Cute didn't, and it would mean maybe freeing up another skill slot for something better down the line!

There was literally no way for this to go wrong!

**Do you wish to Merge Cute and Friendmaking
to unlock the Seduction skill?**

## Chapter Thirty-Nine
# Guild Me Up, Buttercup

I glared at Mister Menu.

> Congratulations! Through repeated actions
> your cute skill has improved and is now
> eligible for rank up!
> Rank E is a free rank!

"Meanie," I said as I slid out of the bed and dismissed the prompt with a wave. Sure, I was going to accept the free rank, because duh, but it wasn't a nice thing to see right after waking up. It wasn't even like I had done anything all night.

Did I snore?

My eyes narrowed.

Did I snore cutely?

It couldn't be. I slept just like any other girl.

After rubbing my eyes and making sure that Orange was okay after a night spent cuddled up in my arms, I wiped my lips clean of any drool, then unknotted my blouse which had ridden up as I tossed and turned.

Then I got up, picked my underthings off the floor, and got ready for the day.

The free room that Juliette had promised turned out to be quite a bit nicer than the one I had over in Rockstack. It had a single bed tucked up against the far wall, with a dresser and a little desk for my stuff, as well as a window that opened up onto a small courtyard at the back of the inn. The Rock Inn and Roll Inn was shaped sort of like a C, with two large bar areas that were on opposite streets connected through an addition that looked newer than the rest of the building.

Apparently, it had once been two inns. The Rock Inn and the Roll Inn, but after years of competing for the same customers, Julien and Juliette had fallen in love and they combined their inns into one big establishment.

Once I was all kitted out and ready to go, I picked up Orange—which meant I was now all kittened out, haha!—placed her in her place of pride on my shoulder, adjusted my awesome hat and stepped out of my room.

Julien was up and about already, serving breakfast to the few people already in the room with a jovial smile. "Ah, Broccoli! How did you rest?"

"Really well," I said. "Your beds are super comfy. Is there a really rare innkeeper skill that makes your inn so cosy?"

"Oh-hoh! Zat's a trade secret," he said with a tap to the side of his head. "Breakfast?"

"I'd love some!" I said as I pulled up a stool at the counter and dropped my backpack to my side. "How much would it cost to rent the same room again tonight?"

"One sil a night," he said. "It comes wiz breakfast and a smile. For a little more you can get two smiles."

I laughed as he returned from the kitchen with a plate covered in eggs and sausage and some freshly baked bread. "Thanks. I think I'll take you on that offer. Though I thought that one silver a night was for a place like Rockstack."

"Ah, it is more zan what you would pay in ze West end of Port Royal. And zat's more zen a room near ze docks, zough a pretty young zing like you shouldn't go anywhere near zere," Julien explained.

"Huh. Well, I don't mind your price, especially not if the food is this good." I stuck my fork in a sausage and took a big bite of it.

"Ah, no wonder Juliette took a shine to you," he said with a hand placed over his chest. "So, what adventure awaits you today?"

"I need to find the Exploration Guild and then I'm going to see about joining them," I said. "After that… I guess I'll head over to the docks. I want to look at the airships."

"Ze guild is easy enough to find," he said. "The docks… it would be best to avoid zose unless you have business zere. If it's the ships you want to see, zen zere is a viewing platform just some streets down. A few cop and you'll have a perfect view of any ship coming in, and wiz none of the unpleasantness of ze docks." He slid a blue card with a lanyard across the counter. "Zat's for you, when you want to come back."

"That sounds like a plan!" I said as I took the card and watched Julien move off to greet some other customers.

The card was a pass allowing one access across the East gate. I guessed that they tried to limit the number of people passing by at any given time.

Breakfast done, I rushed back to my room and deposited most of my stuff. I wouldn't need hardtack and such for a journey across the city. At least, I hoped! My spear was also a bit much, though I had seen plenty of people armed with all sorts of things. I decided that my belt knife and my spade hanging over my back would have to do. That and Orange of course!

I tucked a single gold in my bandoleer and two dozen silver and copper pieces, in case I caught sight of something neat to buy. Then I was off.

The East side looked a bit different in the full light of early morning. There were more people moving about and snooping through the windows along the central avenue and plenty more carts being pulled by horses and donkeys and sometimes giant toads. There was even a trolley with a bell that jingled as it stopped every few hundred meters to pick people up and drop them off.

Grinning, I moved over to the East gate. It was easy to forget that the city smelled a lot like poop when it was otherwise such a vibrant and colourful place. People were laughing and talking, some argued over the things written in the newspapers being hawked by young grenoil boys on street corners.

It felt like a scene out of a movie set in Victorian England, but also completely wrong.

Mages with big staves appeared in the middle of the street with pops, entire teams of adventurers with them, and the guards patrolling in twos wore full plate armour and carried long halberds.

I moved over to one pair that had paused to let a trolley pass. "Excuse me," I said.

They looked over to me, two pairs of froggy eyes hidden under thick metal helmets.

*An attentive grenoil City Guard (level ??).*

"Yes, ma'am?" One of them asked. I assumed he was the senior of the two because he had a colourful tassel over his shoulder. "Can we help you?"

"Maybe. I'm looking for the Exploration Guild headquarters," I said.

"Then shouldn't you explore for it?" the younger of the two asked. It earned him a smack against the breastplate.

The older guard pointed northwards. "Just down Guild Row, ma'am. It's the building with the large compass rose before it. You can't miss it."

"Thank you!" I said with a wave as I ran off in the direction they pointed-ed. I slowed down a little bit later, because if I was running then I would miss all the sights and I didn't want that.

Guild Row was an entire street that climbed up at a fairly steep angle. There were strange and colourful buildings on both sides, from the rather plain but homey Culinary Association building, to the Courier's Union that had a strange tower sticking out the top with a bunch of panels on pulleys that were moving this way and that, to the Mages Guild building that had a collection of floating pillars before it.

I found the Exploration Guild headquarters near the middle of Guild Row. It was a simple but stately building with a huge compass rose built into the front with a stylized bandoleer running across it and the name of the guild beneath it.

"Cool," I said as I moved towards the large double doors at the front. They opened just as I was reaching for them and I had to take a step back to avoid running into a pale skinned and paler-feathered harpy girl. She looked down at me, then scoffed.

"Get out of my way, nobody," she growled.

"Hey," I said as I did the exact opposite of getting out of her way and stood my ground with hands on hips. "I'm not a nobody."

The harpy girl snorted. "You look like an overstuffed pillow in that get-up," she said before shouldering her way past me and stomping down the street.

"Rude," I muttered before looking down at my gambeson. It was rather... pillow-coloured. And fluffy looking. But if I looked fluffy that just meant that I also looked more huggable. And while I wouldn't hug just anyone, it did mean that I looked more like friend material. I hoped.

Shaking off the thoughts about my lame equipment, I stepped into the lobby of the Exploration Guild and paused to take it all in.

It looked like a museum. There were shiny weapons behind glass displays and huge, old maps hanging off the walls next to tapestries and banners that looked positively ancient. Jars and urns sat atop pedestals with little plaques telling of their stories and in one back corner was an entire scale model of something with a bunch of rooms connected to each other in a big spiral, each one with a cut-through on the side to reveal the interior. It took a moment to realize that it was a model of a dungeon in three dimensions.

I stopped gawking after a bit, made a note to come back and read every little plaque, and moved to the far end of the entrance hall where a waist-high desk hid a Grenoil woman. "Hello," I said as I approached.

She looked up from what looked like a newspaper and smiled at me. "Hello miss. How may the Exploration Guild help you today?"

"I was curious about joining, actually," I said.

"Oh, I see. One moment, I'll go verify if anyone can assist you with that," she said.

"No need."

We both turned and watched as a man rounded the corner at the end of the hall and strode toward me. He was a human, tall and dressed as I imagined a nobleman would, with a big fluffy ascot and a suit jacket that clung tightly to his chest.

He smiled at me. "I couldn't help but overhear, young miss. You hope to join our guild?"

"I think I do," I said. "I have a bunch of questions still. Oh, but I do have this!" I reached into one of the bigger pockets of my bandoleer and pulled out the letter Leonard had given me all of a few days ago.

The man took it and stared at the seal. "Unbroken. From one of our more senior members. Leonard Chand'nuit?" he asked.

"That's him, yeah," I said. "We met in the Darkwoods."

"Well, well," he said with a growing smile. "Would you mind following me to my office? I think you might be just what I need." He looked over to the secretary. "Oh, and could I have a copy of the registration forms, please?"

"Of course, Mister Rainnewt," the secretary said before handing over a couple of sheets of parchment.

I followed mister Rainnewt (and wasn't that a neat name) over to a large and lavish office not too far from the entrance. He had maps on the walls and a few smaller displays with strange knick-knacks, but he gestured me to a chair before his desk before I could really start poking at things.

"So, miss…"

"I'm Broccoli, Broccoli Bunch!" I said.

"Well, Miss Bunch, I'm Tarragon Rainnewt, one of the senior members of the Port Royal branch of the Exploration Guild," he said while sitting down across from me. He crossed all his fingers together above the forms he had requested. "Do you mind if I read the letter? It'll take but a moment."

"Go ahead," I said.

While he read, I resisted the urge to kick out my legs while I slowly sank deeper and deeper into the plush chair.

"Well, well," he said as he set Leonard's letter aside. His smile was dazzling. "You're an interesting one, aren't you? I think I might have an interesting offer in return, Miss Bunch, if you're keen to listen to it."

# Chapter Forty

# An Offer

Mister Rainnewt shifted some papers around on his desk. "I think it would behove me to explain the situation. Most who come here and ask to become members of the Exploration Guild come from places like the Scumways. They have no experience out in the field, have no referrals, and are generally not equipped with a class suitable to work as members of our guild. From what I've read you are... unfamiliar with our way of doing things?"

"Pretty much," I said. "I like exploring, and I have some skills related to that, but Leonard and Emeric's party were my first time meeting members of the guild."

Tarragon nodded. "I see. The Exploration Guild holds a strange place in the world. You'll find that we, more than any other guild, have members of a certain... prestige. The adventurous and wild who occasionally have too much time on their hands and who want a river named after them or some such. These members make up a sizable portion of our guild. After these we have those who do genuinely love exploration and architecture and archaeology, who want to discover ancient secrets and unearth hidden ruins. Then we have those who are merely in it for the gold and the lower risk. We lose far fewer members than most guilds whose activities are beyond the walls of a city."

He made a dismissive gesture in the air.

"But enough of that. The point I'm trying to get to is that we don't just let anyone join. When we get new members, we usually give them a few rapid training sessions with some more veteran members before sending them off on a few simple, low-risk missions. Right now, I'm in a bit of trouble."

I took a moment to digest everything he said, then tilted my head to the side. "Trouble? How so?"

"I have an odd number of applicants. With few exceptions, new applicants are sent out in pairs. Usually a noble and a talented new recruit. I happen to have a new noble member but no talented recruits to go with her."

"I... see," I said. "Do you get that many noble members?"

He nodded, an easy smile still in place. "A full third of our membership is made up of people with good blood. Which is why your appearance today is such a boon. Telling a new member that their first exploratory mission will be delayed would be a hassle."

I raised a hand, one finger up in a 'one moment' sort of gesture and Tarragon made a 'go ahead' gesture in response.

The Exploration Guild, as he had explained it was... not what I was expecting. I thought they were scouts and explorers, sent out to find and discover all sorts of new things. Not an old boy's club. The more he talked the more I recalled images of rich old gentlemen out in the Savannah with huge rifles next to the bodies of dead lions and elephants.

Not that I had anything against pith helmets, they were pretty cool.

I was still willing to try it out. "What can you tell me about my, um, partner?"

There was a shrewd look in Mister Rainnewt's eyes that faded almost as soon as I noticed it. "She's a young noble lady from the Nesting Kingdom from the north. A scion of the Albatross family who wants to spice up her life a little. A Thunder Mage, if that helps any."

"That sounds nice," I said. "Okay, I was already interested. But I have questions."

He nodded. "I'm here to answer them, of course."

"Alright. Are there any responsibilities associated with joining the guild? Are there any entry requirements I should be aware of? And do we get to wear cool hats? Oh, and what kind of pay do we get?"

He blinked a few times then chuckled. "There's a standard yearly membership fee, five lesser gold or a percentage off any gains until such a time as the fee is paid. Most missions pay one or two sil per day in the field. The missions available for more senior members double that; any discoveries made are handsomely rewarded. Most members who come in at your financial level still manage to make a tidy profit, though those who do the best are usually those who join a peer's party. As for your headgear, that is up to you, I'm afraid."

I nodded along. The membership fee seemed steep, but they had to pay rent, and it sounded as if I had time to pay it off. Judging by how liberal the party I had met in the Darkwoods had been with their gold I would still be making my money back.

"As for responsibilities. There are some, many even, but not for an entrant as you would be. You're still in your first rank?" he asked.

"My first rank?"

He chuckled. "Between levels one and ten. Past the tenth level you enter your second rank, past your twentieth level, if you become one of the few to make it so far, you enter your third rank."

"Oh, yeah, I'm level six."

"Six? Well well, I'm certain you'll have an opportunity to grow stronger with us."

I had the distinct impression that Mister Rainnewt wasn't laying down all his cards here. Still… if he was going to give me what I wanted. "I'm looking forward to it!"

He grinned and pulled the stack of sheets closer before drawing a small case out from his desk and opening it to reveal a very pretty pen. He started making notes and checking things off with a flourish. "Do you have any skills pertaining to exploration, Miss Bunch? Scouting, Cartography, Pathfinding?"

"I have Archaeology. It's still rather weak, but I think it should help. Other than that most of my skills are based on support and, um, movement." No one had to know that I had the Cute skill. No one. "Oh, and I have Insight at Rank C. Um, that is, Disciple."

"Interesting," he said as he made a few more notes. "I think you might actually fit in nicely. Beyond just coming in at an opportune moment. Once you've returned from your first expedition come and see me, I might be able to place you in a team that will better be able to use your skills."

"Alright?" I said.

He turned the document over and slid towards me. "Do you know how to write your name?" he asked.

I blinked. Did he think I was illiterate? Maybe that was normal with poorer people. I took the document, snapped it so that it held itself up, and then read the entire thing to the tune of a clock in the back of the room going 'tic tock.'

The contract part was fairly simple. It marked me as a temporary member for the Exploration Guild for a period of one month or until I had fulfilled certain requirements. It outlined the protections available to members, including some discounts available at certain other guilds and reductions on travel costs. I could even demand a return for some expenses like food and special equipment.

It wasn't a very big or complicated contract, nothing like the end user agreements back home.

I tapped a line near the end. "This says that the guild will be taking a fifty percent cut on all profits I make for three years to recoup the cost of admission," I said. "But the admission cost is probably way lower than what I would lose over that same period. Also, the temporary membership period is only for those that chose not to pay their first year's membership fee up front."

"That's correct," he said. His smile hadn't so much as twitched.

"What counts as a first year? Is it from the date I join to the same date one year later? Or is it from now until the start of the next year?"

"That latter," he said.

"In that case, shouldn't the fee be reduced by the amount of time that has already passed this year?" I asked.

His smile grew into a full-on grin. "I'll see what I can do. Is there anything else on the contract that bothers you?"

"Nope," I said as I picked up his shiny pen and wrote 'Broccoli Bunch' in big happy letters. There was nothing that prevented me from just quitting whenever I wanted to or if I felt the guild wasn't a good fit. And there was a grace period in which I could pay my admission fee. I would make my final choice after my first mission was done.

"Then that's done," he said as he took the papers back, tapped them down to make sure they were neat, then set them to the side. "I do suspect that's all for today. I'll be giving you a badge. Most members of the Guild have a bandoleer, something of a tradition, but I see you're already equipped. The pins and medals on a member's clothes will usually give you an idea of their rank and accomplishments." He tapped his lapel where a small compass rose was sitting with a few pins all around it.

"Neat," I said. It was like the girl scouts all over again, but with more dragons and less cookies.

Mister Rainnewt stood up and reached over to the table for a handshake, which I eagerly returned. I just hoped that he didn't notice the fizz of my cleaning spell after we had shaken. "Welcome to the Exploration Guild, Miss Bunch. Now, I'm aware that your entrance is a little… abnormal. But it does provide some opportunities that I hope you will use to your benefit."

"I hope so too," I said.

"Very well. If you can present yourself at the lobby tomorrow two hours before noon, with any equipment you would need for a week-long voyage, I would be ever so grateful."

I froze. "Tomorrow?" I squeaked.

"Opportunity waits for no one," he said.

"I… can do that, I guess. Um. A voyage to where?" I asked.

This was way too soon, and with far too little warning.

"The new members are travelling by airship—"

"I'll be there!"

"I… see, that's wonderful. Do pack for a rather swampy area."

"No problem!" I said. "Though I will have to leave now if I'm to have the time to get all the things I need."

"Of course. Here," he said as he opened a drawer and pulled out a small compass rose pin. "The stores that offer discounts are all marked, I'm certain someone as shrewd as you will figure it out."

"Thanks," I said as I took the pin and ran a thumb over it. It was just simple steel with some porcelain embossing over it, the design little more than a deep blue compass rose with a tiny brown bandoleer running across it.

I pinned it right over my heart, then, because my hands were already close, I gave Orange's sleeping head a rub.

"Okay then." I said. "I guess that means I'll be off. Until tomorrow?"

"Until tomorrow," Mister Rainnewt agreed.

I left the guild house with a skip to my step and a bunch of plans percolating in the back of my mind.

The next day I was going to meet my partner, and we would go on a grand adventure together. Which meant that I would have plenty of opportunities to turn her into the very best friend ever.

No more travelling with people for a few days only to be torn apart or meeting cool new people only to have to move on.

This time I was determined to make the best of my opportunity!

Also, I'd get to ride an airship.

People looked at me as I cheered and skipped down Guild Row.

**Congratulations! Through repeated actions your Cute skill has improved and is now eligible for rank up!**
**Rank D is a free rank!**

...

"No!"

# Chapter Forty-One

# Booksie

I was pretty sure all the equipment I had already would be perfect for my first exploration mission. Still, it wouldn't hurt to be even more ready. If I was going to be trekking around in a swamp, then there were some things I would want. Boots that were made for hiking and one of those anti-bug rune things that Milread had used were both at the top of my list.

My first step was to walk back down to Central. The street was lined with shops that sold all sorts of things. Now that I was looking there were lots of small logos on walls and next to shop signs that matched the pins worn by the employees within.

I supposed that the guilds served as a sort of union. I hoped that they had something to say about quality as I entered a store with a large shoe-shaped sign at the front. It was filled with boots and shoes of all sorts and, probably because of the before-noon hours, completely empty of clients.

The only person in the shop was a nice grenoil girl who helped me find a pair of hiking boots. She kept looking at my shoes with something akin to wonder though; I guess sneakers weren't all that common. My new boots didn't fit perfectly and they didn't have the grippy rubber soles that I expected from boots, but they did look nice, with carefully tooled leather that had been polished to a shine.

I left with a box tucked under one arm and two silver less in my pocket.

Next was a stop in a general store half a dozen times bigger than the one in Rockstack and with hundreds of strange items within. It took a lot of focus to just pick out some foodstuffs and a magic bug-repelling amulet, which were apparently quite common.

Then, arms full of stuff that I would need to repack later, I headed back to the Rock Inn and Roll Inn.

"Ah, Broccoli," Julien said as I walked in. "How did your adventure go? See any pretty ships?"

"I'm a temporary member of the Exploration Guild now!" I said as I moved over to the bar. "And no, I didn't get to see the ships yet. I'm going to go drop this stuff off, alright?"

"Go ahead, go ahead."

After dropping off my things, I returned to the dining room to find Julien sitting at one of the tables with two hot meals before him. One at the seat he was perched on and the other before an empty chair. He gestured to the chair as soon as he saw me.

"So, tell zis old gossip how it went," he demanded.

I grinned as I sniffed at the meal. "It went well, I think. I met a Mister Rainnewt and I joined as a temporary member for now. I'll see about joining in full in a little bit."

"Good on you, girl," Julien said. "Now you'll begin your training I suppose?"

"Nope. I'm heading out tomorrow on my first expedition."

"Truly? Zings have changed zen."

"I think it's an exception being made. I did come in with a recommendation." I blew across a spoonful of some sort of potato-ish soup before munching down on it. Just like all the food I'd had in Julien and Juliette's Inns, it was heavenly. "I bought a few things for the trip tomorrow. We're travelling by airship!"

"Oh? Do you know where to?" he asked.

"Somewhere swampy," I said.

"Zat narrows it down to anywhere in Deepmarsh!" he said with a laugh. "You'll want to pack a few good books for ze trip. Else you'll be bored."

"On an airship?" I asked.

He nodded. "Oh yes. It's quite exciting for the first few hours, zen you get used to it. It's like anyzing else, really."

"Well, I guess," I said. I didn't believe him, but I wasn't going to tell him to his face. Then again, I did have a bit of silver to spend still, and a couple of books wouldn't hurt. I had read most of my herbology book cover to cover, even if some parts I'd just skimmed. "Do you know any bookstores in the area?"

"Zere's one along Central zat has a good reputation, but it is quite expensive. And zere's one two streets down zat is owned by a bun. She is quite nice. Less books, but better price."

A bun? Like a Cinnamon Bun? "Can you give me directions?" I asked before noticing that my bowl was empty. I pouted at it while Julien laughed. He picked up the dishes as he got up and rattled off a few simple instructions. Most of them were about turning left at a red building and past a barber shop instead of just street names, but I didn't mind.

Tummy full, and a way to waste the rest of the day away at hand, I walked back out onto the main streets of Port Royal.

I couldn't get enough of just walking around the port city. There were so many strange people out and about. From grenoil aristocrats to people that looked like adventurers. I crossed before a group of five armoured people that I suspected were human, but couldn't tell because of the thick black plate armour they were wearing, and at one point I almost bumped into a floating crystal that apologised to me in a chiming voice for blocking my path.

The further I got from Central the quieter the streets became. There were still horses and toads moving about and people walking to and fro, but the number of shops decreased. Instead the area was filled with big homes.

And then I found the bookstore, a narrow-but-tall building tucked between a butcher's shop and a normal home. There was a sign hanging off the front of an opened book with a big pair of bunny ears sticking out of it.

A bell jingled when I pressed into the shop, and the same anti-stink enchantments must have been active because instead of smelling like sulphur and horse-poop, the interior smelled like books and fresh paper. There might have been something to dampen the sound too, because the constant hiss of steam through pipes was lessened into only a faint murmur in the distance.

"Just one moment, I'll be right with you," someone called from deeper in the store.

"Take your time," I called back. Books, I knew, were a lot more expensive here than they were back on Earth. Probably because producing paper and bindings was complicated and fewer people were literate. A richer clientele and more complexity in making a product meant it was more expensive.

The store had a few rows of shelves, some filled with scrolls, others with leather-bound books. There were display cases with glass fronts filling most of the front of the store, a few books on plush cushions with little placards with their titles next to them.

I walked around, inspecting the names of the books one by one with a growing smile. A Rose Among Marshy Thorns looked like a harlequin romance while Silverto's Compendium of the Arcane looked like a fascinating book about magic. The titles said a lot about the books, which helped since other than some occasional gilding on the edges, the books didn't have covers with pictures on them.

"Hello there. Ah, a human."

I turned and took in the woman that I assumed owned the store. She was young-ish, maybe still in her twenties, with a nice dress and, most attention grabbing of all, a big pair of floppy black bunny ears atop her head. She didn't even have normal ears that I could see.

"Whoa," I said before I remembered that I had to be polite to everybody if I expected the same in return. "Ah, hi, sorry, I never met someone with such pretty ears before. I'm Broccoli!"

The girl grinned. "Hello Broccoli. I'm Booksie. Or, well, that's what my friends call me."

Were we friends already? I was really starting to like this shop. "My friends call me Broc sometimes," I said. "But Broccoli is okay too. After all, broccoli is good for you."

Booksie giggled at that. "Well then, Broccoli, how can I help you to-day? Are you looking for something in particular?" She looked down at my chest. "Or are you here for something to help you with an exploration mission?"

"Oh," I said as I touched my pin. "No, just something to pass the time. I have an airship trip tomorrow; I need reading material. Do you have anything on magic? For people who are really bad at it?"

"I might have a thing or two," Booksie said.

"Oh, and apparently my mana is cleaning-type. So any neat spells that would be easy to cast would be really neat too."

"Hmm," Booksie said as she tapped her chin. "Wait right here!"

I continued looking at all the books for the two or three minutes it took for Booksie to bounce around. She returned with two books and a pile of scrolls that she placed on a table that was free of any books.

"Alright! I forgot to ask you about your budget." She tapped a knuckle to the side of her head and stuck her tongue out. "Sorry! But I picked some books that aren't too expensive. This is A Guide to Manipulating the Es-sence, it's a primer from the Deepmarsh magic academy. Simple, used to teach younger students. Thirty silver. It won't have anything too advanced in it, but it should come with explanations. The diagrams are simple to fol-low and there are sections with practice exercises to help you refine your control."

"Oh, neat," I said as I picked up the book and leafed through it. There were lots of illustrations and the language used seemed almost... conde-scending, but maybe that was for the best.

"This is Larson's translation of a Pyrowalkian combat instruction manual. It's quite popular. One lesser gold."

I took the next book more carefully and opened it up. The text was split down the middle with the same words written above and below but in different handwritings. "Why does it just say the same thing twice?" I asked.

Booksie blinked at me. "Because it's a translation. The top is in the language spoken in Pyrowalk, the bottom is in Deepmarsh. They share a linguistic root, so some words are similar. Can you… read either?"

"I can read both," I said. How could I read both? Was it some sort of cool translation power given by my class? Or maybe because I was from another world? That would be super neat! The only problem was that I couldn't see the translation at work. Which begged the question, which language was I speaking now?

"Oh!" Booksie said. "Well then, maybe wait for an original copy of the manual then. I hear that it has wonderful illustrations."

"It is a bit much for a translation," I said. I couldn't afford to spend too much on books, not when I would probably be coming back in a few days with even more money. "What about the scrolls?" I asked as I gave her back the one book and moved the other closer to my end of the table. I was certainly going to read it.

"I brought a bunch. Unfortunately, there are many, many cleaning spells, but they're rarely written in scrolls. Too… common, I'm afraid. But cleaning mana is close to holy, light and water, so I have a few staples of those aspects. This is Holy Light, which irritates the undead and can dissipate a ghost. Good for lighting up dark rooms too. Lightball, which creates a ball of light that moves with the caster. And this is Draw Water. It's made to draw water from the ground, but it's a staple spell of water mages everywhere. Learning it should help you learn more water-aspect spells later."

"How much for all of them?" I asked.

Booksie looked a little flustered for a moment. "Ah, well, um, two sil each?"

"I'll take all three and A Guide to Manipulating the Essence," I said.

"Oh, wow, okay. Yes, let me just get you a bag!"

As Booksie ran around and looked for a bag and then counted out the silvers I gave her, I looked at all the books around me and promised myself that I would be back. I had a lot of catching up to do, after all!

# Chapter Forty-Two
# Sorry for Harpy Rocking

I arrived early, because I wanted to make a good first impression, and be-cause Julien said that if I paced across his bar one more time he was go-ing to make me sweep the floors while I was at it, and when I offered to do just that he kicked me out and told me to have a safe trip.

I shifted from side to side before the doors of the Exploration Guild building, hands running over my armour to make sure everything was in its place and that I was as neat and tidy as I could be. I needed a haircut, and maybe a nice bath. But I was clean. Very clean.

It was just nerves that had my tummy twisting up inside me with tension.

There had been a few opportunities to make friends already since I had arrived in this world, opportunities that I felt like I had missed or messed up. Heck, I could have just stopped people on the streets and asked them to be friends, but that would have felt forced. This—being given a part-ner—felt like it was my big chance. I would be spending some time with them, which meant plenty of opportunities to buddy up! We were even supposed to be of roughly the same age!

I took a deep breath and opened the door.

The lobby was nearly empty except for Mister Rainnewt, the secretary behind her desk, and an unfamiliar grenoil man. The two men were talking, the grenoil while leaning against the counter and Mister Rainnewt with his hands folded at the small of his back.

I didn't want to interrupt them, especially after they both looked my way then dismissed me to continue talking, so I took a circuitous route around all the displays, making sure not to bump any with my bulging backpack or the haft of my spear. The vases were quite… vase-y, and the big display with the dungeon inside of it certainly looked neat, and the monsters in the tiny rooms looked fearsome, but in the end I found myself itching to get it over with.

"Hello!" I said as I walked across the carpeted room towards Mister Rainnewt and his friend. There was a faint but persistent smell of alcohol in the air that had me recoiling a little.

One look at the grenoil man had me pinning all my suspicions on him.

He looked like an adventurer, with a bandoleer across one shoulder and a coil of rope over the other. He wore simple but tough looking clothes with plenty of pockets, and a cloak over his shoulders, the hood rolled up around his neck to let him see better. The cloak did a good job of hiding the knife and the two flasks around his waist. "Who's zis munchkin?" the grenoil asked.

"This," Mister Rainnewt said. "Is Broccoli Bunch. She will be Amaryllis' partner for the expedition. I expect you to take care of her as well, though she does have some experience under her belt."

I swelled up with pride at that. I also took note of the name. Amaryllis. Was that my partner?

"Experience wiz what? Walking in a straight line? She doesn't look like she knows how to handle zat spear," the grenoil said

"I don't," I said. "Know how to handle the spear, I mean. I got it from a dryad in the Darkwoods and just… kind of kept it. It's a good walking stick."

The grenoil blinked, then guffawed and pulled one of his flasks from his belt until Rainnewt cleared his throat and he stuffed it back. "Well, at least zere's zat. I'm not saddled wiz ze usual batch of no-good nobley sorts. If you can't use ze spear zen what do you use?"

He was eying the knife in my bandoleer and the one by my hip. "I have a makeshift weapons skill," I said.

"Huh. Dangerous one, zat. Hard to predict. I'm Gabriel."

"Broccoli, Broccoli Bunch," I said before extending a hand to shake. Gabriel shook with a grin.

"So, you ready for a week of babysitting, hardships, long nights, and more babysitting, Broccoli?" he asked.

"Babysitting?" I repeated.

He gave me a froggy grin. "Oh yeah, just you wait." He turned towards Rainnewt. "What kind of brats do we have zis time?"

"They are hardly brats. They are respectable new members of our esteemed guild. The Brack twins are actually quite capable," Rainnewt said.

"From ze Bracklands?" Gabriel asked.

I felt like a third wheel in the conversation, but stepping back would have been awkward, so I just stood and listened as they spoke over my head.

"Exactly. Cousins of the duke," Rainnewt said.

"Snobby little shits, you mean," Gabriel grumbled.

I didn't call him out on using bad words because this wasn't the place for it, and we weren't friends (yet), but I made a note to be sure not to copy his vocabulary. Also, he was judging people before even meeting them, which was never a nice thing to do.

"You didn't read any of the files we gave you, did you?" Rainnewt asked. He rolled his eyes back as if looking to the heavens for help.

I gave mister Gabriel a very disapproving look of my own. He should have done his homework, especially if his job, as I understood it, was to take care of us.

He noticed my pout and huffed. "Don't give me zat look. You've no idea what zeir files look like. Right nightmare to read. Besides, I've got Inspect, it'll tell me everything I have to know. Like you're a… level six Cinnamon Bun? What in ze world is zat?"

"It's my class," I said as I crossed my arms. "It's a support class." Which was far better than admitting that it was a class that had skills like Cute.

"Right," he said.

Since he had used something on me, I didn't feel that bad using Insight on him. It was only fair, after all.

*A mostly sober Grenoil Pathfinder of the Midnight Marshes (level ??).*

He wasn't even sober! This man was a bad influence!

My thoughts were interrupted by the doors near the entrance opening and two people stepping in with the sort of confidence I wish I had. They were both grenoil, and even though they were a boy and a girl, there was something about them that made them look similar. Probably the patchy pattern across their skin.

The boy had robes on, with expensive looking boots and a fine cloak. The girl had form-fitting armour that looked like leather over padded cloth, a pretty sword hung by her hip that bounced with every step. They both had backpacks on, sleeping bags rolled up atop them and a staff sticking out of the boy's.

"Ah, France and Florence," Mister Rainnewt said. "You're right on time. Let me introduce you to the man that will be leading your expedition. This is Gabriel, a senior member of the guild. Don't let his demeanour fool you, he's quite talented. And this is Miss Bunch, one of the others going through her first expedition."

"Hrm," Gabriel said as he nodded to the twins.

"Hello!" I said.

The boy, Florence, grinned at me. "I didn't know we would be in ze presence of such cute company," he said.

His sister was kind enough to elbow him in the side for his comment.

I was not cute; I was attractive.

The door opened again, and a final person entered the room.

"And here we have our last participant," Mister Rainnewt said. "Hello, miss Albatross."

"Hello," the girl said as she moved deeper into the room. I stared at her with a strange feeling in my chest. It was the same harpy girl that I had run into the day before, the one that had insulted my outfit and who had been rude to me.

That exchange had been fast, with barely a few seconds to see what she looked like. Now I had a moment to really take her in. She was tall, especially with her messy white hair-feathers and her head turned up so that she was looking at everyone else along the length of her sharp nose. She was pretty though, in the more classical sense. Sharp cheeks and a thin figure under well-fit clothes.

All she had on her was a blouse covered by a sleeveless leather jacket that had a feathery ruff and a pair of shorts that left her long taloned feet exposed so that her every step dug into the carpet. No weapons that I could see, and no gear.

"Are we ready to get this over with?" she asked.

"Do you want me to make introductions?" Mister Rainnewt asked.

"We can do that on the way. Which one is my partner?" she eyed France and Florian appraisingly.

"Miss Bunch here," Rainnewt said as he placed a hand on my shoulder.

"Hello!" I said, snapping to attention. "My name is Broccoli Bunch! I hope we become the best of friends!"

Amaryllis Albatross stared at me for a long moment, one eyebrow rising. "Is this the best the Exploration Guild has?" she asked.

"Hey!" I said before Mister Rainnewt could say anything. "I'm more than capable of handling myself, I'll have you know."

Gabriel snort-croaked. "C'mon, featherbrain, we're wasting time. You join up with Broccoli here or you stay here. Your choice."

Amaryllis huffed and crossed her arms. "Very well. Let's get going then?"

"Fine by me," Gabriel said as he pushed off the counter and started towards the door. "Stick close kiddies, we're heading to ze docks. Doubt anyone is fool enough to mess with us, but you never know."

The twins followed, and soon I was walking next to my partner as we made our way onto the streets. It was just about noon, which meant that the streets were pretty quiet. The sun was beaming down from above and cutting through the slight steamy fog around the city. It warmed up otherwise-chilly roads.

It was good weather for setting off on an adventure.

"So, you're Amaryllis, right? That's a very pretty name," I said.

Amaryllis ignored me.

"What made you join the guild?" I asked, and when I didn't receive any answer other than a dry look, I went on. "I joined because I like exploring. I met a party from the guild next to a ruined town and thought it would be neat to try and join myself. Now here I am!"

"Do you have to talk so much?" Amaryllis asked. "I don't know who sent you, but I doubt they paid you to become my friend."

"Paid me? Nobody needs to pay me to be their friend, that's a free service!"

The harpy next to me crossed her arms. "This is going to be a long week. Isn't it?"

"It's only going to be long if you're not enjoying yourself," I said. "Maybe… maybe you're not ready to be friends yet, that's okay. But if we're going to work together then maybe we should make an effort to get to know each other? And if we do become friends, then that's just for the best."

"Ze human's not wrong," Gabriel said. "If you're going to share a tent wiz someone, best to be on good terms. Ze ozer options aren't always pretty."

I saw the twins glancing at each other, then back to me and Amaryllis.

"Fine. I'm Amaryllis Albatross, of the Albatross family. I'm the third daughter, which means I have two older sisters. I'm a Thunder Mage. My specialty is mid ranged area of effect magic. Is there anything else you need to know?"

"All sorts of things," I said. "Like what your favourite colours are, and your favourite food, and your favourite books, but those things can wait," I said. "I'm Broccoli Bunch, of the Bunch family on Earth. I'm an only daughter, and I'm a Cinnamon Bun. My class is about support, though I don't have that many useful skills yet. I'm really bad at combat, and I'm pretty good at talking. This is Orange Bunch." I pulled the flap on a pouch of my bandoleer open and accidentally woke up Orange who stuck her head out and glared. "She's a spirit kitten companion. She's not that good at combat yet, but she gives great snuggles."

I looked at Amaryllis and found her staring at me as if I was a snake she found in her boot.

"I hope we become good friends!"

# Chapter Forty-Three

# The Silver Boot

With all the warnings I had received about the docks I had kind of built a mental image of what the place would look like. There would be rough people on every corner and graffiti all over, and some people peddling drugs and stuff out of long trench coats.

Instead the docks were merely a very busy place. Hundreds of people moving about between wagons and carts. Formations of guards stomped across the middle of the road with plenty of space around them and the only groups I saw waiting on the corners of streets were grenoils and some humans with signs saying they were looking for work.

The place even smelled a bit better than the rest of the city, maybe because the road ended with a railing overlooking a huge cliff and that meant that there was a constant wind blowing past to take any smells away.

With Gabriel at the front, we had no trouble cutting through the crowd. People seemed to just get out of his way, and when he did deviate from his straight path it was always to avoid a wagon that would have blocked our path in a few steps.

"So cool," I said as I looked to my right where a huge zeppelin-like ship was coming into dock. It was the size of a modern jet. One big balloon with some green banners on its side and a bunch of ship-like parts protruding out of the bottom. I could see people running around inside through small portholes.

There seemed to be two kinds of airships: Big blimp-y ones—basically large balloons with some engines sticking out of them. And airships that looked like sea-going ships but with a whole lot of crystal bits jutting out of the hull and big engines that spewed blue-grey smoke out of big pipes.

"Stop staring like a country bumpkin," Amaryllis said. "We're getting close. If you fall behind, I'm not coming back to fetch you."

"Oh, right!" I said as I snapped back to attention. It didn't last very long, my eyes kept darting around to take everything in.

The docks were built on a few levels, with a wooden pier one level up that shook and thundered with the footsteps of the people moving about and another level below ours that stuck out of the cliff face and stretched out into long piers that ships were docking at.

"Zat's our ride," Gabriel called out as he pointed down one pier.

The ship docked there was one of the smaller airships around, maybe thirty meters long. It was one of those strange hybrid sorts with sails folded by its sides and a large engine sitting in its middle. Two huge propellers stuck out of the back, spinning idly in the breeze.

The crew crawling over the rigging and running across the deck all wore deep blue shirts and, wonder of wonders, were nearly all human—save for a few grenoil.

"Hoh there!" a man called as he stepped across the gangplank leading to the ship without so much as a glance at the fall below. "Are you the group from the Exploration Guild?" he asked.

"Yeah, we are," Gabriel said. "You're Isaac?"

"That I am," the man said. He doffed his big tricorn hat and placed it over his chest as he gave our group an extravagant bow.

I couldn't resist, even if it was a little bit rude…

*A proud Sky Captain (level ?).*

"Is that your ship?" I asked, pointing to the vessel next to us that was gently bobbing in the air. "It's gorgeous."

The captain, Isaac, rose up and stared at me. "Um," he said.

*The Silver Boot, a Mattergrove airskiff captained by Isaac Pinewood, well-maintained.*

"It is, yes," the captain said, his chest puffing out a little. "She's been with me for some years now. The sleekest skiff east of the Seven Peaks. We've fought through storms and flew out of the grasp of air pirates on more than one occasion together, and she's never once failed me."

"Sky pirates," I repeated. "You are the coolest person I have ever met," I said.

Isaac scratched at his chin right next to his really cool moustache. "Well, thank you, I suppose."

"Right," Gabriel said. "Enough fawning over ze dry skin, let's get aboard and get out of zis hole." He crossed the gangplank then shouted over his shoulder. "Where're ze cabins on zis zing?"

"Let me show you," Isaac said before jumping ahead of Gabriel and leading him, and us, over to the back of the ship. It took a few steps to get used to the swaying underfoot, but that was a small price to pay for stepping onto an actual airship.

"You really are a country bumpkin," Amaryllis said as she looked at me. Her expression was hard to read, but it was somewhere between horror and disgust.

"We don't have airships where I'm from," I said truthfully. "We do have aircraft, but it's not the same. And what's wrong with looking for the wonder in the things I see? Isn't that the whole goal of the Exploration Guild?"

"I suppose," Amaryllis allowed. "Just don't get in my way. This expedition will be over soon enough, I hope."

I let the comment go. I didn't want to push her just yet.

Isaac showed us to a lower floor of the airskiff where there were tiny rooms with hammocks strung between the walls and tiny portholes to see out of. The inside of the ship was a bit cramped, and there was a persistent smell like burning rope and motor oil, but I could live with it. "And this leads onto the gallery," he said as he opened a door onto a balcony. I followed eagerly, then gripped the edge of the rails as I suddenly found myself looking down at a drop of hundreds of meters to the rocky ground below. "Watch yourself there," he warned.

"Right!" I said.

"I can give you a proper tour once we've taken off and the ship has settled. In the meanwhile, please keep to this deck. The galley is towards the bow and the head is on the port side. Don't use it until we're no longer docked. It's a bit of a faux-pas to empty the head at port." He grinned at the group and pressed his hat down on his head a moment before a gust of wind blew past. "I need to get things sorted up top. It might be better if you wait in your rooms."

"Yes sir," I said with a sloppy salute. I wasn't about to get on his bad side, especially if it meant losing any privileges aboard the Silver Boot.

We returned to our rooms. The twins France and Florian had their own, and Gabriel had a bigger room all to himself. That left me and Amaryllis to bunk together in a space that was smaller than my closet back home.

Not that that was too bad. I had a pretty big closet.

"I'm taking the top," my partner said without a second glance before she tossed herself onto the hammock above.

"Okay," I said. The bottom had a better view out of the porthole anyway. I stashed my things to the side then pulled out my copy of A Guide to Manipulating the Essence and sat on the ground with my legs stretched out. The hammock wouldn't let me feel the rumble of the airskiff and it would be harder to read with the heavy book hanging above my head.

The first few pages were filed with warnings about practicing magic without proper supervision and some of the dangers that came from un-controlled magic. The kinds of things that I expected to see in any manual for a complicated machine, but with a magical edge to it.

Of course magic was dangerous, all the best things in life were a little risky.

"You know magic?" Amaryllis asked.

I looked up just in time to see her shifting around to stare back at the ceiling. "Not really," I said. "I'm hoping to learn though. I've been prac-ticing really hard and trying my best, but I'm not very good at it. Cleaning spells are pretty much the best I can manage for now."

"Tch. Cleaning spells are for peasants."

"I practice mine on the undead. It's really effective."

Amaryllis looked down again. "What?"

"I think it's because cleaning magic is close to holy? Or maybe it has some sort of purifying effect? I'm not sure, but I'm positive I'll find out if I read enough about magic." I looked up a big grin. "You're a mage, right? You must be super good at magic stuff!"

The harpy crossed her arms (or were they wings?) over her chest. "Of course I'm good. I went to the greatest academies in the Nesting King-dom. I certainly know more about magic than some peasant like you."

"Neat," I said. "Maybe I'll know something you don't, and we can trade lessons later. I'd love to learn more about magic and how it all works." The skiff shuddered and I felt it starting to move underfoot. "We're taking off!" I said as I dropped my book to my side and rushed to the porthole.

The docks were slowly receding as we moved backwards out of the port, the propellers behind the ship whirling like mad to pull us away. Then we slowed to a stop and the entire ship shifted so that its front was pointing to the sky.

"Whoa," I said as we shot forwards. I had to hold onto the walls to stop myself from falling. The city outside of the window flew past. Not at the kinds of speeds a plane back home could reach, but still plenty fast, and we were far closer to the city than any plane would dare fly over back home.

After a moment, the skiff stabilized, and its flight became a little more even. That's when someone knocked at our door.

"C'mon, kiddies," Gabriel's gruff voice called out. "Get to ze galley. We've got missions to talk about and I want to get it over wiz before I drown my sorrows."

"Is he the one that smelled like alcohol?" Amaryllis asked.

I nodded, then because she couldn't see me, answered aloud. "He is. It's really not a good example to set. Still, I trust that the guild wouldn't send someone too bad to accompany us."

Amaryllis landed on the ground next to me. "I hope you're right," she said.

I tucked away my book which had slid across the floor, then followed Amaryllis out into the corridor and to the front (bow?) of the ship. The area was little more than a very basic kitchen with a desk and a few chairs, all firmly bolted to the floor. Gabriel was at the head of the table, two stacks of paper before him with a knife through each to prevent them from moving.

The twins had beaten us to the mess and were already sitting down.

"Hello again," I said as I sat between Gabriel and Amaryllis.

"Hrm," Gabriel said. He pulled a flask from his belt and took a swig. "Alright tadpoles, let ze old man chat for a bit, and zen you can run off to do whatever."

He tapped one of the folders before him. I was mildly surprised to see paper being used for such frivolous stuff, I thought it was more valuable, but maybe there was some sort of paper-making magic out there? Or a paper dungeon with paper drops?

"Zis is an easy one. Even you brats ought to be able to pull it off. Twins, zere has been a shift in ze magical ley lines. Can either of you sense mana well enough to track ze source down?"

"I can do zat," Florien said.

"Good, zen do it," Gabriel said as he removed the knife holding one file in place and slid it to the twins. "As for you two. Zere is an old fort, made when we zought zere would be war with ze Trentans. It's been decommissioned and left to rot. Check it out, map ze roads around it."

He pulled the second knife out of the table and handed me the file.

"Now I'm going to go get very drunk. Don't bozer me."

# Chapter Forty-Four
# A Step Around the Boot

"I want to look around and get the big tour," I said to Amaryllis as soon as we were back in our little room.

"And leave me to do all the paperwork?" she asked acerbically while waving the file we had been given around.

I shook my head. "No, no! Let's look at it now, then… we could take the tour together? It sounds like a lot of fun?"

The harpy rolled her eyes and sat down onto my hammock to place the folder onto her lap. "No. But you're not wrong about looking over these now rather than later." She fumbled with the edge of the folder, her talons not exactly suited to handling the paper, but when I reached out to help, she glared and tore the folder open. There were only two sheets within, and they seemed identical. "Here, tell me if you don't understand anything," she said as she passed one over.

"Thanks!" I took the page and sat down on the ground next to my backpack to read over it.

**Exploration Guild Official Expedition Summary**
*Expedition No.124 of Year 398PC, Port-Royal Branch*
*Mission Statement: To explore, scout, and map the region around decommissioned Fort Froger and return to meeting point.*
*Estimated time: Approx. 3 days*
*Difficulty: Low to Negligible*

That left me with a few questions. Notably, what did the PC in the year stand for and who named the fort we were going to explore? Asking about the year would be suspicious so… "Did they really name the fort 'Fort Froger'?" I asked.

Amaryllis looked up from the page and shrugged. "Why not?"

"Isn't that a bit racist?"

She tilted her head to the side in a way that immediately made me think of a bird. "I think it would be speciesist, actually. And no, it's okay if the Grenoil themselves named it, I think."

"I guess," I said. "So, this isn't really heavy on the details. Do you know anything about this fort?"

"No, I don't. It sounds like one of the projects that went up just after the skirmish with the Trenten Flats. I know Deepmarsh went mad building fortifications for a few years, only for half of them to go unmaintained when nothing happened."

"I'm not familiar with the history," I said.

Amaryllis sighed and pinched the bridge of her nose with her talons. "I'll tell you once we're on the ground again. Go do your country bumpkin routine with the captain."

"Alright!" I said. She didn't need to tell me twice. I scrambled to my feet and tucked the page into my bandoleer before I noticed Orange's head looking around. I bit my lip. "Hey, before I go, can you watch over Orange for me? I don't want her to get hurt while I'm looking around the ship. Thank you!" I tossed the spirit cat onto Amaryllis' lap, the kitty looking none too pleased by the sudden motion, then walked out of the door.

Now I just needed to find the captain…

As it turned out, that wasn't too hard. The moment I climbed onto the deck I spotted him with his awesome hat standing next to the ship's wheel, a collapsible telescope in one hand and a folded map in the other.

I made sure that I wouldn't bump into anyone on the crew as I made my way to the rear section of the ship. I knew it was called a castle or something, but I wasn't quite sure. I had to brush up on my nautical terminology before I became a sky captain myself.

"Ah, hello there, Broccoli," Captain Isaac said over the rumble of the Silver Boot's engine and the whistle of the wind.

I pulled my hair back out of my face, then started to tie it into a rough bun. "Hello, captain!"

"This is excellent flying weather," he said. "We should be making it to Green Hold just before nightfall."

"Green Hold?" I asked. Since he wasn't looking right at me, focused as he was on his map, I decided to take a moment to scan the ship. Other than a few people coiling up ropes or sitting back and taking a break, there were few people on the deck.

The rest of the space was taken up by the big magic engine thing in the middle, two shirtless men both working around it with shovels in hand, occasionally tossing some glowy rocks into a burner at the back.

The front of the ship had another man with a telescope who was leaning against a large ballista while looking around. There weren't any canons or anything like that, which was a little disappointing.

"I take it this is your first time aboard an airship?" Captain Isaac asked.

"It is!" I said. "And it's wonderful."

He laughed, full and from the belly. "Count yourself lucky that the trip isn't even a day long. I love the Boot, but people who aren't born for the sky can find it hard to stay aboard a ship for a long while."

"That's ridiculous," I said. How twisted and evil would someone have to be to not enjoy time spent on an airship of all things?

"It is what it is," he said. "Did you want a bit of a tour? We still have a good six hours before we make landfall."

"Wait, we're arriving today?" I asked.

"You thought the trip would take longer?"

I shifted from side to side and pressed my fingers together while fighting a bit of a blush. "Well, I was kind of hoping for a grand airship adventure. You know, sky pirates and maybe a fight with an evil dragon?"

The captain blinked, then tilted his head back to laugh. "No! No, I'm afraid there's a dearth of sky pirates over Deepmarsh. And as for dragons, well, we have our banners."

"Banners?" I repeated. Captain Isaac pointed to the rigging where a pair of big green banners with a strange symbol in the middle. It had wavy lines that probably represented water, and a big mouth like a crocodile's chomping its way out of the waves. Its long, forked tongue was shaped a bit like a mangrove tree.

"You didn't hear it from me, but most dragons are on the wrong side of greedy. The sky belongs to them, so if you want to pass through their territory you need to pay a tax. The banners are a sign that you've paid your part. They're imbued with the dragon's own magic. They see the banner, they leave you alone. They don't and your ship is fair game. Worse, if they see a rival's banner then you'd best hope you know the featherfall spell because your ship is going down."

"Whoa," I said. "You can't fight them off?"

Isaac laughed, but this time it had a tinge of actual horror in it. "No, no you can't. A young dragon will usually be in its fourth tier. A match in sheer level for the Kingsguard. The older dragons are, well, no one knows."

"Cool," I whispered. I couldn't wait to find one and ask it if I could ride it. It didn't even need to be into battle. "Oh, so about that tour?"

"Of course, young miss, I would never forget a promise I made only a scant few minutes ago. Let me show you the Silver Boot in all of her glory!"

What followed was some of the most fun I'd had in weeks, and it was the best kind of fun, the sort where I learned a whole bunch.

"This is our gravity engine," Isaac said as he tapped the side of the big motor in the middle of the ship. "Careful, it's hot."

"How does it work?" I asked. I didn't know all that much about motors. My dad had shown me how to boost a battery and change the oil, and that was about where my experience ended. Everything else I knew was from television and books.

"I haven't the faintest clue," the captain said with good cheer. "I do know that it burns through quite a lot of mana-rich coal, which boils an alchemical reagent that, in turn, flows through a complex array of runes inside the metal casing. That's what gives us our lift. The boiling reagent gives off heat that pushes out of a cylinder. That also makes a flywheel turn, ah do you know what that is?"

"It's a big heavy wheel that soaks up energy and keeps turning for a while," I said. "I know what it is, yeah."

"Smart girl. There are belts leading below deck and to the control mechanism for our two propellers, and we have a switch that allows the pilot to change the direction they're turning in. It breaks quite often, but most of our forward momentum comes from our sails and some rune work. The propellers are merely more convenient than playing with the wind."

I waved goodbye to the two young men working on the engine and they smiled and waved back.

"Does working on an airship pay well?" I asked.

Isaac made an indistinct gesture in the air as we moved to the front. "For myself and the officers it's decent. Most of the crew are quite mixed. I've got blacksmiths and bakers and farmhands. There aren't that many classes suited to the work we're doing here. Still, the pay is better than what they'd get in some little town and they get to travel. It has its perks."

We got to the very front of the ship where the lookout stopped staring ahead with his binoculars to give us a jaunty wave.

"This," Captain Isaac said as he gave the big ballista a proud pat. "Is a Rever mark four. Imported all the way from the Snowlands. Cost me a pretty copper but it's worth it."

"You don't use cannons?" I asked.

"Cannons? I don't think placing a heavy lump of steel on my ship, then loading it full of explosives would be a good idea. Besides, cannonballs cannot be aimed with the assistance of marksmanship skills. At least, I haven't heard of enemy-seeking cannons yet."

"Sir," the lookout said while pointing to something out ahead. "Grey clouds on the horizon, dead ahead."

"Ah, damnation," Isaac said. "I'm sorry Miss Broccoli, but perhaps it would be best if you returned to your cabin for now. I wouldn't want to have to explain to that grenoil gentleman accompanying you why one of his charges had gone overboard."

"Ah, yeah, alright," I said. I wanted to stay atop the ship, but it wouldn't do to be impolite and end up dead, or worse, in someone's way. "Thank you for the tour. Your ship is wonderful!"

"It was truly my pleasure."

When I returned to the cabin it was to find Amaryllis swaying lightly in her hammock, one leg over the side and her head leaned forwards until it was almost tucked into her armpit. She was snoring lightly. Orange was rolled up in a ball on her tummy, back to sleep again.

I held back a giggle at the 'chuu chuu' noises she was making and slid into my own hammock with my book on basic magic. The day so far had been plenty productive, and I looked forward to seeing all sorts of new places later.

My first mission had so far been exciting, but it lacked… something to make it truly awesome. I figured it would come eventually, maybe as we finally hit the road and started on the adventure proper.

My hammock rocked from side to side, accompanied by my new partner's 'chuu-chuuing' and I tried to imagine what the future could bring. There were dragons to ride, and airships to travel on, and sky pirates to battle. There was magic to learn and awesome skills to discover.

I was smiling like a very silly little girl as I refocused on my book. The adventure was underway, but that didn't mean I could slack off. I had to work hard to make the best of friends and to see all the wonderful places the world had to offer.

# Chapter Forty-Five
# Upskirt Down

Green Hold was tiny.

Or at least, that was the impression I had of the town from what had to be about two hundred meters in the air.

From all the way up on the Silver Boot the houses looked like big rectangles and the walls were only a rough outline around the town. The layout reminded me a bit of Threewells, but with many more homes set around a central square. The area around the town was filled with little farms, most of them with homes close to the roads leading into town.

"You kids all have your stuff?" Gabriel asked. He was standing right next to the edge of the deck, heels over the side and his weight on the balls of his feet. The crew had removed part of the railing, the spot where the gangplank had been when we arrived. "We can't come back to ze ship if you forgot anyzing."

I hefted my pack, certain that I hadn't left anything behind. Amaryllis who was next to me didn't have anything to begin with, something that I was growing increasingly nervous about. Was she going to buy all of her gear in-town?

I set that aside for the moment and raised my hand.

"Yeah?" Gabriel asked as he pulled a flask and took a sip from it.

"How are we getting down?" I asked.

"Did you ever rappel before?" he asked.

"I have," I said. "But there's usually something to, ah, kick off of. And a mountain." Not two hundred meters of empty air. A glance over the side—where I had a railing to lean on—showed that a few people in the town below were eagerly looking up to us.

"First time for everyzing," Gabriel said. He secured his flask to his belt and then kicked a rope off the side. It went taut against the metal bar it had been tied to and the grenoil dropped four handles with little pulleys on them on the ground. "You set zem like zis," he said before expertly doing something with the device. Then he walked off the edge.

France gasped, but I had the opportunity to look down and see that he was slowing down his fall with his rappel. It was still fast, and he didn't have a harness, but he still made it to the ground without going splat.

"Well okay then," I said as I grabbed one of the other devices and waited for the rope to loosen up enough to grab it.

"Just like that?" Amaryllis asked.

"Do you want to go at the same time?" I asked right back. "We could hold hands on the way down if you're afraid."

The girl rolled her eyes and, without so much as picking up her own rappel, she walked off the edge.

"Amaryllis!" I screamed.

"Ah," Florian said. "She's a harpy, she'll be fine."

I looked over the edge and saw that she was, in fact, perfectly fine. Her arms were outstretched and, while she wasn't flying exactly, she was slowly drifting towards the ground, the long feathers on the ends of her arms twisting this way and that to control her fall.

"Oh," I said. I felt a bit silly after that. "Well, see you guys at the bottom," I said as I made sure my rope was taut and that my rappel was secured properly. "Bye Captain!" I called out with a wave.

Captain Isaac was near the wheel, but he heard me and gave me a parting wave. "We shall see each other again, winds willing," he called back.

I didn't have a way to say goodbye that sounded cooler than that, so I just hopped off the side.

The rappel went taut, then something went very wrong. The device slowed my fall, a little, but not nearly as much as I wanted to. I screamed as the ground reached up to me and suddenly two hundred meters didn't look that far away.

I shot as much stamina into my legs as I could and at the very last moment prepared to jump.

I hit the ground feet first.

My stamina went from completely full to just shy of empty.

The ground cratered.

"Zat was a good landing," Gabriel said from a few feet away. "But next time, don't rappel wiz a skirt on unless you want to give ze whole town anozer show."

I squeaked and pushed my skirts down, then I stepped out of the crater I had left in the road. "Did you do that on purpose?" I asked him.

"Look at your rear? You're not my type, dry-skin," Gabriel said.

"Not that!" I said as my anger warred with my embarrassment to warm up my face. I could have died and I was mightily miffed about it.

"Don't get yer panties in a knot," Gabriel said. "I'd have caught ya if ya didn't catch yourself."

I tightened my fists but didn't have time to give Gabriel what for before a scream from above had me looking up. France was rushing down towards the ground at a breakneck speed. I shifted, ready to jump up and at least try to catch her when she suddenly glowed and slowed down before landing on her feet with both eyes wide open.

Gabriel lowered a hand that had been pointing right at the grenoil. "See?" he said.

"You can do magic?" I asked.

The older grenoil snorted. "Featherfall. In our line of work, you learn how to cast it or you learn how to pick up your insides after zey go splat."

"Right," I said. I made note of that. My anger had faded a little in the time it had taken to watch him slow down France's fall.

"Go see to your partner. Ze fool girl wanted to leave before the sun set. Not zat I care."

"Oh, okay," I said before turning around and looking for Amaryllis. The harpy girl had landed at some point because she wasn't in the skies above. I took the chance to inspect Green Hold from the ground. It was a simple little town, more homes than Threewells, but most of them had mud walls and they were barely more than a floor tall.

Just because they were made of mud didn't mean they were poorly crafted though. Most of the homes were built into neat squares and they had little gardens out back with flowers blooming within. Red roofs all gleamed in the almost-orange light of the waning evening and the air smelled like firewood and supper, unlike the rancid odour that had permeated Port Royal.

I ended up wandering along the main street until I found an irate Amaryllis waiting before what looked like the town's inn, arms crossed and talon tapping at the ground. "You finally decided to show up. Good. Let's go," she said before bending down and picking up a bag that had a bedroll and tent tied to the top.

"We're leaving already?" I asked. "And where were you hiding that? Do you have an inventory?"

"An inventory? I'm not giving you a list of my belongings," she said. "And yes, obviously we're leaving now. The sooner we get this over with the better."

I didn't sigh because that would have been rude, but I certainly felt like sighing. I had kind of hoped that we could become friends but so far that hope had turned into mush.

I followed after Amaryllis as she aimed for the town gates.

No. No I couldn't just give up. "I won't give up."

"You won't give up what?" the harpy girl asked.

"I won't give up on trying to be your friend, even if sometimes you're a little rude," I said.

The girl stopped a few steps ahead of me and gave me a look so filled with confusion that my determination to become her friend soon turned into determination not to giggle in her face. "My partner is an idiot," she said before walking on.

"I'm not an idiot. We just think differently," I said.

She huffed as she marched out of the gates, the man on guard duty not even giving us more than a passing look. "Different is right. Your intelligence stat must be in the negatives you're so different."

"There's an intelligence stat?" I asked.

"And you're gullible too." She stopped and looked around, then pulled a tiny compass from an inner pocket of her leather jacket. "North and East," she said.

"You know where the fort is?"

"Unlike someone, I purchased a map. You do know what a map is, don't you?"

"Being rude won't stop me from becoming your friend," I said, a huge grin splitting my features when Amaryllis turned to glare at me. I only smiled harder.

"Tch." She stomped off along the road, head darting this way and that as we moved out of the area with little farms and into what was almost a forest. Almost, because for every tree there was a deep puddle of brackish water.

The bugs must have sensed us, and they knew that we were a snack, because soon enough there were swarms of mosquitoes flying our way. I stopped and searched my bag until I found my bug-repelling rune, the one I had purchased in Port Royal. It came with a thin leather strap that made it easy to wear as a bracelet. A bit of mana pushed into it and the bugs coming our way suddenly whooshed back.

"Hrm. Not completely useless," she muttered.

"I strive to not be completely useless," I said as I pulled out a runelight next. It came with a handy strap that went around the head, but it fit around the brim of my cool hat just right. It wasn't full dark yet, but it was getting dark enough that a bit more light would be appreciated. I pinched the tip of my tongue between my teeth and focused. A second trickle of mana had a cone of light flashing out ahead of us.

```
Health 120/120
Stamina 31/125
Mana 109/115
```

I made a note to keep an eye on my mana reserves. Maybe I could cycle the bug-repelling rune.

Amaryllis snapped her arm to the side and a knife appeared in her hand, a strange leaf-shaped blade that had two tines at the end instead of a point. She glared at it and then the tip lit up like a flashlight.

"Neat," I said.

"Even an idiot ought to be able to use a spell like that," she said.

I smiled, happy that she was willing to talk, at least. "You're a lightning mage, right?"

"Thunder mage," she corrected.

I fired a stealthy Insight at her.

```
An irate Thunder Mage (level 9).
```

So, she was three levels ahead of me, which probably meant that she had at least one more class skill. I was willing to bet that she had skills that were way cooler than Cleaning and Cute.

Especially Cute.

"So, is thunder-aspect mana close to light?" I asked as I scanned the marshes around us. They were surprisingly noisy, with frogs croaking and bugs humming and the occasional splash or gurgle from the water. As the sky darkened even more my paranoia went up a notch.

"It's adjacent, yes," she said.

"So it's only two steps away from Cleaning magic?"

"I do not use that kind of peasant magic," she huffed.

I shook my head at that. Cleaning was useful. I mean, it wasn't fireball, but it was alright.

We reached an area where the road forked, and Amaryllis pulled a small map from a side pocket of her backpack. "I think there's a spot that's a little dryer up ahead."

"We can set up camp then," I said. "It'll be hard to light a fire around here."

"Best not to then. It would attract the slimes."

The what?

But I didn't have time to ask as she kept on moving and I had to jog to follow behind her. As it turned out, she had been right about the dry spot. It was just a more elevated position that overlooked some of the swamp around us, but it was a bit further from the many little tributaries running down from the east.

We set up only one tent, both of us quiet after Amaryllis insisted that we use her superior gear for the night.

And then, after flipping a copper and drawing first watch, I was left alone again. It was okay. I was making steady progress. I knew that in no time at all Amaryllis would dislike me a little less!

**Congratulations! Through repeated actions your Friendmaking skill has improved and is now eligible for rank up! Rank D is a free rank!**

# Chapter Forty-Six
# A Slimey Situation

"Wake up!"

I shifted around, turning my back to the noise that had disturbed me.

"Wake up you blasted idiot!" Someone hissed before I got a rough shove against my shoulder.

"Huu?" I asked as I looked around and tried to piece things together. It took a while for the memories to return and for the sleep to wear off. I had gotten first watch, which meant I got to listen to Amaryllis' cute whistling snores again while hugging my knees in the near-dark.

She had told me not to play with any magic because it attracted monsters, so I had basically spent a few hours all alone in the dark with nothing to do. No lights to read by and just the sky to watch. At least so far from any civilised places the skies had been truly spectacular. It was easy to look up to them and just… drift away.

Then Amaryllis had relieved me, and I got to go to sleep on her surprisingly soft mattress in a tent that I was pretty sure was enchanted to make a person sleep really well. Or maybe I was just really tired.

"Wake up you moron!"

Thunder boomed.

The ground skipped out from under me.

I screwed my eyes shut and let out a squeak as any hints of sleepiness fled.

The flash faded away as suddenly as it had come, and we were left in the dark once more. "My night vision is shot," Amaryllis said.

"What's going on?" I asked as I scrambled to my feet, bumped against the walls of the tent, then stumbled out into the spot we had chosen to camp in. It was still completely dark out, without even the barest hint of sunlight on the horizon.

"Get your gear; leave the tent," Amaryllis said. "Slimes!"

"Slimes?" I asked. Some part of me, still mostly asleep, wanted to flop down and go right back to napping, but an electric buzz startled me and I looked up to see Amaryllis, both wings glowing with static sparks and hair-feathers standing on end.

She flung an arm out, her little knife held at the end, and a long forking jolt of lightning shot out and into the marshes.

I stared at the creature it hit.

The thing was big and bulbous, wobbly, and most of all, dirty. It was as if someone had taken the biggest ice-cream scoop in the world to a bowl of jelly then rolled the ball in some mud and twigs.

*An unemotional Marsh Slime (level 8).*

Electric shocks ran across its body and it seemed to wilt on the spot. Then another rolled out of the woods, and another came after it.

I rushed to the tent, grabbed my backpack to fling it on, picked up Orange, plopped my hat on, and grabbed my spear. An afterthought had the rune-light at the front come on to illuminate our surroundings.

"Oh no," I said.

"We need to make a run for it," Amaryllis said. "There are too many to kill."

"You were going to kill them?" I asked as I watched the dozens of slimes that had surrounded us as I slept. I couldn't blame Amaryllis for not noticing them sooner, other than that gurgling sound they made while moving they were hard to spot against the marshy ground. "What if they're nice?"

"Nice? They're slimes!"

"They could be nice slimes?"

"All they do is eat things. They don't even have brains! World smite me, you could pass for one of them." Amaryllis' arm shot out and another bolt of sizzling electricity shot out and splattered a tiny, basketball-sized slime that had bounced towards them. "Follow the road north!" she said before running off the little cliff we were on.

I followed, leaping off the ground with a burst of stamina that had me overshooting Amaryllis and landing on the path. A flash of my light on the road ahead revealed that it wasn't quite cleared, with a few slimes blubbering about, but not so many that we couldn't avoid them.

The path towards Green Hold, on the other hand, had far fewer.

"South?" I called out, pointing to the easier path.

"No, North," Amaryllis said as she landed and immediately started running that way.

I followed, stumbling a bit as I got used to the weight of my pack, but I caught up with a few quick bounces. We avoided the bigger slimes, both of us taking to the air to pass over them even as they sent out little slimy tendrils to try and catch us.

I thought we were in the clear when I heard a 'whump' and Amaryllis disappeared from my side.

My feet dug into the dirt road with a scrape as I stopped and whipped around.

Amaryllis was on the ground, electrified hand slapping at a large gooey tentacle wrapped around her face and neck. A huge, bulbous slime gooped out of the nearest tree, still hanging onto Amaryllis as it moved towards her.

I ran at her. First trying to pull her away from the monster, but when that didn't work I slapped a hand against the slime, then winced as it felt as if I had stuck my hand in a pot of hot water. It prickled against my skin and I caught a faint burning odour in the air. "Clean!" I screamed as I fired the quickest cleaning spell I could muster.

The tentacle burst apart into motes of light and Amaryllis stumbled onto her knees, gasping.

"Here," I said as I pulled out the trifecta potion I had in my bandolier and pushed it into her hands.

The slime grabbed me, a long limb slithering around my waist.

"Oh no you don't," I said.

Mister Menu flashed before me.

```
Cleaning
Rank C - 100%
The ability to Clean. You are exceptionally
good at tidying up and washing off.
Effectiveness of cleaning is marginally
increased. You may now use mana to clean
things you touch.
```
**Eligible for rank up!**
**Rank B costs two (2) Class Points**

"Yes!" I said.

It was a long overdue upgrade, and I still had two more class points to spend. Really, I should have done it a while ago but there had never been a reason until now.

```
Cleaning
Rank B -00%
The ability to Clean. You are exceptionally
good at tidying up and washing off.
Effectiveness of cleaning is marginally
```

*increased. You may now use mana to clean
things you see.*

Things I could see? I brought my arm up and aimed it at the slime. "Clean!" I'd come up with cooler attack names later.

I felt my mana rushing into my hand, then it formed into a tight ball, hundreds of swirling strands of interwoven magic, like a three-dimensional kaleidoscope. The ball burst forwards and slammed into the slime with a dull thud, like a potato canon smacking a brick wall.

The slime exploded.

I stumbled back, gasping as the bits of slime still on me faded away. That had cost a chunk of mana, but it had certainly been worth it.

**Congratulations! You have caused Marsh Slime, level 9, to get washed! Bonus Exp was granted for splattering a monster above your level!**

I sighed, but my relief was cut off as more gurgles came from the forest around us. "Come on, we need to go," I said as I crouched down next to Amaryllis.

"I'm fine," she said before pushing me off. She got to her feet on her own and shook her head. "It merely caught me by surprise."

"It happens," I said. "You'll have to show me those spells of yours some time, they were awesome!"

"Yes well, that spell, that was a cleaning spell?"

"Yup! I've got it to Rank B! Um, I mean, journeyman."

"It was adequate," Amaryllis said, which set me to beaming. She huffed and turned away. "Let's keep moving. Marsh slimes are mostly nocturnal. There are still some hours of night left."

We did just that, first jogging along then slowing down to a steady walk after we both stumbled one to many times on the puddle-covered and uneven road. I got to practice my new and improved cleaning spell a few times too. It seemed as if it came with a sort of ingrained knowledge on how to fire it, either as a ball-like projectile or a bigger cone. The latter took a lot of mana, but it was fun to use. Like a flame thrower but for cleanliness.

Firing big bursts of cleaning magic at the littler slimes that tried to jump at us was a fair bit of fun, and even Amaryllis joined in, blasting them out of the air with well-aimed shocks and crackling electrical whips.

The sky started to lighten to a paler blue and the marshes changed, the slimes receding away and into the swampy waters while birdsong filled the air and all sorts of animals came awake. "We made it," I said as I stumbled to a stop.

I was running on a couple of hours of sleep and had been walking and using magic for the past couple of hours. My batteries were all spent.

"We have," Amaryllis said. "There are some rocks over there. We can take a break. Eat."

I followed her pointing finger to find a big hill with a few stones jutting out of it. It was just off the road a little ways. "Alright," I said, too tired to voice any other opinions. "You don't have your pack though. But… but we can share the food I have!"

She snorted and shook her head as she took off.

I checked my notifications, making sure to do so quietly because the last thing I wanted was for Amaryllis to think I was the sort of crazy person that talked to her system menu.

```
Congratulations! You have committed minor
genocide! Your kill tally amounts to:
Marsh Slime, level 1 x 4
Marsh Slime, level 2 x 2
Marsh Slime, level 3 x 3
Marsh Slime, level 4 x 1
Marsh Slime, level 5 x 1
For refusing to spare the children you have
been granted Bonus Exp!
```

"Ah," I said. "Ah… ah-ah. Ah!"

Amaryllis stared at me, pausing halfway up the hill. "Did your last two braincells bounce apart?"

"I… ah," I explained. Then, because words were failing me, I made gestures.

"If you need to piss just go behind a bush." She sniffed. "It's not exactly luxurious, but this place is already a swamp."

"Ah!" I tried again. There was a sting in my eyes as tears gathered.

```
Congratulations! Through repeated actions
your Cute skill has improved and is now
eligible for rank up!
Rank C costs one (1) Class Point
```

"Ahhhh!"

"And you've lost your mind," Amaryllis said. She dragged me the rest of the way up the hill, then pushed me down onto a rock. "You sit there and... keep doing whatever."

"Ah," I squeaked back.

"Right... and... thanks. You know, for back there. I'll pay you back for the trifecta potion."

She moved off to the centre of the hill and I saw her bringing her feathery arm over her head to mask her face from the sunlight.

"Th-the slimes," I said. "Were they sapient? Sentient? Do they have little slime homes and little slime families?"

"What? No. They're made from concentrations of ambient mana. It takes a particular kind of mana to make them. Then they roll around and stick to anything magical they run across, including people. They're a nuisance."

"Oh, okay," I said.

It still took a while, and maybe a dab at my eyes, to really calm myself down. Knowing that the slimes weren't people made it... better. Not okay, but better.

"We can see the fort from here," Amaryllis said. "It's actually quite close. I think the scale on my map is off."

I sniffled, then fired a cleaning spell at my face, which tingled and made me sneeze, but at least it cleared my nose up. "Um. We were sent to map out the fort's location. Where did you buy the map?"

"It's from the Golden Nest Bank. They're a Nesting Kingdom institution, can't blame them for being wrong about misplacing such an ugly building."

I climbed up the hill so that I was next to her and took in the distant form of Fort Frogger. It was a large squarish building some ways away, with a single stubby tower and dull grey walls around it, most of them looked cracked and broken even from afar.

And between us and the fort was a good couple of kilometres of swampland.

It wasn't going to be fun getting there.

## Chapter Forty-Seven
# Mud and Bone

I could feel my nose wrinkling up and had to stretch my neck back as I sank into the mud until it tickled my chin. It wasn't too deep, and my hands easily found the bottom, so there was no danger of staying stuck. There was even a lethargic current flowing past that made it... not easy, but possible to move around.

"Lower," Amaryllis hissed right next to me. "Do you want to be found?"

I sank just a bit deeper in the mud until it was just short of my lips. Orange, who was tucked into the nape of my neck, walked around so that she was standing right next to my head in the shadow cast by my helmet. Standing on the air to avoid the mud was cheating!

The sound of loose-fitting boots clunking past had me freezing on the spot.

Amaryllis and I had picked the nearest spot to hide in. There were plenty of bushes and more mud than anyone could want. A great hiding spot, but not a place that I would want to fight in. Getting out would be tricky, which meant that I couldn't afford to be spotted.

The feet thumped closer and soon the noise of footfalls was competing with the thudding of my heart to be the loudest noise around.

I saw a pair of boots move past, then another behind that one. They stopped.

My heart started beating faster.

The boots turned my way and I shut my eyes, almost expecting to feel an attack coming.

The renewed thumping of feet had me letting out a held breath. I slowly turned my head and looked in the direction the patrol had moved in. From further away I could see more than just boots.

The group was made up of four grenoil skeletons, each in simplistic armour and carrying an ill-maintained spear and buckler. Glowing undead eyes scanned the marshes and occasionally stopped to stare at a marsh bird or a swaying tree.

"Let's move," Amaryllis said.

Amaryllis looked kind of silly, her white feathers plastered to her head by an entire layer of caked-on mud and her pale features tinted brown by brackish water. I couldn't imagine it would be fun for her to clean her feathers later, some of them even stayed in the mud as we crawled out of it.

"Did you see another patrol?" I asked.

"No. It could just be the one," she said. She didn't sound so certain of that.

The fort was close. So close that I could actually make out the lights lit from within despite the full morning sun. There were people manning the walls, some of them walking around, others standing stock still.

I had the impression they weren't living people.

"Did you see their level?" I asked. I had forgotten to use Insight while in the mud.

"Between six and eight," she said. "Not too strong for a normal monster, but powerful for an undead."

"Are undead common around here?" I asked. "I've seen some before, but it was in an abandoned town."

Amaryllis eyed me for a moment before looking towards the fort. "No. No it isn't normal. Let's get closer to the fort. We might be able to see where they're coming from. Most of the time undead spawn where there are plenty of bodies and certain types of... unfavourable mana."

"Could it be an undead dungeon or something?" I asked.

"Let's hope not," she said before skulking forwards. She kept low to the ground, her task made easier by the lack of backpack or any gear. I still hadn't gotten a straight answer out of her about that.

We kept as close to the few patches of dead trees as we could. Amaryllis even touched a few of them with a talon and frowned at them. We saw another patrol, just three grenoil skeletons this time, and they were heading away from us. We waited for them to get out of the area before moving on.

Soon we were before Fort Frogger, hiding near the lip of a hill with just the tops of our heads sticking out to take in the entrance of the fortress. The large wooden doors were open, one of them broken and ripped free of its huge metal hinges. The inner courtyard was filled with the undead, mostly grenoil skeletons, but a few that looked like strange horses with human upper bodies. Centaurs?

Two larger skeletons, both in plate armour and holding up Broccoli-sized swords were waiting at the gate.

*A Skeleton Knight (level ?).*

"I can't even see their level," I said.

Amaryllis sighed. "Ten. They've hit their evolution level, the undead can't really go beyond that, not without some very unusual circumstances."

"Evolution?" I asked.

She turned to me. "You really don't know anything, do you?" she asked.

I shrugged before lowering myself down. The little hill we were on was surrounded by a good number of trees, so I wasn't too afraid of getting spotted by a passing patrol. Still, I had yet to remove the layer of mud that covered me. It was good camouflage.

"I'm going to go say hi," I said.

"What?" Amaryllis asked.

"Look, our mission is to scout the region, right? We've sort of done that. Now we just need to see inside the fort, but that can't happen if we have to fight our way in. You're very strong, I'm sure you could take the two skeleton knights at the door. But then there are a whole bunch more inside. So we try the nice way."

"The nice way? Is that what they call suicide where you're from?" Amaryllis asked.

I figured she was being rhetorical. And rude. Mostly rude. "Let me try? If it doesn't work, then we go back to Green Hold and tell Gabriel and that's that."

Amaryllis glared at me, looked over the hill at the fort again, then back at me. "Are your stats back up to full?"

```
Health 120/120
Stamina 79/125
Mana 115/115
```

"Most of them, yeah," I said. "My stamina is a little low, but it's not too bad." I took Orange off my shoulder and handed the kitten over to Amaryllis.

She took the kitty in both taloned hands with surprising care. Orange didn't even protest at the contact.

Then I shucked off my backpack and searched within. I found a potion and refilled the pocket that had held the trifecta potion I had given Amaryllis. "Okay. Can you watch over my bag? It's not too heavy."

"I can," she said. "If this goes south and you die, I'm keeping the cat."

I grinned at her, then scritched Orange behind the ear where she liked it best. "She likes you, so it's okay. You can have my stuff too, I guess."

"Idiot. Do try not to die. I might be stuck with an even bigger fool next time."

I grinned so hard my cheeks hurt. She did care!

I fired a cleaning spell at myself and felt all the mud and gunk rolling off me like water off a hot pan, then I poked Amaryllis and did the same for her. She shivered as my magic washed over her, and even let out a little 'oh' when it was past. "See you soon!"

The knights spotted me before I was even halfway to them, but other than shifting so that their swords were in a sort of guard position, they didn't really react. I stopped a dozen meters away from them and waved. "Um, hello! My name is Broccoli Bunch, I'm with the Exploration Guild. I was hoping to talk to your leader. Or your boss, I guess. Um… rarr?"

The skeleton knights paused, then as one they turned and stepped to the side, leaving the path into the fort's courtyard open.

"Is that an invitation to go in?" I asked.

I didn't even get a 'rarr' in response.

"Can I go get my friend?" I asked.

The skeletons didn't seem to mind. Or if they did, I couldn't tell from their complete lack of motion. I waved at the hill, and soon enough a very cautious Amaryllis stepped out from over the edge and walked over to me, eyeing the skeletons the entire time. "What did they say?" she asked when she came closer.

"I don't know. I can't speak skeleton."

"Skeleton isn't a language," she said.

The skeletons shifted and one of them let out a low 'rraarrg.' I pointed at it, my point obviously made.

I wanted to grab Amaryllis' hand to pull her in—it wouldn't do to leave the leader of the skeleton's waiting—but didn't know if it was okay to touch her feathery arms, and her taloned hand looked hard to hold. So instead I just pouted at her and gestured inside.

She sighed, but followed after me as I moved in.

There were skeletons in the courtyard, both grenoil and the strange four-legged ones. They were too slight to be actual half-horse half-humans, though maybe centaurs were just small-boned. I made a note to ask Amaryllis about them later.

No one stopped us as we reached the entrance of the fort proper. It was a large, squarish building, made of big stones that looked like they had been fused together, probably by some sort of fancy earth-magic. The tower we had been seeing for a while stuck out of the middle; small slit-like windows all around probably gave anyone within a spectacular view of the area.

I paused before the door and checked myself out as best I could, running fingers through my hair, dusting off my gambeson a bit and making sure that my skirt was on straight.

"What are you doing?" Amaryllis asked. She was switching between looking at me, and at the listless skeletons around us.

"I'm making sure that I make a good first impression. People judge you a lot based on how they meet you for the first time, even though judging people like that is wrong. But if I want to make lots of friends then I need to put my best foot forwards."

She stared at me for a moment, then raked her talons through her own hair-feathers and plucked a few crooked feathers out of her arms.

I was grinning as I knocked. Five quick taps of shave and a haircut boomed out.

We waited, both of us shifting uncomfortably while my knock echoed within the building. Footsteps sounded out, low and heavy as if something big was approaching. As it came closer, I could just barely make out the clatter of something like nails scratching against wood in a frenzy.

The door opened with a whoosh.

I stared at the rather plain man within. Sure, he was a ghoulish-looking man with glowing blue eyes behind a pair of spectacles, but he was wearing a cardigan over a sweater-vest and had big fluffy loafers on. Next to him was a dog.

Most of a dog.

A dog skeleton. One the size of a small car.

It stared at us, tail helicoptering through the air so fast I could feel the wind from where I stood. When the tip hit the ground, it cut thin grooves into the stone floor.

"Yes?" the man asked.

"Ah, hi!" I said. "My name is Broccoli Bunch! Let's be friends!"

Amaryllis smacked me behind the head.

"Are you the... lord of this estate?" she asked, voice far haughtier than it had been just a few minutes ago.

"And if I am?" the man asked. He stood taller, and his big puppy stopped shaking with repressed happiness. I fired off two quick Insights while he stared down Amaryllis.

*An Undead Human Bone Setter (level ??).*

*A Bone Hound of the Long Slumber, (level ???).*

I wasn't sure what to do; the tension was rising, and I could literally feel the danger in the air. I didn't know if it was mana leaking out of the two near me or just bad vibes, either way it had to stop, and I knew just the thing!

"Do you like tea?" I asked.

# Chapter Forty-Eight
# A Good Boy

I stared at the undead lord of the tower and his glowing blue eyes stared right back.

The tension in the air grew thicker.

The undead dog let out a long, low growl that made the ground vibrate underfoot.

Then the man placed a hand on the dog's snout without even looking, and it stopped. "What kind of tea?" he asked.

"Oh, I have milk-thistle which is great for the liver, chamomile for relaxing, and I even have some honey!" I said. "Amaryllis, where's my backpack?"

"I stored it," the girl next to me said. "I thought you wouldn't need it, but I can retrieve it in a moment."

"O-kay?" I asked.

Stored? Was there an inventory system all along and I had been lugging things around despite it all this time? Why couldn't I get a handy tutorial that explained all of these things?

"Well, I suppose some tea wouldn't hurt. We'll need a pot to boil the water," the man said.

"I have a kettle in my pack," I said. "Just one cup though, I'm afraid."

The man looked at me, eyeing my most earnest smile (it was extra earnest because I had nothing to hide!) and then he looked over to Amaryllis and sighed. "Very well. Come on in. Don't mind Throat Ripper here, he's a good boy."

The man stepped back to allow us to enter the dark halls of his fortress. His slippers made swishy sounds as he walked towards a room just past the entranceway. It was a lounge area, with a nice carpet. and a single chair next to a table that stood beneath a pretty chandelier.

"Chairs, two of them," he said to a skeleton in a frumpy suit in one corner. The skeleton turned around, bare feet clickety-clacking as he walked off, presumably to get some chairs.

I walked in before Amaryllis, head twisting this way and that to take in the entire room. The fort wasn't built to be pretty, that much was plainly obvious, but some efforts had been made to make it feel homelier. Banners had been added to the bare stone walls and plinths with simple vases stood here and there, usually close to paintings.

I approached one painting and took in the scene. It was a big skeleton dog, teeth bloody as it smiled towards the viewer while standing atop a pile of furry corpses.

"Do you like it?" the man asked. His voice was flat, but I had the impression the question meant a lot to him.

"Is that Throat Ripper?" I asked. The dog's head perked up at the sound of his name. "It's a very evocative image. I wish it was over a more peaceful scene though. Maybe a nice field of flowers or something? This is really well made though, the proportion and perspective are nice."

"Bah, everyone's a critic," he said, but I had the impression he was pleased by the answer.

"It's horrific," Amaryllis said. "And I've seen better from a drunk amateur in Farseeing."

"We can't all measure up, I suppose," the man said, his voice returning to a flat drawl.

I tried giving Amaryllis a look, but it didn't seem to catch on. "So, we haven't introduced each other yet," I said. "I'm Broccoli Bunch!"

"I'm Amaryllis Albatross. Pleasure."

The man crossed his arms, then nodded. "I'm Gunther. No last name, I'm afraid."

Amaryllis snorted at that, earning her a glare from Gunther. I kicked her shin with the side of my shoe. Why was she being so antagonistic to the nice undead man?

"You said the puppy is called Throat Ripper?" I asked.

Gunther shifted, chest puffing out a bit. "Yes. This is Throat Ripper the Marrow Eater. Just Throat Ripper is fine. He's quite nice."

"Does he like scritches? Oh! Wait, I have a pet too! Her name is Orange and she's the best kitten… Amaryllis, where's Orange?"

"She's here," Amaryllis said as she lowered the front of her jacket over her chest a little. It revealed Orange's fluffy head.

"You carry your pet around with you?" Gunther asked. "In such dangerous places?"

"Orange is a spirit kitten," I said as I patted her on the head. She gave me a look and nestled deeper into Amaryllis' chest. "I don't know what can hurt her, but I can unsummon her if things get dangerous."

"Ah, I see. That's quite clever. Incidentally, you may pet Throat Ripper. He's quite fond of being scratched over his sternum."

I gasped and moved closer to Throat Ripper and raised my arm up close to his face to present my fist. Usually dogs were smaller than me, but it was okay. He looked at my hand, then nudged it towards the side of his head. What followed was a whole minute of me making cutesy noises at the big puppy until he crashed to the ground hard enough that the entire fort shook and presented where his tummy would be if he had any flesh.

I didn't even need to get on my knees to scratch him.

Two skeletons ambled into the room hefting big chairs that they placed around the table before they moved off to stand by the wall. "Can I sit next to Throat Ripper?" I asked.

"I don't mind," Gunther said. He was smiling now. I think being friendly with his puppy made him like us a little more.

We sat around the table and I brushed my hands over my skirt to clean them off. I wasn't sure if using cleaning magic around a bunch of friendly undead was a good idea. I didn't want a repeat of what happened to Bonesy. "My stuff?" I asked Amaryllis.

She brought her hands up, revealing a ring around the base of one talon. With a deft flick she did something with the ring and with a poof, a pen and a piece of paper appeared on the table.

I stared. So did Gunther, but he didn't look surprised at all.

Amaryllis picked up the pen which looked like it had been shaped to be held by taloned hands and scribbled something on the page. Then she tapped both to the ring, and they poofed away. She stretched her arm out to the side, and a moment later my pack poofed into existence on the ground.

"Wow! That was great! What did you do?" I asked.

"Are you not from a city?" Gunther asked.

"Not one that has magic rings like that," I said as I stood up to fetch things out of my pack. The kettle came out and was placed on the table next to a stack of cups brought in by the skeletons who had left once again.

"It's a banking ring," Amaryllis explained. "For a small transaction fee, you can store things at a bank in any proper city. You can send a mana burst through the ring requesting pen and paper, which of course is free. Then you request whatever it is you want withdrawn from your storage and they'll teleport it to your ring. They sell certain items too, but the mark-up is exorbitant."

"So it's not like a dimensional storage pocket linked to your ring, just a sort of teleportation beacon?" I asked. It still sounded awesome, but not as great as a personal pocket dimension.

"What? Dimensional storage? That's obviously not possible," Amaryllis said.

I shrugged as I poured water into the kettle and then added some herbs to it.

"Actually," Gunther said. "It might be possible. Dungeons certainly don't care about things such as limited spaces. If you could learn how that functions and tie it to an item... I suspect you would make a killing."

Amaryllis scoffed. "Impossible. And the only killing that would happen is your own when the banks find out you're cutting into their margins."

I poured out three cups of tea, making sure not to spill any, then looked in my bag, and found some bread and a bit of cheese I had bought for the trip. It wasn't the best of either, with the bread going hard and the cheese being a bit strong, but it was better than nothing. "Alrighty," I said as I placed my jar of honey in the middle of the table.

I took a sip of my tea and licked my lips as I savoured the taste. It was really quite good. Amaryllis, after a bit of fumbling to grab her cup with her talons seemed to think so too, and Gunther made an appreciative noise.

"So, what brings you girls to this swampy backwater?" Gunther asked as he lowered his cup and took a piece of cheese to nibble on.

"We're with the Exploration Guild," I said. "We're both new, so they sent us here to map the area around the fort."

"I see," Gunther said.

"An area that belongs to Deepmarsh," Amaryllis said.

"If they want it back, they have but to ask," Gunther said. "But seeing as this area has been unoccupied for some years, I don't think that is likely."

"How did you come to live here?" I asked.

Gunther looked at me over the rim of his cup. "It's quiet. I don't mind the wildlife, and the nearest people are a day's walk away."

"That must be so lonely. You would need so many hobbies to pass the time," I said

"I have Throat Ripper," Gunther said before patting the big dog on the head. The creature had laid itself down on the ground next to him.

"You must be very close then," I said.

Gunther paused, cup held halfway to the table for a long time before he looked up and gave me a wry smile. "Throaty here is why I am the way that I am. When he passed… I couldn't accept that. So I embarked on a self-imposed quest to correct what I saw as a cruelty laid down upon me by the world itself."

"What did you do?" I asked.

"Oh, nothing too extreme. I was once a well-regarded arts dealer in Cinderrun. I gave all that up in order to change my class and become the seed of what I am now. It allowed me to bring back my one true companion, even if it meant cutting ties with neighbours and… well, I didn't truly have any friends, or family that I cared for."

Throat Ripper stood up and booped his master in the side with his head.

"And so, we set to travelling the world. Unfortunately, any class with a penchant for undeath is generally poorly regarded. Either by superstitious fools or those who know what death mana can do in a region if left there too long. We go from place to place, finding quiet little areas to settle down in for a decade or so before moving on. We have only been in this fort for a year and change. The skeletons you see around us are surprisingly easy to find. Throat Ripper has a knack for digging them up."

"You poor thing," I said. I pulled the collar of my blouse out from behind my gambeson and dabbed at my eyes with it. "I'm so sorry that people are mean to you. But sacrificing everything to bring a friend back is… it's beautiful."

"I… thank you?" Gunther said. He looked a bit uncomfortable, which I guess was normal after sharing such an intimate story. "You mentioned that you were here to scout out the region?"

"Yeah. We're supposed to map the area around the fort and explore it a little. We won't do that, of course. The exploring the fort bit, I mean. It would be way too rude to just trample around your home. But if you don't mind, we'd like to see what's around and maybe map that out. Is there a way to do that without bothering your skeletons?"

"You don't mind the skeletons' presence?" Gunther asked.

"Should I?" I asked right back.

Amaryllis covered her face with her hands. "My partner is an idiot, and yet the world conspires to keep her alive," she said.

# Chapter Forty-Nine
# Rift

I spent some time cleaning out my kettle with a cloth and setting everything away in my pack. It was just me and Gunther on the first floor of the fort. Amaryllis had left with Throat Ripper to go to the top of the tower to draw a map of the region, something that Gunther didn't seem to mind at all.

Gunther stayed in his seat and watched me work. It wasn't an awkward silence; we had shared a meal and some tea together, which meant we were more than halfway to being friends already, and a little undeathiness didn't bother me at all.

"You never said where you were from," Gunther said. It was a question, but without the tone of one. I think he wanted to make it easy for me to back out if it was awkward to answer.

"I'm from Earth," I said. "A place called Canada. It's very cold."

"Interesting," he said. "Which dungeon did you appear with?"

I paused mid-motion. "Eh?"

"You're not from Dirt, are you?" He gestured my way with a still steaming teacup. "I couldn't pin it at first, but you're not from this world."

"How did you know?" I asked as I stood up. I… didn't know exactly what to do. Fighting was out of the question, Gunther was a friend, or had the makings of one, and denying it was pointless when it was the truth. Still, of all the things I didn't know, how people treated someone from another realm was… well it was somewhere in the big pile of unknowns.

Gunther coughed. "Every sentence I just spoke was in a different language and you didn't bat an eye. I don't doubt that even someone your age could speak four tongues fluently, but I do think that most would be curious about the switches."

"You… what?"

"You didn't even notice? Interesting. There's a Skill called Tongues that at the expert rank does something similar. Though it's an advanced skill, and a difficult one to acquire. I don't have it, I learned to speak a few languages the hard way, but people like you, Riftwalkers, the rumours all agree that you have the gift on arriving here."

"Wait, there are more people like me?" I asked.

Gunther shrugged his shoulders. "One for nearly every new dungeon. Not always people. Those that can speak usually talk of some difficult or impossible quest. Most go on to live rather mundane lives. I've heard of strange and unique animals and creatures appearing next to new dungeons as well, so perhaps it is not just the sapient who are summoned."

"Whoa," I said. "Ah, I don't know what that means for me though."

Gunther hummed and took a long sip from his cup. "Nothing, I suspect. You're not the first, you're unlikely to be the last. The world might bless you or it might not. I know little more than rumours, truly. Even if a new dungeon appears every day, they appear so far apart and in such inhospitable locations that it is unlikely that most will meet someone like you."

"Oh," I said. "Well, thanks for telling me, I guess."

He nodded over his cup. "I was merely curious. I have lots of time to wonder over things."

I wanted to ask more, but Amaryllis and Throat Ripper both returned, the dog with a clatter of boney paws across the stone ground. "We're done," Amaryllis said as she waved a rolled-up sheet around.

"Oh, good work Amaryllis!" I said.

She scoffed. "Don't praise me for drawing something so simple." She shook her head. "We should be off soon, we've spent a fair deal of time here. We need to get back to Green Hold."

"In that case," Gunther said as he stood up. "I'll escort you ladies to the door."

"Thank you so much for your hospitality, Mister Gunther and Mister Throat Ripper. I'll cherish the memories. And I do hope we meet again."

"It was nothing. A welcome distraction, in fact. And you, at least, were a welcome and interesting guest," Gunther said.

Amaryllis snorted and crossed her wings at that. "This could have been worse," she said.

Gunther, true to his word, escorted us all the way to the door. "Goodbye, big boy," I said to Throat Ripper before giving him a pat. Gunther only got a handshake because he was an older man and those were serious people that you weren't supposed to hug. "We'll see each other again!" I declared.

"Goodbye, miss Bunch," he said. "And you as well, miss Albatross."

We left by skipping out the front gate.

Well, I skipped. Amaryllis walked like the boring no-fun person she was.

After taking our bearings for a moment, we aimed southwards along a well-trodden dirt path and started heading out. I soon stopped skipping, because even with my awesome calves bouncing around so much was taking a toll and I needed to even out my breathing if I wanted to be able to talk while walking.

"That went well," I said.

"I suppose it did. A little unorthodox, but the results speak for themselves," Amaryllis said. "Is walking up to strangers and threats and talking to them your solution to every problem?" she asked.

"Pretty much, yeah," I said. "I was raised to be as nice to people as I want them to be to me. You know, do nice things for your neighbour and they'll help you out in turn."

Amaryllis made a strange trilling noise, almost like a hum but more… birdlike. "That wouldn't fly where I'm from."

I had to restrain myself to stop from skipping again. This was my chance to dig into Amaryllis' past and learn all about her. If I knew more about her then I could become an even better friend. I was already breaking through her antisocial walls! "You're from the Nesting Kingdom, right?" I asked.

"Most Harpies are. It's our race's birthplace."

"Birthplace?" I repeated.

Amaryllis sighed. "You really do need an education. It's a wonder you know how to read at all."

"Sorry. Where I'm from it's pretty much just humans all the way."

"Ah," she said as if she understood, though I kind of doubted that. Unless knowledge of Riftwalkers was more common than Gunther had suggested. "Well, regardless. If we do end up staying partners in the future, then I'll have to make sure you read at least the basic history texts."

A smile burst onto my face and I grabbed Amaryllis in a side hug that had her squawking. "You do want to be friends!"

"Not if you don't unhand me right this moment, you damnable ape!" she screamed.

A few skeletons on a patrol nearby turned towards us and we both froze. Then they kept on trudging by without so much as a 'rarr.'

"Sorry," I said. "Um, change of topic then. What was it like in the Nesting Kingdom? Are you some sort of big shot?"

"I'm the third daughter of the Albatross family," she said.

"So… you have two big siblings?" I asked. That answer had been sort of strange.

Amaryllis stared to the skies. "You know nothing. And to think I suspected you were a spy."

"I wish I was a spy," I said. "It sounds so cool." I put on my suavest voice. "The name is Bunch. Broccoli Bunch."

"You would make a horrible spy," she said. "Unless this is all an act, in which case you're being paid far too well to spy on someone like me."

"Was that an insult?" I asked.

"You can assume that when I'm talking about your qualities it is in an insulting manner, yes." She smiled as she said it though, and I didn't feel any sting. "To get back to your earlier questions, no, I'm not important. My eldest sister Clementine is set to inherit everything. Which will make her a member of the ruling council of the entire kingdom in a few decades. My second eldest sister, Rosaline, has begun to run the family shipyards and she's quite talented at it."

I recalled her mentioning something about Nesting Kingdom airships being the best, and her family being big in that industry, so Rosaline's position had to be important. "And what about you?"

"I'm the spare."

We walked a little bit more in a silence that grew increasingly uncomfortable. "What do you mean?"

"Don't get emotional on my account," she said. "Spare me your pity. I merely mean that I was trained from birth to replace either one of my sisters if the need ever, in some nightmarish circumstance, arose and one of them needed to be replaced. The spare. Then I turned sixteen and I was let loose, so to speak. My sisters are both in good health, they're wonderful people, in fact, and there's no need for any sort of drastic measure. So I was told to just… mind my own business."

"Is that why you joined the Exploration Guild?" I asked.

"Well, if I'm going to make my family proud it won't be by sitting pretty in a mansion," she said.

I really wanted to hug her and tell her that she wasn't just a spare or something like that, but we weren't quite close enough for that just yet. Instead I made sure to walk close by her side so that she knew that she wasn't alone.

I was looking for something more to say when Amaryllis broke the silence. "Do you really not have magic rings where you come from? I thought they were common with humans, especially since you have fingers." She brought her hand up to demonstrate the lack of fingers.

"Ah, well," I said. I wasn't quite ready to tell the whole world that I wasn't from this place. "We had some. They were called mood rings. They told people how you were feeling and stuff. But mine were useless. All they said was that I was happy all the time."

"That does sound useless," she said.

I suspected that if she wore one it would be a nice irritated orange most of the time, but I didn't say as much. There was a layer of sadness under her prickly exterior, and I suspected that deeper still there was a core of niceness that was just well-buried. I would need to dig for it if I wanted her to become an even better friend.

"Do you have any neat magic trinkets?" I asked.

"I have plenty of them, though I wouldn't call them mere trinkets," Amaryllis said. "You have a few yourself, that kettle and that collar you're wearing."

"Oh, they both came from a dungeon," I said. "I think I got really lucky."

"Lucky that you survived?" she asked wryly.

"Yeah. I really wasn't as ready as I should have been for that one. But it's done now."

"I'll buy that collar off of you," she said.

I wrapped my hands around my neck. Sure, it was really ugly, but it would mean losing Orange. "No way," I said.

Amaryllis made that trilling noise again and shook her head.

We were leaving the area around the fort now, our trek so far having been mostly downhill since the fort was built at the end of a chain of hillocks, probably for the better view they offered. I couldn't imagine an army fighting around the fort, not with the amount of mud and swampland all around.

There was a small stone bridge ahead that ran over a river. It wasn't a very deep river, but judging by the marks left on the banks it was fairly dry at the moment. I didn't want to imagine what the wet seasons around the area were like if this was a dry spell. The trees around us seemed a little parched though, so maybe some rain wouldn't hurt.

We were crossing the bridge, Amaryllis answering inane questions about growing up as a harpy, when the shadows of the deadened trees shifted.

Three creatures stepped out before us. They were tall, horse like beings covered in loose clothes that draped back over their long bodies and over their more human-like torsos. Not horses, I realized as I looked at them, deer.

"Cervids?" Amaryllis asked.

She looked over her shoulder and I did the same. There were three more of them.

All six were armed, and I didn't like the looks they were giving us.

# Chapter Fifty
# Ambush

"Drop all of your weapons and equipment and get onto your knees," the deer-person—cervid, Amaryllis had called them—in the middle of the pack before us said.

"This isn't good," Amaryllis said. Her knife-wand slid into her hand from somewhere and began to crackle with an electric hum. "Cover the rear," she said.

I nodded and spun around, my backpack coming off to be tossed to the side as I pulled my shovel off my pack and held it before me. "Insight," I muttered.

```
A confident Cervid Lancer (level ?).
A confident Cervid Runner (level ?).
A bored Cervid Plains Speaker (level ?).
```

"They're pretty strong," I said. That had just been the three that snuck up behind us. I was willing to bet the leader was even stronger.

"We can take them," Amaryllis said, her voice brimming with confidence that I didn't doubt for a moment was fake. "It's just three on six."

I wondered what she meant for a moment before I saw Orange wriggle out from her shirt to come padding through the air. She stood floating at shoulder height next to me.

Licking my lips, I stepped up towards the nearest group of deer people and raised my voice so that they could all hear. "Hey everyone. My name is Broccoli. My friend and I were just travelling by here. If this is your bridge, we apologise."

"Five, Six, you're on the secondary target. Two, Three, Four, you're with me on the primary," the one I suspected was the leader said.

Judging by the way the Cervids shifted, the numbers were their names. Or at least, code names. Most of them were wearing helmets of one sort or another, and all of them had padded clothes on, like my gambeson but stretched out over their entire bodies. No markings that I could tell except for thin orange lines on their shoulders. Their equipment looked uniform, all made of the same materials and with the same cut.

Were these soldiers?

"Broccoli," Amaryllis said. "You should run. It's me they're after."

"No," I said. That wasn't going to happen. I didn't abandon friends, especially not when they were about to be attacked by some bandits or something.

"Break!" the leader said, and that ended any hope that we could have a civil discussion.

Amaryllis was the first to act, her knife hand stabbing at the air even as a thunderous boom sounded out and a pillar of bluish light as thick around as my wrist shot out and hit one of the deer folk.

He screamed as his body convulsed and his charge turned into an ungainly flop to the ground.

I didn't have time to feel pity for him.

Two of the deer people rushed straight at me. One with bare hands, the other with a long spear. The Lancer and Plains Speaker.

I froze for just a moment, the cracking of their hooves on the stone bridge like machine gun fire in my ears and the focus on what I could see of their eyes in the slits of their helmets rooting me on the spot.

Then Orange collided with the Lancer's face and his spear slid past me, cutting a hot line into my sides as it caught on the edge of my gambeson.

I screamed and did the first thing that I could think of. I jumped.

The Plains Speaker looked up to me in time to win a foot to the face. I used him as a springboard to land on the hip-high stone railing of the bridge.

This wasn't some fight in a dungeon where the enemies were only mostly real. This was dangerous, truly dangerous.

Amaryllis was ducking and weaving around a pair of spears trying to hit her, sparks flying out of her talons and skittering across the skin of her enemies. She was taking them four on one and, somehow, was holding her ground.

One of the Cervids was a mage of some sort, throwing translucent shields around that took Amaryllis' attacks without so much as a shudder. "Orange, help her!" I screamed.

I didn't want to fight; I didn't want to hurt people. I didn't want to be attacked. And I especially didn't want to fail a friend.

I swallowed and tightened my grip on my spade.

The Lancer spun around, and his spear darted towards me. I batted it aside, jumped off the railing so that I was right up in front of him, then I fired a blast of cleaning magic right in his face. He stumbled back, which gave me all the time I needed to hop up so that I was a bit above him. I came down with my entire weight swinging the head of my spade down on his helmet.

The 'bong' of steel meeting steel was like music.

The Cervid Lancer said some rude things as he took a step back.

I didn't have time to follow up as the Plains Speaker flung his arms out at me, a net opening wide in the air between us.

Eyes widening, I flung my spade at the net and, fortunately, slowed it down enough that I was able to side-step it.

The Lancer shifted his helmet back in place with one hand and looked ready for more.

And now I was without a weapon.

I jumped, flying over the Plains Speaker.

He raised both hands to catch me, but I brought one arm up and pointed it at his face. "Fireball!" I screamed.

The Plains Speaker shielded his face.

No fireballs happened.

I did get to land on the opposite railing without any issue though. My spear was next to my backpack, but I didn't have time to grab it. Instead I pressed both feet against the rail and shot backwards as hard and fast as I could, my legs springing out to trail behind me.

I crashed into the Plains Speaker shoulder-first.

The breath escaped from his lungs with an 'oomph' and he stumbled backwards until he was pressed up against the rails.

The Lancer had moved out of the way and was stabbing for me again. I don't know how I avoided the stab; it was all a blur of scrambling limbs to try and not get poked by the shining tip of his spear.

I grabbed the end of the lance just behind the metal spike at its end and, with my entire weight behind it, swung it around and into the Plains Speaker's side.

The Plains Speaker yowled as his partner's spear cut through his cloth armour. The Lancer yanked it back and out of my grip, but the damage was done.

I froze for a moment as blood spurted out of the wound and onto my hands.

It was hot.

The Lancer's foot kicked out and I coughed as a steel-shod hoof buried itself in my side.

I crashed to the ground. Rocks dug into my palms and knees as I tried to gather my breath and fight through the pain.

A shadow moved above me. The Lancer, his spear raised up to strike.

I rolled backwards, a move that I hadn't done since gym class some time ago. I was soon under the Lancer, on my back with my legs above me.

My stamina dropped to near-empty. "Meanie!" I screamed as both feet crashed into his chest in what would have been the strongest jump I ever made, were I standing up.

The Lancer went flying.

He was lighter than I would have thought, barely heavier than I was when wearing my full pack and gear.

The last I saw of him were flailing limbs as he went over the railing and splashed into the water.

No 'ding' that announced that I had killed anyone. Good.

I was panting and rolling onto my feet when a hoof rammed into my side and sent my rolling across the bridge. "Ah!" I tried to scream, but my lungs hurt too much.

With tears in my eyes I looked up to find the Plains Speaker walking up to me. He was favouring his injured side and had taken off his helmet. It was laying off on the ground some feet away.

His expression wasn't pretty. "Filthy human scum," he spat out before lashing out with another kick.

I couldn't do much to stop this one either except to curl into a ball around the impact to my stomach and try to keep my lunch inside as pain roiled across my chest.

"Making me look like an—" he began, then stopped.

Amaryllis screamed.

We both looked over to see her pinned to the ground, the long shaft of a spear through her thigh.

"No," I said.

"Hah, see what happens when—" the Plains Speaker began to say as he turned back to me.

I wasn't where he had left me.

My shaking hand clenched the edge of the helmet he dropped.

The Cervid turned around just as I swung with every last bit of strength I had left in me. His helmet caught him full in the side of the face.

I saw a tooth fly.

"Don't!" I said.

I swung in the other direction and caught him in the forehead.

"Hurt."

This time the point of the helmet caught him across his deer-like nose. It crunched.

"My."

He was falling back, eyes watery and wide, blood spurting out of his nose as he exhaled. I couldn't reach his face anymore. I let my hand fall into the helmet, wearing it like an oversized glove as I pushed what little stamina I had left into a forward lunge.

"Friends!"

My wrist snapped.

I cried out and pulled my hand back to my chest. The helmet, with its pointy edges, stayed stuck in the Cervid's chest armour.

I was breathing in gasps as I cradled a wrist that wasn't bending the right way.

The four remaining Cervids were moving closer. One had Amaryllis bound and unconscious on his back.

"Kill her?" One of them asked.

"No," the leader said. "She's a witness. Where's Five?

One of them, the mage, snorted. "Went over the edge. He's swimming to shore."

The leader looked over the side of the bridge and sighed. "Against a level six. Sad. Four, knock her out. Two, give Five a healing potion."

I watched as one of them raised a wooden wand my way. Light gathered at the end of it.

I tried to jump but my legs only wobbled.

The ball of light crashed into my chest and sent me flying back.

I wished that the world went black, that I would fade into the abyss of unconsciousness. No such luck. I writhed on the ground, tears streaming and teeth grit against the pain. I saw the Plains Speaker, looking the worse for wear, stopping above me.

His hoof came down and planted itself on my leg and twisted.

"Six!" the leader called back over my scream. "We're going. Leave her."

"Tch," Six, the Plains Speaker said.

He spat on me and walked away with a limp.

I heard them all moving off, five sets of hooves clacking across the bridge. They were joined by the lancer I had thrown off the edge.

Then their voices faded away into the distance. It didn't matter to me.

My hand, my left hand that still shook, reached into my bandoleer. Fingers scrapped across broken glass as I pulled out my broken trifecta potion. The remains had leaked out.

I flung the glass aside with a cry.

My backpack was still there. Someone had kicked it, but it was otherwise untouched. They weren't bandits here for our stuff.

I crawled to it.

```
Health 31/120
Stamina 02/125
Mana 79/115
```

I wasn't bleeding, not much that I could tell, but I was hurting all over. I didn't want to wait and see if I would heal over time.

Reaching my pack was hard, looking through it was harder.

Then Orange came closer and I saw the kitty climb into the backpack. She came out with a potion between her teeth.

"Thanks," I said. The cork came off. I downed it in one swallow. It was surprisingly sweet.

```
Health 37/120
Stamina 02/125
Mana 79/115
```

My health was ticking upwards, a point every few seconds. I found a second potion and drank it too.

The pain left, but it was slow. A soothing warmth that banished the hurt.

I sat against the side of the bridge and waited for my health to climb back to full. And in the meantime, I allowed myself to cry.

## Chapter Fifty-One
# Fetching Help

"Gosh… Darn it," I swore as the tracks in the ground just sort of stopped. Between one muddy step and the next there wasn't so much as a trace of the six sets of hoofprints left.

My left fist tightened, my right… sort of flopped uselessly and sent a nauseating wave of pain through my entire body.

I carefully held my broken wrist and turned back to stare at the bridge, still well in sight.

The Cervids had truly gotten away.

Not that there was much I could do even if I caught up. I didn't doubt for a moment that they had been holding back. Their leader wanted to leave behind a witness. I couldn't quite piece together the why of it. It didn't make sense.

I looked back and forth from the bridge to the path they might have taken.

It felt as if someone were grabbing my heart and squeezing, as if something were trying to crush my lungs in my chest and, for a long moment, I had a hard time even breathing. This wasn't leaving a potential friend because our paths split. This was losing a friend because someone had taken her away from me to do… do horrible things to her.

Orange pushed her head into my neck and looked up to me with eyes that reflected my sadness right back at me.

"Why?" I asked. I'm not sure who I was asking. The empty air. The world itself? It didn't matter. Things like this shouldn't have happened, not in my fun fantasy world with magic and dragons and fairies and…

I wiped my eyes again. I didn't have time for this!

Amaryllis needed saving, now more than ever.

If I had to… to hurt people to save a friend, I would.

Still, I had to find her first. There weren't any tracks left, and I didn't have the ability to see them from too high above. Even jumping as high as I couldn't didn't reveal anything. Orange was a cat; she couldn't track by scent the way a dog could.

And that gave me an idea.

I didn't run so much as I sprinted. I only stopped by the bridge to fling my backpack off to reduce my weight. I only kept my spear and spade.

Then I was off again, legs kicking out with constant jumps, the road flying by under me as I ate away at the distance.

What had taken Amaryllis and I two hours to cross at a leisurely walk took me twenty minutes.

In the end I collapsed into an ungainly heap at the front of Fort Frogger, my legs wobbly and inflamed from the constant impacts against the ground. Jumping so much couldn't be good, not if the twinges of pain travelling up my legs meant anything, but I didn't have time for anything like that.

It took a moment for me to catch my breath and finally get to my feet. The skeletal knights by the gate hadn't so much as flinched on my arrival.

I walked past them, wincing as the many, many aches across my body that two healing potions hadn't cured. I had one left, but it was for Amaryllis. She would need it more than I would.

"Gunther!" I called out as I knocked on the door with a closed fist. "Mister Gunther, please. I need help!"

The door to the fort opened. Mister Gunther stood in the entrance, flanked by Throat Ripper and looking quite unamused. Then he took me in and his expression shifted. "What happened to you?" he asked. "No, wait, come in, come in."

I followed him in. I wanted to talk right away, but he just kept walking until he was in the lounge and sitting in one of the chairs. The other two had been packed away already, so I was left standing before him. "Amaryllis was taken. Um, we were attacked. At that bridge."

"Not by my skeletons?" he asked.

"No. No by deer people. Amaryllis called them Cervids? There were six of them. They were in uniforms."

Gunther looked at me, an eyebrow rising. Then he saw my wrist. "Come closer. Give me your hand."

"It's broken," I said without approaching.

"I had assumed as much," he said drolly. "Is your class suited to mending bones?" he asked.

"No?"

"Then listen to what I say and come here." I came closer and extended my hand to him. He wasn't very gentle, and I had to hold back a hiss as he turned it over. "Apologies. Most of the time when I'm handling bones the… owner isn't capable of feeling pain any longer." He gripped my hand and pulled.

There was a sickening pop, and I gasped. Then a wash of warmth raced through my wrist and arm and the pain faded to a memory. I yanked my hand back and hugged it close, but a few motions revealed it to be back to normal.

"Tell me of your encounter."

I swallowed. "Oh, okay," I said. I recounted the story of what had just happened. By the end I was breathing hard and I didn't know if I wanted to throw a tantrum or start crying. Throat Ripper helped by standing next to me and pushing his big head into my side.

"I see," was all Gunther said in the end. He arched his hands together and leaned back into his chair. "What are you going to do now?"

"I… I wanted to ask your help," I said while looking to the ground. I was still idly scratching Throat Ripper's neck, but that didn't require much thought.

"To return to Green Hold unbothered? I could let you take a pair of skeletons with you. It would serve as a good deterrent."

"No, to save Amaryllis. I can't track them down. I don't know where they went," I said.

"Didn't you already lose against them? What makes you think you stand a chance now?" he asked.

I sniffled. I wasn't going to start crying again. "I don't know. But I have to save her! She's my friend!"

Gunther looked at me for a long while, then he let out a sigh. "I suppose we could assist you."

"Thank you!" I said before I launched myself across the room and hugged him. "Thank you so, so much!" I repeated.

Gunther didn't seem to know what to do, so he settled with patting me on the head as if I was Throat Ripper. "Yes, yes. Well. Throat Ripper will be the one doing the assisting. And we won't do it for free."

I stood back up and nodded. I was smiling again, for the first time in hours. It had been a long time since I'd gone so long without a smile. "Yes, anything."

"Any— don't make such open promises," he said. "We'll help in exchange for a favour."

"What sort?" I asked. I was eager to get going now. With Throat Ripper helping I was sure I could find Amaryllis.

"Nothing uncouth, I assure you. Just return here and you'll see what I wish of you."

"I can do that," I said. "Can we leave now? Please? I don't know what they're doing to her. We need to save Amaryllis."

"I'm not sending my best friend out there with only you for support," Gunther said. "I'll gather my swiftest skeletons and send them as well. If there truly are six adversaries that have reached or passed the first rank, then you'll need a far greater number of skeletons to hold them back. Cervids are no pushovers."

Gunther stood up and I followed him as he started ordering skeletons around. First he told Throat Ripper and a few of the butler skeletons to go get the dog's armour, then he stepped out and casually pointed to half a dozen skeletons, all of them cervid, and told them to go and get equipped for battle.

It was a little disconcerting to see how much power Gunther had around his little fort, but that power was on my side and would help me save Amaryllis, and Gunther didn't seem like a bad sort of guy.

"Your goal is to save your friend?" Gunther asked me as we both moved back into the fort.

"Yeah, of course," I said.

"Then the moment you arrive, focus on that and nothing but. Take your friend and run back here, or if you must, towards Green Hold. The cervids aren't welcome there, nor is anyone else from the Trenten Flats."

"Is there some history there?" I asked. "Or is it just, uh, speciesism?"

Gunther blinked, then smiled as he rubbed at his nose. "Ah, yes I suppose you wouldn't know. The United Republic of the Trenten Flats is the largest nation on the continent. They're also fiercely expansionist and rather troublesome to have as neighbours. Some decades ago, they invaded Deepmarsh. Or rather, they tried to."

"Deepmarsh stopped them?" It wasn't time for a history lesson, but I was waiting and maybe learning a little about the kidnappers would help.

"They will certainly claim so. I believe that the truth is more nuanced. The Trenten invasion was large, outnumbering any force Deepmarsh could bring by three to one. But they were led by an inexperienced general, didn't have many scouts, and the army they fielded was green. The swamps, unfiltered water, and the insects of the marsh did more to whittle down the army than the resistance Deepmarsh rallied to defend their borders."

"That sounds messy," I said. I could imagine a huge army trying to trek through the same swampy land Amaryllis and I had walked across. With wagons and horses and a lot of people walking over the same muddy ground all day. It wasn't hard to imagine the average soldier's morale taking a hit.

"I still find bodies to this day," Gunther said. "Ah, Throat Ripper is ready."

The big, rather silly bone doggy had changed a whole lot over the course of the last ten minutes. He was now covered from head to tail in thick padded armour, with a layer of what looked like the scaly hide of some sort of crocodile. His head was covered in a helmet that only left the burning embers of his eyes visible and there were boney spikes sewn into the material of his armour all along his sides and back and haunches.

"Oh, wow," I said. "You look so scary Throat Ripper," I said. "Yes you do, yes you do!"

The bone doggy wiggled his butt and his tail, now equipped with a thagomizer, swung from side to side in glee.

"There's a seat built into the top of his armour. It's far from comfortable, but it works well enough as long as you hang on tightly."

I don't know what my expression was like, but Gunther took one look at me and chuckled.

"Remember what I said. Grab your friend and return. Don't dilly dally. Don't try and fight the cervids unless you have no other choice. And if it comes to the choice between you and them, do pick yourself. It would be insulting if you were unable to pay back your favour because you managed to get yourself killed."

I swallowed, the joy that learning that I'd get to ride Throat Ripper into battle snuffed out by his warning. "Alright," I said. "I'll do what I can."

"Good," Gunther said. "Now, don't worry about the skeletons. They're immensely disposable. And Throat Ripper is likely stronger than most everyone but the elites among the Cervid army. He can take care of himself. And if he does pass on, I can always bring him back."

"Thank you, Gunther. I… just thank you."

"Go save your friend, little Riftwalker. You can thank me later."

I grinned at him, and when Throat Ripper bounded out of the front door I followed after the big pup. With a bounce, I landed on the bone dog's broad back and grabbed two spikes that were placed so as to be handholds for the rider. "C'mon Throat Ripper, let's go save Amaryllis."

## Chapter Fifty-Two
# Hard to Ignore

Riding on Throat Ripper was not nearly as neat as I thought it would be. For one thing, he had a really wide back, and while I was able to hook my ankles around some of the spikes behind me, it still left me with my legs stretched out uncomfortably.

Then there was the constant bumping gait that had me almost bouncing off of the bone doggy's back with every step.

Behind us a group of a little over a dozen cervid skeletons formed up into a rough line, each one hanging onto a spear and shield, their eyes glowing even in the midday sunlight.

"Faster," I told Throat Ripper. It didn't matter that it hurt, if I wanted to save Amaryllis I had to get there before they did anything nasty to her. Throat Ripper complied, huge claws digging into the earth to shoot up forwards at a speed that would have had me whooping with joy were the situation any different.

We soon arrived at the bridge and I pointed ahead towards my bag. "That's where I left my stuff," I said. "We can take it later, but Amaryllis was taken around here."

Throat Ripper, being the very smart and good boy that he was, understood and slowed down his mad dash to a trot, then a slow walk that allowed me to sit back down and rest my behind on the saddle built into his armour.

The skeletal doggy crossed the river, then spun around a few times, nose close to the ground. There wasn't any sniffing, and I wondered how he was managing to make out any smells at all without a nose, but that didn't seem to matter as he perked up and started moving off the road.

When we stopped a little while later my heart sank. I was afraid that he had lost the scent, but Throat Ripper was the best and, with a growl that made my entire body vibrate, he pounced forwards and hopped from one little marshy island to the next.

Soon I caught signs that the cervid had been around. Hoofprints in the soggy soil, bushes that had been cut apart in unnatural ways and patches of the ground that seemed... lifted.

I guessed that they had stopped caring about stealth after a little ways.

The sun was high overhead when I heard a distant sound. Talking. Too far away for me to understand, but that didn't matter. Voices meant people and the only people I thought we would be meeting were the villains we were chasing.

"I'm going to scout ahead," I told Throat Ripper. "Can you and the other skeletons wait here?"

He nodded his big doggy head.

"Alright. Hide. If they spot me they might chase me, and it might be best that they don't see you."

The doggy growled. Not one long continuous rumble, but a series of grumbles that were interrupted a few times. The skeletons all darted this way and that. Some splashing into the muddy waters and submerging themselves until only the top of their heads were visible. Others jumped into the skeletal branches of some nearby trees and then stood frozen on the spot, completely immobile. The rest burrowed into bushes and hid in their shadows.

In under a minute the only plainly visible skeleton was Throat Ripper. He padded back a way and sat behind a rock.

"Right," I said. "I'll be back in no time at all, but if I don't return... then save Amaryllis for me?"

The dog looked my way, then let out a whine.

I could only respond with a sad smile.

The area wasn't as marshy as some of the spots we had passed over the last day or so. There were more rivulets here and fewer large ponds, and the ground was rockier. I could see the mountain range to the east a whole lot clearer, which meant that we were probably on the edge of Deepmarsh's territory.

That was both good and bad news. It meant that moving was easier. It also meant that the bad guys would be getting further away faster.

I scowled. I couldn't pin the moment I had decided that the cervid, at least this group of them, were the bad guys. It was probably because they were no-good meanies who kidnapped my friend.

Still, thinking of people as 'bad guys' was dehumanizing. Or whatever the word was for dehumanizing something that wasn't a human. It made it too easy to think of them as non-people, which in turn meant that hurting them was easier to justify.

That was the kind of mindset that started wars and racism and it wasn't a nice way of thinking.

I was better than that.

So, these cervid, bad as they might be, might have had good reasons to kidnap Amaryllis. Maybe her family was secretly evil. Maybe their loved ones were being held hostage. Maybe… there were lots of maybes.

Did it matter?

I hopped over to the edge of a hill and immediately fell to the ground as I heard talking nearby. They were close. I recognized Amaryllis' voice.

On hands and knees, I snuck up to the edge of the hill and slowly looked over it.

"—And then, once we're done ruining your economy, pitiful as it is, we'll ruin that filthy misogynistic culture of yours!" Amaryllis was saying.

I grinned. She was still alive.

Sure, she had ropes wrapped all around her chest and was slung over the shoulder of one of the cervid—The Lancer I had fought—but she was in one piece. Her wounds even looked better, with a strip of cloth wrapped around her leg. Her jacket was long gone, and it looked as if they had frisked her, but she was in good enough shape to complain.

It was as if a stone had been lifted from my shoulders.

"Can we shut her up yet?" One of the cervids asked. The mage that Amaryllis had fought. "We have some cloth laying around."

The leader shook his head. "No. She might choke herself just to spite us."

"When we stop," the Plains Speaker spoke up. "Can I have a bit of fun with her?"

This time the leader took a while to reply. "The client didn't specify if she needed to be intact or not."

"Is that a yes?" he asked.

The leader shook his head. "Not until we get confirmation."

"Stop talking over my head in your barbaric tongue!" Amaryllis shouted.

"Can we at least slap her until she stops screaming?" one of them asked. "She's going to attract trouble. And she's giving me a headache besides."

I loosened my hand. It had been clenched so tight that my nails were digging into my palms hard enough to leave marks. They were going to… to do bad things to her.

"Someone's watching us," one of the cervid said.

I looked up in time to see a few sets of eyes looking my way. "Oh, shoot."

"Two, Four, after her!" the leader said.

I didn't wait to see which cervid that meant. I just shoved off the hill and jumped away, pushing enough stamina into the motion that I practically flew across the landscape.

I heard hooves thundering after me. They were catching up, even with my head start.

A glance over my shoulder showed a cervid waving a staff in the air, a sort of almost transparent whip flicking up and out above him. Then it shot forwards.

My next jump threw me sideways and around a tree, one that I knew held a skeletal cervid in it.

The whip-crack was like a rifle going off behind me, and the tree's trunk exploded into a shower of splinters that had me covering my head.

Any doubt I had that they hadn't been holding back at the bridge fled.

I jumped over the rock where Throat Ripper hid and backed up into it.

**Congratulations! Through repeated actions your Jumping skill has improved and is now eligible for rank up!**
**Rank B costs two (2) Class Points**

"Not now," I muttered to Mister Menu.

Throat Ripper tilted his head at me.

"Come on out, girl, and we'll only kill you slowly," one of them said.

Were they trying to sound like B-rated villains?

Throat Ripper made a noise deep in his bones that shook the air around him. It sunk into me, and soon I found myself having a hard time just breathing.

Then he roared.

You have heard the roar of a fearsome creature! Your soul is shaken.

Throat Ripper grabbed onto the edge of the stone we were hiding behind, claws digging into the rock hard enough that little pieces of it rained down around me. Then he leapt over the edge.

I heard two screams, then one.

The mud to the side exploded apart as a skeleton ran out of it and I heard another dropping from a tree.

Soon there were no more screams.

**Congratulations! You have killed Titan (Wind Runner, level 12 / Wind Tear, level 4) and Rex (Flaming Lancer, level 10)!**

**Bonus Exp was granted for killing a person above your level! Due to not being the primary combatant your reward is reduced!**

"No," I whispered.

The prompt—the accusation—disappeared.

**Bing Bong! Congratulations, your Cinnamon Bun class has reached level 7!**
*Stamina +5*
*Flexibility +10*
**You have gained: One Class Point**

"No," I said. "Take it back? Please?" I begged to Mister Menu. I didn't deserve a level; I didn't deserve to get stronger.

The level up prompt just floated there.

Maybe I did deserve it.

Maybe it was my condemnation. Absolute proof that I had done the worst thing a person could do.

Titan and Rex. Two people that wouldn't be going home. That wouldn't be seeing their families. They wouldn't spend any more time with their friends. Two people that I had killed, that I had taken everything away from.

I was having a bit of difficulty breathing. My heart couldn't decide if it should be racing or seizing and I felt torn up, as if some huge monster was tugging me every which way.

A nose to the side had me looking up.

Throat Ripper didn't have eyes, not really, but there was still concern radiating off of him.

"A-Amaryllis," I said. "We still need to save her."

Throat Ripper opened his mouth. I looked away. There was too much blood there.

I moved out from around the rock, eyes firmly shut. I didn't want to see. I should have looked. I should have allowed the scene to sear itself into my mind for the rest of my life.

But in the end, I was a coward.

We moved past, Throat Ripper guiding me as I held onto one of the bony spikes on his armour.

"Wh-when we arrive," I began. "Let me talk. Please? There's still a chance. We can negotiate, or… or I can apologize. At the very least? To their friends?"

The skeletal dog didn't seem to understand most of what I had said, but I think he knew that I wanted to go ahead on my own again. We moved a little slower, with me setting the pace and the skeletons moving in a wedge behind us.

We were giving the cervid time to prepare, time to get ready to attack us as soon as we showed up. That was okay. It gave me time to breath too, to… bury what I had caused. Not very deep, but enough that I could function for a little bit.

Mom had always told me not to hide how I felt about the world, that I should always let my tears and my smiles run free.

So, while we walked, I mourned for two men whose names I knew, but whose faces were still unknown to me, and would probably remain that way forever.

And then we were near the hill, and the time for sadness and such was over.

# Chapter Fifty-Three
# **Buntimidation**

I crested a hill to find all four remaining members of the cervid group set in a loose formation on an opposite hill. A little rivulet ran across the ground between us, the water flowing along and masking the tense atmosphere with gentle murmurs.

They had set Amaryllis aside, the Lancer holding his spear close to her neck in an obvious sign that they could hurt her at any moment.

"Level check," the leader said.

One of the cervids glared my way. He wasn't one of the two that had attacked me at the bridge, which meant he had to be Three. "She's… level seven. Cinnamon Bun class. Disposition: dreary and resolute," he said.

He must have had a skill similar to my Insight. Since he had used it on me…

> *An anxious Cervid Lancer (level ?).*
> *An angry Cervid Plains Speaker (level ?).*

Those were the two that I had fought on the bridge.

> *A calculating Cervid Slip Spear (level ??).*
> *A rational Cervid Wind Warrior (level ??).*

The leader, and then the one that had just used something like Insight on me. I was expecting a mage of some sort, not a warrior, but maybe that didn't matter.

"I just want to talk," I called out. The distance between us wasn't that great, but it was enough that I thought I could dodge any attacks that they flung my way.

Amaryllis glared at her captors, then her eyes softened as she looked towards me. She shook her head minutely, only stilling when the Lancer shifted his spear.

"What happened to Two and Four?" the leader asked.

"I…" I swallowed down the bile rising in my throat. "I'm sorry about Titan and Rex," I said. "They didn't… I'm sorry."

The leader shifted a little, his hand straying to his hip where a long, curved sword was hung. The others reacted a little too, but the Plains Speaker reacted most of all. "There's no way. There's no way someone like you got to them,"

"Stop it, Six," the leader said. It was low, but it still carried over to where I stood.

"She's just a human," Six hissed.

"Now's not the time," the leader said, and it was the final word on the matter. He turned back towards me, his eyes set, and I had the impression he was weighing me. "What do you want?" he asked.

"I want my friend back," I said.

"You idiot!" Amaryllis finally shouted. Keeping quiet for a whole minute was obviously too much for her. "You should have just run. Go tell the oth—"

She collapsed to the side and the Lancer pulled the butt of his spear away from her as she coughed and spat and tried to sit back up despite her arms being tied up behind her back.

"I'm afraid we can't just return the target to you. It would go against the parameters of our mission."

"I could pay you?" I tried, but the cervid shook his head. My few measly gold pieces wouldn't be enough for that anyway. "M-maybe you could take me instead?"

"I'm afraid not," the leader said.

"Please?" I asked, begged really. I didn't want to have to take the next step.

"Five, Six, flanks, Three, you're with the target," the leader said.

I shook my head. "Please? I don't want to fight."

"Gutting you is going to be a pleasure," The Plains Speaker said. "If you killed Titan, then there's no need for me to hold back."

I closed my eyes and tried to think of something else, but I was tired and weary and nothing came to mind.

So I whistled.

Throat Ripper landed atop the hill just behind me, then jumped forwards so that he was next to me, his huge body blocking most of my view of the other hill, but I could still see the widening of the Cervid's eyes behind their helmets and the way Amaryllis began to grin, sharp and vindictive.

The dog began to growl, the noise almost enough to drown out the rivulet below. Armour clunked as every skeletal cervid Gunther had sent with me lined up atop the hill.

"Three, level check," the leader barked.

"The dog's... a Bone Hound of the Long Slumber, level in the upper twenties, secondary class is Skeleton Lord and its third class is Good Boy.

The skeletons." Three scanned the hill, eyes jerking from walking corpse to walking corpse. "They're all first tier, below ten."

The leader's confidence was gone now. He didn't seem ready to charge in a fight, especially not when Throat Ripper placed a paw on a rock jutting from the hill and it burst apart with little more than a flex of his toes.

I stepped up around Throat Ripper, one hand still hanging onto his side to keep him back, not that I had any doubt that if the doggy wanted to jump across the hill he would. "Um, I would really, really rather not fight," I said.

"You didn't tell me she was a necromancer," the leader hissed.

"She isn't. I thought her class was baking based," Three said.

"It's actually a nature support class," I said, defending my class, even if it wasn't the best. "I don't know if I could learn baking." But it was a great idea. If Baking was anything like Cleaning it might be my path towards fireballs.

The leader shifted. I could tell that he wasn't actually paying attention, a skill I had honed with much practice while prattling at friends. Still, that was okay because he took a small step back and shook his head. "Five, Six, prepare to pull back. Three, get the smoke ready."

"You're not going to try and run, are you?" I asked.

"Smoke!" the leader screamed.

Throat Ripper tensed.

Three tossed something on the ground.

I was expecting some smoke from that, but not the amount that burst out and filled the air as if we were suddenly in a thick fogbank. At least it didn't seem to have any effect on my breathing.

Without being able to see, there was no way to know if they were right before me or to learn if they were running away.

I aimed a hand away from Throat Ripper and fired a small burst of Cleaning magic. The fog around my hand faded away, then returned as the air shifted. So, it was something dirty, something that I could clean away.

"Stay, please," I said to Throat Ripper as I took a few steps before him, planted my spear into the ground next to me, and raised both arms in front of me. When casting a spell, there was a sort of prompt in the back of my mind that asked, 'how much?' It was the same for Jumping and Cleaning, though both took resources from different pools.

When Cleaning I had an idea of how much mana I would need, exactly, to clean something, it was a sense that had been growing keener over time.

Now I aimed the largest and widest Cleaning spell I could before me, and when my mind, or the system, or the world asked me 'how much?' my answer was just 'yes.'

The burst of magic fired out of me with a kick, shoving me back half a step.

The effects before me were a whole lot more impressive.

The magic travelled in a wave, expanding and bursting forwards across the grassy hill, past the rivulet and burst against the opposite hill.

The cervid stared at me.

Between us, the smoke bomb let out a pitiful puff and went inert.

Throat Ripper growled.

"Last chance," I said. I yanked my spear out of the ground and turned it so that the point was hovering between us.

They hadn't even gotten Amaryllis onto the Plain Speaker's back yet, probably because she was fighting them the entire time.

"Please?" I begged past the wash of tiredness. My mana was spent, I didn't have another chance like this one if they had another smoke bomb.

"Push her down the hill," the leader said.

The Plains Speaker grumbled, but he shoved Amaryllis back toward me.

My friend screeched as she tumbled down the grassy hill, hair flying every which way as she flopped downhill. She stopped in the steam with a splash.

"This operation's cost has passed what we were being offered. We're leaving," the leader said across the emptiness between us.

"I… I hope we never meet again," I said. It was the meanest thing I could think to say.

He nodded and backed away. When he and his men were a little ways off, they started to gallop away with surprising deftness.

I waited just a moment before racing down the hill. I almost tripped as my shoes skidded over wet grass and mud, and my spear slipped out of my grasp, but I didn't care. Amaryllis was right on the shore of the little stream at the bottom, coughing and sputtering out a faceful of muck.

I landed next to her and fell to my knees. "Don't move, don't move," I said as I pulled a knife from my bandoleer. A few careful tugs undid the ropes holding her in place.

"About time. I can hardly feel my *oomph!*"

I grabbed the harpy and crushed her to my chest, then held her at arms' length to inspect her up and down. "You're okay?" I asked. She didn't have time to answer. "You look okay. Oh, thank you." I hugged her closer, arms around her waist to hold her close as I buried my head in her neck.

"Don't hug me," she said. "You're a mess."

"I'm sorry," I said. I didn't stop hugging.

She paused, then sighed and started rubbing my back. "What are you sorry over? You saved me. That was probably the single stupidest plan I have ever had the misfortune of being part of, but it succeeded, somehow."

I opened my mouth to speak but the words caught in my throat. I took a deep breath, and then it came spilling out in a rush, words tumbling over words and I don't think my story was linear, exactly, but it didn't matter. I told her of looking for her, of going to Gunther and of making a deal and then I paused.

"And then what?" Amaryllis asked. "Or did you finally realise that being knee-deep in mud isn't the place for this kind of conversation?"

"I killed people," I said.

Amaryllis shifted and I slowly pulled away. I didn't want to. The hug was nice. I missed hugs. But I didn't deserve them.

I looked up and into Amaryllis' eyes, only to see her staring back, confused. "You're talking of those ruffians, aren't you?" she asked.

"The, the cervid mercenaries, yeah," I said in a whisper.

"Okay, and?"

I blinked. "Eh?"

Amaryllis shifted, then pushed herself up so that she was standing above me. From where I knelt on the ground, she practically towered above me, especially with her talons on her hips and her muddy wings flared out around her. "Don't be an idiot. They were mercenaries. Mercenaries that tried to kidnap me for the world knows what reason. This was targeted. What you did was just taking out weeds. You even got a level from it."

I was breathing deeply, almost panting now. I swallowed and tried to control the beating of my heart. "No. No it doesn't matter that they were doing a bad thing. No one should die, ever. Killing people is wrong."

Amaryllis knelt back down and met my eyes for a long moment. "Idiot," she said before hugging me back. "You're just one big idiot, Broccoli Bunch. To think that you'd compromise yourself for someone like me. You're the dumbest person that has ever been." She tightened her grip a little, and I think that she might have sobbed, just a little.

I didn't know what to feel, so I just fell into the hug and held my friend close.

Amaryllis shook her head and the hug ended, but I did feel a little better. Not that I wouldn't have a proper cry later, but now wasn't the time for it. "We need to get back to Green Hold," Amaryllis said.

"I promised Gunther we'd go back to see him," I said.

"And that's wise?" Amaryllis asked.

"Is going back to Green Hold wise?" I asked right back.

The harpy tilted her head to the side like a curious bird. "Maybe not *that* big an idiot. Let's go then. I've had a long morning and could use some of that tea of yours."

# Chapter Fifty-Four
# **The Return**

Despite everything that had happened the sun was still a good few hours away from setting. It beat down on my head from above, warming me where the cooler winds from the mountains to the West sent chills down my spine.

Amaryllis wasn't better off. She had lost her thick jacket at some point and was hugging herself for warmth.

"There it is," I said as I pointed off to the side of the bridge.

We had ridden on Throat Ripper for a little while, at least until we reached the bridge. At that point Amaryllis had declared that there was no way she was riding any further if it meant being 'jostled around by a big brute like Throat Ripper.'

I didn't mind walking, but I didn't think she needed to word it the way she did. Throat Ripper wasn't a big brute, he was a very good boy.

We both paused when we were on the bridge, and I think Amaryllis noticed that I was watching her watch the surroundings because she huffed and crossed her wings again. "Well? Get your things."

I fetched my backpack, but instead of slipping it on, I pulled out a blanket and held it out to her. "It'll be okay," I said.

"What's that for? And what, exactly, will be okay?" Amaryllis asked.

"Everything?" I tried.

The harpy pinched the bridge of her nose. "You are a fool, Broccoli," she said. It sounded halfway between exasperated and fond. "Give me that."

She took the blanket and wrapped it over her shoulders while I collected my things. Having both a spear and a shovel was growing to be a bit of a hassle. At the same time, I didn't want to get rid of either one. The shovel was a memento of my time in the Wonderland dungeon, and the spear a gift from a friend. I supposed that when I found myself a nice place to stay in, or purchased my first airship, I would have a place to store all of my neat high-level gear.

"What are you standing around for?" Amaryllis asked. "We have ground to cover."

"Right, sorry," I said.

We continued walking along the road, both of us much more alert than we had been that morning, but also a lot quieter. That is, until Amaryllis broke the silence. "Thank you," she said.

"For what?"

"Don't be a fool. Thank you for coming back, and for hatching such a featherbrained scheme to try and save me."

"I don't think you should say 'try to save me' when it worked," I pointed out.

She huffed again. "Yes, well, I would have freed myself eventually. I was merely waiting for my mana supplies to be replenished naturally. Then I would teach those idiots a lesson on how to handle a nob— a lady."

"Oh, right, I didn't ask about your leg, are you sure you should be walking?"

She made a dismissive flapping motion in my direction. "I had enough healing points to take care of it."

"Okay, good," I said. I still eyed the way she was walking for a bit, but she didn't show any signs of limping.

"Why are you smiling like that?" she asked.

I hadn't even noticed that I was grinning from ear to ear. It wasn't even my normal 'life is okay' smile. This was a much bigger, brighter grin, and it took me all of a second to figure out why. "It's because I made a friend."

"A friend? You think that just because we've been through some harrowing experiences together and that you saved me, we're suddenly nest buddies?"

My smile faded and I looked at Amaryllis with tears gathering in my eyes.

"F-fine. I… suppose I could deign to call even someone as dumb as you a friend—get off me!" she said when I glomped her from the side.

"But we're friends now!" I rubbed my head against hers so that our cheeks squished. "Oh, I've been looking forward to having friends ever since I came here, and I'm super happy that you're my first real-deal friend, Amaryllis."

"Do you do this to all of your friends? No, don't answer that. Keep the sordid details, and your hands, to yourself," Amaryllis said as we started walking again. She might have made a fuss but when I held her close to my side she didn't complain, and we were soon walking in sync with each other through the swampy marsh.

The last few hours had been a roller coaster, with more ups and downs than I had been prepared to deal with, but now it felt as if things were settling into a comfortable, straight path. I could really use a friend in a moment like that, and now I had one.

"So, which backwater are you from?" Amaryllis asked.

"Are you asking because you want to know more about your friend?" I wondered.

"No. I'm asking because if you are going to follow me around like some sort of enamoured chick, then I ought to at least discover how woefully unprepared you are so that I can cram some knowledge into that thick skull of yours. World knows I'm starved for intelligent conversation already."

"Ah, that's sweet of you." I could see the fort a little ways ahead of us. There were quite a few more skeletons on the walls. "How about I tell you my life story later?"

"I'm sure it's riveting," she said.

"It's not as interesting as being a harpy princess," I said.

She snorted, though it sounded more like a sort of whistle. "I'm no princess," she said.

For just a little while, we slid into a comfortable silence, one that lasted until we were nearly at the gates of the fort. Throat Ripper bounded ahead of us, full of happy doggy energy. I wanted to skip after him, but I decided to stay next to Amaryllis in case she needed more morale support.

"I meant it," Amaryllis said.

"Meant what?"

"My thanks, earlier. I don't think most would have tried to do what you did, especially not for a stranger. I wasn't always as kind to you as I could have been."

"It's okay. A lot of people are like that when I first meet them. And you don't need to thank me, it's the least I could do for a friend."

Her eyes narrowed and for a moment I wondered if I had said something wrong. "How can you sound so condescending when you say that?"

"Eh? But I'm not!"

"Yes, well, your idea of friendship is utterly bizarre."

"I prefer to think that I have an outside context on the subject," I said. "Hey, do you think there's such a thing as friendship-aspect mana?"

"What? No, what kind of backwards, uneducated idiocy is that?"

We reached the front doors of the fortress with Amaryllis prattling on about how mana was a tangible thing and how I really, really needed to read a book someday. Before we had even crossed the courtyard leading into the fort proper the door opened and we were greeted by Gunther.

"Ah, hello again, Broccoli. Miss Albatross. It's good to see that you're both well."

"Yes, I suppose it would be," Amaryllis said.

I poked her in the ribs, which earned me a glare. "Don't be rude. Mister Gunther went out of his way to help us today. He didn't need to."

Gunther hid a smile behind the act of scratching his nose. "Quite. Would you ladies step in? I'm ready for that favour you owe me, miss Bunch."

"What favour?" Amaryllis hissed at me as I began to follow Gunther back in.

"I don't know, he wasn't very specific."

"You… you absolute moron."

I didn't know what to expect from Gunther, but it wasn't to find that the furniture in the living room had all been shifted about. A few extra torches were sitting in sconces and a large tarp was placed across the floor. In the middle of the room, next to a Throat Ripper that was being fussed over by a couple of skeletons, was a large easel.

"Please, stand over there," Gunther said as he gestured to the end of the room.

"Oh, is this like some sort of painting magic?" I asked.

"There's no such thing," Amaryllis said.

"There isn't?" I wondered. "Not even… like painting the future, or using colours to manipulate a person's emotions?"

"What? No, that's preposterous."

Gunther hummed as he moved to the back of the easel. A skeleton was standing there holding up a platter with some paints on it and a case that had all sorts of brushes and glass jars of various pigments. "You would do well to set aside what you think is correct, Miss Albatross, especially around someone like Miss Bunch here who… well, the world most certainly has plans regarding her," he said.

"Plans?" I asked. "Like quests?"

Gunther paused, hands hovering over the brushes and paints. "Yes, like quests," he said. "I haven't had anything new to paint in some time. I hope you don't mind being my subjects. I'm quite rapid with the brush and oils."

"No problem!" I said. "Did you want to paint Amaryllis too? We could be sitting next to each other, or posing in a cool way, or hugging or something."

"I am not being painted in some sort of… debauched pose. Nor am I suitably dressed for a painting," Amaryllis said.

"While you are perhaps a… little dishevelled," Gunther said. His hand began moving across the entire canvas, laying down the background layer of paint. 'You do have a certain ferocious look. The adventuress after a difficult ordeal."

Amaryllis stood just a tiny bit taller at the compliment and I had to stifle a knowing grin. "Well I think you look great," I said. "Here." A bit of cleaning magic later and we were both freed of all the mud and gunk that covered out clothes. Amaryllis even passed her talons through her hair to straighten it out.

"Very well. Just stand naturally," Gunther said.

Amaryllis shifted, her arms moving up, her back bending a little and all of her feather floofing out.

"What are you doing?" I asked.

"I'm getting into the proper pose for a painting."

"Oh," I said. Then I hugged her. "Paint us like this!"

"No, you idiot!" Amaryllis protested. "Is this how you want people to see you when they look at the painting? Some, some hug-giving harlot?"

"Hey! I would never charge for a hug!"

"Wh-what's that's supposed to mean?" Amaryllis sputtered.

"You're a friend. Friends get free hugs!"

Gunther sighed as he lowered his brush then moved over to place us both shoulder to shoulder. It wasn't the most active pose, but I suppose it wasn't all bad.

It was kind of awkward to just stand there, like taking a family photo, but with the world's slowest camera. "Um, can we still talk?" I asked.

"Of course," Gunther said, though he sounded distracted. "Tell me about how your rescue went? Did Throat Ripper do a good job?"

"He was the best," I declared. Off to the side of the room, Throat Ripper replied with a

thump-thump of his tail on the floor. "I don't know if undead doggies have snacks, but if they do, he deserves all of them."

"I'll see what I can do," Gunther said. "And the cervid, they've left?"

"They did," Amaryllis answered. "You might find yourself in some trouble if they decide that you're a threat."

"Perhaps. Perhaps not. I am difficult to be rid of, and my home here is well-guarded. Nonetheless, perhaps I shall increase the number of patrols. Just to be cautious."

"That would be wise," Amaryllis said.

They actually began to talk politics, Amaryllis questioning Gunther over his views of the laws pertaining to necromancy, and while that was interesting enough, I had my mind occupied by other things.

Sure, the day had gone… well. I might have lost a friend and I didn't, instead I had made one. But at the same time, I was left wondering just what was left in store for us in the coming days. Amaryllis' near-kidnapping hadn't been a coincidence, which meant that someone had deliberately targeted my friend.

I… we would need to get to the bottom of it. Together!

"What are you smiling about now?" Amaryllis asked.

"Nothing," I said.

# Chapter Fifty-Five
# **Revelations**

"It's beautiful," I said.

Gunther shifted a little, the compliment making his deathly pale skin flush just a tiny bit. "It is adequate," he said.

The painting was fairly simple, with a stone wall illuminated by torchlight behind both myself and Amaryllis. It reminded me just a little of American Gothic, but Amaryllis was the only one scowling, her sharp eyes looking at me sideways and there was just a hint of humour in her gaze, probably a trick of Gunther's brushstrokes that made her eyes pinch at the corners.

Standing to Amaryllis' left was a Broccoli Bunch that I hardly recognized. Sure, that was my smile, the one I always wore when taking a picture with a friend. And I had my trusty spade over my shoulder and my bandoleer on and my spear held up by my side. But something had changed. There was a lot of happiness there, but also… guilt. "It's really nice," I repeated.

I hated lying.

"You can take it with you if you want. I merely needed the practice," Gunther said.

"We couldn't," I said.

"Nonsense, it cost me nothing to make," Gunther insisted.

"No, I mean, we literally can't. It's too big to carry through the swamps. It'll get all mushy," I said.

Amaryllis poked the painting and it poofed away. "There. Done. Favour's paid, painting is in storage, sun is still shining. We should go."

"Amaryllis!" I said. "That was rude. Gunther's a friend."

"No, no, she is correct. Rude, but correct. If you intend to reach Green Hold by nightfall, then it would be best if you left now. A direct route west-southwest will have you intersecting the road leading into the town in… oh, six, seven hours at a fast jog?"

That was a lot of jogging. "Um, but that would mean just… leaving, like that."

Gunther's smile was a little wry, but it was still genuine. "Yes. But no worries, I'm certain we'll meet again someday. Else I suppose I'll read of your exploits in some book of myths and tales."

Amaryllis snorted. "Hardly," she said before eyeing Gunther. "You weren't all that bad, for a necromancer."

"And you're passably tolerable, for a harpy," Gunther replied just as easily.

"Aww, you're getting along," I said.

Amaryllis huffed and walked past me. "I'll be waiting outside."

I watched her go for a moment before turning back to Gunther. "It really was nice to meet you— and Throat Ripper," I said. I walked over to the big bony lump. The doggy was laying on his side and looked asleep... or maybe just more dead, though one of his eyes started to glow when I started patting his side. "Thanks for your help earlier," I said.

He replied with a thump-a-thump of his tail, so I gave him some extra pats.

"Be safe, and may the world watch over your journey," Gunther said.

I smiled. "And may it, um, watch over you as well?" I said.

He laughed. "Ask your friend about proper greetings, I'm sure she can talk your ears off about it. Good luck, Broccoli Bunch. We'll see each other again, I'm certain."

I found Amaryllis eyeing a skeletal harpy, her head tilted to the side as she stared at the only bird-like skeleton in the area. I looked at its thin-boned arms and the way its legs connected to a strange pair of thin hips, then I eyed Amaryllis who was, by then, glaring at me.

"Stop staring at me like I'm some sort of chicken," she said.

"Um, but aren't you just a little bit chicken?" I gestured at her white hair and feathers.

Amaryllis squawked and stomped off and out of the fort so fast I had to jog to keep up. "A chicken! She calls a member of the purebred Albatross family a bloody chicken! Why, world? Why did you saddle me with this idiot?" Amaryllis asked the skies.

"Is being called a chicken an insult?" I asked.

It was a strange way to start our voyage back, but Amaryllis' loud and gesture-filled rant about the inferiority of the Chicken clan and how they did little more than scratch at the dirt all day and eat grubs, was entertaining at least.

Apparently, humans weren't the only ones that didn't like insects in their lunch. Most harpies were on the same page.

With Orange pouncing ahead of us to scout, we moved down the same path we had that morning. Amaryllis' rant only stopped when we recrossed the bridge. Nothing happened though, and soon we were walking along at a good clip towards Green Hold.

Amaryllis went dull-eyed for a moment, then scowled at the air. "I'm going to be hitting my class evolution soon. I'll need a second class in abeyance if I want to keep progressing."

"What's that mean?" I asked.

"It means that… if you decide to remain my partner in the guild, which if you have any wisdom in that thick human skull of yours you will, we'll have to make a detour to a suitable dungeon to pick up a second class."

So, second classes were a thing for real then. "And what's a class evolution?"

Amaryllis stopped walking so suddenly that I took three steps before noticing. I lowered my spear and started to prepare some cleaning magic.

"How do you not know that?" she asked. She was eyeing me like I was a bunny and she was a hungry bird of prey. "Everyone knows about it, even peasants. Especially peasants since it's what keeps them that way."

"Is it that big a deal?" I asked.

"It's the only way to level past ten. Without guards and warriors in the second tier and beyond civilization would collapse in a week."

"Wait, you can't level past ten without an evolution thing?" I asked. I was beginning to worry. What if they were really expensive?

"Broccoli," Amaryllis said. "Where are you from? How did you survive with such an abysmal education?"

"Ah," I said as I hesitated. I didn't want to share too much. No, that wasn't it. I was afraid to share too much because that knowledge might shove a wedge between Amaryllis and me. But now my lack of knowledge was doing the same thing. "It's a long story?" I tried.

"It's a long walk."

"Right." There went that excuse. I decided that I might as well bite the bullet. "Do you know what a Riftwalker is?"

"Yes… no," she declared. Suddenly she was eyeing me up and down as if I had started dancing a naked jig. "You are not… oh but that would explain a lot."

"So you know what a Riftwalker is? Gunther knew, somehow. He was very mysterious about it, but he didn't seem to think it was a bad thing."

"The only person for whom it's bad is me. If some of the professors back home learned that I was with a Riftwalker and didn't question her thoroughly they would clip my wings and fling me off the highest tower in

Farseeing." Amaryllis slapped her talons over her face. "That explains why you're so wildly incompetent at everything."

"Ah," I said.

Amaryllis went on. "Your complete cluelessness about magic. Your ignorance about the local cultures. And to think I thought that you were merely struck in the head."

"That's rude, I think," I said.

"You must be from some incomprehensibly backwards world where the young are coddled and protected," Amaryllis said.

"Hey! Canada's not... too backwards. We have the internet in some places," I defended.

Amaryllis made a high-pitched trilling noise, one that I had never heard from her before. "Well, now I'm slightly less disappointed that we've become... friends."

She had been disappointed? "You are?"

"Oh yes. The last Riftwalker that I learned about was an unassuming man of little talent and worth, or so every test suggested," she said.

"That doesn't inspire much confidence," I said.

"He went on to be a professor of the Snowland's greatest academy and pioneered the creation of the gravitic engine that airships use today. That was some hundred-odd years ago."

"Oh," I said.

Now the glint in Amaryllis' eyes looked kind of scary.

"Well, don't expect anything like that from me," I said. "I think I already did the thing this world wanted. But we can still be friends anyway."

Amaryllis deflated a little. "Truly?" I nodded. "Well, regardless, you're still a trove of possibly interesting, if mundane, facts."

"I'll tell you about my world if you help me learn about the magic you use here," I said.

"Deal!" Amaryllis said. She puffed out her chest, and when she began walking again it was with something of a strut. She really did remind me of a chicken. "With me at the helm of your education you'll have caught up to the world's standard in no time."

"Awesome!" I said with a laugh as I jogged to keep up. "So, what's a class evolution?"

She waved a hand dismissively through the air. "A class evolves when it hits its tenth level. This is universal across all classes that I'm aware of. At that point, the world gifts you with some choices on how you guide your future development. Some require certain actions to be taken beforehand, others are more common and are available to everyone. Most classes have the default option to continue with the same class."

"Okay?" I said. "So level ten lets you evolve your class. Got it. I've met a lot of Grenoil who are Fencers, is that because they all evolve into that?"

"No. There's a dungeon in Deepmarsh, the capital, that gives anyone that clears it the Fencer class. It's a low-level dungeon, purposefully kept that way so that younger grenoil can obtain the class. For a lesser gold you can be escorted to the boss and someone will beat it near to death for you," Amaryllis said. "By participating in the fight, you can replace your main class with Fencer, which is what quite a few grenoil set out to do. It's a well-documented class with some clear and easy progressions."

I couldn't keep the smile off my face as I listened. These were the kinds of things I wanted to know for a while now. "So, back to the evolution thing. Can a Fencer become a Sword Dancer?"

Amaryllis nodded slowly, as if uncertain. "I think that's one of the class evolutions from Fencer, but with a focus on two blades?"

"That sounds right. I met a grenoil from the exploration guild that had two swords and that class," I said. "So when I get to level ten, I'll get to pick from a bunch of classes?"

"It depends on your accomplishments, but essentially, yes. There are some progressions that are very well documented. Fire and Thunder Mages for example. There's another evolution at level twenty, and every ten levels after that."

"Brilliant. I can't wait to find out what my class will evolve into at level ten," I said.

"Probably something suitably droll. Your class sounds like something a peasant might obtain from cleaning the lavatory."

"You can get classes from cleaning lavatories?" I asked. "I thought you needed to fight a dungeon boss."

Amaryllis sighed. "No. Your first class is always a gift of the world. And it's usually awful. That's why I switched to Thunder Mage about a year ago."

"What were you before?" I asked.

"That doesn't matter," she said with a lofty wave of her hand. "As of right now, I'm level nine, which means my evolution approaches. Once it's done, I'll be bottlenecked until I unlock a second class and can start levelling both it and my primary class again. The next bottleneck will be at level twenty for the primary and ten for the secondary class."

"Okay?" I said as I tried to imagine it. Maybe it was like those glass jars in chemistry class, then the first one filled up the excess would pour through a spout to the second and so on. Or maybe not.

"I just need to find a suitable dungeon to tackle and I'll be set for a while. We can even share a secondary class, if you want to come along."

"That sounds like a lot of fun!" I said.

I wasn't too sure where my friendship with Amaryllis stood, but I was hoping for the best.

# Chapter Fifty-Six
# Dreaming Big

"Cleanthrower!" I shouted as I stretched an open hand towards the nearest slime.

Cleaning magic poured out of my palm as if I had opened the tap on a garden hose. It splashed over the greyish blob of gelatinous magic, melting it apart.

"There's another ahead of you," Amaryllis said as she raised a hand. She was holding onto a ball of light, kind of like those I had seen Arianne make the first time I ever met a grenoil, only these were a bit brighter and she managed to cast a stronger light forward, like a flashlight that illuminated the way ahead.

I looked up ahead, and she was right, a huge slime, bigger than any I had ever seen before, was blubbering its way ahead in the middle of the road. I could see the entire half-digested body of a rabbit near its core. "I got it," I said as I stepped up. I brought my hands together, palm flat by my side, "Kame!" I took a wide stance. "Ha… meee…" Then I shot my arms out before me with a loud. "Haaa!"

A white ball of cleaning magic puttered along through the air in a meandering course that ended when it booped into the slime's chest. Then it kept going, carving a hole through the entire monster.

The slime collapsed.

"What was that?" Amaryllis asked.

"It's a, uh," I flushed. "Magical chant from my homeland. It makes you way more awesome."

"It makes you louder," Amaryllis corrected. "We're lucky slimes are deaf else you'd have called every creature across the entire region with your incessant screaming."

"Oops?" I said. I was a little sorry. It wasn't nice to put myself and Amaryllis at risk like that. On the other hand, that was one more slime down, which meant just a little bit more experience towards the next level. I would need it. I had to be stronger, strong enough that the next time there was a fight, I could fight on my own terms, or at least make people think twice about hurting my friends.

Walking through the swamps at night—with only the rune-light on my helmet and Amaryllis light to guide us—was a bit scary, but it wasn't so bad, especially after getting rid of just about every slime on our path.

Amaryllis used her thunder magic liberally at first, but she then suggested we pace ourselves and switch every so often to keep at least one of us topped off with mana.

The moon above made the clouds glow silver and refracted off of the humid fogbanks rising up all around us. All the noises of the marsh were damped by the fog, which only made it harder to tell where something might come from.

Amaryllis said that monsters could usually sense that messing with a person was a bad idea, but we were also both in our first tier, which made us prime midnight snack material.

I had to get strong enough that no one would eat me.

"Hey, Amaryllis?" I asked.

"What inane question do you have for me now?" she asked as she panned her light across the woods.

"What level was Throat Ripper at?" The cervid mercenaries had backed off instead of fighting the bone doggo, so aiming to be at about that level was a good start.

"Third tier," Amaryllis said. "That's above level twenty of his primary class."

"So he had… three classes total?" I asked as I worked out the information in my head.

"To get past twenty he would need his second class at level ten, and a third class, yes," she said.

"How long do you think it would take me to get that strong?" I asked.

Amaryllis' light shifted until it was illuminating me. She didn't stop moving though, so nor did I. "Is this a Riftwalker thing?"

"It's a Broccoli Bunch thing," I said.

She snorted. "Getting past the first tier is simple enough. A few years with safe and well-paced training. Far less with situations like ours where we're fighting for our lives. Second tier can take anywhere from two to ten years to get past. You'll rarely see anyone younger than thirty past level twenty. The pinnacle of most civilisations are those in their third and fourth tiers. It can take decades to move past those. Most people succumb to old age before hitting their fifth tier. Mostly because to keep growing at a decent rate you need to start facing challenges that are frankly ridiculous."

I processed that for a bit. Amaryllis was really a fountain of knowledge. I think some people would have pegged her as a nerd back home, and they would have been very rude for placing her in a box like that.

So, the more one levelled up, the harder it got, and most people didn't make it to level forty unless they tried really hard for a long time. That just meant that I had to either work even harder, or I could aim for a point where I'd be respected and stop there.

That sounded good enough, and it lined up with my goals in life.

"Why are you asking?" Amaryllis asked. "Not that the question is terrible. I'm merely curious as to what brought you to it."

"I want to know how strong I need to be to carry out my dreams."

"And what are those?" Amaryllis asked.

"I want a small house with a little fence around it. A dog, two cats, a gentle husband with a really nice chin, and two kids. A boy and a girl," I said.

Amaryllis tripped over a root or something and her light went out. She said bad things while recasting the spell. "That's it?" she asked.

"Well, I'd like it if I lived near my friends, that way I could visit them every night. We could do rotations where every night a new friend cooks supper. I think it would be cute."

"What kind of peasant aspirations are those?" Amaryllis asked. "Don't you want… more?"

"Not really?" I asked. "I want plenty of little things, but they're not my dreams. Oh, I do want to learn fireball, does that count?"

"No, no it doesn't!"

Amaryllis flashed her light ahead of us, illuminating a couple of slimes that were sliming their way closer. She muttered something and arcs of lightning flashed out of her fingers and sizzled as they dug into the slimes.

If I ever found a glowing red sword, I was giving it to her to complete the image.

We continued our trek through the woods at a sedate pace until, finally, I could see a faint glow in the fog ahead. "Is that Green Hold?" I asked.

"It might be," Amaryllis said. "I'm not going to look for a hill to use as a vantage in this lighting."

"Stop here for a bit," I said. Crouching down, I took off my backpack and shifted my bum like a kitty looking for just the right balance. Then I pushed a chunk of my stamina into my legs and shot into the air.

I resisted the urge to scream in delight as the wind whipped at me. Then, when I was at the apex of my jump, I looked ahead. The town was covered in a thin layer of fog, but it was easy enough to see the little towers around it and the plumes of smoke rising into the sky.

I landed with an 'oomph' and resettled my skirts. "It's Green Hold," I said.

"Handy skill that," Amaryllis said. "Just normal Jumping?"

"Yup," I said. "Rank C. That's, um, disciple?"

Amaryllis shrugged a shoulder and began walking again. "Most would try to get rid of it or find a skill to merge it with. But if it works for you."

"It's got enough experience to rank up to journeyman, actually," I said.

"Hrm. What's your skill distribution look like? You only have so many skill points to go around before you hit your class evolution."

"Do I get more after?" I asked.

"You do, but it's slower. It's best to plan these things out," she said.

"Ah, okay," I said. It made sense. What did I want to focus on? Having Cleaning at rank A would require three levels worth of skill points. I could do that as soon as it was ready to rank up. Or I could move other skills up a few ranks or save some points for the next skill I'd unlock at level eight. So many choices.

| Name: Broccoli Bunch | | Race: Human (Riftwalker) | | | Age: 16 |
|---|---|---|---|---|---|
| Health | 120 | Stamina | 130 | Mana | 115 |
| Resilience | 30 | Flexibility | 35 | Magic | 20 |
| First Class: | Cinnamon Bun | | First Class Level: | | 7 |
| Skill Slots | 0 | | Skill Points | | 3 |
| General Skill Slots | 0 | | General Skill Points | | 1 |

| General Skills | | Cinnamon Bun Skills | |
|---|---|---|---|
| Insight | C - 33% | Cleaning | B - 12% |
| Makeshift Weapon Proficiency | E - 58% | Jumping | C - 100% |
| Archaeology | F - 57% | Gardening | D - 13% |
| Friendmaking | D - 58% | Cute | D - 100% |

"Skills unlock a secondary thing at disciple, right?" I asked.

"They do," Amaryllis confirmed. She zapped a little slime with a wave. I was noticing fewer and fewer of them as we came closer to Green Hold.

Maybe there were patrols, or the mana around the town was different enough that they didn't spawn every night?

"One more question," I said as I looked at Mister Menu's display of my profile. "How many General Skills can you have?"

"Five initially," Amaryllis said. "You'll get another five at the same time as you hit your bottleneck. You can't really get General Skill Points."

"Only from doing something for the World, right?" I asked.

Amaryllis slowed down. "You got some?" she asked.

"Um," I said.

"World curse your ignorant luck," she muttered.

"Just two of them," I said.

"Yes, yes, just two. Two enough for some people to kill you."

"What?" I squeaked.

She huffed. "Killing someone with General Skill Points lets you take them for yourself. But the people with those are… rare. Dungeon core breakers, who are fair game. Some champions that did extraordinary deeds. Sometimes the people who get a rare, an exceptionally rare, quest. They're usually strong enough that killing them for the points isn't worth the hassle, but when nations go to war those champions become targets."

"Ah," I said.

It sorta made sense. As far as I could tell, any skill could be acquired by anyone. That meant that you could have a skill that wasn't part of your class. But Rank D was… lame? Not that great? It certainly helped, but it wasn't beyond what a person could do naturally.

Jumping at Rank D made me good at jumping and helped with the timing and balance. Cleaning at that same rank made me a more efficient cleaner. But it had all been within human limits—with a bit of help. The moment those skills reached rank C they became… more. Magical.

So a person with lots of General Skill points could start unlocking plenty of new ranks in a hurry and would become a lot stronger in a short period of time. Assuming they got more than just two points, of course.

"Ahh, my head is stuffed," I said.

"Yes, I'm sure Thinking isn't one of your skills," Amaryllis said.

I glared over at her, but the glare fizzled and died on contact with her smug grin. "You're mean. I'm not an idiot."

"You're certainly smarter than most of the fools I have to deal with," she said. "That doesn't make you a genius by any measure though."

"Who was it that needed saving yesterday?" I asked as innocently as I could.

Amaryllis did that cute huffing thing she did when I scored a point and started walking a little faster. "Those were exceptional circumstances. Circumstances that I will get to the bottom of."

As I watched the walls of Green Hold grow closer, I started to have a really bad feeling in the pit of my stomach.

# Chapter Fifty-Seven
# Pomf

Green Hold's gate was guarded by a single older grenoil with wrinkly skin and a quarterstaff by his side. When he saw us coming from within his tower, he turned on a magical light and brought it around so that it illuminated the pair of us.

Amaryllis had to shout up to him that we were with the Exploration Guild and that we were returning from a mission before he opened the gates a crack and let us in.

"I wouldn't normally let folks in at zese sorts of hours, but it ain't right to keep two young ladies out when it's dark out," the guard grenoil said.

"Thank you, sir," I said.

I was a little disappointed that I didn't get to see Green Hold during the day when it was no doubt bustling with activity, but I still got to admire the pretty stone and mud homes. Some of the buildings were a little strange, big rounded things that reminded me of the Roman colosseum but way, way smaller, with the words 'Tadpole House' on a few signs above the doors. Others were simple enough, shops and homes and, of course, a large inn.

We made our way to the last of these, the tallest building in town - apart from some of the guard towers - all stone and wood with a blue-shingled roof. The sound of gentle chatter drifted out of the building, mingling with an instrument that sounded a bit like a bagpipe but higher in pitch.

"Let's find that bastard," Amaryllis said as she kicked the door open and stomped into the inn.

I was caught flat-footed for a moment. I knew Amaryllis was a little miffed, but I didn't expect her to suddenly turn as angry as she did.

The crowd in the inn hushed up, dozens of froggy faces turning towards the entrance where Amaryllis stood, hands on hips and face set in a furious scowl. She scanned the room and I could pinpoint the exact moment she spotted Gabriel because her arm shot up and she pointed to the man.

Gabriel was sitting by the bar, a few empty cups before him and his big flabby cheeks tinted a nice rosy colour. The patrons around him edged away from him as Amaryllis spoke up. "You! You toad-skinned, no good bastard!"

I walked in behind her and waved at all the nice grenoil sitting around and watching the show.

"Come here you slimy jerk!" Amaryllis said as she stomped across the entire floor, grabbed Gabriel by the scruff of his jacket and dragged him off to the back of the inn. There were little booths to the side, but she walked right past those and straight up the stairs, presumably to reach the rooms upstairs. Gabriel started to fuss and fight a bit, but his swings were all wild and not very strong, and Amaryllis had a lot of pent up rage fuelling her.

"Ah," I said the moment they disappeared at the top of the stairs. Every eye turned to me. "I'm sorry about my friend," I said. "We had a bit of a day, you know? So, um, I heard some nice music from outside, who was playing that?" I smiled at them all.

No one answered, but they did return to their meals and beers and I heard more than one person speculating on what Gabriel had done to earn a young girl's wrath.

In the corner, a large grenoil man started to blow into a strange sort of bagpipe while another pulled up an accordion and a third started plucking the strings of what sounded like a stand-up bass but looked like a very large fiddle.

I wanted to stare some more, but I heard a bang from upstairs and decided not to dilly dally too much.

"Oi!" the grenoil behind the counter said. "If she breaks anything, you're paying for it!"

"Yes sir!" I said before taking the steps two at a time.

The top of the stairs opened into a cosy lounging area, though it was empty save for one grenoil that looked to be knocked out on a couch. One of the bedroom doors was wide open and I could see Amaryllis shaking Gabriel within.

"Tell me! Tell me who paid you off you slimegoblin, you lily-livered amphibastard bug-eating... mudlicker!"

I blinked as I tried to parse what she was saying. I was quite certain that at least half of those had been hideously speciesist. "Um," I said as I walked into the room and placed a hand on Amaryllis shoulder. "It's okay? Maybe don't kill him? Please?"

Amaryllis puffed up. Literally. Her feathers poofed upwards and even her hair stood on end a little. She suddenly looked twice as big as she had, but it was all fluff. "He betrayed me!" she squawked.

I slapped a hand over my mouth, but it was too late, a giggle had already escaped.

She turned her glare onto me. "What are you laughing about?" she asked.

I couldn't keep it in. Maybe because I was tired, or because of the long day, but when she turned towards me all I could think of was the little 'pomf' sound her feathers made.

I bent over double, hands clutching at the sides of my tummy.

Amaryllis puffed up even more. "Why are you laughing?" she demanded.

Gabriel started to croak too. "Ya look like a rooster," he said.

"I do not!" Amaryllis said.

But she did.

Gabriel and I looked at each other and we both started laughing together. It took Amaryllis stomping her foot and calling us both all sorts of foul things for an entire minute for the two of us to calm down.

"Now," Gabriel began as he wiped an eye clear of tears. "What's zis about a betrayal? I haven't drunk enough to deal wiz your snitty attitude."

"Someone tried to kidnap Amaryllis," I said.

"Oh. Well zey didn't succeed," Gabriel said.

"Not just someone," Amaryllis said. "Cervid mercenaries. They were after me specifically."

That sobered the grenoil up a bit. "Zat's bad news. Cervids on zis side of the border means zat zey've found a way to cross over wizout being spotted. Not zat ze patrols have been all that sharp lately. You sure?"

"Of course I'm sure," Amaryllis said. "If it wasn't for Broccoli, I'd be halfway to Manamere by now, or wherever they wanted to ransom me from."

"Our ship back to Port Royal is passing early tomorrow," Gabriel said as he moved over to the room's bed and sat down. "It's meant to wait for all of us to board before heading out. We can get on it first zing in ze morning and move back to Port Royal. I'll leave a missive wiz ze mayor of Green Hold. Cervids... zat's bad news."

"They were here for Amaryllis," I said. I didn't know the whole context with the cervids and the grenoil yet, but I could guess. Fort Frogger had been built to watch for an invasion a long time ago, so obviously there was some bad blood there. "Someone had to know where we would be."

"Broccoli's right," Amaryllis said.

"Well, I just got my mission parameters from Rainnewt. Didn't much care for zem since babysitting missions like zis one isn't my sort of zing," Gabriel said.

"Tch. Come on Broccoli, we'll get a room and set up a watch for the night," Amaryllis said as she walked out.

I looked after her departing back then over to Gabriel. "Sorry about that, she's a bit stressed," I said. "By the way, drinking while on the job is very rude."

"Bah, piss off kid," Gabriel said. He let himself fall backwards onto the bed and I just hoped that it was his as I walked out and shut the door behind me.

I followed Amaryllis back downstairs. It felt that, ever since we had arrived in Green Hold, Amaryllis had taken the reins and was tugging me along. It was okay for now, but I had kind of gotten used to the idea that I was the mistress of my own fate. I would need to think about it some more and maybe set some boundaries with Amaryllis before she decided to drag me into something I didn't want to be part of. Peer pressure was not okay, after all.

I found Amaryllis talking to the innkeeper. She placed a handful of silver on the counter and received a pair of keys. She tossed one over to me. "We have a room on the third floor," she said.

"Together?" I asked.

"I would usually prefer my own room, but seeing what happened today, I think bunking together would be for the best," she said.

"Right, if something happens, we'll be two fighting it off," I said.

She nodded. "I'm heading up now, are you coming?"

"I'm going to grab something to eat first," I said.

She shrugged her shoulders, and I noticed that at some point her feathers had unpoofed themselves and were back to lying flat across her arms. "Suit yourself. Knock twice and call out your name before entering. I'm going to set a spell on the door."

"Zat spell of hers had better not damage my door," the innkeeper said.

I smiled and pulled up a chair. "I know it's a bit late, but are you still serving supper?" I asked.

"Aye, we are," the innkeep said. "What'll you have?"

"Something filling," I said. "Um, but no bugs."

"Bah, humans," the innkeep said before he waddled off to the back. I fetched a handful of coppers out of my backpack while he was gone and had them waiting in a neat stack by the time he returned and placed a tray before me.

It was simple fare. Some chicken, some potatoes and gravy and a few other veggies to the side. Still, it smelled good and the glass of milk he set next to it was chilled to the touch. Did they have magic to keep food fresh? It would make sense.

"So, you're wiz ze exploration guild like zat scoundrel Gabriel?"

"Yup, but I'm not a scoundrel," I said as I dug in.

The innkeep laughed. "You don't look ze sort, no. I'm Jules, ze owner of zis fine hole in ze wall."

"Ah, I'm Broccoli, Broccoli Bunch. Sorry for not introducing myself earlier. I was hungry and a bit nervous. What's the name of your inn?"

"Zis is ze Croak and Stagger," Jules said with obvious pride. "My grandpa was a rogue with ze army for some time. Build zis inn, married my grandmozer and my family lived here ever since."

"That's a sweet story," I said. I took a sip of the milk. It was a little strange tasting, but maybe it was just not pasteurized, so I fired a bit of cleaning magic into it just in case. "Hey, Jules, could you tell me anything about the cervid?"

"Ze cervid? Zose no good horse-wannabes? Bah. Can't tell you too much. Zeir entire nation is bent on taking up as much space as zey can. Weird folk. Not a good one in ze lot of zem."

I didn't believe that, but I wasn't about to say so aloud. "Is it true they came here once?"

"Zey certainly tried. But we gave zem a good thrashing and zey never tried again, ze cowards couldn't handle a bit of a tussle in ze mud."

"Hrm, so if there were cervid around now it would be unusual, wouldn't it?" I wondered.

Jules looked at me long and hard. "Yes, yes it would be."

I finished the last of my milk and set the cup aside, then brushed the back of my hand across my mouth to get rid of my milk moustache. "Thanks Jules, the meal was super good. See you in the morning!"

"Aye, I'll make sure your breakfast is just as good," the innkeep said as I stood off the stool and made my way upstairs. I had a lot to think on, and some sleep to catch up on. I hoped that half a night's rest would be enough.

# Chapter Fifty-Eight
# Opportunity Comes Kicking

My second ride on an airship was nothing like the first. The *Silver Boot* had been a naval-looking ship with a magical means of lift and propulsion. It wasn't meant to fly, but it did so anyway and with a lot of panache and flair.

The airship that hovered just over Green Hold and which we boarded via some dropped rope ladders was nothing like that. Its name, the *Marshy Gasbag*, was proudly emblazoned on its cloth sides and on the small nacelle at the bottom of it. The entire vessel was a huge greenish grey balloon, oblong and pointed at both ends with a few engines in boxy protrusions at its sides.

It was more of a Zeppelin than a flying boat. If it wasn't for the bluish smoke pouring out of its four motors, I could have imagined it back on Earth way back when people still flew in style instead of all cramped in the passenger seats of a jet.

I sort of wished that the experiences I had aboard the Silver Boot would repeat, with a cool captain showing me around, but we were greeted by a harried looking grenoil First Mate who showed us to our rooms then ran off to get the ship ready to depart.

I found myself waiting in a tiny lounge, too small for the five tense occupants within, and with chairs that weren't all that comfortable. The only saving grace were the windows looking out of the sides of the ship, seeing the world roll by beneath was always a treat, especially from inside a warm room with no wind in my face.

I sat with my knees crossed and Orange on my lap and, after some poking and prodding, got the twins to spill out the details of their adventure. Not that it was all that adventurous an adventure. Unlike Amaryllis and I, their mission had gone on without a hitch. They had been surprised by the slimes at night, but Florine was a Marsh Wizard in a marsh, so he took care of them.

When I had exhausted that bit of discussion, I tried prying some things out of Amaryllis, but she was busy glaring at Gabriel who, in turn, was busy nursing what I suspect was a hangover.

In the end I ended up resting my head against the cool glass of the window, fingers rubbing at Orange until the lack of sleep and yesterday's adventure caught up with me and the world slowly, gently went dark. I was serenaded to sleep by the rocking of the airship and the distant rumble of its engines.

Something touched my shoulder and I snapped awake, the momentary confusion as to where I was fading away when I saw Amaryllis standing above me. She had Orange tucked into the crook of a wing and my backpack was slung over the opposite shoulder. "Hey, you. Good, you're awake," she said.

"Eh?" I asked. I twisted around to look at the landscape beyond the window only to find that it had been replaced wholesale by the bustling docks of Port Royal. Our ship was floating next to a sort of vertical pier, part of what was essentially a parking garage for airships. Ropes were latched to the side and grenoil in harnesses moved over to check the surface of the balloon or do other maintenance-y things.

"Oh," I said. "How long did I sleep for?"

"Three or so hours? Maybe a bit more. The height makes it hard to tell how the sun's moving," Amaryllis said.

"Right." I got up and stretched, rubbing my neck to work out the pang that had grown in it. We were alone in the lounge area, which might have explained why Amaryllis looked so eager to get a move on. "Lead the way?"

"We can talk while we walk," Amaryllis said.

I agreed with a nod, then followed her as she led me through the ship and onto a ramp that reached over to the port proper. There was a customs agent of sorts waiting at the bottom of the ramp, but one look at the pin on my bandolier and the one Amaryllis wore on her belt and we were let through.

"I'm… sorry about last night," Amaryllis said. "I lost my temper and that was inappropriate."

"Okay," I said. I didn't like it when she acted that angry, but I could understand where she came from. The apology was nice, though it did feel as if she was trying to put some distance between us with it.

"That kidnapping attempt was suspicious. Obviously. It wasn't done by my family. They wouldn't have sent cervid after me. Which means it came from elsewhere. I don't think anyone but the guild and the bank would be able to tell where I was at the time, and only the guild knew where I would be ahead of time, which has some very disturbing implications."

"You didn't tell your family where you would be?" I asked. I wasn't going to fling rocks from my glass house, I hadn't exactly told my family that

I was heading off on a grand adventure either, but I was curious about her homelife.

"That is unimportant," Amaryllis said.

She walked through the docks as if she owned the place, her fierce scowl clearing the path before us until we were out of the docks and onto the streets proper. The Port Royal smell hit me then and I had to hold back a gag.

"Lovely," Amaryllis drawled like someone that had just stepped in dog poop. "It's traditional that the director of the guild be there to greet a team returning from their first mission. I intend to get to the bottom of this."

"You mean Mister Rainnewt?" I asked.

"Who?"

"The man that worked at the guild," I said. "Tall, human. Kind of nice?"

"No, that man's just some sort of clerk or administrator, he's a paper pusher," Amaryllis said.

"He's the one that assigned me as your partner," I said. I didn't want to think ill of someone, but I couldn't help but begin to think that Mister Rainnewt was just a little suspicious now. Hopefully, it was all just some horrible accident and my imagination was running wild, but it wouldn't hurt to verify.

Trust a whole lot, but verify anyway, my dad used to say.

It was usually about the price of groceries, but I think it counted here too.

I got to see a part of Port Royal that I hadn't visited yet as Amaryllis took us up one set of stairs, then another. We crossed arches made of rattling pipes and then into an area where the homes were far larger and seemed to have been carved out of the mountain itself and then had flowers and gardens planted around them to add embellishments. There were more guards here, and yet fewer people on the streets.

I wanted to gawk around a bit like the tourist I was, but Amaryllis was setting the pace and she was relentless.

We marched onto Guild Row, coming onto the street from the opposite end than I was used to and walked down to the front of the Exploration Guild.

"Let me handle this," Amaryllis said as we reached the doors.

I had a bad feeling all of a sudden as she raised one taloned foot and kicked the door.

Her foot bonked against the solid wood and barely rattled it.

Amaryllis' face went an interesting shade of painful-white as she lowered her foot, but she didn't say anything as she reached up and opened the door properly before limping in.

I expected a crowd in the lobby, but it was completely empty save for the grenoil secretary behind the counter at the far end of the room.

"Where are Gabriel and the twins?" I asked.

"That's what I want to know," Amaryllis said. She stomped her way across the lobby and to the desk. "Hello. Do you know where the team that just returned is?"

The secretary looked up from a stack of papers and blinked a few times. "In the lounge, I believe, with the director."

"Good," Amaryllis said before turning to the left and stalking off.

"Thank you and have a nice day!" I called out to the befuddled secretary as I followed my friend.

Amaryllis seemed to know where she was going because she didn't so much as pause until she arrived at another door. She poked this one a few times, glared at the door frame set into a stone wall, then nodded to herself.

"Oh no," I said as she took a step back.

This time, when she kicked the door open, it crashed into the wall. Splinters flew where the frame busted, and the pretty ivory-capped handle went ballistic.

Amaryllis stepped into a room that was arranged to look a little like a cross between a lounge and an inn's main room. There were tables and chairs all over, a huge hearth on one side with the skull of what might have been a dragon over the mantle, a stuffed six-legged bear looked tall in one corner and there was a bar at the far wall.

There was a persistent smell in the air, like strong alcohol, but more refined, mixed with a thick herbal scent that I suspected came from the men sitting off in one corner enjoying cigars while staring at the spectacle that Amaryllis was starting.

Gabriel and the twins were closer to the middle of the room, talking to a Grenoil woman that was surprisingly short for a female grenoil, at least, as far as I could tell. She had a long scar running across her face from just above an eye to below her mouth, it made her lips curl up strangely to the side.

She raised the ridges above one eye as she looked to Amaryllis. "You're paying for that door," she said without a hint of a grenoil accent.

"Come on, Mathy, let the lass have some fun. It's just a pinch of destruction of private property," A big human sitting off to the side said while waving a cigar around.

"Shut it, Abraham," the woman, presumably called Mathy barked across the room. She turned back to the pair of us and I could feel her eyeing me up and down for a moment. "So, you've made your entrance, Miss Albatross. What I hear from Gabriel is concerning enough, but I'd like your version of things."

Amaryllis stood a little taller and I noticed that her feathers were starting to puff. "Our mission parameters were simple. I imagine you know what those were; we were to scout around Fort Frogger to the North-East of Deepmarsh. Our initial journey went without issue. The Fort was and is occupied by a single man who has been inhabiting the region for some time, I presume. After completing our objective, we started trekking back towards Green Hold to report."

"Haha! I can hear the stories she's not telling you, Mathy," the big Abraham guy said.

I didn't speak up. I appreciated that Amaryllis wasn't saying anything about Gunther and Throat Ripper already. I didn't need to ruin it by opening my mouth.

"What happened before doesn't matter," Amaryllis said. "It's what happened when we were crossing a bridge that's concerning. We were waylaid by kidnappers on the road."

The Mathy lady made a dismissive sound. "Bandits? I'll report it to the guard and—"

"No bandits," Amaryllis said. "Kidnappers. Six of them, with military equipment. All six were cervid using false names, unless the cervid had taken to calling their children numbers while I wasn't paying attention."

The room had resettled to a sort of calm after Amaryllis' entrance, the men returning to their cigars and the few women around speaking in low murmurs. Of the dozen or so people in the room, only a couple actually seemed to care at first, but Amaryllis' declaration had all of them paying attention.

Mathy croaked. "I see. In that case, let's talk in my office. Just you, Gabriel, and I, Miss Albatross. Abe, make sure the… other one stays here. She might be complicit in this whole thing too."

I noticed all the suspicious looks turning my way and gulped.

## Chapter Fifty-Nine
# Lord Abraham Bristlecone!

I was super curious about what was happening with the Mathy lady and Amaryllis and Gabriel, but it seemed as if I wasn't wanted, and snooping was so far from polite that I didn't give the idea more than a passing thought. Instead I just stood in the middle of the lounge room and shifted my weight from foot to foot, uncertain as to what to do next.

Then Abraham saved me.

"Oi, girlie, come on and sit with us old timers. You'll pretty up our corner of the room just by being here and you won't wear a hole in the floor, haha!"

I smiled, my reservations melting as Abraham's gregarious voice boomed across the room. He gestured to an unoccupied seat made of dark wood with big fluffy cushions. It was quite similar to his own throne-like seat, though with fewer stuffed animals surrounding it.

"Now, what brings a young lass like you to this backwards port?"

"Um," I said. "Adventure, mostly."

"Haha!" Abraham roared. "A girl after my own heart. Oh, I do love a spot of adventure in the morning, then a bit of exploration in the afternoon and maybe a bit of a tussle with some big beastie in the evening. That's the true man's life! Isn't that right, boys?"

The other men sitting around the hearth weren't all so Abraham-like, but they looked wiry and dangerous in their own ways. All of them were older, and all of them had a scar or two on their hands or faces. The nearest, a grenoil with a wrinkly nose, shook his head in exasperation.

Abraham himself looked like… well he looked like Santa Claus if Santa hit the gym six days a week and spent the last day prowling around in the savannah looking for a lion to wrestle. He even had a pith helmet!

"I overheard a little about your adventure with those deer lads from out East. Oh, that reminds me of that time the princess of Manamere got her grubby hands on an ancient Crys statuette and I was tasked to fetch it. I spent a whole week crawling on my hands and knees across the Trenten Flats themselves, then I snuck in through the royal privy pipes until I was in the castle proper. Found the princess too. Poor lass got quite the fright when I stuck my head out in her private toiletry room. Haha!"

I held back a giggle and sat on the edge of the seat. "Then what happened?" I asked.

There was a chorus of 'oh no' from the old men around us, but they were wearing secretive little smiles of their own, especially when Abraham lit up as if I had just announced that it was his birthday.

"And then, lass, I climbed out of the bowl, quite the stench on me, let me tell you. Cervid sewers make the ol' Port Royal perfume smell like fresh roses. The princess beat me on the head a few times. Solid whaps of her little princess-y make up kit. Haha! It didn't help the smell any!"

"Oh no!"

"Oh yes indeed little miss. But no fear! It takes more than some perfume flung into his face to take out the great Abraham Bristlecone!" He tugged his big manly moustache, the sort I would no doubt have if I were a cool old man instead of the exact opposite. "I ran out of the little princess's room, without harming one hair on her furry little hide of course, I'm a gentleman, not some lowlife ruffian! Then I was accosted by the royal guard and we had ourselves a bit of a scrap! Tough fight too, all I could carry with me in the sewers were my knickers and a spoon!"

I slapped my hands over my mouth. "Were you caught?" I gasped.

"Haha! No one catches Abraham, not unless he wants it!" he declared before giving me a wink. "I ran off the guard, defeated Folsom the Spear Champion himself and left the boy covered in spoon wounds. Then I raced off into the princess' quarters and found the Crys statuette. Then it was up to the roof where Raynold here was pissing his britches."

The old grenoil snorted. "No sane man would execute a plan that involved skimming over an enemy's castle roof with a ship as clunky as your Shady Lady," he said.

"It was a perfect plan!" Abraham said.

"You exited right next to all of their anti-dragon siege equipment!" Raynold shot right back.

I had the impression the fight was rehashed a few times already. "How did you guys make it out if there was a bunch of anti-dragon stuff around?" I asked.

Raynold stopped and, when Abraham went to talk, flung a wooden cigar box at the man's head to shush him up. It bounced off without so much as making Abraham flinch. "Ah, let me explain this one, Abe, the little miss might actually learn something, unlike with most of your sordid tales."

"Hah!" Abraham said. "You're merely jealous that my life was a little exciting, you damned paper-pusher!"

Raynold shook his head. "You see Miss…"

"Broccoli, Broccoli Bunch," I said.

"Miss Bunch. Most cities that install the kind of weapons needed to fight off threats in the air expect them to come from the air. But I, being both brighter and less keen on suicide than Abe here, calculated their firing arcs and discovered that the primitive canons the cervids use couldn't depress low enough–that is, they couldn't fire downwards. I merely needed to guide our air skimmer through the widest roads in the city and over some of the walls."

"You tore off half the rudder," Abraham complained.

"That chimney moved!"

The two started to bicker back and forth over which one of them was the greater fool. I didn't like seeing friends argue, even if it didn't seem like it was in bad faith. "Did you accomplish your mission?" I asked.

"Oh-hoh!" Abraham said as he cut himself off halfway through the act of flinging the cigar box back at Raynold "Did we ever! Have you seen the Screaming Mountains, little Bunch?"

"No, what are they?" I asked.

"They're these mountains, far off to the Southeast and just off the continent. The people there are made of crystal and when the sun rises, they begin to hum. By the time midday hits a man can hardly hear himself think!"

I wanted to ask Abraham for some more tales, because his stories so far had been wonderful, but Amaryllis and the others chose that moment to walk back into the lounge area. Amaryllis was wearing a smug grin, Gabriel looked like he needed a stiffer drink than usual, and the Mathy lady looked like she was a step away from tearing someone's head off.

Then she locked eyes on me. "You're still here?" she asked.

"Yes ma'am," I said as I got back onto my feet.

"Hmm, good. Gabriel, get the girl a coin-purse. Standard mission pay, then show her out."

It took a moment for the words, and their meaning, to register. Was I being kicked out of the guild? "Is this because I haven't paid yet? Mister Rainnewt implied it was okay to pay when I returned."

"No, it's because you're a liability. You should never have been allowed to join anyway," the woman said.

"What are you talking about?" Amaryllis said. "She's perfect for this guild. She even saved my life."

"Be that as it may," she continued, "Her level is far too low, her class doesn't seem suitable to the work, and with the amount of suspicion going around it's wiser to show her out than to keep a possible snake amongst the tadpoles."

Amaryllis squawked. "Fine! If Broccoli can't join your guild, then I'm heading out too!"

The grenoil woman stood a little taller at that. "I'm afraid I can't let you do that. Your parents—"

"Will hear all about your incompetence," Amaryllis interrupted. "The only one here that managed to actually help me was her," she said while pointing right at me. "I'm not going to let you just... get rid of her."

The woman's eyes narrowed. "You're making a spectacle of this."

"And yet the only clown here is you," Amaryllis shot back.

Mathy looked ready to tear Amaryllis' head off when Abraham cleared his throat. "Care to share with the rest of us, Mathy?"

"My name is Mathide, Abraham," the woman said. Abraham's moustache twitched and I suspected he was trying not to smile. "And I suspect we have... had a spy in our midst. Has anyone seen Rainnewt?"

There was a long moment of silence that seemed to say 'no'.

"World damn us all," she muttered.

"So, because of that skinny little snake you're going to punish poor Broccoli here?" Abraham asked.

I took a small step back as Mathide looked my way. The woman was downright terrifying. "It's okay?" I said. I couldn't just let everyone else speak over me. "I really wanted to join your guild, but if you won't have me, I can just... go?"

"No, you can't," Amaryllis said. She was glaring at the back of Mathilde's head as if she could set it on fire with her eyes alone.

"How about a compromise then?" Abraham asked. He pulled the cigar box—now resting on his lap—open and took out a cigar. A snap of his fingers had a small flame dancing on his index which he used to slowly light the cigar. "If the girls need to be safe, well, I happen to be heading out west, to Greenshade. I can take them with me and drop them off at the guild there. It's about as far from Trenten as you can get without running through the desert or swimming the sea."

Mathilde frowned at that before she turned to Amaryllis. "Would that be acceptable? The Exploration Guild branch there is smaller, but there's plenty of work to be had. I'll even let you bring your human friend here if you trust her so much."

"I do, and it is," Amaryllis said.

"Hoh-ho! Abraham Bristlecone, saving the day once more! And I didn't even need to stand up for it. Raynold, fetch me a glass of that scotch you've been hiding away!"

"Jump off a cliff," Raynold said.

I raised a hand, just like I had been taught to do in class and waited for Mathilde and Amaryllis to both look my way. "Um, I'm sorry, but what exactly is going on?"

Amaryllis was the first to answer. "Rainnewt has gone missing. He accepted you as a member without going through the proper channels and is the one who arranged all the missions. Mathilde here thinks he's some sort of troublemaker. I think he ought to be hung for trying to have me kidnapped. This so-called leader here thinks the solution is to kick you out of the Guild even though you've done more work to stop their own mistakes than anyone else. I, as a person that isn't an idiot, am keen on pointing out how utterly devoid of sense that is."

Mathide croaked and it didn't sound all that happy. "We'll get to the bottom of it, Miss Albatross. If the Exploration Guild is good at one thing it's discovering things." she looked my way. "Miss Bunch… I wish we had met under better circumstances."

I smiled right back. "It's never too late to become friends, and I think I understand why you, um, tried to kick me out. It's okay."

"Too damned nice," Amaryllis muttered.

"Right-oh!" Abraham said as he jumped to his feet with surprising spryness. "The *Shady Lady* will be ready to depart first thing in the morning. You ladies just need to ask around to find it. It's like a small adventure!"

Things were moving a little fast, but I nodded anyway and tried on an even bigger smile for size.

From what I could tell the business with Mister Rainnewt was suspect. He had seemed nice, but nice people didn't kidnap girls, to say the least. It kind of soured my impressions of the guild a little bit, but going on an adventure of sorts with Mister Bristlecone sounded like a jolly good time. That, and Amaryllis had stepped up to defend me, which… Well, I had happy little butterflies fluttering in my tummy at the thought.

"That doesn't leave us much time," Amaryllis said. "Come on Broccoli, let's go. We have things that need doing before we set off."

"Oh, um, right. See you tomorrow then, Mister Bristlecone?" I asked.

"Sure thing, young Miss!"

# Chapter Sixty
# Pretty Dresses

Exiting the Exploration Guild building was like dropping a heavy load off my back. Suddenly I went from being scrutinized and under someone's careful watch to entirely free to do as I wanted in the space of a few steps.

"Whaa, that was stressful," I complained to the open skies. Even the stinky Port Royal air was more welcome than the tension in the Guild.

Amaryllis shifted next to me. "That it was," she agreed. "We should head out. We have a lot of things to buy and only one day to do so."

"Buy?" I repeated. "I was thinking I would go to an inn. There's a nice one in the East quarter, the owner's a sort of friend."

"That's fine, but the day is still young and you need better equipment," Amaryllis said. "That spear is... usable, but you're carrying a shovel as a weapon. I don't think I need to tell you why that isn't the brightest idea."

"But I like my shovel," I said. I wanted to grab my shovel and hug it safe, but it was on my back, so instead I hugged Orange who was trying to shuffle her way out of my bandoleer. The poor kitty was already growing too big for the biggest pouch I had.

"We can get you a sword, or perhaps a dagger. Though those are traditional Harpy weapons. Humans like heavier blunt weapons, right? Maybe a war hammer? We'll get you something nice and proper." She started walking downhill towards the areas that I knew had more shops in them, so hiking up my backpack I jogged after her.

"Amaryllis," I said. "We're friends, right?" I asked.

"I... yes, we're friends," she said. She didn't sound completely sure, but I suspected there was a good reason for that. Amaryllis struck me as the sort of girl that had never had that many real friends. Which meant that it was up to me to teach her the joys of friendship!

"Amaryllis. Friends don't make friends do things. Not unless those things are vitally important. I like my shovel, and unless it's putting me and you at risk, there's nothing wrong with it."

The harpy slowed to a stop. Her face was blank for a while, then she huffed. "Well, fine, you can keep the shovel I suppose. But that armour of yours..."

"It's been good for me," I said as I looked down at my gambeson. It looked nice enough.

"It's clean, certainly, but it's got holes and cuts all across it, and I can't feel a single enchantment on the entire piece."

I blinked. "There's enchanted clothes? Wait, no, of course there's enchanted clothes. That's brilliant! What sort of enchantments are there?"

Amaryllis resumed walking, this time with her nose inching up into the air. "That depends entirely on the quality and age of the garb. That and the ability of the craftsman. There are a few good stores even in a backwater like Port Royal that ought to have something serviceable."

I felt a grin growing. Shopping did sound like a good way to get rid of some stress. Plus, I could find some totally awesome new stuff to wear while we gossiped. "Is it really a backwater?" I asked as I looked around. Port Royal seemed pretty big and pretty new. The buildings were all well-maintained and the area had a vibrancy to it that made it feel active and alive.

"It's not the worst place. The smell could certainly be improved upon. But compared to the likes of Farseeing or Fort Sylphrot this is a quaint little city. The grenoil truly are trying their best but their culture is still... lesser."

I hummed as I thought about that. It sounded a little... a lot racist. But maybe it wasn't entirely wrong. Maybe this area was like a third world country compared to the rest of the world and I was just too ignorant to know any better. "I guess it is kind of old fashioned."

"Yes, I suppose it would be, even to you."

I shook my head at that. "I think you'd be amazed by the sorts of things we have back home," I said. "I know that I sometimes miss the internet and phones... and toilets."

Amaryllis laughed, high-pitched and birdlike. "I suppose some amenities are missed no matter where you're from. The Nesting Kingdom has these great big bathhouses that I sorely miss."

"I haven't taken a bath since I came here," I said. "Or a shower. I've been meaning to but... well, there's always more adventuring to do."

Amaryllis scoffed. "If we visit my home one day, I'll show you the bathhouses; you'll certainly enjoy them. The better ones have professional preeners. It's excellent. Though I suppose they couldn't do much for you."

I shrugged. "So, um, back to enchantments." Conversations were always speeding past the sorts of things I wanted to know.

"They're a way to twist ambient mana into a specific shape. Essentially constantly casting a weak spell," Amaryllis explained.

I touched the collar around my neck. Was there a spirit-kitty summoning spell out there? Was there one for puppies? I had so many important things to learn still.

Amaryllis seemed to know where she was going and led us across Central and to a small side street filled with shops laid out in a rough circle around a large fountain appropriately filled with statues of frogs.

There were people standing around or sitting on benches, lots of grenoil ladies in big dresses and men in suits carrying canes. I couldn't help but gawk a little at the people passing by, though I did try to keep it to a minimum.

A human lady walking past us pulled up a black and green speckled handkerchief and pressed it to her nose as she strutted past. It wouldn't have really caught my attention except the pattern on her handkerchief was distinct, and the moment it came to my attention I was suddenly seeing it everywhere. Ascots and those little puffs of cloth in men's breast pockets, even the lace of the dresses we passed were made of the same material.

Fortunately, I had an Amaryllis to help. "What's with all those similar clothes?" I asked.

"Ah, you noticed that?" Amaryllis said. She lifted her neck a little to look extra haughty. "It's a product from the city's dungeon. Some sort of cloth dropped by the monsters that occupy the first floors. The material is pulled out by the cartload every day and the locals have taken to wearing it."

That... sort of made sense. "Does that happen a lot?"

Amaryllis shrugged a shoulder. "It depends on what the dungeon makes. There's a dungeon in one of the independent cities where the first level monsters drop knives once in a while. Everyone there has the same sort of knife. They're practically free."

"Huh," I said. I was from a world where things were always, by necessity, made or grown or at the very least gathered. Things didn't just... spawn from monsters. I already had some things just like that on me, but I hadn't thought to connect that to the economic repercussions of easy to obtain and somewhat free... stuff.

"Here we are," Amaryllis said as she stopped before a shop. Unlike the others in the square—was it a square if it was round?—this store didn't have mannequins in pretty dresses and nice suits, but instead had leather armours and tough-looking but handy clothes on display. There were even heavier things like plate and mail sets within.

"I kind of expected a blacksmith for armour-related things," I said.

"Only if you want to be weighted down all the time. Us harpies can't afford to be lumbering brutes like you humans," Amaryllis said. "This place has good equipment. Quality stuff."

The shop didn't exactly look like the kind of place where I would find a good bargain. Still, I followed when Amaryllis stepped in.

The inside smelled like leather and oils and a bit like perfume, as if the owner wanted to fight off the city's stench. There were lanterns hanging over displays, but unlike the stores back home there weren't that many things on sale compared to the size of the main floor.

A pair of grenoil at the back were measuring a customer's arm length, one of them taking notes while the other worked the tape, and an older grenoil lady wearing an apron over a sundress was manning the counter off to one side. She was the one to step up when we entered. "Hello and welcome to ze Rising Shield, how can I help you?"

"My friend here needs some better equipment," Amaryllis said.

"Oh, and you should get a bandoleer," I added. "Nearly everyone else at the guild has one."

"Explorers!" the old grenoil lady said. "Excellent. We have all sorts of zings zat will keep you safe, warm and fashionable in any deep dungeon or far off land."

I was already enjoying my shopping experience more than most of the times I'd gone shopping back home.

"What do you suggest?" I asked.

The grenoil lady looked me up and down. "Do you mind if I ask you some questions?"

"I don't."

"In zat case. How do you fight, how do you move and what is your position on your team?"

"Um. I don't fight very well. I do have a makeshift weapon proficiency and a lot of Cleaning magic for that undead and such. I move a lot by jumping, it's one of my best skills. As for my position, I want to be the ranged DPS."

"A what?" Amaryllis asked before her eyes narrowed. "Is that one of the strange things from your… home?"

"Yup," I said.

"I zink I see," the grenoil lady said. With that, she moved back to the counter and opened up a large book, one filled with images. She looked back up to me a few times, then back down to the book.

"What is she doing?" I muttered to Amaryllis. I didn't want to interrupt the lady, but I was starting to get weirded out a little.

"She's creating an outfit," Amaryllis said. "It's what good tailors do."

"From scratch?" I asked. "What about all the things on display?"

"Zose," the lady said without so much as looking up. "Are pieces zat are ready for some discerning clients and ze occasional experimental piece. Now, what do you zink of zis?" She turned the book over and revealed a sketch of an outfit.

It was simple enough, a leather chest piece over a tight cloth gambeson that flared out at the bottom into a nice skirt. The sleeves were big and poofy and the armour seemed to incorporate a bandoleer already. There was a single pauldron over the left shoulder and a matching steel plate on the right hip. "Whoa," I said.

"Ah, my eye hasn't failed me yet," she said. "Zis is a simple enough outfit. Ze skirt makes it a little unusual but some young ladies seem to favour zem. Ze price is for ze unenchanted version."

Price? I looked over the page, then found a number at the bottom right and almost winced. One lesser gold, two pure silver. That was a fair amount of my gold. "How much do the enchantments cost? And what sort can you provide?"

"On a piece zat's so new? It's not very expensive."

"New?" I repeated.

Amaryllis huffed next to me; it was her 'of course you don't know' huff. "The older something is the better magic takes to it. The harder it is to add something like an enchantment to it."

"Is that why Insight tells me the age of equipment?" I asked.

"Yes, actually."

The grenoil lady picked up right where she had left off. "As for enchantments, ze most popular ones are durability and cleanliness. We can also make the cloth fireproof or wick off humidity. Zere are mana absorption enchantments as well. If you want somezing specific you need just ask and we can find an enchanter for a fee."

"I think the fireproofing, durability and mana absorption would be best for you," Amaryllis said. "No need for the cleanliness enchantments, of course, and the more specialized kinds of enchantments are all rather, well, specialized."

"Ah, okay," I said. "Can you tell me how much those three would cost?"

"Zree enchantments working concurrently, and none zat use ze same spell structure? Zat would be…" She scribbled some notes on a loose leaf, then opened a smaller book and raced through it, occasionally stopping to make a mark on the side. "Zat will be… two lesser gold, and seventeen sil."

"That's just for the enchantments?" I asked.

"Zat's right."

"Ah, well, I think that I can't—"

"We'll take it," Amaryllis said. "But only if you can have it all ready within the next two hours."

I almost choked. "H-hey, I don't have that kind of money," I said.

Amaryllis rolled her eyes. "I'm well aware. I, on the other hand, am not some poor peasant like you and do have some gold to my name. Consider it a gift for not letting me get kidnapped and ransomed."

"Ah, but it's too much!" I said.

"Don't be an idiot, this is nothing. And now you'll at least look like you can stand next to me without being an embarrassment with that torn up armour of yours."

"Well zen miss, all zat's left is for you to pick ze colour."

# Chapter Sixty-One
# Spending the Night Inn

I spun to make my new skirt flare out, as one does, and then giggled as I went dizzy for just a moment.

It was a very pretty skirt and deserved to be spun a whole lot. The lady in the shop had given me a whole selection of colours, and while some were sensible and even reasonable to wear while out adventuring, I couldn't help but pick a bright blue. It was the same pale hue as the sky a moment after the sun rose on a cloudless morning and I loved it.

"Stop doing that, you idiot, you're going to run into the path of a cart and you'll ruin your new dress when you cover it in your bloody remains," Amaryllis said.

I stopped myself in the act of preparing for another spin, then patted down my skirts. "Right!"

The armoured cuirass squeezed everything in place while emphasising other things, and the thick cloth armour beneath somehow managed to be fairly loose and flexible and soft. It probably helped that a couple of weeks of running around and fighting for my life and walking for what felt like hundreds of kilometres had done away with the little bit of tummy I had come into the world with.

Not that I was vain or anything, but I did now have the beginnings of a six-pack and that was something to be proud of. My friends back on Earth had always told me boys were into that sort of thing, which meant I was putting all of the chances on my side that I'd find a nice husband. Also, I bet I could do so many sit-ups!

"So, what's next?" I asked as I walked next to Amaryllis. "I have some coins left, we could go and grab a bite to eat, or we could buy some more books."

Amaryllis looked up to the skies which were just starting to turn pinkish. "Perhaps it would be best to head back to an inn. I have a bit of research to do and we skipped both breakfast and lunch. I can stand to go a day without eating but I'd really rather not."

We walked past a street vendor who was hawking 'genuine Brackland beetles' that were fried in some sort of oil. "I know a nice inn," I said. "They even make food without bugs in it."

"That is a good selling point," Amaryllis admitted. "The cuisine in Deepmarsh isn't awful, but it's not exactly to my liking."

I looked down both ways of the street, because we were about to cross, then grabbed Amaryllis' by the talon and pulled her across at a quick trot to avoid a passing trolley. The moment we were on the other side, Amaryllis tore her hand back and shook it. "You humans are all so touch-y feely," she muttered.

"I would have thought that harpies would be the same way," I said. "What with you all being bird people. Do you have nests and such?"

"Only the truly impoverished would sleep in a nest," Amaryllis said. "Or those incubating an egg the old-fashioned way, as some clans still do."

I almost tripped. "You can lay eggs?!" I asked.

Amaryllis gave me a flat look. "Of course I can."

"Yeah, but eggs! How does that even work?"

A passing group of grenoils in worker's overalls gave us a look and I noticed the feathers on Amaryllis' arms poofing a little. Was that her version of a blush? I hadn't meant to embarrass her.

"You idiot," she said. "That's… well I suppose it isn't common knowledge where you're from." She coughed to clear her throat. "Traditionally, when a man harpy and a woman harpy get married, they prepare a nest, and when they enter their breeding period, they… consummate their relationship. The egg that the woman lays next is fertile and it is incubated until it hatches. If the female harpy isn't in that sort of relationship, then the egg she lays will be infertile and the clan will dispose of it. It's all quite civilised I assure you."

"You have a breeding cycle?" I asked. This was way more interesting than that one class in school with the horrible videos.

Amaryllis huffed. It was her 'I'm better than you' huff. "Unlike you humans who just mate whenever, we actually know that there's a time and place for such things. Usually in the spring when the winter snows melt away."

"Neat," I said. "Wait, does that mean that you lay eggs every spring? Can they be eaten?"

Amaryllis was giving me a very flat look. "I'll have you know that eating eggs is extremely taboo. That's like… offering to eat a human baby because the meat is tender."

"Ah, wow, okay sorry." I was fortunately quite used to placing my foot in my mouth though. "Are there any other taboo subjects? Just in case?"

"Not really," Amaryllis said. "It's considered quite rude to bring up certain subjects around strangers though. You don't talk about eggs with a person that isn't a close family member, and it's usually something handled amongst the womenfolk."

"Ah, okay."

"And talking about religion in a public gathering is a faux-pas. Politics and economics and other such contentious subjects are fine."

"You'll have to show me your home one day," I said.

"I dread the idea of presenting you to my sisters," Amaryllis said. "They would take a shine to you that I find frankly terrifying."

"That sounds like a lot of fun," I said. "Oh, that's the inn!" I pointed to the Rock Inn and Roll Inn just a little ways down the street.

"Seems respectable enough," Amaryllis said. "We should get a room for the both of us. It will save us some money."

I eyed her from the corner of my eye. She had been throwing money around without a care earlier. Sure, her biggest purchase was my awesome new armour, but she had also purchased a new leather jacket with a fur-lined neck similar to her last one, and a thin bandoleer with slips for potions to go underneath.

It wouldn't have surprised me if she was really just a little nervous to sleep in a room alone. She had been through a lot in the last couple of days and I think that she had yet to decompress. Really, what Amaryllis needed was a good hug and some tea and maybe a warm blanket. But if all she wanted was to share a room that was okay too.

"It'll be like a sleepover!" I said.

Amaryllis hummed. "One of my sisters was terribly keen on those. She used to drag out the most ridiculous outfits and makeup and make me parade around in them for her amusement." She sounded cross about it but was wearing a melancholic smile.

"Do you miss your family?" I asked.

"I hardly left on bad terms," Amaryllis said. "I just needed some… time to my own."

I didn't have time to dig into that as we arrived at the inn and slipped in to find a busy floor. Not every table was filled, but it was a near thing. Julien's inn seemed to attract a lot of upper-crust sort of people, grenoil in nice suits and people with spectacular hats and colourful outfits who seemed okay with the idea of bumping shoulders and sharing a pint.

I had the impression that that was a purposeful thing, that Julien wanted people here to let go of some of their social pretensions while in his inn.

The fat grenoil in question was talking animatedly to a customer behind the bar, but as soon as he saw us his eyes lit up and he raised both arms as if to hug the air. "Ah, little Broccoli! You made it back."

"Hello Julien!" I said. "I did! We had a few close calls, but we made it out alive. This is my friend and partner Amaryllis."

"Hello," Amaryllis said.

"Any friend of Broccoli is a friend of Julien's. How can I help you ladies?" he asked.

"We need a room for the night," I said. "Um, a room with two beds?"

"Something nice would be welcome," Amaryllis added. "With a desk and some room to think would be preferable."

"I have just ze zing," Julien said.

I nodded. "And food," I added. "Your food's the best."

"Oh hoh, zis one knows how to warm an old frog's heart," Julien said. A moment later he called over one of the barmaids and gave her some directions to lead us off to a room way off on the other side of the inn. Amaryllis slapped a single gold coin on the bartop and that had Julien's eyes sparkling in greedy delight.

Our room, as it turned out, was a whole lot bigger than the rooms I was used to, with a small washroom, two big beds and a little living room. It reminded me a bit of a modern hotel room, but with a most rustic charm. I could still hear the soft murmur of the bar below and the windows overlooking the street ahead of the inn gave a nice view of Port Royal.

"Bed!" I cheered as I jumped into the air and crashed onto one of the beds side first.

Orange, who didn't seem amused by my jump, stood hanging on nothing above the bed before she strutted off to the window and started grooming her little paw-paws in the sunlight.

"You idiot," Amaryllis muttered. She turned to the barmaid that had accompanied us and huffed. "We'll have our meals as soon as they're ready," she said.

"You're supposed to tip!" I called from the fluffy surface of the bed.

"Tipping? Really?" Amaryllis asked.

"I have some coins if you don't have any," I said as I got ready to jump off the bed.

Amaryllis grumbled something, but she pulled out a pair of silver coins and gave them to the now-smiling barmaid. "Here you go. Just… get our food. And no bugs."

"Yes ma'am," the barmaid said before scooting away.

"You're supposed to say 'thank you'," I said.

"She's help, you're supposed to pretend they don't exist," Amaryllis said.

I supposed that that was one of those cultural differences that I would have a hard time reconciling. Sitting up, I watched as Amaryllis pulled a chair from the table to one side of the room, then pulled a pen and sheet of paper from her ring with a poof. A moment later she scribbled something and they both poofed back.

"Whatcha doin'?" I asked.

Amaryllis made a gesture with one talon raised that I suspected meant 'give me a moment,' then, with a poof, a small notebook, a pen, and a larger book appeared above the table and fell. "I've been meaning to look over known dungeons for a proper second class. Something that will complement my primary class."

"Ohh," I said as I bounced off the bed. Beds were fun, but shopping for magical classes sounded a lot more fun. I pulled up a bench next to Amaryllis and, with my legs kicking out to bleed off some of my excess energy, waited for her to open up her book.

She did so, but not before rolling her eyes. "There are a few different schools of thought when it comes to second classes. Generally, a class will level up for doing things that are in-line with that class' purpose. A warrior will level from training at arms or from sparring. A chef will level from cooking. Do you follow so far?"

"That makes sense, yeah."

"So, as I said, the two major philosophies are split along two ideas. The first suggests that you find a second class that matches your first. A warrior might get a spearman class. A chef a cook class. That way you can continue doing the same sort of training and so on to level both classes up. Since the experience is more or less evenly shared between the two classes, this means that your second class will level far faster."

"Because levels eleven and up take more experience points per level?" I asked.

"Experience points?" Amaryllis asked.

"Uh. more… experience in general?" I asked. "Experience points are an Earth thing, I guess."

"Yes, I suppose," she said. "The second school of thought suggests finding a class that's utterly dissimilar to your first. That way you can practice both separately. It's both more and less efficient seeing as how the first method, the two similar classes way, tends to spend a long time with their second class at its bottleneck while the first reaches level twenty."

"Oh," I said. "That's kind of annoying. But then if you have two entirely different classes you need to spend time training two things?"

"Exactly. It's something of a toss-up as to which is best and matters for much furious debate in some circles."

"I can imagine," I said. "So what will you do?"

"I don't know yet," Amaryllis admitted. "Which is why I have this." she tapped a talon on the surface of the book.

*Midhve's compendium of Dungeons and Associated Classes*, I read. "Well then, let's pick you a class!"

Amaryllis huffed, but she opened the book all the same.

# Chapter Sixty-Two
# The Dungeon Book

"This compendium doesn't hold as much information as you would think, but it's nonetheless one of the most useful books out there. Most noble families, academies and guilds have a copy at their branch offices and mansions," Amaryllis explained.

"Does the Exploration Guild have one?" I wondered as I scooted closer.

"The Exploration guild are the ones providing most of the information being published here," Amaryllis said.

She opened the book to a page near the start and I leaned closer to read.

**The Pit of a Hundred Traps**
*Approx. Dungeon levels 5–7*
*Suggested levels 10+*
**Party composition:** *3+ Healer Necessary.*
**Special warnings:** *Poisons. Traps.*
*Located south-southwest of Stormshark near the Bay of Storms in lands belonging to the Kingdom of Endless Swells.*

*At ToW this dungeon has seven floors. The path from floor to floor is built along a series of tall plinths above a basin of predator-filled waters. The delve room is otherwise safe. Special care should be taken while using the bridges from one plinth to the next as some have trapped boards.*

**First Floor:** *Large area with key at one end. Simple pitfalls.*

**Second Floor:** *Rows of pillars meant to be jumped over. Pit beneath contains venomous spiders (common). Key at end.*

**Third Floor:** *Maze-like tunnel. End returns to start. Key hidden within. Layout changes daily. Pitfalls, blow darts.*

**Fourth Floor:** *False treasure room. Mimics. Key in one of the chests.*

**Fifth Floor:** *Use keys marked with symbols on the door to open. Remaining keys to be kept. Lesser boss is a large brass boar. Must be baited into traps or killed with overwhelming power.*

**Sixth Floor:** *Puzzle room. Bait large turtles into eating poisoned fish. Key at end of room.*

**Seventh Floor:** *Dungeon Boss. Large animated bear-trap. Needs to be baited into setting off different traps across the room. Each broken tooth summons an iron bear (uncommon).*

**Loot rewards:**

*Various traps. Ropes. Poisons. Fishing rods*

**Class reward:**

*Master Baiter class*

*Specializes in setting off traps from afar and tracking.*

"What's ToW? And what's a delve room?" I asked as I held back a giggle. I really hoped that Amaryllis didn't pick that class, or else I'd never be able to look her in the eyes again. Instead of looking up to see her no-doubt unamused look, I looked at the maps on the next page. They were small, and not that detailed, but they showed the rough shapes of each floor of the dungeon, and there were even some notes to the side.

Amaryllis hummed. "ToW stands for Time of Writing. This one is nearly a year old." She tapped a date at the bottom of the page. "No doubt the dungeon has gained at least a floor since. Some of the traps may have moved. And the delve room is the main room of a dungeon. Some dungeons have a room that allows you to access each floor. You can't actually skip ahead, and the dungeon punishes you for trying, but it does mean you can leave if you need to."

"Neat," I said. The Wonderland dungeon in Threewells had that, then. The large room with the shaft had to be its delve room.

"Indeed," she said. Amaryllis began flipping through the pages too fast for me to do much more than stare at some of the maps or read the passing names of the dungeons. She seemed to know what she was looking for.

But I didn't. "Ah, what kind of class do you want?" I wondered.

"Something that will synergize with my Thunder Mage class."

"Another mage class? Or something thunder and lightning related?" I wondered.

She hummed, then shook her head. "No, not quite. I want something that will work well with my class, shore up some weaknesses, but not something too close. Ah, this one is interesting."

The page she stopped at had a bit less information on it. I noticed that she had been skipping right past some of the dungeons with too many levels. They were probably a bit beyond us anyway.

**Toyland**

*Approx. Dungeon levels 4–7*

**Suggested levels:** *8–10*

**Party Composition:** *3+ Area of Effect Specialist Suggested*

**Special Warnings:** *Golems. Horde Enemies*

*Located next to Port Hazel, the capital of the Kingdom of Mattergrove.*

*At ToW this dungeon has five floors. The delve room is built to resemble a long, large castle room, with a glass ceiling (always near dusk) and hundreds of dust-covered boxes. All are empty. Excessive tampering or destruction in the dungeon will replace some boxes with traps. Otherwise safe.*

**First Floor:** *A long, narrow playroom. Hundreds of toys within. Upon crossing the middle of the room, the toys rise and begin to charge the delver in waves. Attacking prematurely awakens all toy golems at once.*

**Second Floor:** *Nutcracker room. Defeat toy knight in joust atop provided mount or fight soldier golems.*

**Third Floor:** *Room is filled with large plush animals. Deceptively dangerous. Will be invited for 'tea.' Accept and pass. Otherwise fight. Enemies resilient and strong for level. Slow-moving.*

**Fourth Floor:** *Room is built like a theatre. Large Marionettes act out a play on stage. Participating unlocks special reward (Toy wand, rare) Otherwise simple combat against large wooden foes. Focus cords.*

**Fifth Floor:** *Dungeon Boss. Large room filled with broken toys. Large armoured 'teddy bear' in centre. Will summon toys from sides of the room to aid in combat. Suggest fire.*

**Loot rewards:**
*Various toys. Small children's trinkets. Enchanted playthings.*

**Class reward:**
*Toymaker class*
*Class specializes in making small trinkets and toys and animating them with mana.*

"Oh," I said. "That class does sound like a lot of fun."

"You're merely saying that because you want to play with the toys I would make," Amaryllis said.

"I'm a bit old for most toys," I defended myself. "Though I wouldn't mind a teddy bear that hugs back. I'd call it Threadbear and I'd love it lots."

She shook her head and seemed about to tell me off, but the door opened and our supper arrived. The book was pushed aside as a pair of trays laden with all sorts of small plates with artfully arranged meats and veggies and breads were placed before us by a pair of barmaids. They left as quickly as they had come, leaving the room smelling heavenly.

"Let's eat!" I said as I immediately began digging in. Amaryllis went a little slower, at first, but she soon tossed her cutlery aside and began spearing her food with her talons.

When we finally finished eating some time later, I had to lean back into my seat to pat down my overfull tummy. There was still some food left, and I wanted to eat it, but there was no room.

I was almost dozing when Amaryllis dragged the book closer and started shifting through the pages. "Found it," she said a little while later.

"Eh?" I muttered as I sat up straighter.

"Look," she said as she pushed the book my way.

**The Palace of Strings**
*Approx. Dungeon levels 4–7*
**Suggested levels:** *8–10*
**Party Composition:** *2+ High Mental Resistance and Perception Suggested*
**Special Warnings:** *Body Snatchers*
*Located at the base of the cliffs of the independent town of Rosenbell.*
*At ToW this dungeon has 4 floors. No delve rooms. The entry point is a garden around an ancient palace.*
**First Floor:** *The garden hedges. Attempting to pass over the walls summons (rare) gargoyles. Large spiders near the ceilings will try to ensnare delvers.*
**Second Floor:** *The main halls of the palace. Knights patrol the corridors, held up by strings. Focus fire on the strings to disable.*
**Third Floor:** *Ball room. Filled with child-sized humanoid puppets in dresses. Hidden weaponry. Will demand to dance.*
**Fourth Floor:** *Throne room with a large 'puppet king' that uses multiple weapons and hidden compartments on the body to unleash different effects on the battlefield.*
**Loot rewards:**
*Strings, Spider parts, Dresses.*
**Class reward:**
*Puppeteer class*
*Ranged control of a single target or golem. Minion control.*

"That sounds… kinda spooky," I said.

"Don't be a coward, it's a normal enough dungeon. And a low-levelled one at that," Amaryllis said. "And, best of all, Rosenbell isn't too far from Greenshade. A week on foot. Less if we rent a carriage."

She flipped the book to the very back where a map was laid out. I 'oohed' and started looking at it. I used to love the maps in fantasy novels, they were some of the best parts, and now I could trace my own journey across Dirt.

"The class is a little… unusual, but I think it might have its uses, if I unlock the right kinds of skills for it." Amaryllis stood up, then stretched her back until it popped. "I'm going to go rest," she said.

"Ah, I should go to sleep too," I replied. The filling meal had done a number on what was left of my energy, and the sun was about to set outside besides. "There's a shower here, right?"

Amaryllis snorted. "There is. Enjoy yourself, I'm going to get changed."

I woke up to a sniffling noise, like two pieces of cloth rubbing together. It was faint, and I decided that it had to be from some other room in the inn. It was a busy place after all. That, and I had just had a nice warm shower and was tucked under a veritable pile of cosy warm blankets. Moving was not an option.

I was almost back asleep when I heard the snuffle again. It sounded as if it had come from Amaryllis' side of the room.

Carefully, I turned around and snooped out of the top of my blankets and looked around.

Other than Orange who was curled up next to me I couldn't see anyone.

Then Amaryllis' bed shook, and the sniffle returned.

Someone was crying. Quiet, lonely sobs, the sort that are trying very hard to remain quiet but just can't help but escape.

Pulling Orange up, I sat on the edge of my bed, then stood up with the kitty cradled to my chest. I was glad that I chose to sleep with some clothes on for a change. It meant that I didn't lose all of my warmth as I padded across the room.

Amaryllis had her head buried in her pillow, eyes closed and face pressed into the soft white fluff.

"Amaryllis?" I asked.

She tensed.

Swallowing, I placed a hand over the blankets where her shoulder was. "Amaryllis?"

"What's wrong, Broccoli?" Amaryllis asked.

If she was trying to sound self-assured, she was doing a poor job of it.

I, on the other hand, didn't know what to do. When I was sad and lonely, I asked for hugs, but I wasn't sure if that would happen with Amaryllis, and maybe her problems weren't the kind that could be fixed with lots of hugs and cuddles. "Are you okay?"

"I'm fine."

I winced. "Oh, okay," I said.

"Go back to bed," she muttered.

I did as she asked and sat on her bed.

"What are you doing?"

"I'm going to bed," I said.

"Your own bed, you moron!"

Sighing, I plopped a disgruntled-but-too-sleepy-to-care Orange on Amaryllis' other side, then glomped down atop of her. There were a bunch of blankets between us, so I did my best to make my hug as awesome as I could make it.

"Wh-what are you doing?" she asked.

"I'm giving you a hug. It's supposed to make you feel better."

"It's not working."

I chuckled. "I think it is," I said. "Did you want to talk about it? That makes it feel better too."

"The only thing I want to talk about is how stupid you are," she grumped.

"We can talk about that too, if you want."

Amaryllis was quiet for a very long time, but she didn't squirm and she didn't fight off my hug, so I stayed where I was even as my back started to get a bit chilly.

"It was just a nightmare," she said.

"Nightmares can be scary."

"It was... the cervid. They took me, and my family didn't want me back. Which is ridiculous." She snorted and it didn't sound as if she thought it was all that ridiculous.

"That's awful. But it didn't happen, right? And even if your family didn't want you, you're still my friend. And friends are a family that you pick."

The room was quiet for a while, and I thought that maybe she had gone to sleep when at last she spoke. "Do... do you want to get under the blankets?"

"If you want?" I asked.

"My... my sisters used to do this. It was immature and childish, but when one of us had a nightmare..."

"I get it," I said.

It took some doing, and I tried to be fast not to let all the warmth escape, but soon enough I was tucked up beside Amaryllis and hugging her close. Her wings were surprisingly soft from so close.

"I'm a mess," Amaryllis said.

I snorted and fired a bit of cleaning magic at her. "There, now you're not," I said before tightening the hug. "It's okay. Go to sleep."

"Idiot," she muttered.

"Yup."

The night grew darker as more lights outside the window were snuffed out, but it was okay.

"Thank you," Amaryllis said.

I fell asleep smiling.

# Chapter Sixty-Three
# The Shady Lady

When I woke up it was to find that Amaryllis was already up and about. She must have taken a shower because her feathers were still drippy and she had a towel wrapped around her head. "Oh, you finally decided to wake up," she said.

The words were biting, but the tone didn't match at all. She sounded... softer than she would have yesterday. I smiled a little, then hid myself in the warm pile of blankets until only the top of my head stuck out. "I'm not coming out until someone brings breakfast," I said.

"You moron," Amaryllis said. "I didn't take you for the lazy sort."

"I'm not lazy. I'm merely highly unmotivated to leave my warm snuggle cocoon," I said.

Orange, who had slipped under the blankets, poked her head out and gave us both a glare that seemed to say 'really, at this hour?'

"Come on, we should grab something to eat on the road. There are vendors out all over this city. Or do you want to miss the opportunity Lord Bristlecone is giving us?"

Somewhat reluctantly (I wasn't lazy, but it was really comfy under there) I pushed the pile of blankets until they smothered Orange and I hopped off the bed. I was only in my blouse and underthings, and all of the rest of my clothes were near my bed. It took a disproportionate amount of effort to trudge over and start getting dressed though.

"Is Abraham really a Lord?" I asked.

"He is, technically," Amaryllis said.

"How can someone technically be a Lord?" I wondered.

She sighed. "He has something of a reputation. He earned the title through some, shall we call them, exploits. He's not one of the founders of the Exploration Guild, but he was one of their big names for a long while. There are towns named after him, and landmarks that he discovered cover most maps. He's quite famous in some circles."

"So going with him is a big deal?" I asked.

Amaryllis huffed. It was a new huff that I hadn't heard before. "He's a bit of a washout. No, that's not the correct term. He merely grew old, and instead of retiring in grace he still leads the occasional daring mission into the frontier or goes on some hare-brained adventure. There are characters in children's books that bear a striking resemblance to him. He's a fossil."

"I think he was nice, and maybe a little lonely," I said. "No one wanted to hear his stories."

"I can't imagine why," Amaryllis deadpanned.

Shaking my head, I slid on my shoes, then tied them up. I was still keeping a set of boots in my bags. My Earth shoes were just a whole lot more comfortable, though they were starting to show some wear.

"And I'm ready!" I said as I bounced to my feet.

"Finally," Amaryllis said.

We went downstairs after I picked up my backpack and cradled Orange in the crook of my arm where she would at least be snug and warm, or as warm as a spirit cat could be, I guess. Julien wasn't behind the bar, instead it was manned—grenoiled—by a young lady who waved us goodbye as we went out the front.

It was still early enough in the morning that the streets were mostly bare, the sun hadn't even fully risen over the distant mountain range to the East. The few people around looked like workers rushing to get to their jobs, or people that had just finished a night shift and who looked more than ready for bed.

Amaryllis was right about the vendors though. As soon as we were off the main street and heading towards the docks, we ran into a few carts that were still preparing to take off, their owners adding oils and arranging things before their first clients arrived. We both agreed, with no prior discussion, to avoid all of the stands that sold bugs in any shape or form and aimed for the ones that had colourful signs that displayed drawings of local favourites.

We ended up with two bowls made of some round loaves of bread with the middle scooped out. The bread was still soft, perhaps owing to the strange sort of fridge they'd been stored in. Hot minced meat, beef if I had to guess, mixed with some beans and a savoury sauce was placed in the middle. We didn't get spoons, but a peek at a grenoil using his tongue to eat out of the bowl showed me how to eat the snack.

I shrugged. "When in Rome," I muttered before slurping out the stew. It tasted pretty good. Nothing like the food at the inn, but still hearty and filling, and then I got to eat the bowl too, which was nice.

"Your face is a mess," Amaryllis said.

I looked at her shirt which had a few stains on it that hadn't been there before. "You're one to talk," I said before firing a bit of cleaning magic at myself. Then, because I was nice, I cleaned off her shirt too.

She huffed, but it was her 'I'm too good to say thank-you huff,' which was almost as good as if she had said thank-you.

We aimed for the docks, Amaryllis sometimes taking the lead when we got to intersections that weren't yet familiar to me, but otherwise we just aimed for the big, noisy part of town with all of the flying ships around it. It was hard to miss, really.

"So, do you know what his ship looks like?" I asked.

"Not a clue," Amaryllis said. "The *Shady Lady* is supposed to be quite popular. It was one of the first airships ever built in Mattergrove, some five or ten years after the Nesting Kingdom started producing their own."

"Ah, Mattergrove is a human place, right?" I had seen it on the map yesterday, it was to the West of Deepmarsh, but that was about all I could remember without looking at the map again.

"It is. It's a large enough nation, but rather impoverished. Their lands don't lend themselves well to cultivating any useful crops and the Seven Peaks, that is, the mountains around which the kingdom is built, don't have anything worth mining in them. They're not as advanced as the Nesting Kingdom or Deepmarsh, so they're behind there was well."

"What do they sell?" I asked.

"Wine, mostly. They have good vineyards. That and plenty of fish, though other than a few rare breeds that Harpy nobility enjoy there's not much of a market for it. Endless Swells, another human-centric kingdom to the North, sell more fish for less."

"Ah," I said. "That kind of sucks for them," I said. I would have asked a few more questions, but we arrived on the topmost deck of the docks. Piers stretched out before us to reach out to various ships that hung over empty air. Seagulls were flocking around in big groups, eyeing passersby in case they dropped anything tasty and men and women in overalls and working clothes moved about with a sense of urgency.

I could have spent hours at the docks just gazing at the airships taking off and smelling the weird sizzly tang from the magical engines they used, but time wasn't on my side.

I spotted a grenoil who looked important, with a tag over one breast that read 'Dockmasters Association'. "Excuse me, sir. We're looking for a particular ship," I said.

"Zen I suggest the registry," he said a bit dismissively. I walked up alongside him and matched his pace.

"She's called the Shady Lady. She belongs to one Abraham Bristlecone."

The grenoil stopped in his tracks. "Is she leaving?" he asked.

"Um. I think so? As soon as we get to her, I mean."

"Zank ze stars. Ze Shady Lady is over at dock fifty-one." At my confused look he pointed off to one side. "Two levels down. Look for the plaque at the base of the pier." He then pointed to a nearby dock where a plaque was stamped onto the ground that read 'Twelve' in big letters.

"Thank you, sir!" I said before I jogged back to Amaryllis. "Follow me!"

"I have a bad feeling about this," Amaryllis said.

"Oh, don't be a worrywart," I said. "We're about to go on another adventure! Just imagine how much fun we'll have."

The moment we arrived at pier fifty-one I started to have the same bad feeling that Amaryllis had mentioned. I wondered if it was contagious, or if she just knew something I didn't.

The Shady Lady was hard to miss. Mostly because the ship at the end of the pier had her name emblazoned on its side in foot-high letters. The fact that the words ran half-way across the length of the ship said much about its size.

The airship was small. Tiny even. With a long hull made of wood and a bunch of triangular sails mounted on poles that stuck out every which way from the ship. There was a little cabin at the back, with exhaust pipes sticking out of it, and a small area above that cabin with a large wheel that probably served to direct the ship. The very back of the ship ended abruptly with a huge propeller stuck to a shaft.

And above it all a sort of oblong balloon whose original colour I could only guess at. It was covered in so many patches and nets and bits of tarp that it was impossible to tell what it was supposed to look like.

One thing was immediately obvious: The Shady Lady deserved her name. Too many of her planks were mismatched to be original, and there were some nasty scrapes along the bottom. There was even a pole sticking out of the bow that I was pretty sure was a spear that had stayed lodged in the front of her.

"I can glide," Amaryllis said. "So when she goes down, ditch that bag of yours and do try to hang on."

"I'm sure it'll be fine," I tried to assure her. And myself.

The door to the ship's cabin burst open and a spotless Abraham stepped out of it. On his heels was Raynold, who looked just as spiffy now as he did at the guild.

"Broccoli! And you brought your feathery friend!" Abraham said as he raised both arms in an enthusiastic greeting. "Welcome, come aboard, come aboard. We're all ready to set sail, to maraud across the clouds and maybe get into a bit of a scrap with some wild drakes or a griffon or two."

I felt a grin tugging at my lips. "Hello, Abraham," I said. "Mister Raynold. It's a good morning to meet you two!"

"Ahaha! A good morning indeed. Come on, the Shady Lady doesn't bite, not when I'm around at least. Hoh-oh!"

Laughing, I hopped over from the pier to the ship, and took a few steps to steady myself once aboard. A few steps were all I could take since the entire vessel was only five meters or so wide at its middle. The entire deck had things on it. Poles for ropes, pulleys, a few seats with fishing rods next to them. There were even small cannons tucked next to the rails where they couldn't be seen from outside of the ship.

It looked like the Shady Lady had had parts added and removed and changed all throughout her life as a little airship, and despite my reservations I was growing to like her a whole lot. She had personality.

"C'mon birdy," Abraham said. "If we want to make it to Greenshade sometime this week we ought to head out sooner rather than later!"

Amaryllis hopped over to the ship, then jumped down the rails to land next to me. "If I die on this death-trap, I'm returning as a ghost to haunt you," she said. "And my name is Amaryllis, not birdy."

"Very well then, Lady Amaryllis," Abraham said. "Welcome aboard the Shady Lady. Let me show you girls around right quick. We're short-handed, so we'll all have to do our part else we'll drop out of the sky like a sack full of lead bricks. Why, that reminds me of the time I encountered the dread air-pirate Golden Rogers..."

# Chapter Sixty-Four
# **Physical Manakinesis**

"Pull, little lass!" Abraham shouted from the other side of the ship.

I planted my two feet on the railing, wrapped my upper arm around the rope and pushed off as hard as I could until my entire body was horizontal. The rope came with me, but only with some effort and I had to grit my teeth against the strain on my arm.

The sail whose line I was pulling finally deployed, and with a 'whap' its canvas caught the wind and expanded.

In moments Abraham was by my side and he caught me before I fell onto the deck. Then, with deft hands, he grabbed the rope and tied it into a quick knot on a nearby metal hook. "Haha! We almost died there!" he cheered.

I was grinning like a loon as I tried to keep my feet as the Shady Lady shifted and began to turn, the sail I had deployed allowing the airship to twist around a little and change course. That was handy, because right in the direction he had been heading in was an entire flock of whales.

A pod of whales?

I wasn't sure which word was the right one to describe gigantic flying fish the size of semi-trailers. They were big, grey, and moved through the air in much the same way as whales moved through the ocean. "Insight."

*An Eastern Skim Murqh (level 9).*

"Whaa," I said as I leaned against the rails to take in the entire group of gigantic flying creatures. They were majestic, in their own way. Like fat people in a supermarket.

"You're easily impressed," Amaryllis said. She was looking a little dishevelled, with her hair tossed this way and that and her clothes already covered in stains from being near the big blubbering engine at the back of the ship for too long.

"How can you not be, this is great!" I cheered.

"Oh-hoh, a lady after my own heart. My, if I was forty years younger I'd be smitten on the spot," Abraham said before he moved to the back of the ship, pulled a bottle of something from a rack, took a swig of it, then emptied the rest into a hole above the engine. "Raynold! Remind me to get the engine checked again."

The dapper grenoil, who was currently behind the wheel, shook his head. A head that looked rather strange with a pair of elongated aviator goggles tied to it. "I reminded you at Port Royal, you insufferable oaf!" the grenoil said. "You said you had it in hand."

"I did! I even commissioned a repairman to look at the old monster."

"Did they?" Raynold screamed right back.

"They're supposed to show up this afternoon," Abraham shouted back. "Haha! They'll be surprised that we've left already."

"World save us all," Raynold said.

Amaryllis stared at the two older gentlemen, then glared at me. "This is all your fault somehow," she said.

"Don't worry," I said. "If we die, it'll be while having tons of fun."

"Haha! That's the spirit!" Abraham said. "Why, you remind me of that time Raynold and I were sent to escort a diplomat from the Pyrowalk Empire all the way to Mattergrove! Easy trip, and the lass they sent was a nice enough lady, but the Shady Lady had a bit of a ballast problem."

"A ballast problem?" Amaryllis repeated.

"Yup! We lost our balloon when we flew through a flight of sabre sparrows!"

"You, you lost your…" Amaryllis looked up to the balloon above us, the thing that was currently keeping us afloat. "That's unbelievable."

"Oh? Sabre sparrows are a well-known threat. And they taste great roasted over a campfire," Abraham said.

Grinning, I hopped over to one of the metal doodads on the deck and sat down to listen, the whales flowing past us to one side serving as a backdrop and the rushing winds as music to accentuate the tale.

"What's unbelievable is you surviving that kind of crash."

"No worries! I have the jumping skill! I merely hopped off the Shady Lady before we crashed. Raynold here had some newfangled idea with a tarp and some rope—"

"It's called a parachute, and it's safer than jumping off the ship a league in the air."

"And I carried the envoy. We all made it safely to land. Of course, we landed in the desert, and the Shady Lady's own landing was a little harsh. But Abraham Bristlecone never leaves a friend behind! So Raynold and I carried the Lady halfway across the Ostri desert until we ran across a few of the desert folk. When they heard our story, why, they were so impressed they helped pull the Shady Lady across the rest of the desert wastes until we reached Pisshole."

"Pisshole?" I asked, then slapped a hand over my mouth.

"It's the name of an oasis to the Northeast of the desert," Amaryllis said. "The Ostri have… unique naming conventions."

"Haha! They truly do. Nice folk though. Always good for a bit of manly sparring. Why, when I reached Pisshole one of their bigger chaps challenged me to a wrestle! I lost an arm!"

I blinked, then looked at his arms, both exposed because of the pocket-lined vest he was wearing, and both looking rather whole.

"I got better," Abraham explained.

"So cool," I said. "Hey, you have the Jumping skill too?" I asked.

"I do! Quite useful that one. I hear that at Master rank you can teleport short ranges, but I never got it past Expert myself. Other things to invest the time in, you know?"

"That's wonderful. I'm trying to learn a bunch of new skills too. Oh, and I really want to learn how to use magic, but I'm terrible at it, and I haven't practiced at all in a few days," I said.

"Oh-hoh! I can't help you there, I'm afraid. I've always been more keen on punching things into submission before lighting them on fire," Abraham said.

Amaryllis sighed. "I suppose I ought to keep up my end of the bargain on that one and actually teach you a thing or two. How far along are you with that Fireball spell of yours?"

"I'll leave you ladies to it," Abraham said. "The engine's making a clicking noise, usually it's more of a rattle, and I think we've dropped a quarter league in the last few minutes. I'll call you if I think we're going to crash."

"Okay, thanks Abraham!" I said.

Amaryllis stared at me for a long while. "How are you less concerned about crashing than I am?" she asked.

I shrugged. "I don't stress easily. Stress is bad for you, so I try to just… not stress. If we're going to crash, there's not much I can do about it."

Amaryllis massages her temples, then gestured to the fore of the ship. "It must be nice, being so daft that no problem sticks to you. Come on, we can practice over there. I don't want you lighting the ship on fire."

The Shady Lady had a figurehead shaped like a pretty lady who was wearing far too little clothing, but I guess that was par for the course with ships.

I sat next to the figurehead, then, because the Lady was a nice ship, I gave its figurehead a pat.

I didn't like getting pats myself, but this was a ship, which I figured was kind of like a pet, so it was okay. Maybe? I'd have to ask a sailor later.

"So, magic!" I said.

"Yes, magic," Amaryllis said. "Show me what you can do."

I nodded and brought my hand up. I had been practicing a little, but not nearly as much as I would have wanted to. It was magic after all, and that alone made it deserve my full attention. My mana gathered in my palm, then spread out to cover my entire hand until it was like I was wearing a translucent, glowing glove. I focused a little and brought it all to a hover over my hand and started to make it take the basic shape of the Fireball spell.

It was tricky to get the rotating shape just right while also keeping the cone-shaped tail in place, but, after a solid minute I almost managed. Then Amaryllis hummed, I looked up, and the entire spell broke apart and did little more than release a bit of hot air.

"Well... you're terrible," Amaryllis said. "But I suppose it makes sense if you never came into contact with our magic system before. I was trained since I was... honestly, I can't remember. I had toys that required manipulating mana to make them work, and my early classes on reading and writing were broken up by exercises with mana. You'll find that's the case with most noble families and plenty of wiser non-nobles too."

"Ah, darn, so I have years of catching up to do?" I asked.

"Essentially, yes. Don't despair too much. When I went to the Farseeing Academy some of the students in my first year were just as bad as you are now, and by the end of their first year they had done much to bridge the gap between their skill level and that of the students like myself who had practiced their entire life."

"Oh, neat, so I can learn Fireball."

Amaryllis huffed and took my hand in hers. Far from being romantic, she moved my arm up and pointed it off the side of the ship. "Push mana out," she said.

I did as she asked until I had a rough ball of my mana in my hand.

"Good, now shift its aspect."

I did that too, frowning as I thought hot thoughts and the mana warmed up in my hand and started to flicker and dance like a flame.

"Not bad. A bit slow, but that is Fire-aspect mana if I've ever seen it. You were using Grigori's Fireball, right?"

"I was?" I asked. "I got it from a scroll. It's in my bag still."

"It doesn't matter. I think I recognize the spell, not that it's terribly complex. Start forming it again," she instructed.

I focused and started to form the ball part of the fireball, then I noticed little tendrils of mana snaking around my own, these charged with an almost humming, electric quality. When the tendrils touched my skin, it was like I was pressing my hand against a transformer.

"Are you doing something?"

"I told you to make the spell, not ask foolish questions," she said.

I decided to trust that Amaryllis knew what she was doing and continued to form the Fireball. The tendrils of Amaryllis' magic pushed and prodded the magic into slightly different shapes.

"Look at the new form, pay attention to it," she said.

"R-right," I said.

Soon I had what definitely looked like a translucent Fireball floating in the air just above the surface of my hand.

"Good. Cast it."

"Um. How?"

Amaryllis sighed so hard it ruffled the hair by my neck. "The trigger on this spell is near the cone. Pull on that and push it out with your mana at the same time. Some people like to push their hand forwards too."

"Got it," I said.

I found the thing I thought was the trigger in the spell, then at the same time as I yanked on it, I closed my hand into a fist and punched forwards.

The spell launched.

A trail of heated air followed after the fist-sized ball of fire. I laughed as the Fireball rushed ahead, screaming through the air. Then it started to spin out of control like a deflating balloon. For a moment I was worried it would come back, but it exploded a dozen meters away into a ball of fire with tiny electrical sparks flashing throughout.

"I did it!" I cheered as I got up.

"Congra—" Amaryllis began, but she was cut off as I hugged the air out of her lungs.

"Thank you! Thank you!" I said.

***Ding! For repeating a Special Action a sufficient number of times, you have unlocked the general skill: Physical Manakinesis!***

# Chapter Sixty-Five

# Storytime

```
Physical Manakinesis
Rank F - 00%
The ability to push mana out of your body
using motion as a focal point.
```

"Huh?" I said.

"What?" Amaryllis asked.

My confusion must have been showing, or maybe she just noticed that my hug and thank-yous had stopped for a moment as I tried to figure out the skill I had just unlocked.

"Um, I got a new skill," I said. "It's a General Skill called... Physical Manakinesis."

"Manakinesis?" Amaryllis asked. She frowned as she seemed to think about that for a moment, then gave up with a shrug. "Never heard of that one. I expected you to unlock Fireball, or perhaps Mana Manipulation or Mana Shaping. The latter are valuable skills for anyone who wants to practice magic."

"Yeah, I can imagine. The skill description is kind of strange too. It says something about using my body as a focal point for pushing out mana?" That didn't quite parse for me. Or maybe I just didn't know enough about magic to make sense of it.

"Let's go ask the fossils. I'm loath to admit it, but they are both rather experienced, even if they seem somewhat uneducated. Abraham especially," Amaryllis said.

I didn't comment on how rude it was to say that kind of thing, Amaryllis was who she was, and maybe one day she'd learn to look past that, but it wasn't my right to try and change her, really. Instead I hopped to my feet and skipped across the deck to the back.

Abraham was squinting at a grease-and-oil covered book, a tiny set of spectacles perched on the end of his nose. His brows rose and his look of deep concentration faded as soon as he saw us coming closer. "Ah-hah! Figured out your little spell, did you? I bet you can't wait to launch that monster into some unsuspecting beast's maw and see what happens!"

"Not yet," I said. "I unlocked a skill, and I don't know what it does."

"Oh, what sort of skill is it?" Raynold said. He locked the ship's wheel in place with a metallic device and came to stand on the edge of the castle so that he could look down on us. "I might know a zing or two."

"Ah, it's called Physical Manakinesis," I said. "Do you know anything about it?"

Abraham frowned and started tugging at his moustache, but Raynold didn't have any such problems. "Ah, I know zat skill, yes. I don't have it myself, but we've fought people who did. Abraham, do you remember zose fish-people in the Hoofbreaker Woods?"

"The scaly little bastards with the weird dancing magic?" Abraham asked.

"Story time?" I wondered. I didn't clap my hands like a five-year-old, because I wasn't five.

Abraham laughed and nodded. "Haha! There's always time for a good tale or two. Raynold, let's fix something to eat that isn't some poor dead insect, and we can tell the girls all about our adventures in the far East."

I think we were all getting a little hungry, because no one disagreed. Soon enough Amaryllis and I were trying to help as the boys pulled some meat out of a rune-covered cooler and, after wiping the top of the engine clean, started cooking the meat right on the metal top-plate.

It was a little weird, but I couldn't argue with the mouth-watering scents that I caught every so often. There wasn't any room for a table on the deck, but Raynold pulled a plank from somewhere and set it on some of the strange equipment and we found some stools tucked away in one of the little cabins at the back.

In no time at all we were having a barbeque a league over a grassy plain, the bright blue skies all around and the distant call of the flying whales serving as a counterpoint to the Shady Lady's thump-thumping engine.

"So," Abraham said after taking a bite of steak and swallowing it whole. "Here we were. Out beyond Trenten lands because we ran into a bit of a kerfuffle with some of their royal guards and had to make a bit of a run for it. Unfortunately, they were on the persistent side and wouldn't just let us go off to mind our own business."

"This is a few years after the Cry statuette heist," Raynold said.

"It's not a heist if you're stealing something back," Abraham said. "Now, we were off in the deepest end of the forest known as the Hoofbreaker Woods. Nasty terrain there. Lots of very small cliffs and ridges, and the soil is rocky and hard to travel over."

"Hence the name," I guessed.

"That's right," Abraham said.

"What does any of this have to do with Broccoli's new skill?" Amaryllis wondered.

"Ah, but see, we encountered people with that skill deep in the woods. We reached the end of the forest after losing our cervid pursuers, and being just a mite lost, we decided to follow the coast South until we encountered the Grey Wall."

"The Grey Wall?" I wondered. I knew I was just adding more and more delays until we got the important part of the story, but the little tangents were just too much fun not to dive into.

"A huge wall made of grey stone, built to cut off the advance of those pesky deerfolk," Abraham explained. "So, here we were, walking along a long shore, mostly well fed because the monsters in those woods were only in their twenties and they made for good eating. And then we encounter a group of strange savages!"

"I'd hardly call them savages," Raynold said. "They had their own culture and were fairly well educated in magical matters. They were merely behind in other things."

"They walked around as naked as they were born, haha!" Abraham said. "Little fish-like folk, no taller than my waist, and they didn't carry a weapon on them. Nice enough folk, all things said."

"And the skill?" Amaryllis asked.

"Ah, yes. See, they didn't have weapons, they fought with arms and legs and kicks and, most of all, magic. Instead of casting proper spells though, they would shape their magic and strike out with that. It was a little crude, but some of them were exceptionally talented."

Raynold shook his head. "It's not like more traditional casting, where a spell is built and zen activated to unleash an effect. Not zat zey didn't have zat as well. Zey just coated zemselves in mana and used it to supplement zeir fighting prowess. Like zis," he said as he brought his hand up. Mana gathered around his closed fist in a blink, and then his entire hand started to drip with wet-looking mana. Raynold punched the air off to the side and a burst of mana shot out, then he brought his hand back and the mana returned.

As the grenoil man waved his arm about in the air, the watery mana flowed after it, dancing through the sky like one of those tassels gymnasts sometimes used.

"That's pretty," Amaryllis said. "And it shows decent control, but it doesn't look… weaponizable."

"Hrmph," Raynold said. He brought his arm up, then sliced it down along his side. The watery mana shifted into a narrow band and sliced through the last few inches of our makeshift table. The wood clunked to the floor. "Ze issue is range, but some of zose fish people could imbue zeir mana into the world around zem and use it all as a weapon. A kick to the ground would unleash somezing similar to ze earth pillar spell, a punch would launch a weak fireball and so on."

"It reminds me a bit of fighting a terramancer, only with water," Abraham said. "Tough fight those."

"Wow," I said. So, if I understood things correctly, I had just unlocked the ability to become the avatar, and I was totally okay with that. Though I did hope that it came without tattoos.

Amaryllis gave me a strange look. "You're thinking stupid thoughts again," she said. "It's sad that I already recognize that look on your face."

"N-no," I said. "It's just that the way Mister Raynold describes the skill reminds me of something, and I think it sounds really awesome. I should practice until I hit apprentice rank with it!"

"That's the spirit!" Abraham said. "We've got another day and a bit before we crash over Greenshade, that's plenty of time to hone your skills."

"Crash over Greenshade?" Amaryllis asked.

Abraham laughed. "It's a figure of speech!"

Amaryllis glared at him for a while, then sighed. "So, Broccoli, do you have any skills that aren't topped off?"

"You mean that I can still improve? Um, yeah, a few. Most even," I said as I poked Mister Menu.

| Name: Broccoli Bunch | Race: Human (Riftwalker) | | | Age: 16 | |
|---|---|---|---|---|---|
| Health | 120 | Stamina | 130 | Mana | 115 |
| Resilience | 30 | Flexibility | 35 | Magic | 20 |

| First Class: | Cinnamon Bun | First Class Level: | 7 |
|---|---|---|---|
| Skill Slots | 0 | Skill Points | 3 |

| General Skill Slots | 0 | General Skill Points | 1 |
|---|---|---|---|

| General Skills | | Cinnamon Bun Skills | |
|---|---|---|---|
| Insight | C - 33% | Cleaning | B - 12% |
| Makeshift Weapon Proficiency | E - 58% | Jumping | C - 100% |
| Archaeology | F - 57% | Gardening | D - 13% |
| Friendmaking | D - 68% | Cute | D - 100% |
| Physical Manakinesis | F - 00% | | |

"Um. In my general skills I have Insight, Makeshift Weapon Proficiency, Archaeology, Friendmaking and Physical Manakinesis that all need more experience to rank up. And in my class skills I have Cleaning and Gardening that could use more training. Um. I have three class skill points, but I thought I should save them to get Cleaning up to Expert rank."

Amaryllis slapped a hand over her face.

"What?" I asked.

"How are you so far behind?"

"I'm behind?" I asked.

Abraham seemed to think that this was hilarious because he guffawed and slapped the table a few times. Only Raynold's intervention saved the plank from flopping to the ground.

"Most people, sane, intelligent people, work on any new skill until it's as good as it can be. Accumulating so many skills without actually working on them is just so irresponsible," she said. "Come on, get up. We can practice magic when you have the time to waste on that. We need to get your other skills up to par."

"Ah, okay?" I asked. "I'm not sure how we'll grind any of them, though," I said.

Amaryllis had a dangerous and frankly kind of scary look in her eyes. "Why, Broccoli, we'll just need to figure out how to practice as many skills at once as possible. I'm sure that weapon proficiency of yours can be trained anywhere on this ship while you're cleaning and inspecting it from top to bottom."

"Um," I said.

"We can even practice that new skill of yours. I'm pretty sure pushing mana up against a mana-heavy attack will negate... some of the damage, at least." She raised her talons and an electric buzz filled the air.

"Um," I said with more feeling this time. The feeling was terror.

"Haha! That's the spirit," Abraham said. "Why, you remind me of that time I trained with an ancient monk atop the Jade peak. I nearly died three times on that first morning alone."

"But we're on an airship," I pointed out. "Isn't this a terrible place to fight."

"No worries, Miss Bunch, the Shady Lady is one tough old ship. She can endure a bit of a scuffle with your feathery friend."

Amaryllis jumped to her feet, and I did the same just in case. "Wait, wait, Amaryllis why are you doing this?" I asked as she started to advance towards me.

"To make you even stronger, of course. That way if we're ever in trouble again we'll be able to handle it better."

That... was actually a pretty good reason to train a little bit. And sharpening my skills didn't sound like a bad idea. I just wasn't keen on getting hurt.

"Don't worry! If you lose any limbs, I'm great at sewing," Abraham said. "And Raynold here knows a healing spell or two!"

"I... I'm more of a lover than a fighter!" I said.

"Then you'll love sparring!" Amaryllis said.

That day, I learned that dodging someone who could fly on an open deck was rather difficult.

# Chapter Sixty-Six
# A Place to Park Airships

I bounced over to the figurehead and glomped it from behind so that I could better see ahead of us.

The Shady Lady was coasting along quietly through the mid-afternoon sky, carried along by the breeze at our back and navigating thanks to Raynold's expert twists of the rudder this way and that. I suspect that he was aiming for thermals that I couldn't see because we would occasionally ride up as if on a large swell for a little ways.

I rather enjoyed the quiet now that the engine was off. Amaryllis didn't, but that was probably because she had been spooked when the motor exploded and sent the ship's propeller flying off into the distance and left a bit of a hole in the side of the cabin.

The smoke trailing behind up was kind of pretty, and it also meant that no matter what happened, we would be super easy to find.

I turned around and looked ahead again, then I felt my eyes widening and my smile growing wider. "I can see a city!" I called back while pointing the city in question up ahead.

"Haha! We'll make it to Greenshade after all! Didn't I tell you as much, Raynold!" Abraham shouted. He didn't need to shout over the engine anymore, but I think he was just used to talking at that volume.

"I'm ze one zat calculated our descent, not you," Raynold said.

"Bah, that's merely a detail, you old frog!" Abraham said. "It doesn't matter, in a few hours we'll hit land and I can finally be rid of you!"

"I zink I am ze one zat it most looking forward to having some time wizout your... loudness," Raynold shot back.

Grinning, I leaned against the Shady Lady's figurehead and allowed the wind to toss my hair back (I hoped that Greenshade had a hairdresser or two, I needed a snip). The adventure so far had been plenty of fun. Flying across the sky and playing tag with Amaryllis across the entire ship and just having fun and making new memories. It was all I had hoped for.

And soon we would be landing in another city and setting off on another adventure, it was going to be wonderful!

"Hey, Amaryllis, have you ever been to Greenshade?" I asked.

"I haven't," the harpy said as she walked up to the front of the ship and then brought a wing up to shield her eyes from the sun. We would need to find her a nice hat at some point. "I learned a little about it. I had to learn about most cities, but Greenshade is… not inconsequential, but nearly so."

"Oh-hoh, if my little brother heard that he would be crippled!" Abraham said.

Still smiling, because there was never not a reason to smile, I turned towards Abraham. "You have a little brother?" I could already imagine a younger, slightly more handsome Abraham in my mind.

"Indeed! Little Lewis was a little brat when I ran off to have my first great adventure. Too bad he never followed in his big brother's footsteps. He's unhappily married now, with three little ones of his own! My niece is my favourite, but don't go telling the others! Haha!"

I grinned. Having someone like Abraham as an uncle must have been great. "I can't wait to meet them all," I said.

"Your brother is the lord of the city, isn't he?" Amaryllis asked.

"He is?" I wondered.

"Bah, it's a silly title. I didn't want it and Lewis always did want to make a name for himself while hiding behind as many walls as he could manage. I'm sure he'll be out to greet us when we crash into his backyard, haha!"

"Oh, great, nobles," Amaryllis muttered.

I stared at her but didn't have the energy to point out the bit of hypocrisy in her words. "So, Greenshade, what's it like?"

"It's a trade city. A sort of centre of overland travellers moving into or out of the Ostri desert," Amaryllis said. "It's also one of the only proper cities near to Deepmarsh where goods can be loaded onto airships and sent over the Darkwoods. A few nearby independent cities trade with Mattergrove through Greenshade, so does the Nesting Kingdom. Just about all of the goods moving into Mattergrove do so through this one city. It's a wonder it's not the capital by now."

"We built the city there because it had a nice view over the cliffs overlooking the desert," Abraham said.

"There're lots of humans there, right?" I asked. It would be nice to be surrounded by a bit of normalcy for a little bit. Not that I minded seeing people of all sorts of species around. "Um, except for the travellers, I guess? Wait, do a lot of people travel over land?"

"It's mostly human, yes," Amaryllis said. She leaned over the railing next to me and squinted into the distance. "There are some grenoil, but they tend to dislike the dry air. Plenty of ostri and some harpies too. Some sylphs too, but they don't travel this far from their mountains too often."

"Awesome!" I said.

"And as for the travel, well, airships don't run on happy thoughts. They're faster than overland trade, but you can't move as many goods, the risk is nearly as high that the cargo will be lost and while faster, a large enough caravan can move more goods in a year than a dedicated airship. In the end it comes down to the terrain and the wildlife. In some regions, airships are almost always better, in others it's more cost effective to send goods over land."

That was good to know, I supposed. It felt as if the world was going through a slow and steady change, pushing the boundaries of what the people inhabiting the world could do with their magic and creativity. And I got to ride along with that wave of enthusiasm!

Greenshade started to appear in more detail as we dipped through the clouds and came closer to the city. The city seemed to sprawl out every which way, with only the far western end where a large drop lay acting as a natural wall. The road to the west seemed neat and orderly, but the further out they went the more they zigged and zagged. The houses also didn't share the same colours as those in Deepmarsh, where nearly every roof was red. Here there was a rainbow panoply of roof colours.

There were also roads leading out of the city and through what I suspected were vineyards and small patches of forests among rolling hills. Small homes with smoke trailing from their chimneys dotted the countryside.

"Pretty," I decided.

"Hang on!" Raynold called from the very back. "We'll need to dip and pull up to gain some speed, else we'll never make it."

I grabbed onto the rail, then saw that Amaryllis was having a bit of difficulty doing the same with her talons, so I wrapped one arm around her waist and hugged her from behind. Orange, who had been snuggled up near the still warm (and still smoking) engine, padded up to us and perched atop the figurehead's head just as the Shady Lady dipped down.

Amaryllis squawked, Abraham roared with laughter, and I cheered with glee as we dove towards the ground. The entire ship rattled and clanked, the sails snapped in the wind and I saw some rope and a few odds and ends take off into the air.

My knuckles went white as I hung unto the sides and I felt my stomach dropping inside of me.

The only one that seemed unconcerned was Orange who began to lick a forepaw as if none of this mattered to her.

"And up!" Raynold screamed.

Sails shifted and the Shady Lady rumbled in protest as she began to right herself.

The ground shot past beneath us, much, much closer now than it had been earlier.

Things clanked, the ship wobbled, and I couldn't continue cheering even though I wanted to because my lungs were busy being crushed against my ribcage.

The Shady Lady levelled off, but at a speed that still had us pushed back by the wind alone. It was, I judged, a small miracle that we had held onto the big balloon above.

"Haha! Good flying, Raynold my old chum!" Abraham cheered.

"We haven't made it yet!"

Greenshade, which had been a sort of blurry mess of indistinct rooftops from above, was now far closer. Perhaps a little too close.

My next cry was one of alarm as we shot past and between a pair of towers, the guards atop them jumping to the side to avoid us.

The city didn't have all that many tall buildings, which only meant that the people in the streets had a perfect view of the Shady Lady as she shot past and almost rubbed against the roofs below.

Then we were over the fancier parts of town, the place with the nicer homes that had little gardens and greenhouses and, best of all, lots of room between each other.

"That's my brother's estate!" Abraham said as he pointed to a building off to one side. It was nice enough, from what I could see in the ten or so wild seconds before we shot past. Kind of like a palace with big wings on either side and a hangar of all things behind it.

The Shady Lady bobbed up, as if catching a thermal. I blinked as the air suddenly went dry, and when I looked back ahead it was to find that we were now off the edge of the western cliff and over a huge expanse of desert that stretched out for as far as I could see.

"Whoa!"

"The Ostri desert," Abraham said. "Driest, warmest, and sandiest place I ever ran across. More nasty beasties than you could shake a stick at, and nothing worth fighting for entire leagues!"

"Do lots of people live there?" I asked.

"Just the Ostri folk. Nicest people you'll ever meet. Everyone's a friend to them, as long as they're fair," Abraham said.

"We should visit!" I told Amaryllis who was still tucked up against my chest. I think she might have been shivering a little.

Poor thing. They probably didn't have roller coasters back in her kingdom.

We shifted around, Raynold spinning the wheel until the Shady Lady was coming around and back towards the cliffs.

Just like the airship port of Port Royal, there were dozens of vessels berthed alongside piers on the rocks side of the cliff, with wooden docks and elevators that were moving up and down along the walls.

"World damn us, ze doors are closed!" Raynold screamed.

"Haha!" Abraham said. "They didn't see us coming in time to roll out the welcome mat. That or my little brother's friends want me dead again! What a great way to try and kill me!"

"What?" Amaryllis screeched.

"Oh, no worries! They only succeeded the one time," Abraham said.

We were now flying straight towards the cliff where I could see large doors built into the stone face. Most were closed, some were opened to show that there were smaller ships, like the Shady Lady, sitting in wait. None had a free open spot.

"My, that was quite the week. See, there's the countess that—"

"This is not the time for one of your stupid stories!" Amaryllis yelled.

"I like his stories," I defended.

"You're an idiot too!" Amaryllis barked.

Abraham, far from being insulted, started to roar with laughter. "Raynold, aim for that one!" he said as he pointed to one of the closed doors.

"Aye!" Raynold said. "Got a plan?"

His plan had better be short because we were approaching fast.

"Ramming speed, my lad!"

"Zat's not a plan!" Raynold screamed.

"Haha! One way or another we're ending this in a cliff hangar!"

Made in the USA
Monee, IL
26 January 2021